A FEARSOME DOUBT

Also by Charles Todd

A Test of Wills

Wings of Fire

Search the Dark

Watchers of Time

Legacy of the Dead

A FEARSOME DOUBT

AN INSPECTOR IAN RUTLEDGE MYSTERY

CHARLES TODD

BANTAM BOOKS

A FEARSOME DOUBT

A Bantam Book / October 2002

All rights reserved.
Copyright © 2002 by Charles Todd.

Book design by Lynn Newmark.

No part of this book may be reproduced or
transmitted in any form or by any means, electronic
or mechanical, including photocopying, recording,
or by any information storage and retrieval system,
without permission in writing from the publisher.
For information address: Bantam Books.

LIBRARY OF CONGRESS
CATALOGING-IN-PUBLICATION DATA

Todd, Charles.
A fearsome doubt : an Inspector Ian Rutledge mystery/
Charles Todd.
p. cm.
ISBN 0-553-80180-5
1. Rutledge, Ian (Fictitious character)—Fiction.
2. Executions and executioners—Fiction. 3. Police—
England—Fiction. 4. Kent (England)—Fiction.
5. Widows—Fiction. I. Title.

PS3570.O37 F43 2002
813'.54—dc21
2002018669

*Published simultaneously in the United States
and Canada*

Bantam Books are published by Bantam Books, a division
of Random House, Inc. Its trademark, consisting of the
words "Bantam Books" and the portrayal of a rooster, is
Registered in U.S. Patent and Trademark Office and in
other countries. Marca Registrada. Bantam Books, 1540
Broadway, New York, New York 10036.

PRINTED IN THE UNITED STATES OF AMERICA

BVG 10 9 8 7 6 5 4 3 2 1

For L., and for B. and C.,
with much love.

A FEARSOME
DOUBT

AUGUST 1912

LONDON

THE PRISONER WAS STANDING IN THE DOCK, FACE STRAINED, eyes on the foreman of the jury. His fingers gripped the wooden railing, white-knuckled, as he tried to hear the portly, gray-haired man in the jurors' box reading the verdict. But the roaring in his ears as his heart pounded hard enough to suffocate him seemed to shut out the words. He swallowed hard, then leaned forward a little, concentrating on the juror's lips.

"—guilty on all charges—"

The foreman's voice rose on the last four words, as if he found them distasteful, his glance furtively flicking toward the accused and away again. A greengrocer, he was not sympathetic to theft and murder.

The prisoner's face swung toward the judge as he lifted the black silk square and settled it neatly on his heavy white wig, prepared to pass sentence.

". . . taken from this place . . . hung by the neck . . ."

The prisoner blanched, and turned in anguish toward his wife, seated in the gallery watching, her gloved hands clenched tightly in her lap.

But she offered no comfort, staring straight ahead. Her face was closed and empty. He couldn't look away. His sister, on the far side of his wife, was weeping into her handkerchief, hunched into her grief, but he hardly noticed. It was his wife's coldness that riveted him.

He thought, "She *believes* it now—"

Inspector Ian Rutledge, the young officer from the Yard whose evidence had all but placed the rope around Ben Shaw's throat, turned away and quietly left the courtroom.

He did not enjoy sending any man to his death. Even this one, whose crimes had shocked London. At such a time he was always mindful of his father, a solicitor, who had held strong views on the subject of hanging.

"I don't believe in it. Still, the dead had no choice in *their* dying, did they? The murderer did. It's on his own head, what becomes of him. He knew from the start what justice would be meted out to him. But he always expects to avoid it, doesn't he? There's an arrogance in that which disturbs me more than anything else—"

Ben Shaw hadn't been arrogant. Murder hadn't set well on his conscience. Hanging might come as a relief, an end to nightmares. Who could say?

Certainly not Rutledge himself—he had never taken a life. Would that alter his view of murder, would it in any way change his ability to understand a crime, or his attitude toward the killer? He thought not. It was the victim who had always called out to him, the voiceless dead, so often forgotten in the tumultuous courtroom battle of guilt versus innocence.

It was said that Justice prevented Anarchy. Law established Order.

Cold comfort to the elderly women Ben Shaw had strangled in their beds.

Still, the silenced victims had not gone unheard in this courtroom. . . .

THE BONFIRE HAD BEEN PILED HIGH WITH THE DEBRIS FROM a dozen gardens and enough twigs and dead boughs to outlast the Guy. The celebrants were gathered about the square, talking and laughing as if the gruesome spectacle they were about to witness was far more exciting than frightening. The match had yet to be tossed into the pyre, but two men in flowing wigs and faded satin coats awaited the signal. Their sober faces were flushed with wine and duty. The taller leaned toward his companion and said in a low voice, "All this hair itches like the very devil!"

"Yes, well, at least your shirt fits! This lace will end up strangling me, wait and see! I'm ready to kill whoever thought up this charade."

"Won't be long now."

It was the close of Guy Fawkes Day, and tonight the stuffed effigy of a traitor was about to be paraded around the village square and then thrown into the flames.

Bonfires were a long-standing English tradition, marking the Gunpowder Plot of 1605 when the real Guy Fawkes had been caught with his coconspirators attempting to blow up the Houses of Parliament and King James with them.

A macabre way of reminding schoolchildren, as they went round their villages and towns collecting pennies to buy Roman candles, what becomes of traitors.

As a rule it was a family affair, held in the back garden, the fire as fat or sparse as the family could manage, the Guy dressed in cast-off clothes stuffed with straw. In too many households during four and a half years of war the celebration had dwindled to a token affair; the dearth of able-bodied men and the hardships of families struggling to survive without them made the effort increasingly a burden. The village of Marling had decided to revive the custom with a public flourish.

Ian Rutledge had given his share of pennies to the local children this morning, while Hamish, in his head, disparaged the whole affair. *"It's no' a Scottish tradition, to waste guid firewood. It's too hard to come by."*

Remembering the barren, stone-scarred mountains where Hamish had grown up, Rutledge said, "When in Rome . . ."

"If ye came for Hogmanay, now, a good fire on the *hearth* was hospitality after a long ride in the cold."

Rutledge knew the Scottish holiday, the last day of the year, when the children demanded gift cakes and the whisky flowed freely—and not necessarily whisky upon which any tax had been paid. He had commanded Scottish troops in the war, and they had brought their traditions as well as their traditional courage with them. He had turned a blind eye on more than one occasion, the policeman subverted by the compassion he felt for his homesick men—many little more than boys—trying to forget how short their lives were destined to be by remembering home.

Tonight, 5 November, he wasn't on duty in London; he was standing among the revelers in an attractive village high on the Downs, and beside him was the widow of a friend who had died in the Great War. She had invited him to come down for the occasion. "You must, Ian! It will do both of us a world of good. It's time to put the war behind us, and try to rebuild our lives. . . ."

He had no life to rebuild, but she did, and Frances, his sister, had urged him to accept the invitation. "Elizabeth has mourned for two years. It won't bring Richard back, will it? I think we should encourage her, if she's ready to shut the door on all that. And it will do you good as well, to see more of old friends. You've buried yourself in your work for months now!" The last accusing. And then Frances had added, hastily, "No, I'm *not* matchmaking. She would do as much for either of us, if we were in need, and you know that as well as I do."

It was true. Elizabeth was one of the most generous people Rutledge knew. Richard Mayhew had been very fortunate in his choice of wife.

She was a slim woman in her late twenties, with sparkling dark eyes and a wry sense of humor. Her presence was brightness and warmth and a belief that life could be good. It was—almost—contagious.

And just now, he was in need of warmth and brightness, to chase away other shadows. . . .

Clinging to his arm in the press of people, Elizabeth was saying, "Richard loved all this, you know. He loved tradition and the . . ."

Rutledge lost the thread of her words as the Guy, flamboyant in dress and hanging from a long pole, was brought into the square and carried triumphantly around the unlit fire. A deafening shout of approval rose, and as Rutledge glimpsed the painted mockery of a face, its wild eyes and flaring nostrils, the grinning mouth, the bits of someone's wig straggling about the ears, he had to laugh. What was lost in talent had been made up in exuberance.

"Aye, exuberance," Hamish agreed, "with a wee touch of Auld Clootie . . ."

The Devil. Only a Scot with generations of Covenanters in his family tree would make such a comparison.

Rutledge responded silently, "The first James was your king as well as ours. Or have you forgotten?"

Hamish, considering the matter, replied, "We didna' care o'ermuch for him."

The Guy was closer now, dancing a jig on the pole, and Elizabeth was laughing like a girl. "Oh, Ian, *look,* he's wearing those masquerade clothes I found in the attics and donated to the committee. Wouldn't Richard have been *delighted*—"

On the far side of the crowd, someone had lit the fire, and the flames began to fly through the dry brush, reaching for the harder wood. Applause greeted them. In the garish light, the Guy took on a realistic life of its own, the straw-stuffed limbs jerking in time with the booted feet of its minders as it was paraded before an appreciative audience. Shouts of approval and the word "Traitor!" mingled with laughing cries of "Into the flames with him!" and "God Save King James and Parliament." The shrill, giggling voices of children taunted the Guy, a counterpoint to parents warning their offspring not to venture too close to the fire: "Mind now!" or "Stand clear, do!"

And in the light of the flames, lit just as garishly as the Guy, was a face that Rutledge's gaze passed over—and returned to—*and recognized—*

But from where?

He went cold with a sense of shock he couldn't explain. A knowledge that was there, buried deep in the brain, concealed by layers of denial and blank horror. And yet rising to the surface with the full force of his being was a single realization—*He didn't want to know the answer—*

There was danger in searching for the answer—

He stood motionless, his body rigid, his arm stiffening in Elizabeth's grip. But she was entranced by the spectacle, and unaware. He was physically caught up in his surroundings, the voices of people on every side of him, the heavy smell of smoke as the wind blew it his way, the warmth of Elizabeth's hands on him, the coolness of the night air, the rough feel of the wool coat across his shoulders, the shadowed brick facades looming above him—and at the same time, emotionally, he was firmly locked in a private hell that mirrored the flames rising into the black sky above. As the seconds passed, it seemed for a fraction of an instant that the eyes of his enemy sought and found his before moving on. The odd light lent them a ferocity that stunned him.

As if acknowledging a connection between them, a connection built on—what?

And how did he know this was an *enemy*?

"Gentle God," Rutledge whispered under his breath—and then the face vanished, a will-o'-the-wisp in the November night, a figment of murky imagination lost in the smoke. Suddenly he doubted his own senses.

He had seen it—Dear God, surely he *had* seen it!

Or—had it been no more than a fleeting memory from the last days of the war—a moment's aberration, a flash of something best buried in the dim reaches of his mind, best unresurrected?

In this past week uneasy memories had surfaced and disappeared with disconcerting irregularity, as if the approaching anniversary of the Armistice had jarred them into life again. Rutledge was not the only soldier who was experiencing this phenomenon—he'd heard two constables who had survived the trenches warily questioning each other about lapses in concentration. And several men in a pub dancing uneasily around who was sleeping well and who wasn't. There had been the officer sitting on a bench by the Embankment, staring at the river water with such obsessive fascination that Rutledge had stopped and spoken to him. The man had traveled a long way back to the present, and looked up at Rutledge as though wanting to ask, *"Were you there?"* And saying instead, "The water's bitter cold and gray today, isn't it?" It was almost a confession that drowning had been on his mind.

As if uncertain, all of them, whether or not they were going mad, and grateful to discover they were not alone in their fears. As if that made it more tolerable, not being alone. . . .

Just this need had sent him down to Kent.

He found himself searching among the villagers gathered in a ring around the fire's blazing gold and red light, but the face he sought was no longer there. Not now.

Not ever?

Hamish, alarmed and accusing in the back of his mind, was exclaiming, "It canna' be. Ye've gone o'wer the edge, man!"

Badly shaken, Rutledge had lost sight of the perambulating Guy, making a lap on the far side of the bonfire. Now the grotesque effigy was coming round once more, a final circuit while the lengths of harder wood smoked and began to burn hot enough to consume the fire's prey.

Over by the bronze statue of a mounted Cavalier that stood at the point of the square where the main road curved away from the High Street, there was hilarity as a police sergeant gathered older boys around him and gave his orders. The bronze Cavalier's back was turned on the antics of his descendants, his face haughty and withdrawn under the brim of his plumed hat, the aristocratic arch of his nose and the smooth sweep of his cheekbones highlighted by the fire's blaze.

As the first Roman candles went streaming noisily skyward from the cluster of children, Rutledge flinched. At the Front, flares had been used to test the wind—

The *crack!* and the *rat-a-tat-tat* of the smaller charges sent his heart rate soaring. He felt exposed, caught out in the open, as the sounds of war surrounded him again. His immediate inclination was to shout orders to his men, to bend into the run that would carry him across No Man's Land—

Elizabeth, suddenly aware, looked up at the tension in his face and cried, "Oh—I didn't think—are you all right? It's only the children—"

Rutledge nodded, unable to trust his voice.

Just then the Guy went sailing into the heart of the blaze, like a living creature struggling to escape as the heat rushed toward him. The onlookers were ecstatic, roaring at the top of their lungs as the straw-stuffed figure jerked and twisted as if in torment. The candles streamed wildly above the tongues of flame, and the noise was deafening.

Rutledge was still scouring the faces illuminated by the flames. A policeman was trained to observe, to remember the shape of a nose, the width of a mouth, the way the eyes were set, and the height of the forehead.

He couldn't have been wrong, there had to be someone who bore a faint resemblance to the man he'd seen. *Something* had triggered that memory, something had reached somewhere deep in his past and dredged it up.

But there were only strangers here, appearing and disappearing in the smoke like wraiths, none of them familiar, all of them solidly alive, villagers with every right to be here enjoying the night.

In God's name, it had surely been a ghost. . . .

He knew about ghosts—

People were milling around him now, slapping each other on the back, celebrating, calling out to friends, pressing him toward the fire, into the heart of the crowd. Mind-numbing to a man who was claustrophobic. Someone who knew Elizabeth came past and thrust a glass of long-hoarded champagne into their hands, shouting something Rutledge couldn't decipher in the din. He drank the champagne quickly, to steady himself. *What was happening to him? Why had a perfectly normal evening gone so badly wrong?*

Hamish said, "It's November—"

As if that explained everything.

And in a terrible way it did. Last November Rutledge had been in the trenches of France, he and his men abandoned by hope, and bitter, too tired to relish the successes of the Americans or to believe the whispers of a peace.

The doctors had warned him there would be flashbacks, that he would from time to time find himself reliving what was best forgotten. "Sometimes as vividly as life," Dr. Fleming had cautioned him. "And far from unnatural."

Easy for Fleming to say, sitting in his sparsely furnished surgery surrounded by stacks of folders of the living dead, the men who had come home shattered in body or spirit.

Locked in by the crowd, his body confined on all sides by people oblivious to his sense of suffocation as the claustrophobia gripped him, wanting to break through them to space and air, fighting to draw a full breath, Rutledge struggled with panic. Even Elizabeth, chatting with a neighbor, was pressing against him, her body warm with excitement and the heat of the fire.

The nightmare surrounded him, unending, like torment meted out carefully to make the pain last. He felt like the Guy, a helpless spectacle.

And then the Guy was consumed, the flames began to die back, and the euphoria of the evening seemed to wane as well. Women began to collect reluctant children, and men with rakes and brooms went to brush some of the ashes back toward the still-red coals at the center. Voices could actually be heard over the din and the crowd started to move in different directions, freeing him at last.

Elizabeth, her face pink from laughter, looked up at him and said gratefully, "Thank you for coming, Ian! I couldn't have faced it on my own. Although it's time I learned, isn't it?" She was holding his arm again, her fingers like individual bands of steel gripping him.

And then as swiftly as he had seemed to suffocate, his mind cleared and he was himself again. He put his hand over hers and managed a smile.

As she moved away to speak to someone else, Rutledge scanned the far side of the smoking remains of the fire for a last time, but the face was not there. The man was not there.

Surely he never had been—

Elizabeth said, turning to look behind her, "Did you see someone you know? Do you want to try to catch him up?"

"No—!" Rutledge answered abruptly, and then added at Hamish's prompting, "I— A trick of the light, that's all. I was wrong."

It was surely something about the night that had disturbed him, and the noise and the acrid smell of the fireworks lingering in the smoky air. There was no one there—

"He canna' be," Hamish reminded Rutledge. "He's deid. Like me!"

Deid. Like me!

Rutledge hesitated, on the point of asking Hamish what he knew— what he might have seen. Then—or just now.

But before he could frame the words, he stopped himself.

What if this had nothing to do with the war?

AFTER A VERY fine dinner with Elizabeth and three of her friends at the hotel just along the High Street, Rutledge drove back to London. Introductions and the subsequent settling into chairs as everyone exclaimed over the success of the evening had given Rutledge time to collect himself and present a polite, pleasant facade in spite of his unsettled state of mind.

It was something he was becoming increasingly good at doing, finding the right mask for his terrors.

Caught up in their own excitement, no one at the table noticed his long silences or made anything of his distraction. He was the outsider among them, and they included him from kindness, expecting nothing in return. He overheard one of the women as she leaned toward Elizabeth and murmured, "He's absolutely charming! Where did you find him?" as if he were a new suitor.

His hostess had replied dryly, "He was Richard's best man. I've known Ian for ages. He's been a great comfort."

For Elizabeth's sake, he was glad to find himself accepted. He couldn't have borne it if he'd embarrassed her. Yet it could have happened all too easily.

Frances had been wrong—he was not ready to meet old friends and pick up the threads of an old life. There were too many walls that shut him off from people who remembered a very different man called Ian Rutledge.

Still, Elizabeth had not let him go without extracting a promise that he'd be back on 10 November.

"You *will* ask for leave, I hope," she said anxiously, a reminder. "And Chief Superintendent Bowles will agree, won't he?"

"I see no reason why not," Rutledge responded, bending his head to kiss her cheek. "I'll be here. If I can."

What he didn't tell her was that—with or without leave—he had no intention of being in London on 11 November.

But on the long drive home, watching the headlamps pick out the verges of the road and pierce the heavy shadows of trees and hedgerows, Rutledge had found himself seeing again and again the face he'd carried with him since the bonfire.

It lingered against his will, as if once having surfaced it refused to be stuffed down once more into the bleak depths from which it had risen. And there was no respite, for traffic was too light to distract him. The cloudy, moonless night seemed to be its ally, and even Hamish was silent. By the time Rutledge reached the outskirts of London, the shoulders and chest attached to the face had fleshed themselves out, bit by bit gathering substance like a reluctant ghost. They belonged not in the proper English clothing Rutledge thought he'd glimpsed tonight, but in a torn and bloody uniform.

And Hamish said, as if he'd been waiting for Rutledge to reach this point, "I'd no' pursue it. There were sae many . . ."

In the pale morning light, as he made his way to Scotland Yard the next day, Rutledge realized he had arrived at the same conclusion.

IT WAS 9 NOVEMBER. RUTLEDGE WAS AT THE YARD, PREPARING to clear his desk for leave due to begin that afternoon. He was looking forward to returning to Marling, in Kent. Not just as an escape from London to avoid the public commemoration on the eleventh, but as an opportunity to prove to himself that the memories awakened on Guy Fawkes Day were no more than an isolated and unexpected response to the noisy press of people around the bonfire and his own restiveness over the approaching celebration of the Armistice. There had been no recurring episodes. For that he was grateful.

He knew very well that it had become something of an obsession, this celebration. Hamish harped on the date, as did the newspapers, giving him no peace.

For weeks he'd watched the preparation of the temporary structure that London was building to honor the nation's casualties of war. In fact, seeing every stage had been unavoidable as he came and went at the Yard. The permanent memorial would not be completed until the next year, but much had been made of the eventual design and placement.

A Cenotaph: a monument to the dead buried elsewhere . . .

And so many, so very many of them were: a sea of white crosses in foreign ground, some with names, some with no more than the bleak word

Unknown. But *he* had known them; he and officers like him had sent them out to die, young and inexperienced and eager, dead before he could recall their names or remember their faces. . . . Dead before he'd had the chance to turn them into real soldiers, with some small hope of survival. Dead and on his conscience, like weighted stones. And no time to mourn—

Nor did he need a Cenotaph standing close by Whitehall and Downing Street as a focus for his grief and loss. He—like countless others—carried them with him every day. The men he had served with, shared hardship and fear with, bled and suffered with, were as sharp in his memory and his nightmares as they had been before they died. As was the recurring voice that lived in his mind. A reminder in every waking moment of the Scots he'd led and the one Scot he'd been forced to execute during the horrendous bloodbath that had been the Battle of the Somme.

Invading his thoughts, Hamish scolded, "Ye've read the same lines three times, man!"

Realizing he'd done just that, Rutledge finished the paragraph and signed the report, setting it aside to be handed to Superintendent Bowles. His mind often grappled with the long nightmare of the trenches, the blighted landscape of northern France, the narrowed focus of trying somehow to protect the men under him, and the black despair of failing. Sometimes these seemed more real than the paperwork in front of him.

He was reaching for the next folder when a young constable tapped at his door and stepped aside to usher in a florid-faced, middle-aged woman in a dowdy black coat and a black hat that did not become her.

"A Mrs. Shaw to see you, sir! She says you'd know who she is."

The woman stared at Rutledge, her heavy features twisting into a mask of pain. Tears began to trickle down her face, ravaging it.

Rutledge nodded to the constable as the man hesitated before closing the door. It swung shut with a click.

"Please, sit down, Mrs. Shaw," he said gently as he strove to find her name in his memory. But there were no Shaws in the files he'd been reviewing, and as far as he could recall, no Shaws who had served under him in France. She watched him from behind her tears, waiting for the first stir of recognition.

Before the war, then?

And it came back to him as she sank heavily into her chair.

She was the widow of a man he'd sent to the gallows. Shaw . . . Ben Shaw. Convicted of murdering elderly women and robbing them. He had been trusted: a man-of-all-work who came on call to do the small and necessary repairs that aging and ill householders couldn't manage. And when they didn't die soon enough to suit him, he'd eased their going with a pillow, and then ransacked their meager possessions for anything of value. Alone in the world and bedridden, they had had no chance against him.

One of the newspapers had written a sensational account of the scene as imagined by one of their journalists: *"He came boldly to the bed, speaking kindly, offering to plump the flat and lumpy pillows for them, as he must have done a hundred—nay, a thousand times!—and as they smiled gratefully, he slipped the pillow over their faces before that smile could be replaced by horror, and held it there firmly against their weak—futile—attempts to prevent him. And when the pale, flaccid arms fell back to his victims' sides, he had lifted each graying head, slipped the pillow gently back beneath it, and closed the bulging eyes before walking back down the stairs and shutting the door behind him, leaving the pathetic corpse for a cleaning woman to discover in the morning . . ."*

Inflammatory as it was, it had drawn a reprimand from the judge as he charged the jury and bade them ignore the overwrought misconceptions of a writer paid to stir up the public sentiment.

Rutledge, pushing the recollection aside, wondered what had brought her here, to the Yard. It was as unexpected as a resurrection. "You wished to see me, Mrs. Shaw? What can I do to help you?"

"Turn back the clock," she answered tremulously. "But there's no one can do that, is there?" She began to cry in earnest.

As a young policeman, he'd dreaded having to speak to friends and relatives of victims, dreaded the tears that seemed to fall without conscious will, a flood that made him feel exceedingly helpless. How do you offer comfort, where there is none? Experience had not taught him an answer.

Rutledge was silent, allowing Mrs. Shaw a space in which to recover, and then said with compassion, "No one knows a way to do that."

It was, he thought, a prelude to a piteous account of life as the widow of a hanged man, followed by an entreaty for money to pay her rent. She must be in dire straits, to come to the police for help. He tried to recall the name of the clergyman he'd met while investigating the case. It would be in the files. Surely the parish must offer some provisions for the Mrs. Shaws of this world—she needn't be reduced to begging!

She surprised him.

"Turn back the clock to that trial," she said baldly, staring fiercely at him, "and this time find some way of bringing out the *truth*!"

Caught utterly off guard, Rutledge found himself fumbling for words. "I don't quite understand—"

"The truth who it was killed them, the old ladies." She began to dig in the purse she carried with her, and pulled out a small handkerchief. Unfolding it on the edge of his desk, she added triumphantly, "That's your proof, right here! It won't bring my Ben back, nothing will, but it should clear his name!"

Inside the square of cheap cloth was a locket without its chain. In the center was the face of a man in profile, carved in onyx from what Rutledge could see of it, against a pearl-gray background. A lacework of black-enameled laurel leaves framed it. She opened the locket for him next: inside lay a delicately braided coil of graying chestnut hair, protected by a crystal cover.

She watched him as he studied it, guarding it against any intent on his part to take it from her, turning it in her rough hands with the delicacy of a merchant exhibiting his wares.

It was mourning jewelry, worn to remind the wearer of a loved one.

"May I?" he asked. She nodded, and showed him the reverse.

And on the back of the locket were several lines engraved in the gold case: *Frederick Andrew Satterthwaite, loving husband, d. April 2, 1900.*

Satterthwaite had been the name of one of Shaw's victims.

"He couldn't sell it, could he?" Mrs. Shaw was demanding. "Not with that inscription on the back of it! Anybody would have known at once where it come from. What surprises me was that he kept it at all. But I suppose he couldn't think what to do with it. And it's pretty, in a morbid way. That's *gold* it's set in." A red finger with a chewed nail pointed at the setting, tapping it.

Rutledge rather thought she was right, on both counts. This was indeed a piece of jewelry that would have marked the possessor as a thief and murderer.

And it hadn't been found in Ben Shaw's possession—to his, Rutledge's, certain knowledge. It had never come to light at all, and only a distant cousin's memory of the locket had seen it included in the inevitable inventory of Mrs. Satterthwaite's belongings. *"One mourning locket, bearing name of deceased's husband, and date of his death, set in gold, onyx profile. Missing."*

The investigating officer, Inspector Nettle—Rutledge had not been the first on the scene—had written in his notes the query *"Very likely thrown into the river?"*

"How did you find it?" Rutledge asked, leaning back in his chair. The locket was too difficult to fake—too expensive, for one thing. And for what purpose? "More to the point, where had your husband hidden it?"

"God save us, *no!*" she replied in a harsh, frustrated voice. "If he had, would I bring it to *you?* Now? To what end—I ask you, what good would it do?"

"Perhaps to put your mind at ease, in regard to your husband's guilt?"

"I told you, the truth comes out with this, and too late to save Ben! No, this I took from my *neighbor's* house yesterday. Henry Cutter, his name is. The old bitch, his wife, died last month, and he couldn't bear to go through her clothes and such. Finally he asked me. And I found this in the back of the chest where she kept her corsets and drawers. Folded in that handkerchief." The stubby finger stabbed at a bit of color in one corner. "See, it's embroidered: *JAC*—for Janet Ann Cutter. And what I want from *you,* Inspector, is to find out what it was doing in *her* chest, and how it got there! I want to know if Henry Cutter stole it from a dead woman! And if my poor husband is innocent, I want you to clear his name. Do you hear me? My children deserve that—to have the shame taken away—even if you can't bring Ben back to us!"

Hamish said, "It isna' a small thing she wants."

Her small, bright eyes glared balefully at Rutledge, as if he'd hanged her husband with his own hands. Which, in a way perhaps, he had. He'd been the investigating officer, after Philip Nettle had dropped dead of a burst appendix. It was his evidence, built on Nettle's original investigation, that had put Benjamin Edward Shaw on trial for murder, in August 1912. Six years and more ago . . .

4

THE SHOCK OF HER CERTAINTY, THE FEROCITY WITH WHICH
she faced him, were overwhelming.

And as the implication of her words sank in, Rutledge felt cold.

*If this locket had been found in someone else's possession at the time
of the trial, what difference might that have made to the outcome?*

He tried to find something to say. Something that would dispute her
conclusions. Or support his own position—

Hamish warned him. "It's no' wise to be o'wer hasty."

The small, deadly bit of gold jewelry glittered on his desk, mocking
Rutledge, seeming to take on a life of its own.

They had searched the Shaw house from top to bottom—the locket
had never been found. Was not there. He would have sworn to that under oath.

Yet here it was—all these years later—

Where had it been? And why?

And, gentle God, did it matter?

Yes, it mattered—if he had hanged the wrong man.

When Rutledge failed to answer her, Mrs. Shaw regarded him with
disdain. "You don't want to believe me, is that it? Because my Ben was
hanged for a murderer, you think I'm no better than he was!" She leaned

forward. "Well, it won't wash, do you hear me? I've come to ask for my rights, and if you won't help me, I'll find someone who will!"

"Mrs. Shaw," he said, forcing himself to think clearly, "I have only your word that this locket was found among the belongings of Mrs. Cutter. You should have left it there—"

"And risk having *him* find it? I'm not stupid, Inspector. If *he* killed those women and not my Ben, what's to stop him from killing *me*, if I let on what I'd done? As it was, I had to pretend to a faintness, to get out of that house."

"We spoke with the Cutters—"

"Yes, and so you did. Did you expect him to say, 'You've got it all wrong, Inspector, it wasn't Ben, it was me!'?" Her rough mimicry of a man's voice mocked him.

Rutledge said reasonably, "If you are right, why would Mrs. Cutter have kept this piece of jewelry? She must have realized that it was dangerous, given the fact that her husband may have been a murderer."

"Because she was sickly, that's why, and didn't want to be left alone! Better to sleep with a murderer than to sleep alone, and not have bread on the table when you wake up! It was the only bit he couldn't sell, wasn't it? Maybe it was her hold over her husband. And as long as he didn't know what had become of it, she was safe."

"It's not a very sound theory," he argued.

Mrs. Shaw looked him over, weighing up the clothes he wore as if she knew their value to a penny. "You've never known want, have you? Never worried at night where the rent was coming from or how you would pay the butcher, and what you was going to do about worn-out boots. I can tell you what happens to a woman on her own!"

And he could see for himself the suffering in her face.

But how much of what she'd told him about the Cutters was her need to find absolution for her husband?

The truth was, he didn't want to believe her. The bedrock of his emotional stability, the only thing that had brought him back to sanity after France, was the Yard, and the career he'd built there before the war. By 1914, his reputation had been shaped through solid achievement, unlike his undeserved glory in the war, where he had been driven half mad and shaken to the core by endless slaughter. To lose his career now—

He had never been a hero. But he'd been a damned good detective.

Hamish mocked, "Aye, so ye say. You're no' sae perfect, none of us is—"

"You weren't there; you don't know anything about this case!" Rutledge retorted in anger. *"You weren't there!"*

Mistaking the direction of his sudden flare of anger, Mrs. Shaw prodded defiantly, "If you killed my Ben wrongly, you owe me restitution. My children have gone hungry without him, and I've had nothing to give them, no way to offer any life at all. It's my children I'm defending. It's too late now for Ben."

Struggling with his own vulnerability just now when the war seemed to have returned with unexpected and extraordinary force, and against his will already half convinced by the intensity of the widow's determination, Rutledge made an effort to explain how the Yard would see her demands. He said, "We can't reopen a case—"

"You can!" she told him, interrupting. "Here's a wrongful death, and I have the proof. What's to become of me, and my children? Why should Henry Cutter go scot-free while we suffer for what he did?"

The locket lay between them, tearing his life apart as well as hers.

It couldn't be true. He'd been careful. So had Philip Nettle.

How could he destroy the past, when that was all he had?

And yet . . . and yet if he had failed Ben Shaw, what then? Why should *his* past be sacred? Untouchable?

Nell Shaw got to her feet, a middle-aged woman with nothing to be gained by coming to him, except relief from her personal tragedy. An unattractive woman with no graces, who would always provoke dislike and even loathing.

"I've a daughter of marrying age. I've a son looking to be apprenticed. I've done for them the best I could these last years. But there's no money to see them right. I barely kept food on the table. And no one's willing to lift a finger for them—not for the offspring of gallows' bait. We might as well have gone to the hangman along with Ben." She began to fold the handkerchief over the locket, as if shielding it from his eyes. "I see I'll find no help here. Well. There's other strings to my bow."

"I can't turn back the clock," he said, unconsciously repeating her words. "We don't know how this came into Mrs. Cutter's possession. Or why. Or, for that matter, when. It's evidence, yes, but it's not clear proof."

"It's something to be going on with! If you wasn't afraid to find out that you are as human as the rest of us and got it wrong."

The truth was, he *was* afraid. . . .

And at the same time, he knew he was honor-bound to get to the bottom of this allegation.

STIFLING THE TURMOIL that was tearing apart his own mind, Rutledge tried to put into perspective how momentous the finding of this locket must seem to the woman seated in front of him. Providing of course that her story was true—

But he could see no benefit for her in a lie. That was the key. She had nothing to gain by lying. And there was a driving force about her that couldn't be counterfeited. It was there in the way she held her body, and in the small, determined eyes.

He had never liked this woman. From the beginning of the murder inquiry, she had been a thorn in the side of authority. He tried to disregard his dislike now.

Hamish said, "Aye, she's an auld besom. But if it were another inspector's case she was complaining of, what would you do?"

Rutledge picked up his pen and uncapped it, drawing a sheet of paper forward.

"Mrs. Shaw. Listen to me. First and foremost, we can't search the Cutter house on your word alone—"

"What you're saying is that my word isn't good enough—"

"What I'm saying is that you took the locket from its hiding place. If I send forty men there in an hour's time, and nothing else turns up—if there's no more evidence to be found—then it's your word against Mr. Cutter's that the locket was in Mrs. Cutter's belongings. Now or ever."

She said stubbornly, "I left the chain where I found it. To mark the place!"

Rutledge nodded. "I understand that. But the chain could belong to any locket that Mrs. Cutter owned. There's no one who can say with authority that the chain my men discover actually belongs to the Satterthwaite locket. Mrs. Satterthwaite, I remind you, is dead—"

"There's another side to this coin, Inspector. That I'm telling the truth." Her eyes met his squarely. "And you're unwilling to hear it."

She had backed him around again to his own possible guilt.

He had always taken a certain pride in his knowledge of people. He knew how to watch for the small movements of the body or shifts in expression that supported or contradicted what he was told. Only a very few people lied well.

And either Nell Shaw was among them—or she believed implicitly in what she was saying.

Hamish said, "Aye. If you canna' satisfy her, she'll go o'wer your head."

And there were sound reasons why that must not happen. Rutledge was not the only officer who would be brought down if the Shaw case was shown to be flawed. Even if her accusations bore only a semblance of truth, the Yard was not immune from politics or personal vendettas.

"I'm not sending you away," he told her. "I'm searching for a practical way of getting around the rules I have to follow. I'll give you a chit for the locket—"

"No, never!" she declared, shoving it back in her purse and clutching that to her bosom with both arms. "It's all I've got."

He put down the pen. "Then you must let me have a few days to look again at the file, and then to decide how best to go about this problem. I don't have the authority to open this case myself. And it won't do you much good to make enemies—for you will if you begin to annoy my own superiors, or Mr. Cutter. It's to your advantage and mine to proceed with caution. Have you spoken to the barrister who defended your husband?"

"I've got no money. He won't give me the time of day."

"I make no promises, mind you. But I give you my word that I'll do my best. If I can satisfy myself that there's just cause to reopen the case, I'll tell you so and give you the name of someone at the Home Office who will listen to you."

"And if you can't?" she asked suspiciously.

"Then you're free to speak to anyone else here at the Yard."

"That's fair. I never asked more." There was a gleam of gratification in her dark eyes. "I've waited this long. A few more days won't matter, will they?"

5

AFTER RUTLEDGE HAD SEEN MRS. SHAW INTO A CAB, HE SAT
in his chair and stared out the window at the bare branches of trees
that stood out stark and almost pleading against the colorless sky.

He couldn't have been wrong about Ben Shaw. . . .

And yet he had been badly shaken by that locket, and Mrs. Shaw's
ferocious defense of her husband's innocence had rung with conviction.
If he had been so certain of the man's guilt before, how had that altered
so easily?

Hamish said, "Your wits are scattered, man, ye're no' thinking
clearly!"

What if he had been wrong—

Hamish said, "It isna' the end of the world—"

Rutledge retorted angrily, "It was a man's *life*. You weren't
there—"

Hamish agreed readily. "I was safe in Scotland then, and alive. . . ."
After a moment he added, "She willna' be put off."

Nor was he the sort of man who could quietly bury truth under a
layer of lies. Rutledge faced himself now, and with that a possibility
that appalled him. Like it or not, he must get to the bottom of this question of Ben Shaw's guilt.

Like it or not, he must find the answer, for his own soul's comfort.

Hamish growled, "It isna' a matter of comfort, it's a sair question for the conscience." His Covenanter heritage had always projected his world in severe black and white. It was what had brought him to defy the Army and face execution rather than compromise. His strength— and his destruction.

Ignoring the voice in his head, Rutledge considered the next step. How did one go about dredging up the past, without destroying what had been built upon it?

This was not the first time he'd dealt with families whose anger was as destructive as it was futile, when not even a jury's verdict could persuade them of a loved one's guilt. But few of these families had ever brought forward what was in their eyes fresh proof of innocence.

And on that slim balance, he was forced to confront his actions of more than six years ago.

Hamish said, "I saw a magician once. When the troop train was held up in London, he came to entertain us. I couldna' be certain what was real and what was false."

Rutledge suddenly found a memory of Ben Shaw's defeated, exhausted face, when the prison warders brought him to the gallows. Even if he could clear the man's name, there was no way he could restore the man's life. Shaw was *dead. . . .*

Like so many others. The world seemed filled with phantoms, his mind shattered by them.

Suddenly he could feel himself slipping back in the trenches, the Battle of the Somme in July 1916—the watershed of his madness.

HAMISH'S VOICE BROUGHT him sharply back to the dingy confines of his office at Scotland Yard, with its low shelves, its grimy windows, the smell of old paint and dusty corners heavy in the passages. With the sound of footsteps harsh on the wooden floors outside his door, and brief snatches of conversations that seemed to have no beginning and no end.

Rutledge rubbed his face, trying to remember what Hamish had said to him. And the voice repeated, "It's no' unlikely that Shaw himself gave the locket to the neighbor's wife. A love token. Mrs. Shaw willna' care to hear that."

"With that telling inscription on the back? Besides, mourning jewelry isn't the most romantic gift, is it? When Mrs. Cutter's own husband was very much alive."

"A promise, no doubt, that he wouldna' be alive much longer. It could explain why she kept it."

"You didn't know Shaw," Rutledge reminded Hamish.

But then, had he?

All the same, Rutledge did know his superior, Chief Superintendent Bowles. And therein lay a hidden snare that could be as explosive as a mine.

The Shaw investigation had brought a promotion to the then Chief Inspector Bowles, who had used the murders to political and professional advantage. Bowles had kept himself very much in the public eye, repeatedly promising the newspapers that this vicious killer would be brought to justice with all possible speed, assuring frightened neighbors of the murdered women that everything possible was being done, publicly pressing his men to greater and greater effort.

It was Philip Nettle who had stumbled on the connection that linked the three victims—the fact that each had at one time or another employed the services of the same carpenter when work needed to be done. A trusted man, a caring man, one who had trimmed the wicks of lamps, brought in coal for the fires, oiled locks on the doors, kept window sashes running smoothly, and generally made himself indispensable. And then betrayed their trust.

The discovery of the murderer had once more pitched Chief Inspector Bowles into the forefront of public attention. As Philip Nettle lay dying in hospital, Bowles had made half a dozen speeches that cleverly fostered the notion that it was his own intuition that had come up with the crimes' solution. He had given interviews to magazines and newspapers. And he had delivered the eulogy at Philip Nettle's funeral, praising the man rather than the police officer, kissing the grieving widow's cheek with marked condescension. She had regarded him with bitterness, convinced that Bowles's callous demands for results had prevented her husband from making a timely visit to his doctor.

Sergeant Gibson, reading the caption under yet another photo-graph in a newspaper, had said sourly within Rutledge's hearing, "You'd bloody think the man was standing for Parliament!"

Sergeant Wilkerson had answered, "Aye, there's hope he will, and leave the Yard for good!"

To order the Shaw file brought to his office on the heels of a visit by Mrs. Shaw would ring alarm bells at the Yard. Old Bowels would hear about it before the day was out, and send someone down the pas-sage to ferret out what was going on. Hanged felons were finished busi-ness. Even if Mrs. Shaw found a hundred new pieces of evidence.

The Yard, like the Army, demanded obedience and rigorously fol-lowed the chain of command.

"Aye, it's as guid an excuse as any," Hamish taunted, "for doing nothing."

"Or a damned good reason for exercising caution," Rutledge coun-tered, getting up from his chair.

He went himself to the vast cavern where records were kept and, af-ter some hunting among dusty cabinets, located the folder he was after.

With his office door shut, and no one but Hamish to observe him, Rutledge opened the file and began to read.

At the end of it, he sat back in his chair and watched the reflection of pale November light from his windows as it played across the ugly walls.

The sheets of paper and notes and conclusions that had been meticulously written seemed—in the light of Mrs. Shaw's discovery—to lack conviction now. And yet in 1912, they had rung with truth—

No one had questioned one Henry Cutter, or his wife—except in regard to the comings and goings of Ben Shaw, his reputation in the neighborhood, and whether he was capable of killing anyone. The res-idents on either side of the Shaw house had had very little to say about their neighbor. They hadn't seen suspicious goings-on and they hadn't noticed any changes in Ben Shaw's manner after the first murder or the last.

Mrs. Cutter—her given name was Janet—had unexpectedly pro-vided one important clue. The two Shaw children had been taken out of the local school and put into better ones, a small private school for the son, and an academy for the daughter. An inheritance, Mrs. Shaw had claimed, from Shaw's late uncle. Records turned up no such inheritance—the uncle had died in debt twenty years before, leaving his young son no choice but to emigrate. It was not long before Inspector Nettle was digging deeper into Ben Shaw's sudden financial windfall.

This had been the point on which the evidence had turned. The Shaws had been a struggling family until just after the first body was found. A Mrs. Winslow. Many of her belongings had been unaccounted for, but it was believed at the time of her death that most of these had been sold to enable her to continue to live independently in her own home. It was not until the second murder, of Mrs. Satterthwaite, that the police had begun to draw a wider net and stumbled on the Shaws. It was the third murder that had concentrated attention on Ben Shaw's activities on the three nights in question.

Especially after Mrs. Cutter had provided the most important reason to concentrate there. But no one had wondered why she was so cooperative. . . .

Could it have been to her advantage?

A shocking thought. That he could have sent an innocent man to the gallows on the basis of a woman's perverted evidence. Rutledge closed his eyes against the pale light, looking back instead into the darkness of the past.

He had been so sure of his evidence and Nettle's. So thoroughly convinced of the man's guilt was he that his certainty was palpable in the courtroom. A well-thought-out investigation, the judge had applauded in his summation to the jury. For there had been no reason to connect the Cutters with the three women. Certainly, no evidence in that direction!

What could have been Henry Cutter's motive for murder? His style of living hadn't altered, but the Shaws' had.

After the sudden death of Inspector Nettle, Rutledge had interviewed the neighbors again, including Henry and Janet Cutter. Nettle had been in increasingly severe pain for several days, covering it with wry humor and massive doses of cathartics. He often scrawled his notes in a shaking hand that was hard to follow. Rutledge had left nothing to chance. He had backtracked to substantiate each fact.

Mrs. Cutter had not had kind words to say for Mrs. Shaw ("a nosy and overbearing woman with few saving graces"), but she claimed that Mr. Shaw had never demonstrated any vicious tendencies that would account for his killing elderly women. "Kind to animals, and all that," she'd said to Rutledge, bewildered. "A good father, too, and he put up with that wife of his when no one else would. Always after him to do better with his life, provide for his family. It doesn't seem right that the smallest sign of wickedness didn't show in his face or his ways! How are we to know, I ask you, if there's no sign to warn us?"

And then she had added, almost as an afterthought, that last damning sentence. "And he did provide for his children. It hasn't been six months since they were put in better schools, never mind the cost!" She had repeated it for Rutledge's edification. "Not six months!"

The first murder had occurred just seven months before. . . .

Henry Cutter had described Ben Shaw as a man clever with his hands, always called on by his neighbors when something failed to work. "And I've never known him to take a ha'penny for what he done. Never saw him drunk, nor known him to strike his wife. It seems queer that he'd kill helpless old ladies for what he could scavenge in their houses. . . ."

"What he could scavenge" had been over a hundred pounds' worth of jewelry and small, portable treasures that could, in the right quarter, be sold without questions asked.

But Henry Cutter, in the notes, had called Mrs. Shaw a kind and loving wife, "and Ben would have done anything for her, he cared that much for her."

Kill and steal to give her the kind of life she goaded him into providing? Rutledge had, at the time, wondered if Mrs. Shaw wasn't equally guilty for hounding her husband to desperate measures to keep her satisfied. But there was no law in English jurisprudence to cover that crime, even if she had.

Certainly their house had shown an influx of money that their combined income—his as a carpenter and hers as a shopkeeper's assistant—couldn't explain. But there were the small jobs that Ben Shaw did, for it seemed that he did charge when his services were sought by those well able to pay. He had never kept an accounting of what he'd earned in that fashion. His wife had probably spent most of it on clothes for the children, better schools, and certainly better food than their neighbors enjoyed.

Someone had told Rutledge—a neighbor two houses away—that she'd heard that Ben Shaw had come from better stock than his wife, who "had pulled him down, if you want the truth. Common, she is," determined though she was to give her children opportunities to rise above their station. "I'll say that for Nell Shaw, she never tried to hold either of them back, on her own account!"

Rutledge would have put his money on Mrs. Shaw as the killer, if there had been the slimmest chance of that. He hadn't liked her, for one thing, and he'd felt some sympathy for her husband after enduring her sharp tongue in the early stages of the investigation. Nell Shaw had been angry, defending her family like an enraged tigress, accusing the police of failing at their own duty and having nothing better to do than badger a poor man into night terrors.

But neither Rutledge nor Nettle had ever fully explored the background of the neighbors—what opportunities they might have had to meet the three dead women, what reasons they might have had to commit murder. There was no evidence at all that pointed in their direction, even though Henry Cutter's wife seemed to know more about the victims than Mrs. Shaw had. She had read about them in the newspapers . . . so she claimed.

Instead he had focused on two facts: that Ben Shaw was often in the homes of the deceased. And that after he was charged, Ben Shaw had all but admitted he was the murderer.

But what if he hadn't been—what if, afraid from the start that his wife might be guilty, he'd confessed to distract the police from her?

Hamish said, "Or fra' someone else he cared for."

It wouldn't be the first time that a husband or wife risked hanging out of fear of the truth coming out. Or out of fear that the other was in danger. . . .

What if, looking deeper, Rutledge found himself thinking, he'd come across unexpected evidence that proved clearly that the most obvious pointers were not the most likely after all . . . ? In one case in ten, digging deeper brought out new facts. And yet at the time, he was convinced that he *had* dug deeply—

Speaking up after a long and brooding silence, Hamish said, "What if ye find that I'm no' the first victim whose death can be laid at your door? What if this man died a worse death than mine, because ye were no' the clever policeman you thought you were?"

As Rutledge laid the last of the pages aside, he wondered if he would come to regret his decision to retrieve the file.

But he was committed now . . . whatever he learned about himself.

6

THERE WAS NOTHING MORE RUTLEDGE COULD DO THAT DAY about his promise to Nell Shaw. Nor the next, as he drove south of London and back into Kent.

But it was like a sore tooth nagging in the back of his mind. And after he had crossed Lambeth Bridge, he made his way south and east, to the part of south London where the Shaws—and the Cutters—lived. It was familiar ground, and yet as the motorcar turned down street after street, he could see that the once prosperous working-class houses were showing signs of neglect after nearly five years of war and shortages of manpower and materials. England had impoverished herself to win, and Rutledge found himself thinking that here was the invisible cost in human suffering and hardship.

Many of the factories had shut down, and the residential streets were grim in November's gray chill. Not even a dog wandered in the gutters sniffing for scraps.

Those who could escape had done so long ago, especially those who had found a way of prospering from the war. Those who were doomed to finish out their lives here had fallen prey to despair and hopelessness.

Among them, Mrs. Shaw and, so it seemed, Henry Cutter. . . .

Not for the first time, Rutledge asked himself how Henry Cutter's wife had come by that missing locket.

"Ye canna' be sure she did! There's only one woman's word for it."

Rutledge replied grimly, "It wasn't in the Shaw house when it was searched. I'd stake my career on that."

"Aye, it's what you're doing."

"The problem is, why would Shaw have given the locket to Cutter's wife? For safekeeping when the police were crawling all over his house? It would have been safer to pitch it into the Thames." He fell easily into the old habit of answering Hamish, of treating the voice in his head as though the dead man sat in the rear seat of the motorcar, his constant companion and a fearful presence. "Shaw wasn't the sort to stray from home and hearth. But then no one thought he was the sort to commit murder, either."

"People are sometimes verra' different under the skin. If he was clever enough to kill, he might ha' been clever enough to have other secrets."

"The same could be said of Mrs. Shaw—or the Cutters."

Rutledge passed the house on Sansom Street without stopping. Fog was curling in off the river, wreathing roofs and sliding over chimneys, giving the house and its neighbors a sinister air.

He told himself he hadn't yet formulated a strategy for his opening move. Like contemplating a chess game before touching the pieces, he thought to himself. It was very like that—he couldn't afford to choose the wrong move.

Hamish was saying, "In the end, you must speak to Cutter."

But how to go about that without arousing Bowles's suspicions? The Chief Superintendent was a vindictive enemy, when aroused.

Rutledge wished Mrs. Shaw had had the sense to write to him instead of coming to the Yard in person. It would have drawn far less attention. But then he might have read the letter and done nothing, putting it down to a woman's refusal to let go of the past. Her strong presence, tearful and demanding and fiercely certain, had affected him, as she must have guessed it would.

It might yet prove to be nothing more than that. A brooding that had consumed her to the point of believing in her own phantoms.

A widow whose husband had been hanged for murder must not

have had an easy life. Nor her children. He had only to look around him to guess what privations they'd suffered.

Still, she'd survived. It showed in her toughness and her determination. He found it hard to blame her for being bitter and angry. And if she was right, if there *had* been a miscarriage of justice, he was as much to blame as Bowles and Philip Nettle. Perhaps more so, because he had brought the case to trial.

Everything hinged on that locket.

THE AUTUMN WEATHER was at its worst—the clear skies of Guy Fawkes Day had long since given way to a week of heavy clouds and a cold wind. Today, the breath-sucking fog seemed to follow Rutledge out of London, cloaking everything and everyone in a clinging, damp, choking vapor. It ran ahead of him toward the Downs, silent fingers reaching through the hedgerows and shrouding the trees.

He could barely see the verges of the road, and slowed for fear of running into a farm cart or lorry, invisible around the next curve. Hamish, a presence at his shoulder, was restless with the tension of driving.

"It wasna' necessary to leave sae early! Ye'll kill us both before this weather lifts!"

Rutledge wasn't sure he would be sorry to wind up in a ditch, his neck broken. But his sister would mourn. And a handful of friends. And Jean, who had married her diplomat and sailed for Canada, would learn of his death on her wedding journey.

He smiled wryly at that. He had no illusions now about his former fiancée. Jean would read the news and sigh prettily, and say to her new husband, "My dear, I've just heard—a very dear friend has been killed on a road south of London. I—I must believe it's a blessing. He was—he was never the same after the war, you know. I daresay—but no, that's not fair. I should never wish to believe he'd found a way to *end* it—"

And the diplomat, not very diplomatically, would reply briskly, "You mustn't blame yourself, my dear. It's all in the past now."

Hamish commented, his voice clear in the dim interior of the motorcar, "Aye, it's no' a bonny thing to say. But it might be true, nonetheless."

Rutledge concentrated his attention on the road.

ELIZABETH MAYHEW GREETED him warmly, clucking her tongue over the weather, and saying, "I was afraid you might not come. That you'd be glad of the weather as an excuse."

"Nonsense," he told her, kissing her cheek. "It will lift by noon. Frances sends her love, and I'm to convince you to come to London for a few days over Christmas."

"How sweet of her," Elizabeth said, leading the way to the stairs. "I may do that. I've grown so dull of late I'll bore her to death. But perhaps it *would* be good for me. We shall see."

The house was a comfortable Georgian manor on the outskirts of Marling, a pretty village that had enjoyed its share of wealth over the centuries and still maintained an air of quiet gentility.

Set back behind a low brick wall, the gardens bedded down for the winter, the house now seemed to wear its age more starkly, but in summer it glowed with the warmth of the sun and with the rampant colors of perennials, with annuals sprawling at their feet. Then it was timeless and beautiful.

There had always been a welcome here, as long as Rutledge could remember. But without Richard's voice in the passages or his long legs stretched out toward the fire after a day tramping on the Downs, there was an emptiness in the rooms that lamps and Elizabeth's lighter voice couldn't fill.

Rutledge had known Richard Mayhew longer than Elizabeth had, long before Elizabeth had come into the picture. In his youth, he'd played tennis here with Richard, and gone for long walks over the Downs, following old tracks and pathways whose origins were lost in time. It had seemed odd, when the summer light lingered late into the evening, to think of the ghosts whose footsteps they were following. Angles, Saxons, Romans—God knew what other now nameless tribes had passed this way. Richard had called it the spell of Midsummer. "The poets are always writing about it. I daresay the ancients worshiping the sun thought this a magic time."

And so it had been. Before the war had come and swept it all away.

Now the house seemed sad without Richard, and Rutledge found himself wondering if it wouldn't be wiser if Elizabeth closed it for a time and took a smaller place in London. Away from the memories. But perhaps those memories were comforting. . . .

As his own were not.

She was saying, "And I must apologize—but we've been invited out to dine, and I couldn't tell them no. With the Hamiltons—you remember them?—and of course Mrs. Crawford will be there. She's coming up from Sussex, just to see you."

Melinda Crawford was one of the most remarkable women he'd ever met. As a child she'd survived the siege of Lucknow, during the Great Indian Mutiny of 1857. An inveterate and fearless traveler, she had seen more of the world than most men. Rutledge had always been immensely fond of her. Her memory was as sharp as ever it had been, her tongue as tart, and her company as charming.

Elizabeth, reading his expression, said wryly, "Richard adored her, too. I think she took his death harder than I did."

It would be an unexpected treat to see Mrs. Crawford again. But not tonight. He was too tired and his mood too dark for polite conversation. "It was a rather long drive—" he began, and then stopped. "Would you like to go?"

She made a face. "Not really. But Bella Masters has been having a very difficult time, and we've been trying to cheer her up a bit. Raleigh will come to dine, but Bella can't get him out of the house otherwise. She hasn't said, but I have the awful feeling that he's dying. And nobody quite knows what to do."

"What's wrong with him?"

"A very stubborn infection. It cost him his toes, and then his foot, and now he's about to lose his leg close to the knee. Blood poisoning. He has some sort of apparatus to wear in place of his foot, but he hates it. Bella tries to pretend all is well, which doesn't help. It's Lydia Hamilton's turn to entertain them, and she couldn't make up her numbers. I'm afraid Raleigh isn't always very good company. We're the martyrs thrown to the lions."

"In that case, by all means, we'll go," Rutledge assured her.

She seemed relieved, but said only, "Then come into the sitting room and we'll have our tea in comfort, before it's time to dress. I've something to show you—"

Henrietta, the spaniel, had just presented Elizabeth with puppies, five of them, still blind and squirming and noisy. They lay in a box near the hearth, and Henrietta rose to greet Rutledge before warily allowing him to admire her family. Elizabeth was on the floor beside the box, clearly entranced, giving him the name of each tiny ball of fur.

He could hardly tell one from another, except by the liver-colored spots, but dutifully gave his attention to each in turn, while Henrietta licked his hand and watched attentively as Elizabeth lifted her brood one by one and held the newborns up for his inspection. He found himself thinking that Elizabeth herself would have made a wonderful mother, but there had never been any children in her marriage. Richard had been philosophical about it. "Early days," he'd said. But time had run out.

When the maid brought tea, Elizabeth went to wash her hands and Henrietta climbed gratefully back into her box, nosing each of her treasures, as if to reassure herself that none had gone missing. Rutledge leaned back in his chair and closed his eyes.

Hamish, in the back of his mind, was saying something about Richard. He ignored it, and tried to put London and the Yard out of his thoughts for the evening. It would not do to drag the Shaws into Elizabeth's uncomplicated world, and yet Rutledge found himself wishing he could talk to her as he would have done to her husband. A barrister, Richard would have understood Rutledge's dilemma and heard the story out without criticism or comment. Elizabeth would worry over Ben Shaw's innocence as well as his guilt, and leave the subject more tangled than it was. . . .

She came back into the room just then and, seeing him with his eyes closed, said briskly, "You need your tea!" and proceeded to pour him a cup.

Hamish said, "A wee dram o' whisky would do more good."

THE WHISKY CAME at the Hamiltons, a stiff drink that Lawrence Hamilton handed him with the admonition "You'll need this!"

Elizabeth had gone upstairs to speak to Lydia, and the two men were alone in the drawing room.

Rutledge said, "I hear Masters hasn't been well." He had met the man a time or two in the courts, but hardly knew him at all.

"No, he hasn't. And it's been difficult for him. Not only the loss of his limb, but the constant pain and the dragging down of his spirits. He had to give up the law, you know, and that was possibly worse than amputation. He loved his work." Lawrence was square, fair, with a ruddy complexion. "Still, he's a man of uncertain moods. Always was, for all I know, but now it's noticeable. Lydia and Elizabeth and a few other friends have tried to make his illness bearable for Bella—"

He broke off as the maid ushered in another guest. Melinda Crawford swept into the room with grace, a tall woman, slim now with age, and wearing the evening dress of another reign: gray silk, with lace high to the throat and binding the sleeves at her wrists. Her white hair, piled high in shining waves, was still thick, and the handsome blue eyes were unclouded. The beautiful ebony cane in her left hand was more affectation than necessity.

She greeted her host with warmth, and then regarded Rutledge with interest. "You survived the war, then. Why haven't you been to see me?"

Rutledge answered, "First I had to find my way back into civilian life." But it was Hamish that he had wanted to hide from her. Melinda Crawford had seen war, had nursed the wounded and comforted the dying when she was only ten; her experience was so vast that he had been afraid she would instantly read his secret in his eyes.

He went to kiss her cheek, and she held him off for a moment, studying his face. "Ah. And have you found your way?" She let him kiss her then, and took his arm as he led her to the small French love seat.

"I don't know. I expect you'll tell me?"

She laughed gently. "War has done nothing for your manners, I see. But it's good to have you back. Lawrence, is that sherry I see at your elbow?"

He brought her a glass and she sipped it. "One of the privileges of age," she declared, "is to be able to drink a glass or two of wine without a lecture on moderation. This is quite good, Lawrence. I shall require the name of your wine merchant."

Lawrence chuckled. "Indeed. He's the same as yours."

"Ah, but he never treats me as well."

Hamish, taken aback by Melinda Crawford, was silent, trying to make up his mind about her. Rutledge, drawing up a chair next to the love seat, said, "I've missed you."

"At my age," she agreed, "four years is a very long time. I wasn't sure I would live to see you again." She studied his face once more. "But the wicked seem to thrive in this world, and I'm still here. Thank you for your letters, and the books of poems. I treasured both."

"I thought you might like the poet. O. A. Manning."

"She's dead now, I've heard."

He answered simply, "Yes."

"A tragedy among so many tragedies. There's never time to mourn. I remember in India there were so many burials we couldn't cry anymore. It was almost the same here, after this war. And you're back at the Yard, I've heard that as well. You forgot my birthday this year."

"I didn't forget. I didn't know what you would have liked. Frances sent a gift from both of us. Nightgowns suitable for a queen, if I have it right. Silk, in fact, from the East. Appropriate, she felt."

"Very beautiful," Melinda Crawford agreed. "Most of all, I would have liked your company for a few hours. But then I'm selfish, aren't I, when so many people are being murdered these days." Her eyes twinkled, but there was an undercurrent of sorrow behind the words.

The aging face was serene, and told him nothing. But he had a glimpse, brief as a butterfly's touch, of the loneliness of this extraordinary woman.

She would not have wanted him to see it.

7

BEFORE HE COULD ANSWER, THE DOOR OPENED, AND A MAN and woman came in, followed by a young man of perhaps thirty.

Lawrence made introductions, and Rutledge studied Raleigh Masters. The barrister had been heavyset. Now his jowls drooped like a bloodhound's and his clothes fit rather too loosely. His brown hair was streaked with gray and his frame was a little stooped, although that might have been from the crutches under his arm.

He swung into the room, a powerful man still, and undaunted, it seemed, by his infirmities. "Hallo, Mrs. Crawford, good to see you again, my dear. Forgive me for not shaking hands, Mr. Rutledge, but I have not yet learned the knack of these sticks."

His wife came to greet Melinda Crawford, and then spoke to Rutledge in a breathless rush. "Down from London, are you? How very nice!"

Bella Masters seemed to possess a rather diffident nature, and her face was worn with worry, as if she slept poorly. But there was an underlying attractiveness there, and a strength, if Rutledge was not mistaken, that was the last defense against her own weakness.

Lydia and Elizabeth returned to greet the newcomers, and Bella went on in that breathless way, "We are so sorry to be late—the weather was very bad just past Hever."

"Nonsense!" her husband retorted, adjusting his sticks as he sat down heavily into a chair. "I could see perfectly well!"

Bella glanced apologetically at the young man—who must have been driving them—but he ignored the remark and came to speak to Mrs. Crawford and then Rutledge.

Lawrence Hamilton had introduced him as Tom Brereton, and he said now to Rutledge, "Did I hear Mr. Hamilton correctly? You're an inspector?"

"Yes. Scotland Yard."

"Then you're here on duty?"

"Actually, I'm on leave."

Brereton nodded. "I believe Lawrence said you are a friend of Mrs. Mayhew's?"

"Yes. I've known her for some years. Richard and I were at Oxford together."

"I met her in hospital during the war. She read wonderfully well—it was rather like hearing a play. Everyone came to listen. I never had the good fortune to know her husband. They tell me he was an excellent barrister. I was interested in the law at one time, but my eyesight isn't what it was." Brereton smiled wryly. "Shrapnel. They did what they could, but I won't be studying long hours anymore."

"Yet you drive." It was a typical policeman's response, as Hamish was pointing out.

"Oh, yes, I can manage. Now. But they tell me a great many more motorcars will be on the road in the next year or so. That might make a difference." He shrugged. "I know Kent fairly well. It helps."

Mrs. Crawford was chatting with Lydia, and Brereton continued in a lowered voice, "She's a truly amazing woman. Did you know she'd been at Lucknow? During the Mutiny? I can't quite comprehend it. 1857, that was!"

Rutledge responded, "She has several interesting souvenirs, including one of the greased paper cartridges that sparked the Mutiny. And the ball that passed through her skirts one afternoon, as she carried water to the wounded. Her mother nearly fainted at the news—young Melinda was supposedly taking a nap."

Brereton smiled. "I can believe the story. My grandmother told me once that Mrs. Crawford had been quite a heroine. But *she* denies it."

At dinner, they were well into their soup before Masters looked up from his spoon and said, "Mrs. Crawford. I'm told mulligatawny soup is an old Indian specialty."

"I shouldn't know, Mr. Masters. I've never been in a kitchen in my life."

Rutledge nearly swallowed his soup the wrong way. But Masters took her at her word, and grunted. "Well, I've never been one for foreign dishes. Although they tell me the French cook surprisingly well."

Bella Masters turned to stare at her husband, and Rutledge caught a shadow of fright in her eyes. Searching in her pocket she found a small vial of powder, and asked the maid for a glass of water. After mixing the two, she handed the glass down to her husband, on the other side of Elizabeth.

Masters shook his head, and finished the course without saying more, but over the roast of beef, he turned to Rutledge and asked, "Are you here, Inspector, in an official capacity?"

"No, fortunately. I'm on leave and have come down to visit friends."

"Hmm. If the Yard knew what it was about, you'd be looking into these murders of ours." It was said with a proprietary air, as if they were his own.

Bella said, "I don't think we ought to discuss here—"

"Nonsense," her husband interrupted. "They're the talk of the district. You can hardly step into a shop without hearing the whispers!"

"All the same," Melinda Crawford put in firmly, "it can wait until the ladies have withdrawn. Elizabeth, I hear you've been blessed with puppies. How many did Henrietta produce?"

"Five," Elizabeth answered, as Masters said something under his breath. "Would you like one of them? Unless Ian intends to speak up, you have first choice."

"I'm afraid not; there's no garden for a dog at my flat," Rutledge replied. "Let Mrs. Crawford have her pick."

Lydia said, "The children would love one, don't you think, Lawrence?"

"Or two, perhaps. They'll be squabbling constantly over just one," Hamilton drawled, in mock enthusiasm.

Brereton laughed. "I'll take one of them, Mrs. Mayhew. I've got a small house, but the garden is walled. A dog should be quite happy there."

Masters glared at Brereton. "You're not taking it home in my motorcar!"

Elizabeth interposed soothingly, "Their eyes are barely open. It will be weeks before they can leave their mother."

Bella nodded to her husband's glass. The powder was settling to the bottom, no longer in suspension. "Do drink your medicine, my dear. It's long past time for it!"

Masters grudgingly picked up the glass, swirled it irritably, and swallowed half of it with a grimace. "I daresay it could be poison, for all I know. But I trust you, my love."

She seemed to shrivel before his glare. "It was the doctor who ordered it, Raleigh. Hardly poison!"

Lydia signaled the maid to remove the dishes. "Well," she said brightly, "have you heard the gossip? That house on the other side of the church has been bought by someone from Leeds! He made his money in scrap iron during the war, or so they tell me . . ."

The conversation moved on smoothly, and Bella thanked Lydia with her eyes. The powder, whatever it was, seemed to shift her husband's mood, and he joined with good humor in the speculation over the newcomer and what effect he might have on village affairs.

"If he's a bachelor, every woman within ten miles will be inviting him to dine, in hopes of marrying him off." Laughter met his comment. "Ask Brereton, here. He's never at a loss for a way to spend his evenings."

Brereton answered, "If he's a *rich* bachelor, he'll have the edge. I'll be forgotten in a day."

"It's a beautiful house," Elizabeth commented. "I'm glad someone will live there again." For Rutledge's benefit she added, "The last of the family died of influenza a year ago—Oliver Hendricks. He always offered us the pick of his gardens for the church. Oliver lost both sons in the war, poor man. Richard knew both of them well."

Rutledge himself remembered Walter and John Hendricks, but said nothing. What was there to say? Death had not played favorites. . . .

It was after the ladies had withdrawn for tea and the port was being passed that Masters returned to the subject of murder.

"I can't understand," he demanded, "why the Yard hasn't been more forward in this business. Two bodies in a matter of weeks!"

"I'm afraid I know nothing about the murders, sir," Rutledge answered him.

"I wonder what you are about, then! To be giving officers leave when they ought to be doing their duty is the height of stupidity!"

"The Chief Constable—" Rutledge began, but was interrupted.

"I know the law, Inspector. I spent twenty-five years as a barrister, ten of them as K.C. My question is, why does no one take *these* murders seriously enough to put a stop to them!"

"That's unfair," Lawrence Hamilton put in. "You have to remember—"

"I remember only that invalided soldiers are dying, and no one seems to care," Masters retorted. "When my mentor, Matthew Sunderland, was alive, he believed that there would come a time when murder was tolerated, as long as it inconvenienced no one but the victim. I daresay he's being proved right."

Rutledge's attention swung back to Masters. Matthew Sunderland had been the King's Counsel in the murder trial of Ben Shaw. Rutledge remembered him distinctly, a stooped and thin figure in his black robes, his voice and his manner patrician as he conducted the prosecution. Mr. Justice Patton had treated him with cordial respect, well deserved by a man who had served the law for nearly fifty years. Sunderland was seldom wrong when he cited a precedent, and young barristers lived in dread of facing him across the courtroom.

"It's interesting that you knew Sunderland," Rutledge said, shifting the subject to one he preferred to explore. "Do you recall the Shaw trial?"

"Why should I?" Masters countered.

"I wondered if Sunderland had ever spoken of it to you," Rutledge returned mildly. "It received widespread publicity at the time."

"Sunderland was always conscious of his duty," Masters replied. "And convinced that he'd done his best. I never knew him to feel any doubt about the outcome of any trial."

Hamish, in the shadows of Rutledge's mind and quiet for most of the meal, spoke now.

"You didna' ask him that. . . ."

MASTERS, AS IF suddenly aware of the small glass with his medicine in it, stared at the remaining portion for a moment, swirled the contents again, and then drained it at one draught.

By the time Lawrence Hamilton had described a fraud trial in which he was involved, Masters's chin was resting on his chest, and he was breathing heavily. Hamilton glanced at Rutledge. "I think it's time to join the ladies. We'll let him sleep, shall we? It's happened before."

Rutledge and Brereton quietly rose and followed their host to the drawing room. Bella Masters looked up quickly as they came in, and relief spread across her face as she saw that her husband was not with them.

"Is he sleeping?" she asked softly. When Hamilton nodded, she said only, "Well. It will do him good." She had been sitting next to Mrs. Crawford, and now came to take a chair beside Rutledge. "I want to say," she told him, smiling, "that it's wonderful to see Elizabeth out and about again. It's time she put the past aside. She's one of my favorite people, you know." A shadow passed over her face, and the smile faded. "Widowhood is something we all must learn to live with. God knows, every wife must look ahead to the possibility."

"She's a remarkable woman," he agreed, wondering if Mrs. Masters was matchmaking.

But she surprised him by adding, her eyes straying to Brereton, sitting by Elizabeth now, "There's someone—well, I may be speaking out of turn!"

"Someone?" Rutledge prompted, curious. Brereton, perhaps? Or was Mrs. Masters warning him—the houseguest—off on general principle?

"There's a young man she's had lunch with. A time or two. I've seen them in the window of The Plough." The hotel on the High Street. "I hope it's someone suitable—" A worried frown touched her face. He found himself thinking that Bella Masters wasn't the sort who could prevaricate successfully. Her expressions were too easily read.

"I'll bear it in mind," he said, answering the concern rather than her actual words.

He spent perhaps another five minutes sitting with Mrs. Masters, and then was commandeered once again by Mrs. Crawford, who wanted to know what Frances, his sister, was thinking of, letting that handsome major slip through her fingers.

Rutledge laughed. "I rather think it was the other way round. Frances enjoyed his company, but was not in the right frame of mind to accept a proposal."

Melinda Crawford said, "I do wish she would settle. She's a very intelligent young woman, and your father spoiled her. She won't find his like, and she should stop trying—before the better choices are snapped up."

It was, Rutledge thought, a unique way of regarding his sister's spinsterhood. He suddenly realized that he shared it. Caught up as he had been in his own problems, he had not stopped to consider why Frances was still unmarried. Had there been someone during the war—someone he had never known about, and she had not wanted to speak of?

A little more than a half an hour later, Rutledge and Elizabeth took their leave. Masters, rested and less belligerent, had departed with Brereton driving. Mrs. Crawford had gone a little before them, her chauffeur summoned from the kitchens where he'd been gossiping with the Hamilton staff. Lydia had carried Elizabeth off for a moment to review the Christmas flower schedule for church services, leaving the two men alone.

Hamilton said, apropos of nothing, "You said something earlier about the Shaw murders. What brought them to mind?"

"My chief superintendent," Rutledge answered mildly. "He was promoted on the coattails of them. We aren't allowed to forget that."

"Our first cook was horribly shocked by the deaths, even though they occurred in London. I remember she refused to let a man into her cottage after that. She was convinced she'd die the same way. Dreadful to be old and fearful. I went myself a time or two to help nail up the back steps or whatever needed doing, and always took care that Lydia was with me." He shook his head. "The poor woman died in her sleep, and wasn't found for two days."

"Did you know Matthew Sunderland at all?"

"I knew him to nod to, as we passed each other. I was too provincial and too young to have the courage to sit at the great man's feet. Although, to do him justice, he was never as lofty as he appeared. But the man had a regalness about him, the white hair and his carriage. Someone, I forget who, compared Sunderland to General Gordon—that same charismatic belief in his own power." Hamilton smiled. "To tell you the truth, I often wondered how many cases Sunderland carried just striding into the courtroom. And he had a voice to match, deep and impressive enough to read the Old Testament to savages. We won't see his like again this century!"

8

As she stepped into his car, Elizabeth Mayhew said to Rutledge, "Sorry! I didn't mean to keep you waiting so long. But if Lydia and I don't settle the flower schedule ourselves, there's endless confusion. People by nature want to change things, and it takes hours for the committee to draw up a satisfactory list. We've learned to circumvent argument by working it out between us."

As the engine turned over, he got into the car beside her, then realized that earlier she'd folded the rug for her knees and laid it in the rear seat. With a cold shock of dread, he turned and fished for it, his eyes carefully away from the spot that Hamish seemed to favor. As his fingers touched the wool, he drew it toward him. It seemed to come with unexpected ease, as if Hamish had given it a push in his direction. But that was imagination, and he took a deep breath to dispel the feeling of having come close to the one thing he feared—finally confronting the nemesis that haunted his waking hours.

Hamish had died in France in 1916, in the nightmarish days of the first battle of the Somme. He had died as surely as any of the war dead. Shot by a firing squad at Rutledge's orders, shot by the coup de grâce that Rutledge had administered with his own hand, buried deep in the stinking mud that the artillery shell had thrown up, killing men like nettles before a scythe. Rutledge had not wanted to execute the Scottish corporal, but Hamish MacLeod had been stubborn in his refusal to do what he had been ordered to do, and in the heat of battle, disobeying an order in the face of his men had left his commanding officer no alternative but to make an example—and hope with all his being that the young Scot would see the error of his ways well before the threat had to be carried out. But Hamish, worn and exhausted and tired of watching men die in the withering fire of No Man's Land, would not lead them out again. And Rutledge had had to do what he had sworn he would.

Hamish MacLeod had been a natural leader, not a coward, respected by officers and men alike. But he had been battered by too much death and too little sleep. He'd watched the corpses piling up, he'd lost count of the replacements, and the shock of the endless bombardments had left him shaken and tormented. Death had come as a release for him—and had nearly destroyed Rutledge.

And while Hamish lay somewhere in France—buried securely beneath a white cross lost in an alien garden of thousands upon thousands of war dead, hardly distinguishable from the soldiers who slept on either side of him—if his ghost walked, it walked in Scotland, not England. He had loved the Highlands with a passionate intensity, and the woman he'd left behind there. But in Rutledge's battle-frayed mind, there was something that was still alive and stern and real, the essence of the soldier he'd known so well and had—for the sake of a battle—ordered killed. Murdered—

Rutledge shut the thought out of his mind. As Elizabeth was settling the rug over her knees and he was putting the car into gear, he struggled to break the silence that engulfed him. But the first question he could think of was "What were these killings that Masters was talking about?"

"Oh. I hadn't said anything before. You're on leave, and I hadn't wanted to bring your work into this holiday."

"Masters seems to have had no such compunction," he said wryly.

"I've never faced death," she said thoughtfully. "So I can't tell you what *I'd* do if someone—a physician—told me I probably wouldn't live much longer. But Raleigh has fought it bravely. It's just that he's turned . . . bitter—I suppose that's the word. The worst of it was, he's had to give up his work in London. And he's not the man we once knew. I expect that's why we're so tolerant of him. As well as for poor Bella's sake. She doesn't quite know how to cope. He won't let her touch him—they have nurses in for that."

She sighed, drawing herself away from the Masterses' dilemma. "The murders. There have been two ex-soldiers killed. One was found on a lonely road, the other by a field, and no one quite knows who would do such a thing—or why. The pity is, they survived the war, and now it's not a German killing them, but an Englishman. Their own side! I find that rather horrible, don't you?"

ELIZABETH HAD FALLEN asleep, her head against his shoulder. He was no more than two miles or so from her house as the crow flew, and Rutledge could feel the weariness of the long day turning to drowsiness of his own as he drove. Fighting it, he concentrated on the road ahead—and swerved as he realized too late that a man was standing at a crossroads, almost in his path.

As the lamps of his motorcar pinned the figure in their bright beams, he would have sworn in that instant that it was the face he'd seen the night of the Guy Fawkes bonfire.

Elizabeth came awake as the motorcar veered wildly. She said quickly, "What's wrong—?"

Rutledge's heart rate seemed to have doubled as he fought the wheel to bring the car back to the road. He had all but *killed* the man!

"Someone—in the road—I didn't see him until I was on him—"

He must stop, he told himself disjointedly—be certain the man was all right—the wing had missed him—given the idiot a shock perhaps as severe as his own—but done the man no harm—*there had been no contact—*

Yet he didn't want to go back—he didn't want to find that the figure on the road had existed only in his dream-filled brain as he had drifted unexpectedly into sleep.

"I don't see anyone in the road." Elizabeth said it doubtfully, turning to look over her shoulder. "Are you sure, Ian? There's no one there—Ought we to go back?"

Hamish said, "You must go back! You canna' leave him to bleed to death in a hedgerow!"

Rutledge was already slowing the motorcar, and with some difficulty turning it on the narrow road. Dread filled him, a deep and abiding belief that if he was right, there would be no body and no sign of one.

And when they reached the crossroads again, although he searched for a good ten minutes, no one was there—

RUTLEDGE WAS AWAKE before dawn, standing at the windows looking out over the back lawns of Elizabeth Mayhew's house. It was a pretty view, even in the early morning mists. Flower beds laid out asymmetrically formed a pattern that led the eye down a grassy walk to a bench overlooking the small pool at the bottom of the garden. In summer the beds held a wonderful variety of blooming plants, but an early frost had blighted summer's growth, leaving behind only the skeletons of what once was.

But what he saw at this moment was not a Kentish garden; it was the blighted landscape of France. It seemed he could still hear the guns, using up their stockpiled shells in a mad frenzy of noise and destruction. It was as if there was to be no Armistice in a few hours. The rattle of machine guns, punctuated by the sharper fire of rifles, added to the din, and men were still dying, and would go on dying until the eleventh hour. He had tried to husband them, to stop the waste of life and the long, long lists of the wounded, but he could hear the cries of pain and the screams of the dying and the scything whisper of bullets over–head.

A political decision it had been, not a battlefield victory: The Armistice would commence on the eleventh day of the eleventh month, at the eleventh hour of the morning—11 November, 1918, eleven A.M.

It had held no reality for Rutledge. He had stood in the trenches, Hamish alive in his mind, and stared across the bleak, tortured land he had known intimately for four unthinkable years. And the Scot's words kept forming in his head: *"I shallna' see this eleventh hour, I shallna' go home with the rest, I shallna' prosper in the years ahead. And you willna' prosper, either."*

Better to be dead. Better to walk out into that machine-gun fire and be dead, than to go home to nothing. . . .

He could hear the voices around him, men who had survived, talking tentatively about what would actually happen here. But not of home. Not yet. No one could quite grasp an end to the bloody Great War. There was neither jubilation nor hope, only an odd reluctance to think beyond the appointed hour. As if it would be unlucky. He wondered if the Germans in their hidden trenches were feeling the same fatalistic acceptance, or if they, too, counted their dead in their thoughts, and wondered why it had all begun anyway.

He didn't know why it had begun, this war. He understood the political reasoning, the invoked alliances, the assassination in Sarajevo, where the Austrian archduke had died. He had succumbed to the banners and the enthusiasm and the euphoria as all the others had, he had trained and shipped out for France, and gone into battle with a sense of duty and honor. Then he had watched it metamorphose into the most appalling slaughter in living memory. And still the generals and the political leaders and the press had fought on, safe in their cocoons far from the dying . . .

Appalling . . .

Coming back to the present, he watched a wind lift the boughs of the trees and run lightly across the grass.

Was it barely a year ago that this slaughter had ended, with no banners and no enthusiasm and no posturing, in a last barrage of shells and the cold gray November dawn? He shivered. For too many men, this was not a day of solemn commemoration but a day of agonized remembrance.

For him, a reminder that Hamish MacLeod had *not* come home.

WHEN HE WENT down to breakfast, Elizabeth was already there. "Good morning!" she said cheerily, then seeing his face, the tired lines that marked a sleepless night, she went on in a more subdued tone, "Melinda Crawford has asked us to tea. There's a note that just arrived. I'm to send back an answer."

"Yes, why not?" Rutledge answered. "And I'll take you both to dinner afterward, if you like."

"I'd like that," she agreed. She watched him lift the lids of serving dishes on the handsome buffet, and fill his plate. "I'll give the staff the day off. They'll be delighted."

Sitting down across from her, he picked up the napkin ring and then reached for the teapot. It was a quiet domestic scene, far removed from the images that had haunted him only a short hour ago, soothing in a way that he hadn't anticipated. As if it had the power to wipe away the past, simply by being so normal, so undemanding.

As he looked up, he thought Elizabeth was about to say something to him, and he waited, expecting her to suggest plans for the morning. But she finished her toast instead, eyes dropping to her plate.

"I'll just tell the chauffeur we're coming," she said after a moment. "He's waiting in the kitchen for my reply." Rising, she walked gracefully to the door and left him to his own meal. He knew, none better, that an appearance of hearty appetite was an accepted indication of good health. The knowledge had served him well when he had spent more than a week in his sister's home, an invalid after being shot in Scotland.

But Elizabeth had been picking at the food on her plate, and he wondered what was on her mind. The policeman in him was too well trained not to take notice. It would, he thought, come out one way or another in its own good time.

The door opened and she came back into the room, frowning. "Ian. The most horrid thing. There's been another murder—closer to us this time. And on the road we took just last night. Mrs. Crawford's chauffeur, Hadley, was regaling the cook and scullery maid with the gruesome details. He'd come that way this morning—the police stopped him to ask his business—"

Rutledge stared at her. Had he struck the man in his headlamps? Was this the body that the police were examining even now?

"Who was killed? Was the driver told?" He kept his voice steady with an effort of will.

"The police didn't say. But a farmer who was bringing his horse to the farrier had seen the body and told Hadley that it was a one-legged man. Like the others."

"How did he die?"

"I don't think they know yet. It wasn't an accident. Hadley was certain of that. Ought you to do something?"

The last thing Rutledge wanted to do was to go back to that crossroads and look down on the face of a man he might recognize. And yet he knew very well that the figure he'd seen had had two good legs. It was coincidence—and a damned uncomfortable one. He had to believe that. Whatever he'd glimpsed was a trick of memory, a startling but harmless tearing of the curtain between sleeping and waking.

Hamish was saying, *"You werena' asleep at the bonfire . . ."*

"There's nothing I can do to help. I don't have the authority here," Rutledge told Elizabeth truthfully.

She pressed her hand to her cheek as if for comfort. "What a terrifying start to the morning—"

"Come eat your breakfast, and don't dwell on it," Rutledge responded quietly. "There's nothing you can do. Nothing I can do, for that matter. I'd only be in the way."

With a twist of her shoulders as if trying to shake off her unsettled mood, she said, "I'd never realized, quite, how unpleasant your work must be. Dealing with such things."

"No different, in fact, from a doctor's surgery, where one patient has hiccoughs and another has a gall bladder." He lied with a lightness that he didn't feel. But it earned him a smile from Elizabeth. He reached for the jam pot and said in a more cheerful voice, "What would you like to do this morning? I'm at your service."

She bit her lip. "Would it be too much to ask—could you help me go through Richard's things? I haven't been able to face it alone. And that's not why I asked you to come and stay—but this isn't starting out as the morning I'd planned—and—" She broke off, distracted by what she was trying to say. But the words wouldn't come, whatever they were.

"I'll help you," Rutledge told her. "On one condition. That we try not to make it morbid. For your sake, if not mine."

She nodded. "I won't cry on your shoulder. Nor you on mine. This is what one does after a death in the family, isn't it? A practical matter. Before the moths get into the clothes." It was her turn to try for lightness; she failed wretchedly. "Oh, hell!" she ended bitterly. "Why couldn't he have come *home!*"

Hamish answered her, but of course she couldn't hear the words. *"Because the guid died, and left only the dregs to make the new world . . ."*

AS IT TURNED out, the morning passed uneventfully. The clothes hanging in the wardrobes no longer carried the scent of the man who had worn them in 1914. A faint mustiness had crept in, despite applications of lavender, and they had lost the personality that had given them vitality. Elizabeth folded and packed them as Rutledge took them out and handed them to her. The drawers of the chest were easier, their contents already folded, already in neat piles. In the top drawer, Elizabeth came upon a pair of cuff links engraved with initials. She held them for a moment in her hand, then passed them to Rutledge. "You gave him these—a wedding gift. Would you like them back to remember him by?"

He thanked her and took them. He'd liked Richard immensely, and had found in him a good friend. It was kind of his widow to remember that.

As the tall case clock in the hall struck the eleventh hour with its deep tolling chimes, they both paused in silence. Standing where they were, in the midst of their work, as a natural thing.

Rutledge thought he could hear the distant sound of the bagpipes that had buried Hamish MacLeod, but it was only a trick of the mind.

9

TEA WITH MELINDA CRAWFORD WAS TYPICAL.

She was in great spirits and refused to allow her guests to enjoy anything less. She chided Elizabeth for bringing a pot of honey, saying, "You know I'm not allowed to indulge in such things." But the expression of delight in her eyes told them that she would enjoy it hugely.

Turning to Rutledge, she said, "Growing old is not for most people. It's too trying. One daren't eat this or do that, or even bend over to smell the garden flowers, for fear one's back won't straighten up again."

"You seem to thrive on it, all the same," he told her.

"Well, it's most certainly better than the alternative."

He looked around the room, found it unchanged from his last visit before going off to war. There were the personal possessions she'd brought home from India with her, beautiful carvings and silks, sandalwood fans that scented the warm air, and a small teak curio cabinet with ivory inlays, where she always kept smaller treasures. They were as fascinating as the stories she told about them.

It was, in a way, like stepping back into his own past, and he found it unexpectedly soothing.

She rang a little bell at her elbow, and tea appeared like magic, a wheeled cart with a silver service, fine china, and from somewhere, a single yellow rose. She had remembered that Rutledge liked cake, and had ordered two kinds, one with a lemon filling and the other with raisins.

Elizabeth was asked to pour, and as she passed a cup to Rutledge, Mrs. Crawford said, "You met Tom Brereton the other night at the Hamiltons. What did you think of him?"

Rutledge replied, "Sound enough. A friend, I take it, of Mr. and Mrs. Masters."

"Brereton was to be Raleigh's protégé and read the law. A brilliant future ahead of him. The war put a stop to that."

Elizabeth said, "He's nice. We had lunch one day, when he came into Marling to see the doctor. He regaled me with tales about the American Expeditionary forces. He's a wonderful mimic."

"I was thinking," Mrs. Crawford said, "of leaving him something in my will. His life won't be easy if he loses his sight." She smiled. "Of course, it could be a long wait; I'm not in the mood to shuffle off my mortal coil. All the same, it would please me to help someone in need. Brereton doesn't have a great deal of money, and independence when one is blind is important."

"It would be a kindness, certainly," Elizabeth said. "But do you know him well enough? Can you be sure it's for the best?"

"I intend to know him better before making a final decision. But Ian here is a good judge of character. I'd like him to keep my notion in the back of his mind."

Which, Rutledge thought, was a veiled suggestion that he use his resources at the Yard to verify Brereton's worthiness. But why had she chosen to speak of this in front of Elizabeth?

The answer followed on the heels of the thought.

Elizabeth said, "Richard knew his family, of course. Tom's grandfather served in India at one time. Did you ever meet him out there?"

Mrs. Crawford set her teacup on the tray. "We danced a waltz together in Agra. I was all of twelve, and terribly in love. He was quite dashing in his uniform." But Rutledge had the strongest feeling that she was not telling the entire story.

As they finished their tea and he dutifully ate the last of the raisin cake, Mrs. Crawford turned to Elizabeth. "My dear, will you go up to my room and fetch the small box you'll find on the desk there? I don't like to ask Shanta to do it. Her bones are older than mine!"

Shanta was the Indian ayah who had become the housekeeper, much to the shock of the neighbors. She ruled the household with an iron hand, reminding recalcitrant staff that even the Dear Queen had had an Indian servant, and that Mrs. Crawford was following royal tradition. Rutledge wondered at times how Mrs. Crawford kept any servants at all, but they seemed to adore her and seldom left until they were carried out in their coffins.

As the door closed behind Elizabeth, Melinda Crawford turned to Rutledge and asked, "What is troubling you? That silly girl who turned you down for a diplomat?" She was referring to Jean, who had once been engaged to Rutledge and broke it off when he came home shell-shocked.

"No. Besides, she's off to Canada with him."

"Well, I hope he's worthy of her—most diplomats are as shallow as she is."

Rutledge laughed. Mrs. Crawford was nothing if not partisan when she cared for someone.

"Then it's something else? Scotland? I had a long letter from your godfather. He's been worried about you. He says the war has changed you. Well, war has changed us all, come to that. But you more than most, I think. It isn't physical. I can count all your limbs. Therefore they must be in the mind, these wounds of yours. Too many bad memories? Or bad dreams?"

"A little of both," he answered ruefully. "It will pass." He had feared she would be able to see too clearly. He had been right.

"My dear, I lived through the Great Mutiny, when we all expected to die, and most unpleasantly. I've seen things no woman ought to see. No, nor a man either. It does not pass. One just grows—accustomed to it. One learns to crowd it out and put it into the farthest corner of one's mind."

He couldn't explain to her that Hamish already lived there. "I try," he said.

"You're young. And a remarkably attractive man, did you know that? It's time you married, had a family, and looked forward."

"Elizabeth?" he asked, wondering if that was why Mrs. Crawford had sent her out of the room.

But Melinda Crawford shook her head, frowning. "No, Elizabeth isn't right for you, my dear, and I hope you have no thoughts in that direction. Besides—I rather think her fancy lies elsewhere."

His eyebrows flew up in surprise. Was that what had been on the tip of Elizabeth's tongue at breakfast that morning, before the news of another murder had spoiled the chance to speak to him? He wondered. Bella Masters had also hinted at other attachments.

Watching his face, Melinda Crawford nodded in satisfaction. As if pleased to discover no attachment *here*. He knew she was fond of Elizabeth, and was amused.

Still, he was slow answering, unable to tell her why he could never offer marriage to any woman. How would she—*could* she—share his life with Hamish?

Then, hearing footsteps coming down the stairs, his hostess said in a low voice, rapidly and with an intensity that was unlike her, "Remember one thing, Ian. I have seen war at its worst. Nothing you can tell me will shock me or disturb me. If you ever find you need to talk about things best forgotten, I shall be here. For a time, at least. Don't leave it too long!"

THE BOX, INLAID marble, contained photographs of a garden party Mrs. Crawford had given nearly thirty years ago, and Rutledge recognized his parents among the faces, his father stooping over his mother with loving attention as he brought a plate of food to her table. His sister Frances, in a trailing lacy gown that all but swallowed her, stared at the camera with sober curiosity. Richard was there, a fair smiling child with girlish curls to his shoulders, his pose already exhibiting that sturdy, masculine grace that had made him a natural athlete and one of the finest cricket bowlers in Kent. Rutledge sat astride a pony, his shoes dangling high above the stirrups, his face half hidden by a pith helmet tipped over one eye. Mrs. Crawford, in an elegant hat that was a froth of ostrich feathers, was surreptitiously gripping his belt to keep him safely in the saddle.

It was typical of her to have planned an afternoon that would please both her guests. Elizabeth was poring over the photographs with exclamations of delight.

Rutledge, as keen an observer of human nature as Melinda Crawford, wondered if she had also set out to recapture a time far removed from war on this day of all days—as if she knew what was going through his mind. It was an extraordinary kindness.

He smiled and tried to remember that sunny afternoon for her sake, and succeeded in making her happy. Whether he had succeeded in convincing her that she had chased away all the dark shadows he couldn't tell.

Hamish said, "I wouldna' wager my pay on it."

ON HIS RETURN to London on the evening of Wednesday, twelve November, Rutledge went directly to the Yard instead of his flat. At this hour, in a city the size of London, the police presence at the Yard was as strong as it was at midday, and he was greeted jovially as he strode down the passage to his office.

Sergeant Gibson, whose irascible manner concealed a very clever mind, said, " 'Ware the wolf at the door!" as he passed.

And Inspector Raeburn paused to warn, "If you've come for peace and quiet, better leave now."

Indeed, there was an air of orchestrated urgency about the place. Another inspector stopped long enough to say, "Old Bowels scents promotion. He's been summoned to the Home Office tomorrow, possibly something to do with that rash of fires in Slough. They found a body when the ashes cooled this morning, and the hope is it's the fire-setter, not a hapless victim. Seven firms have been burned out so far, and we're frantically searching for a link connecting them."

"You'll find it soon enough," Rutledge responded as he reached his office. With so many men out of work and wages very low as Britain tried to regain her capacity for peacetime industry, bitterness often turned to trouble, and labor disputes became volatile. Fire setting was not uncommon.

Hamish pointed out, referring to the Shaw investigation, "It isna' a good time to bring up the past."

It wasn't. Rutledge shut his door against the mayhem and sat down at his desk. He had made notes from the Shaw file, and with luck there would be a few free hours in the morning to visit one or two of Mrs. Shaw's neighbors. Discreetly.

He drew the sheets of paper out of his drawer and prepared to read through them again, seeking any missed clue. He had given himself two days to find a sense of perspective about the case. Instead, other emotions had driven it from his mind. And yet, with the commemoration of the Armistice safely behind him, almost as if turning a leaf in a mental book, he felt a return to a sense of balance.

Hamish, reflecting Rutledge's tiredness from the drive out of Kent, doubted there would be anything worthwhile to be found in his notes. "For ye read them on Sunday, and you're no' so puir a policeman that you couldna' see it was all trim and proper then."

Still, Rutledge persevered.

But the pages were not in proper order. And an extraneous letter, an invitation to a retirement dinner for another officer, was in among them.

It had been lying on his blotter Sunday when he had walked out of the room. In plain sight.

He stared at the sheets in his hand, trying to remember how he had left them. Hamish was right about one thing—he wasn't so poor a policeman that he would mix up his files like this. He had learned early on in his career that a meticulous attention to detail was essential to giving evidence in court. A muddled record of any investigation was a death knell—the defense would swoop down on the policeman like an eagle after prey, and tear him apart.

Pages two and five had been reversed. He sorted through them again. One. Five. Three. Four. Two. And just after five, that extraneous letter.

A thought struck him then. And with it came cold alarm.

Someone had been in his office and gone through his desk in his absence.

What had they been looking for? And in their search, had they taken note of this sheaf of pages—or simply set it aside while hunting for another file?

More to the point, what present inquiry of his was urgent enough that new information couldn't wait three days for his return?

He thumbed through the copied notes again. He had nothing to hide. The original file had been returned to its cabinet, after he had abstracted the information he wanted. He had disturbed no one—he had left no particular trail.

In fact, he had simply tried to be circumspect, knowing Chief Superintendent Bowles would be the first to be annoyed by any resurrection of his own past—the inquiry that had begun his climb to his present position.

No. It wasn't Bowles; there would be no reason for him to come to Rutledge's office. If he'd needed a folder, he would have sent someone else to locate it.

And whoever it was, no doubt in a hurry, had sifted through the drawer's contents with only one thing on his mind: satisfying Bowles.

Rutledge went through his entire desk with great care. As far as he could determine, nothing was missing. The files he was presently working on were as he'd left them. Whatever had been taken must also have been returned.

Coincidence.

It was the only explanation. . . .

But neither he nor Hamish found it satisfactory.

10

THE NEXT MORNING RUTLEDGE REPORTED FOR DUTY, AND then at midday, after a meeting ended earlier than expected, he found his way again to the street of soot-blackened houses where the Shaws had lived their entire married life. Winter sun splashed the roofs and walls, bringing out every flaw, like an aging woman who had ventured out too early into the merciless morning light. Even the mortar of the bricks seemed engrained with coal smoke, and in the windows, white lace curtains mocked it.

Number 14 was very like its neighbors, upright and lacking any individuality that would offer a hint about the occupants within. The iron knockers on several doors were Victorian whimsy, mass-produced rather than a reflection of personal taste. One house possessed an urn-shaped stone pot that had held pansies in the summer, their withered stems falling over the sides like a bedraggled veil, but most of the street seemed not to care about the image it presented. The white lace curtains were a last pitiful attempt at pride, but there was no money to spend on frivolous ornamentation.

Rutledge left his motorcar a block away and continued on foot, hoping to attract as little notice as possible. But now and again curtains twitched as the women of Sansom Street inspected the stranger with suspicion. He was as much an outsider here as he might have been on a street in Budapest—outsiders seldom brought anything but trouble. Particularly well-dressed ones with an air of authority.

He walked on to the end of the street where a church stood like a beacon, its early Victorian tower rising above the dingy roofs. The door needed paint, and the stained-glass windows were grimy, but when Rutledge stepped inside and opened the door to the nave, he was surprised to find the interior as bright and polished as any church in Westminster. His footsteps echoed on the flagstone as he walked down the aisle, and something large and black rose like a goblin from the chairs below the pulpit.

A scarecrow of a man, his robes flapping and his face flushed, called, "Good morning! Is there any way I can help you?"

The rector rose to his full height, a feather duster in his bony hand and a cobweb across his chest like a lace collar. His white hair, in disarray, looked like a ruff. The smile was genuine, if wry.

Rutledge said, gesturing around him, "This is truly a sanctuary."

"Well, yes, we try to manage that. My wife had a committee meeting this morning, and I'm frightfully poor at dusting, but one tries." He paused. "What brings you to St. Agnes?"

"Curiosity, I suppose," Rutledge said slowly. "I understand you buried a parishioner not long ago. A Mrs. Cutter, Janet Cutter." It was a guess, and apparently on the mark.

"It's been three months since she was laid to rest," the rector said, riffling the feather duster between his hands and sneezing briskly. "Her husband has taken it hard. Not being used to fending for himself, everything at sixes and sevens. Are you acquainted with the Cutters?"

"I've met them. My name is Rutledge. I had occasion to speak with them—some six years ago."

The rector nodded. "That would be near enough to the time that Ben Shaw was arrested. I was at the trial when the verdict was brought in. I recall seeing you there." He left the words like a gauntlet between them.

Rutledge smiled. "Yes. You have a very good memory."

"In my calling—as in yours, I'm sure—a good memory is a necessity." He put the duster down behind the steps to the pulpit and said again, "What brings you here?"

Rutledge took a chair in the first row. "I don't know. Recently I received information that intrigued me. And like a good policeman, I follow my instincts."

"Then Mrs. Shaw took my advice," the rector responded. "I wondered if she would."

It was unexpected. Rutledge asked, "She came to see you?"

"Yes, she was quite disturbed. She wasn't sure what to do, and I told her to begin with the police. *Not* with Henry Cutter. It was, after all, a police matter." The rector's long, narrow face gave little away. He took another chair, moving it slightly to face Rutledge.

Their voices echoed in the emptiness of the church, and Rutledge had an uneasy feeling that if Hamish spoke, the words would echo as well. A shiver passed through him.

The rector was saying, "Toward the end of her life, Janet Cutter was a woman with something on her conscience. It kept her restless, even with the morphine for the pain. But she never spoke to me about whatever worried her, and I have no reason to believe it was murder. I tell you that because I don't want you to jump to conclusions the evidence fails to support."

"Did you believe Ben Shaw was a murderer?" Rutledge asked bluntly.

The rector turned away. "I don't know the answer to that. Truthfully. Ben was not a willful murderer. It wasn't in his nature. But few of us know what temptation will do, when we're faced with it and we think there are no witnesses to it. He wanted more for his family than he could afford to give them. Did that lead him to theft and murder? I would like to think it didn't. But then the facts were quite clear. Still, he could have been led. The opportunity was there. And the temptation."

Rutledge picked up the thread he was following. "The women were old, infirm. It was a kindness to end their pain and their loneliness . . ."

The rector shrugged. "Who can say what went through that poor man's mind?"

"If Shaw *wasn't* guilty of murder, who was? His wife? Mrs. Cutter?"

The rector turned tired but knowing eyes on Rutledge. "I don't speculate on guilt. I try to bring comfort without judgment."

"I'm a policeman. Judgment is my trade."

"So it is." The rector rose. "It has been interesting to speak with you. May I offer a word of advice? Not as a man of the cloth, but as someone thirty years your senior, and therefore perhaps—a little wiser?"

"By all means," Rutledge answered, rising as well.

"Walk carefully. You can't bring Ben Shaw back from the dead. He's long since faced a judgment higher than yours or mine. Better for him to be a martyr than to open wounds you cannot close again."

Rutledge considered him for a moment. "Yet you sent Nell Shaw to me."

The rector smiled, a youthful look replacing the somberness. "Yes, Inspector. It's my earnest hope that you won't fail either of us."

OUTSIDE THE CHURCH, Hamish said sourly, "He prefers riddles to plain speech."

"No. I think he's uncertain of his duty, and passed the problem on to me."

"Or knows a truth he willna' own up to."

It was a cogent remark.

NO ONE ANSWERED Rutledge's knock at Number 14, the Shaw home. He left, walking back to the motorcar, deep in thought. He had no excuse to call on Cutter, and no right. Henry Cutter would be well within his rights to complain to the Yard of harassment if he found a policeman on his doorstep asking questions about an old murder, and his wife's possible role in it. But there was another source of information. . . .

Back at the Yard, Rutledge called Sergeant Bennett into his office. Bennett had been a constable when Ben Shaw was tried, and he'd known the people on Sansom Street better perhaps than they knew themselves. A sharp mind and a sharper memory had brought him to the attention of the Yard and seen him promoted.

Bennett was in early middle age now, of medium height and with nothing to set him apart from the ordinary man on the street he interviewed time and again. It had been his hallmark, this ability to fit in.

Rutledge had seen it at work often enough. The question was, where did Bennett's loyalties lie at the Yard? There was no way of guessing.

Hamish warned, "Then you'd best walk carefully."

Rutledge began circumspectly, "This is in confidence, Bennett. But I've been looking back at the Shaw case. It seems one of the missing pieces of jewelry may have come to light."

Bennett's bushy eyebrows rose. "Indeed, sir!" Curiosity was bright in his eyes. "I'd a feeling he'd chucked them in the river!"

Rutledge was not about to enlighten him. "I want you to think back to the investigation—before I came into the picture. Philip Nettle was in charge of the case. Was there any suspicion that someone other than Shaw had had access to the murdered women? Mrs. Winslow. Mrs. Satterthwaite. Mrs. Tompkins."

"There was a charwoman who did for two of them," Bennett said slowly, digging back into his memory. "Not likely to smother anybody, frail as *she* was. No old-age pension for the likes of her—she worked until the day before she died. The victims went to the same church—St. Agnes, that was—when they could get about on their own. We looked at that connection closely, sir, but it went nowhere. Nor did they seem to have more than a nodding acquaintance with each other. But as it turned out, Shaw came to meet them through the church, after a fashion. The rector asked him to make some repairs for Mrs. Winslow, and on the heels of that, Shaw was contacted directly about the other two."

Which, as Hamish was pointing out, might explain the rector's unwillingness to involve himself in the past. . . .

"Shaw was a member of the same church?"

"He'd repaired the vestry door after a storm warped it, worked on the footing for the baptismal font when it cracked. But he wasn't local, you know. Grew up in Kensington, and still had ties there, even attending services there in preference to St. Agnes. Mrs. Shaw was said to like that very well; she'd not cared for the local church, seeing herself as above it." His mouth twisted. It was apparent he had not been among Nell Shaw's admirers. "But after his marriage, Shaw appeared to have severed ties with his family. Or they severed theirs with him."

"Mrs. Shaw must have been a member of St. Agnes at some time. As I recall, she'd grown up two streets over from Sansom."

"Had been a member as a girl, yes, sir. There's a story that was set about, that she went into service in Kensington, and married the son of the house. The truth was, she worked in a corset shop and took a purchase round to the house one day, for his mother. The mother wasn't at home. When Ben told his future wife that, bold as brass didn't she claim she was feeling faint and could she come in and sit for a few minutes?"

Intrigued, Rutledge asked, "How did you discover all this?" It hadn't been included in the written reports.

"It was told me by the neighbor's wife, Mrs. Cutter. I discounted it until I spoke to a neighbor of Shaw's mother—she was still living in the same house—and she confirmed the corset version." Bennett looked pleased with himself, rocking back on his heels. "Still, that had no bearing on the murders." It was an afterthought, the policeman overriding the man.

"What was your opinion of the helpful Mrs. Cutter?"

"Now, there was a deep one! Butter wouldn't melt in her mouth, but she'd just let slip a bit of the story, see, and then wait for you to pry the rest out of her. As if she was reluctant to finish what she'd begun."

Rutledge had met others of Mrs. Cutter's ilk in his career.

"Did she know the three dead women?"

"Odd that you should ask that, sir," Bennett answered, scratching his dark chin. "She swore she didn't. But she went to that same church, didn't she? Had done, for twenty or more years."

Rutledge smiled. "Any chance that she might have been tempted to murder them? After all, her situation was hardly better than the Shaws."

Bennett considered the question as he studied Rutledge. "As to that, I can't say. But Mr. Nettle, God rest his soul, remarked once, 'I'd not care to be in Mr. Cutter's shoes, if he strayed too far from hearth and home!' "

Interested, Rutledge asked, "And had he strayed? Or been tempted to stray, do you think?"

"He was the only one defended Mrs. Shaw. Most of the street couldn't abide the woman. I was never sure what to make of that, to tell you the truth, sir! Except that she was a strong-natured woman. That sort often attract weak men."

———

As HE WAS leaving the Yard for the day, Rutledge found himself thinking about Bennett's last comment. He wished there was a viable excuse for calling on Cutter, but without making his interest in the Shaw case too apparent, there was nothing he could do at this early stage. As Hamish had warned him several times that day, he ought to watch his step. Bennett was very likely trustworthy, but he was also ambitious. And Rutledge had learned from his first day at the Yard that ambition ran rampant in the passageways and offices.

He himself had never craved promotion. It was a mark of achievement, but he had long since discovered that he preferred dealing with inquiries firsthand instead of rising to the level of delegating authority to others. He had found too often that objectivity was lost with ambition, and pleasing one's superior officer became more important than getting to the root of an issue.

Philip Nettle, who had been the first officer charged with the Shaw case—or the Winslow case, as it had begun—had complained several times that Bowles was pushing him to conclusions. "You can't *know* that," Bowles was fond of saying. "Stick with what you do know, man, and leave imagination to the press."

"Aye," Hamish agreed. "It isna' always wise to look for complexity when there is none!"

Complexity, Rutledge retorted as he walked out the door, was often what saved the innocent. Judging only by the obvious facts could lead a policeman astray.

"It isn't the guilt of a man," he said as he turned the crank on his motorcar, "that we set out to establish, but the truth in a case. And sometimes that's buried deep."

"Aye," Hamish agreed bitterly. "I wouldna' be lying sae deep in a French grave, if there had been time to sort out the truth. . . ."

Wincing, Rutledge put his motorcar into gear and turned out onto the street. "You gave me no choice," he said.

"I couldna' give you a choice," Hamish agreed. "Else there would have been a longer list of the dead on my ain soul. I couldna' bear it. As ye're haunted, so was I."

———

UNSETTLED THAT NIGHT, Rutledge considered what to do about the Shaws. The wisest course was to ask Mrs. Shaw to hand over the locket to Chief Superintendent Bowles and wash his own hands of decision. He could walk away then with a clear conscience. But if Bowles refused to take the matter any further, what then? Push that small, damning piece of jewelry out of his own mind, as if it didn't exist? Pretend that there was no question about Shaw's guilt, even though he knew there was?

He'd seen the locket. He had absolutely no doubt about its authenticity. The truth was, he wasn't as certain that he could trust Bowles.

And whatever he decided, the rearrangement of the papers in his desk drawer had left Rutledge with a feeling that Bowles was already looking over his shoulder. Waiting—for what?

"For you to put a foot wrong," Hamish responded. "I'd no' gie him the shovel to bury you with."

"I've been pitched into doing the devil's work," Rutledge said. "Any way you look at it. Bowles may crucify me for trying to find the truth. Mrs. Shaw will damn me if I walk away. And Shaw himself will haunt me until I *know* what happened."

"Aye. It's a fearsome thing, judgment. I wouldna' be in your shoon."

In the morning, tired and hampered by the restlessness that was Hamish's response to Rutledge's own uncertainties, Rutledge went back to the church where he had stopped on his first visit to Sansom Street.

The rector—the name on the door read Bailey—was in his small, cluttered office at the back of the church, and rose to greet Rutledge with a quiet interest.

"I've come back again," Rutledge said, "because I have more questions to ask. They aren't official; you can refuse to answer them, if you wish. But I need information, and there's no other way to get it except to ask."

"You look tired," Mr. Bailey remarked as the light from the windows fell on Rutledge's face. "Sleepless night, was it?"

One of many, he could have said. Instead, Rutledge admitted, "In a way. I'm on the horns of a dilemma, you see." He set his hat on the chair beside him, and began to explain. Bailey listened in silence. Rutledge, trying to read his man, came to the conclusion that Bailey was not as struck by the events of the last week as he himself was. Or else hid his curiosity more cleverly.

"I can't resolve your problems," the rector said when Rutledge had finished. "I have no reason to think that Ben Shaw was innocent. And no reason to believe that he was guilty. The courts drew that conclusion, not I. I simply offered comfort to the family and helped them survive."

"Pilate couldn't have said it better," Rutledge commented.

Bailey smiled. "If I judge, to what end will that come? Should I have lectured Mrs. Shaw on her poor choice of husband?"

"From what I've heard, he was a cut above her, but a poor provider."

"Or perhaps he'd given her a taste for the kind of life she really wanted to live, and then walked away from it himself," Bailey pointed out. "I never discovered why he chose to work with his hands, when he might have done much better for himself using his mind."

"If his family rejected his wife, he may have rejected their way of life and taken up something more suitable to hers. As I remember, she was left to fend for herself from an early age. She hadn't been given his opportunities."

"It's true. She had no family to speak of. Nor did Shaw, for that matter. There was a sister, but she died shortly after the hanging. And I recall a cousin, who'd run off to Australia in 1900, after a rift with his father. There was no way to reach the man, and no reason to expect that he would come, if someone had tried. I was told he hadn't come home for his mother's services, when she died, and he'd been as close to her as anyone. Neville, I think his name was? And whatever caused the rift, it was apparently severe."

"Was there anything between Shaw's wife and the neighbor, Cutter? He seemed to speak well of her, when interviewed. Few other people did."

"Cutter liked Mrs. Shaw. Why, I can't tell you. And I won't guess. But the odd thing was, she was very different in his company than she was ordinarily. Mary—my wife—even spoke of it, a time or two."

Hamish said, *"Leave it, and speak to Mrs. Bailey . . ."*

For once Rutledge agreed. He asked a final question, clearing up another possible direction, as he stood to bring the interview to an end. "Did Mrs. Cutter visit the poor or the infirm, as part of her duties as a member of this church?"

"Most of the women have served on committees to visit those who are no longer able to come to services. It's considered a Christian duty. Again, Mary would know more about that. She has served on most of the women's committees—the duty of a churchman's wife."

Rutledge thanked him and left. He found the rectory just around the corner on a side street, a fresh coat of paint on the door setting it apart from its neighbors. Mrs. Bailey answered his knock, drying her hands on her apron. "If you're looking for my husband, you'll find him in the church office, this time of the morning."

She was a slim woman—some would say bony—with still-fair hair and a smooth face, though her throat and hands gave her true age away.

Rutledge smiled, and replied, "My name is Rutledge. I've just spoken with Mr. Bailey, and he suggested I might do better to ask you the questions I'm trying to answer."

"Rutledge—" She repeated the name thoughtfully. "We never met at the time, but you must be the policeman who was assigned to the Shaw inquiry." Nodding as she placed him, she said, "My granddaughter told me you were a very fine-looking man, for a policeman. She was eight at the time, and murder had very little meaning for her, thank heavens."

He could feel himself turning red. Mary Bailey smiled. "Oh, dear, I'm afraid I never mind my tongue as I should. In a clergyman's wife, it's a dreadful sin! But I've found over the years that if I attach one interesting fact to someone, I can keep a face and a name in my memory forever. Helpful when everyone expects the rector's wife to know exactly who they are and how important they might be."

She invited him into the kitchen, where she was making bread. The scents of warm yeast and rising dough were comforting. Her hands, moving almost without direction, began to knead the ball in the bed of flour.

"This won't wait," she explained, "and I'm sure your questions won't, either. What do you need to know? Has someone else in our parish been involved with the Yard?" It was as if she had someone in mind, he thought, and was fishing.

"No, just an odd coincidence that occurred some days ago, and when it was brought to my attention, I wanted to put it to rest. A piece of the jewelry missing at the time of the Shaw murders has come to light. I'm trying to find out what—if any—significance that might have."

She studied him, her blue eyes reading more than he was comfortable with. "And as the inspector involved, you want to know if this changes anything that—happened."

"In a word—yes," he replied.

Nodding, she kept her eyes on her hands now. "Yes. Well. What is it you want to know?"

He began indirectly. "Mrs. Shaw. Did she serve on any of the women's committees? Visiting the ill, the poor?"

"She didn't attend services here after her marriage. But she was never comfortable with that sort of need. I called on her once to ask if she might know of anyone looking to be a companion to an elderly man recovering from a leg fracture. I thought at the time it might mean an extra bit of money for her, if she could use it. But she was clear on that point, as well as her dislike of dealing with the infirm."

"Her neighbor, Mrs. Cutter . . ."

"Was very active, until her health broke. We could always depend on Janet Cutter. And she was a very good cook, as well. She'd often bake a little extra and put it in a basket to take to someone under the weather. Still, Janet kept to herself, you know, she wasn't one to sit and gossip. I put it down to shyness. But she seemed to have a kind heart."

"And fingers that stuck to bits of jewelry?" Hamish asked.

"Mr. Cutter was one of the few people who defended Mrs. Shaw when we were closing in on her husband. He thought she was a very different person from the general impression of her. His wife, on the other hand, was not as kind."

"Mrs. Shaw was never a very pretty woman, but she has a very bold and defiant way about her." Mrs. Bailey added more flour to the bowl. "Some men like that."

Rutledge tried to picture Mrs. Shaw flirting, and failed. He said as much.

Mrs. Bailey laughed. "I never suggested she was flirting. But her manner was bold. She could manage tradesmen very well, she could take charge of a situation and deal with it, she was unflappable. If the butcher overcharged her or brought her a less than satisfactory bit of beef, she would face him down without embarrassment or tears. 'Now see here, Mr. Whoever, I wasn't born yesterday, and I know that that chicken is *old,* and if you don't take it back, I shall complain to my neighbors about the poor service you're offering these days!' "

"How do you know this?" he asked, intrigued.

"Because," she said, turning to face him, "the same tradesmen come to my door, and over the years, you hear things." She dropped her voice a level and said in a brusque tone, " *'I fear Mrs. Shaw isn't herself this week. She complained fiercely about my cabbages. I ask you, have you ever had reason to doubt my cabbages?'* It's a way tradesmen have, to play one customer against another, and if I say, 'Your cabbages have always been quite lovely,' then the rest of his route hears that Mrs. Bailey at the rectory is particularly fond of his cabbages."

"What did Ben Shaw think about Mrs. Cutter?"

"Ah, interesting you should ask that," she murmured, giving the bread dough a good thumping. "I think—*think,* mind you, there's no proof—that when he was younger and drinking more heavily, Henry Cutter was not above striking his wife when in his cups. Ben Shaw was not used to the world he married into and came to live in. He was sentimental, and rather nice. He would have been the knight in shining armor, if Janet Cutter had cried on his shoulder. Ready to take on her battles, but not to move into her bed, if you follow me."

"And yet he was accused of smothering three elderly women," Rutledge gently reminded her.

"As a policeman," she reminded him in turn, "you are not easily fooled. Well, after nearly fifty years dealing with a church, one comes to understand politics, human nature, and human frailty in unexpected ways. The infirm are not always pleasant and clean and defenseless. They can be ill-tempered, nasty, and terribly cruel. Their rooms often smell of urine-soaked bedding, dirty bodies, and bits of stale food. They have bedsores and bad breath and suspicious natures. Their caretakers often abuse them, because they're helpless, and because patience wears thin. The knight in shining armor come to nail up shingles and repair windows doesn't last long, even if the first time he'd arrived in full array. This doesn't excuse Ben Shaw, you understand—but it is important to realize how easily such a thing might have happened."

Rutledge had not walked into the scenes of the crimes—Philip Nettle had done that. The women had long since been removed to the morgue, thin and small under their sheets, defenseless and pathetic. "You're telling me," he said slowly, "that anyone might have killed them. A man. A woman. Not a monster."

"What I found most unusual about the crimes was that anyone had killed the three women at all. Why not just randomly take what you like? A silver spoon here, a man's pocket watch there."

"They would have missed something—"

"Yes, but who can say when they missed that spoon just how long it had been gone? We've had cases where men come to the door with apparently respectable intent—selling mousetraps or books of household hints. And then finding no one at home, they break in and take what they like. Easier to do when the inhabitants are elderly, ill women asleep in their beds."

He'd looked into that himself. Chance burglaries, an easy way to add a few pounds to a door-to-door seller's pocket. There had been no reports of any such burglaries in this part of London for a year before the murders. . . .

Hamish, intent and interested, said, "But if they complained, the auld women, and the thief had taken fright—"

Rutledge finished the thought in his head aloud. "If Mrs. Cutter had found herself on the verge of being caught and hanged, would Ben Shaw have volunteered to go back and speak to the old women—and when they refused to be silent, silenced them forever?"

Mrs. Bailey set her loaf in the waiting pan. "It's a shocking suggestion, Inspector. Not one that I care to contemplate, to tell you the truth. Is there anything else you wish to know?"

Still—it made sense. It would explain how a man like Shaw had gotten himself involved with murder. . . .

Mrs. Bailey had been more helpful than she knew.

But Rutledge realized as he drove across the Thames back to the Yard that he might also have underestimated the rector's wife. . . .

In a parish where there were no garden tea parties or Sunday luncheons with the gentry, the rector and his wife had learned how people lived with the small degradations of little money, poor health, hard work, and not much beauty. The Baileys would have had few illusions about their neighbors and over the years acquired a rather pragmatic view of their flock. They had ministered in the truest sense, without judgment.

At what cost to themselves? he wondered.

11

THERE WAS A MESSAGE WAITING FOR RUTLEDGE WHEN HE
arrived at the Yard.

Chief Superintendent Bowles wanted to see him.

Braced for an angry confrontation, Rutledge went along to
Bowles's office.

Anything but angry, Bowles greeted him with his usual cold stare
and brief command to sit down, sit down.

There were papers all over his desk, and he hunched over them
with frowning intensity before saying to Rutledge, "You've been in
Kent, have you?"

"Yes. To visit friends."

"Hmmm. What's your opinion of these murders?"

"I have none. I don't know anything beyond the fact that there have
been more than one."

"Looks bad, damned bad. The Chief Constable is not happy, and
his people haven't found anything to be going on with. Incapable lot,
apparently." Bowles had never held a high opinion of police work outside London. "No, that's not kind. Mainly it's out of their line of experience. You served in the war. You'll have a better sense of what's
happening. I'm sending you down to have a look. Be quick about it, if

you can. The Chief Constable has friends in high places. Needn't say more on that score."

He passed a sheaf of papers across to Rutledge, who began to scan them as he suggested, "I should think Devereaux would be the best man—"

But Bowles paid no heed. ". . . Some bloody foreigner to blame, most likely . . ."

Unexpectedly Rutledge was reminded of the face at the bonfire—in the headlamps of his motorcar. As if in warning.

Rutledge looked up into the yellow eyes of his superior. They were staring at him. Speculative. Watchful.

Deliberately taking a different tack to test the waters, Rutledge replied, "The hop-picking season is over. The extra workers have gone back to London or Maidenhead, wherever they came from. I could deal with that end of the investigation. From my desk."

"Worth looking into," Bowles agreed, taking the remark as a course of action. "But they want someone on the ground in Kent. Hand over whatever you're working on to Simpson. He'll cope."

Inspector Simpson was, as everyone knew, Bowles's latest protégé. A weak-chinned man with a spiteful nature, he was, in the words of Sergeant Gibson, "Generally to be found toadying up to Old Bowels. Right pair, the two of them!" There was rumored to be a wager on how long it would take Simpson to make chief inspector, over the list.

Rutledge found himself wondering if it was Simpson who had gone through his desk.

And as if reading his mind, Bowles added, "I hear a Mrs. Shaw called on you a few days ago." A bland voice, a glance out the window to indicate that this was mere curiosity on the Chief Superintendent's part.

Fishing.

Rutledge chose to be circumspect. "Yes. Ben Shaw's widow. His hanging still haunts her. Sad story."

"Shall I send Simpson along to have a talk with her?" The yellow eyes were mere slits now.

"Short of bringing her husband back, I doubt there's anything anyone can do. Even Simpson." Rutledge paused. "She hasn't prospered since Shaw's death. I expect she was hoping for a handout."

"Yes, well, Shaw ought to have considered his family before taking to murder." Bowles stirred in his chair, preparatory to dismissing Rutledge. "See what you can do in Kent. I've already told the Chief Constable you'll be there smartly!"

It was an unmistakable warning: Get out of London and don't meddle with things best left alone.

RUTLEDGE MADE A point, before leaving his desk, to remove any papers connected with the Shaws. Simpson, if mining for trouble, would find none. . . .

But on his way into Kent, he paused in Sansom Street and again left his motorcar where it would attract less notice. He walked as far as the Shaw house, and then to the neighboring door of Henry and the late Janet Cutter.

"It's no' wise!" Hamish told him. "There'll be someone to see, and in the end, a tale will be carried back to the Yard."

"There may not be another chance." Rutledge found himself wondering if Simpson had already questioned the constable on this street. It would be like him.

A girl-of-all-work opened the door to him, her hands red from laundry.

"Mr. Cutter's not to home," she confided in the tall, attractive stranger on the doorstep. "He's just off to work after his dinner, but I wouldn't look him up there. Mr. Holly is not one to like gossiping on company time."

It had all the earmarks of a quote overheard from her employer. She smiled up at Rutledge with artless interest, then remembered her duty. "Is there a message you'd care to leave, sir?"

"Did you serve Mrs. Cutter, before her death?" he asked. "I don't remember you here, before the war." There had been an older woman, as he recalled, worn down with childbearing and worry, who did the heavy work.

"I came in '17," she said, "when Mum had Tommy. Mum wasn't well, after, and Mrs. Cutter asked if I'd like to work, instead. And a good thing, too, for Tommy was trouble from the start. Colic." A cloud passed over her face, darkening her sunny spirits. "Mum and Tommy were took by the Influenza. Within a day of each other." She nodded wisely. "She never knew he went. Best that way!"

"Was Mrs. Cutter a good employer? Did you enjoy working for her?"

"She wasn't a *bad* employer," the girl said, groping for words to explain how she felt. "Mum said she were different before the stroke. Jollier. It was as if that took the spirit right out of her. And she seemed—sad—when I came here. As if there was a burden she couldn't carry and it was getting heavier with every year that went by. And finally it buried her under its weight."

"Did you have trouble pleasing her?" He encouraged her guileless chatter. The stroke had occurred after the trial. Mrs. Cutter had been well enough the last time he'd come here, to question the couple.

"Oh, it weren't that, so much as the heaviness of her mind. It was like working in a house where there'd been a death. As if black crepe hung on the mirrors and the shades were drawn."

For such a young girl, as Hamish was also pointing out, it would have been a depressing atmosphere.

"And Mr. Cutter? Did he find the house bleak, too?"

"Mum said he was bewildered, but when I came in '17, he was more resigned. The Missus was young for a stroke, Mum said. Came on of a sudden, like a flash of light. Mum heard her calling, and then the sound of someone falling down the stairs. Frightened her witless to find Mrs. Cutter lying up against the balustrades halfway down, and not able to move. Doris and Betsy and I had nightmares, hearing it, but the boys wanted her to tell it over and over again."

"Where was your mother when this happened?"

"Hanging out the clothes. She left a sheet dragging, to run in."

He thanked the girl, still more of a child than a woman, and walked back to his motorcar, thoughtful and uneasy.

"I ought to find Henry Cutter," he told himself as he drove on to the Lambeth Road, and turned toward Kent.

"It's no' been pressing for all these years," Hamish reminded him.

"It hasn't, no," Rutledge agreed, and fell silent. Trying to remember the case not in hindsight but the way it had unfolded at the time—that was what was hard. How he'd felt, how he'd thought, how he'd watched the evidence build.

He had been another man then. Young, idealistic. A stranger to the hollow shell who had come back from the war and for months struggled to rebuild his peacetime skills. He had more in common with the voice of Hamish MacLeod than he did with his prewar self. That Ian Rutledge might have lived six centuries ago, not a mere six years. Somewhere they had lost each other.

NOVEMBER ANYWHERE IN England was a cold and often rainy month. The air was heavy, damp, and chill, and with the sun retreating toward the equator, the shorter days seemed to drag through their appointed hours with a dullness that sometimes made the difference between sunrise and sunset a matter only of conjecture. Had the sun risen? Was it setting or was there another squall of rain on its way? Along the rivers, fog could hold on for a good part of the morning, and heavy clouds finished the late afternoon long before night could fall. The lingering sunsets of Midsummer, when light filled the air well past eight and nine, and sometimes as late as ten, were a thing of memory.

A depressing season . . .

Hamish said, "The rain was worst, in France. I couldna' get used to the rain."

It had soaked their greatcoats and left shoes a soggy, rotting mess, and it had ruined tempers, brought out the miasma of smells from the trenches, and made the heavy mud so slippery that a man could lose his footing and go down as he raced across No Man's Land. Rutledge had fallen more than once, feeling the swift plucking at his shoulder or elbow where machine-gun fire had barely missed him. And then scrambled back to his feet into the steady scything, waiting for the blow to his body that never came, never more than just that ghostly plucking. Living a charmed life had frightened him as much as it had defeated him. He'd wanted to die.

———

KENT WAS A fertile part of the country, covered with pasturage and hop gardens, with orchards blazingly white in spring, and apples or plums or cherries hanging darkly from summer boughs. Agriculture was its mainstay, though there had been iron at one time, and the cutting of the great forests for making charcoal to smelt the iron had opened up the Weald to grass for sheep or horses or the plow. There was still industry along the Medway, and shipbuilding on the coast where the tradition of putting to sea was strong. But most of Kent was green, with ash and beech and sometimes oak in the hedgerows or marching in shady rows down the lanes.

This was also the gateway to England from the Continent, the path taken by invaders, by priests, by merchants, and by the weavers who at the request of Edward III had come to teach the English how to turn their valuable wool into far more valuable cloth. Prosperous and rural and content, most of the villages turned their backs on the Dover–London road, and got on with their lives in peace.

Marling was a pretty village, even by Kentish standards, settled on a ridge overlooking the long slope of land that fell away toward the Weald. A High Street ran through the center, dividing where a triangular space opened up and created the irregular square that had held the Guy Fawkes bonfire. The Tuesday Market here had been one of the village's mainstays for generations, giving it status among its neighbors.

The square had been cleared long since of the last of the ashes, and today lay quiet and colorless in the cold rain that had followed at Rutledge's heels. Even the Cavalier standing bravely in the wet on his plinth appeared to huddle under his plumed hat.

Rutledge knew where to find the police station—it was several doors down from the hotel where he'd dined with Elizabeth Mayhew and her friends after the bonfire. Tucked in between a bakery on the one side and a haberdashery on the other, the station occupied one of the old brick buildings still carrying proudly the Georgian facades that gave Marling its particular character.

The midday traffic was light, a few carriages and carts, a motorcar or two, and women hurrying from butcher to greengrocer to draper's shop—one, pausing to speak to a friend, pushed her covered pram with metronomic rhythm, back and forth, back and forth. Another, carrying a small wet dog in her arms, was lecturing the animal for running into the road, warning it of dire consequences.

On the surface, it was a peaceful scene, a prewar England in some ways, seemingly detached from the hardships and shortages that scarred Sansom Street's inhabitants in London.

Hamish, observing it, said, "You wouldna' think murder had been done here. Or ever would be."

"No," Rutledge agreed, "but night falls early this time of year. It's always after dark that people begin to look over their shoulders."

He left the motorcar by the hotel, and when he entered the police station was greeted by an elderly sergeant dressing down a young constable who was red about the ears.

The constable glanced up with undisguised relief at the interruption and earned another condemnation for not paying strict attention. When the sergeant sent him on his way, the young man scuttled out without looking back.

The sergeant straightened his jacket, squared his shoulders, and met Rutledge's glance levelly, identifying him at once as a stranger. "Sergeant Burke, sir. What can I do for you?"

"Inspector Rutledge, from the Yard. I'm looking for Inspector Dowling."

"He's just gone home to his meal, sir. I expect him back on the half hour." The sergeant studied him. "Come about the murders, then, sir?"

"Yes, that's right."

"Well, the Chief Constable knows best, sir, but I doubt even the Yard can help us. There's no sense to these murders. At least not so far. Unless we've got ourselves a shell-shocked soldier who thinks he's still at war."

Rutledge flinched as the remark struck home.

The sergeant leaned against the back of his chair, thick arms resting on the top to ease his weight. "I've been sergeant here for fifteen years," he went on, "and was constable for ten before that. And I can tell you, this is the first inquiry where I've not got a hint about who's behind it. No whispers in the shops, no words dropped in the pubs, nothing that makes me prick up my ears and wonder, like. There's always a root cause waiting to be found, if you look hard enough, but I'm blessed if we can see it. The only thing the victims have in common, so far as we can tell, is their service in the war. Poor men, all three, who served their country well and came back with little to show for it but the loss of a limb. No hero's welcome nor bands playing nor offers of work. A crying shame, to see the lads lying like old rags by the roadside, and feeling helpless to do anything for them."

"How well did you know them?"

"I watched them grow up, you might say, sir. Never any real trouble from any of them, except what you'd expect from high-spirited lads with time on their hands. Nothing vicious, or mean."

"Yes, I understand," Rutledge responded neutrally, knowing well that it was human nature to praise Caesar after he was dead. "That's mainly why I'm here. Another pair of eyes, another perspective."

"In the war, were you, sir?"

"Four years of it."

Burke nodded. "Then you'll know, better than most, what the lads went through. Well, then, Inspector Dowling'll give you what little we've found. Shall I fetch him for you, sir?"

"No, let him finish in his own good time."

Rutledge left, promising to return in half an hour. He thought for a moment about calling on Elizabeth Mayhew, but instead went to The Plough for his lunch. At a table to himself by the window, he looked out on the square and watched people going about their business in the rain. A bobbing of black umbrellas above black coats, a bowed head here or there, and one man hurrying along with a newspaper held over his hat. Rutledge's own hat sat in the chair opposite him, darkly spotted with rain. It was, he thought, as good a way as any to prevent company— Hamish or someone else—from taking the empty chair. For the dark-paneled room was quite busy with custom, as if the rain had discouraged people from making the journey home for their midday meal.

Hamish said, from just behind his shoulder, "Yon sergeant has a level head."

Rutledge came within a breath of answering the voice aloud, used to its cadence in his mind. Stopping himself in time, he responded silently, "Let's hope Dowling is as competent."

When he'd given his order, he turned again to the window, hoping to put an end to Hamish's conversation. And he saw Elizabeth Mayhew just taking leave of a man in a heavy coat whose back was to him. She was smiling, her face alight, upturned, as she leaned toward the figure.

Rutledge found himself suddenly jealous. Not for himself but for Richard Mayhew, dead now and buried in France. As schoolboys, he and Richard had tramped in the face of cold winds that in winter blew across the Hoo peninsula like a knife, bringing mists on their heels. Or in summer followed the old Saxon ways that crisscrossed the Kent countryside, footpaths now but once the high roads of a dim past, serving settlers, warriors, or pilgrims.

Adventures that had shaped their boyhood, and through that fashioned the men they would become. They'd gone their different ways soon enough, but each had carried with him that mark of self-reliance and independence learned on the Downs and in the marshes—experience that had served them well in the war. They'd discussed that, once, on a bombed-out road in France where they'd briefly crossed paths—unaware that it was for the last time.

Richard had said, "The first thing I'll do when I get home is walk out over the Downs again. When I'm too tired to sleep, I retrace my steps and find that solitude again, and the silence."

Rutledge had answered, smiling, "I never expected that learning to tell time by the stars or guess at wind speed would save my life one day. It was a game then. Do you still have your uncle's compass?"

Richard had dug it out of his pocket, holding it out like a holy relic. "Never without it. Do you remember the night we were washed out by the rain? I thought I'd never be that wet again. But we were, our first week in France. While my men were cursing and swearing, I was standing there laughing. Only, it was summer on the Downs, and a damned sight warmer than December in the lines!"

They had had nearly ten minutes before the snarl of traffic had opened up, and Rutledge had had to move on. Richard's last words had been, "When the war is over, I'm going to have a son, and I'll teach him everything I know about that safe other world. But I won't tell him about this one. It's too obscene . . ."

A week later Richard was dead, and there would be no sons.

In his second year at Oxford, Richard had fallen deeply in love with

Elizabeth. He'd been absent-minded and daydreaming by turns, plotting ways to see her again, driving his tutor to despair when Elizabeth had gone to Italy in the spring, for her mother's health. Rutledge had never seen a happier groom on their wedding day, or a bride more beautiful. Or two people more perfectly suited to each other. It was time for Elizabeth to put her mourning aside—he'd said as much himself—but was it time for her to fall in love again?

For the glow on her face was telling. Rutledge had seen it before.

Hamish said, "There's no accounting for the heart."

But surely, Rutledge countered, a love like theirs lasted?

"The man is dead," Hamish reminded him. "There's wee comfort in memories when the other side of the bed is cold and empty."

Rutledge's own fiancée had deserted him. But the woman who had loved Hamish mourned still. His last word as he lay dying had been her name. Fiona was more faithful than Jean, who had preferred to put the war behind her.

The man walked on, passing the Cavalier's statue without looking back. Elizabeth followed him with her eyes, standing stock-still where he'd left her. Then, lifting the black bowl of her umbrella, she moved on with a spring in her step, as if the rain had vanished.

Rutledge felt an extraordinarily strong sweep of loneliness, as if here in the window of the hotel dining room he was cut off from the quiet voices and soft laughter that filled the room on the other side of him. And cut off, too, from the villagers going about their business in the weather. An observer with no role in the reality of life . . . He lived with the dead, in more ways than one.

Hamish said, "Ye'll never know better. It's the price of what ye are."

12

INSPECTOR DOWLING WAS A THIN MAN WITH A NOSE TOO LARGE for his face. Its weight seemed to pull him forward, stooping his shoulders. But the brown eyes on either side were warm and friendly, like a dog's.

Shaking hands with Rutledge, he said, "I'm glad you're here. Sergeant Burke should have sent for me."

"He was kind enough to suggest it, but I took the opportunity to have my own meal."

"At the hotel? Good food there, is it?" Dowling said almost wistfully. "My wife, dear heart that she is, has never mastered the culinary arts."

Rutledge smothered his smile.

Dowling shuffled papers on his desk with a sigh. "Well, then, on to this business of the murders. Each of the victims lived within a twenty-mile radius of Marling. All were ex-soldiers, men with perfectly sound reputations. The last victim was found close by Marling, but the others were discovered along the road coming in from the south. There were no signs of violence—no wounds, no bruises. You'd have thought, looking at them, that they'd stepped off the road for a brief rest."

"How did they die, if there was no violence?"

"An overdose of laudanum, but in suspicious circumstances. I'm told by the local doctor that amputations often leave behind a residual pain, as if the limb's still there and hurting from whatever it was that made removing it necessary—in these cases, machine-gun fire or shrapnel, and the infection that followed. Amputees, each of them got about on crutches." He shook his head. "Myself, I don't know how I'd deal with that. Thank God, I've never had to find out."

"Suicide, then?" Machine-gun fire and shrapnel tore at a limb, making it nearly impossible to save. Rutledge had seen the aid stations with the bloody remains piled high under a tarpaulin, waiting for disposal.

"It's not likely, for two very good reasons: Each was the sole support of his family, and his pension ended if he died. I don't think any man in his right mind would leave his family destitute, if he could still feed them and clothe them. However bad the pain got."

Hamish quietly agreed.

Rutledge was thinking instead of Raleigh Masters, who resented his lost foot with a bitter passion. And yet he clung to his life as if only to make those around him suffer through the blight of his own.

He wondered if there was a similarity, if these victims had also made life wretched for those around them. That might explain one murder. Not three.

Dowling was saying, "Moreover, I've spoken with each of the widows. They absolutely refuse to consider suicide."

But wives and widows—witness Nell Shaw!—were often the last to accept the desertion of their husbands, even in death.

"And there's one other small detail here. These men had been drinking wine before they died. But no one seems to know where it came from, this wine. Not from home, certainly; there was none in any of the three houses. And no one recalls seeing any of the three men in a public house the nights of their deaths."

"What time of night did they die?"

"It was after eleven, certainly. That's the latest time we've been able to establish. The bodies weren't discovered until close on to morning, when the light was improving. I've sent my men round to talk to everyone who might have been on those roads after dark. They all swore there wasn't a body lying there when they passed."

But dusk came early in November. . . . A dark bundle in the high grass at the side of the road might not be visible.

Hamish said, "How many would stop to ask if a drunk needed help? And the next day, how many of those would admit they'd passed by without stopping?"

It was an interesting point.

"Why were the victims out on the road at that hour? Eleven o'clock or later?" Rutledge asked Dowling. "If they hadn't been visiting a pub, where had they been?"

"For the most part they were looking for work, picking up whatever they could find. All three often went from village to village, accepting lifts when one was offered, walking if they had to. Taylor had been mending a fence, Webber repaired furniture, and Bartlett—who'd been a glazier before the war—had gone to sit by a friend's bedside. The man had been gassed at Ypres, and was dying. Lungs burned out. As a rule, the three victims stayed the night where they were, if there was work. Sleeping in a barn or outbuilding, whatever they could manage. Which also explains why there was no hue and cry when they didn't come home."

Rutledge said thoughtfully, "And all three killed at night . . ."

Hamish said, "What did they see, that they shouldn't have seen?"

Which was a reasonable key to unexpected murder: These men had stumbled on something they shouldn't have. Still, death had come on three different nights, and on three different roads. Kent was hardly a hotbed of crime, where something evil lurked at the crossroads, waiting for dark. Smuggling had once been a cottage industry along the coast, but that was long past.

Dowling tossed his papers aside. "We've combined our efforts, Inspector Grimes in Seelyham, and Inspector Cawly in Helford, and I. Keeping an eye out for strangers hanging about, questioning everyone who'd seen the victims the day before they were killed, making a master list of everyone who admits to being on the roads each of the three nights. And we've come up with what we could have told ourselves before the killings began: The victims knew each other, they were poor, they were wounded in France. But half the ex-soldiers in Kent fit that description, and if that's what the murderer is after, he's got an endless supply of choices. Why these three, and so close to Marling? I can tell you that Grimes and Cawly will be happy to drop this business into your lap, Inspector, but I'm a stubborn man and don't give up easily."

BEFORE LEAVING THE hotel, Rutledge had arranged for a room. His glimpse of Elizabeth Mayhew's face as she stood in the rain on the High Street had made him uncomfortable about staying with her for a few days, although she would have been the first to urge him. Or would she?

She had asked him to help clear out Richard's clothes. In preparation for what?

It was none of his business, he reminded himself, and yet it had left an oddly unpleasant taste in his mouth, as if he had been excluded from what had always felt like a family circle.

Hamish said, "You were nearly sure at breakfast that she was on the point of speaking her mind."

"And she stopped herself. I'd like to know why. It would have been—easier, coming from her."

Instead, it was as if the relationship had changed in unexpected ways.

Taking along the young constable—now silent and shy—who had been dressed down by Sergeant Burke, Rutledge set out to visit the places where each body had been found.

"Put yourself in the murderer's shoes," Rutledge suggested to the young man as they drove past the square and out of Marling on the way to Seelyham. "How well would you need to know this part of Kent, in order to find a quiet place for a killing?"

Constable Weaver brightened, as if no one had asked his opinion before. "I'd say ours are fairly well-traveled roads," he answered after a moment's thought. "Anyone coming down them in the direction of Marling would see the empty stretches. You'd only have to keep in mind where."

Which meant, Hamish pointed out, that the possibilities were wide open.

"Were the three dead men heavy drinkers?"

"They'd not say no to a pint, sir, if someone was buying. They didn't have the money for much else."

"They hadn't developed a taste for wine, in France?"

"There's a story about that, now you mention it. Some of the

Marling men took shelter during a storm in a burned-out French farm-house. It had a wine cellar, and the men helped themselves. They were sick as dogs for two days, after drinking the lot." Weaver chuckled. "Tommy Bilson brought home the silver cream jug he found there under a mattress. And it shined up something wonderful. I told him I ought to arrest him for stealing it." He suddenly remembered who sat beside him in the motorcar and cast an anxious glance in Rutledge's direction.

It was as old as warfare, this propensity to appropriate souvenirs. Rutledge had seen countless small acquisitions while boxing up possessions of the men he'd lost. There had been no way to discover where these objects had come from, much less who might have owned them once. For the most part he'd closed his eyes to them and sent them home. One of the most touching had been silver buttons, for a bride who would never wear them to the altar. . . .

Weaver pointed just ahead, where a line of trees marched along a winding stretch of road, giving some protection from the sun or rain. Rutledge pulled the motorcar to the verge. The constable was saying, "Seelyham's not more than three miles in that direction. Inspector Grimes was called to have a look at what a farmer had found, and he sent for us."

They got out to stand by the trunk of an ash tree. Its thickness offered an ideal place for a man to rest if he was drunk or tired. Shadowed by tall grass and the branches overhead, it was also an ideal spot where a body might be disposed of.

There were no cottages or farms within sight just here, no windows overlooking the road, but a hundred yards or so in the direction of Marling an overgrown drive wound between leaning stone pillars to a house protected from view by trees and a thick shrubbery. Only its roof and several chimneys were visible over the treetops. Too far away to hear anything, too far to see the road. Still . . .

"Who lives there?" Rutledge asked, pointing out the gates.

"Nobody now. The family died, and the lawyers are trying to find the heirs. Gone to New Zealand for a fresh start, or so I'm told."

"Tell me about this first victim. What was his name? Taylor?"

"That's right. Will Taylor. He worked in the hop gardens before the war. But there's not much call for a one-legged man in that line. He'd found a job in Seelyham, putting up a fence that had blown down with the last storm. Good with his hands, and married, with two children."

"Did you know him?" Rutledge asked. Weaver had missed the war by a matter of months, too young to serve, but probably eager.

"He was my brother's age—Simon was lost off Gallipoli, when his ship went down," Weaver replied somberly. "And I know Taylor's wife, as well. Alice was in school with my sister. Too young to marry, but her mother signed the papers."

"The sort of man who'd find himself mixed up with something he ought to leave alone?" Rutledge asked, looking up and down the quiet road.

"I never knew Will to be dishonest. He used to complain about the hop pickers from the East End. Light-fingered and always after the girls, he'd say."

Hop picking was labor-intensive. Help was brought in during the autumn to take in the crop, and sometimes the same workers were called on to do the haying first. They were often the dregs of London's East End, willing enough to work for wages, and sometimes representing the third and fourth generation hired out to pick. It was good income with winter coming on, a little something laid aside for the coalman or a sick child or gin to warm the inside of a man when the cold winds blew. A goodly number of the pickers came from the Maidstone area, bringing with them their dogs and their children, both of which ran underfoot like chickens.

Weaver stared down at the broken stalks of last summer's wildflowers. "I don't see Will Taylor mixed up in anything sinister. He was bent on feeding his family. Took losing his leg hard, an active sort who liked working out in the air. But he was trying to manage somehow."

Rutledge said, "Did his wife have anything to tell you?"

"I questioned Alice myself," Weaver responded. "But she didn't know much. He was staying over in Seelyham to finish the fence, saying he'd come home when it was done. She didn't expect him for another day or two. Sergeant Burke went on to Seelyham and asked about Taylor's work. The fence was done properly, and a day early. Taylor was told he could wait until the morning, but was eager to get home, and set out after his dinner."

"Was Taylor carrying his pay?"

"Yes, sir, and it was still there, in his pocket. You'd think, wouldn't you, sir, that a thief wouldn't fail to find that!"

THE SECOND VICTIM had been found on the road from Helford. It ran into the Seelyham road at an angle, just outside Marling. Lying in a ditch by the side of fields, he was almost invisible until the sun rose high enough to pierce the shadows.

Beyond where Weaver stood with Rutledge, the hop gardens spread out toward a distant farm, tucked into a fold of land. Their frames and their green vines gone for the winter, the gardens looked bare and fallow. An oast house, one of the most recognizable features of the Kent landscape, reared its head like a decapitated windmill close by a stand of trees, its white walls streaked and wet from the rain. Inside it was an oast, the drying kiln that was an essential part of the processing of hops.

"Tell me about this man—Webber?" Rutledge encouraged Weaver as they got out in the rain and stood by the spot. "What sort was he?"

"Most everyone in Marling knew who he was. Not the sort you'd find carousing of a Saturday night. He'd had a strict upbringing, and his mother was Temperance-mad. A carpenter by trade. Made tables and chests and the like, as his father had done before him. He was in Helford, recaning chairs. The caning Webber did was known all over. No breaks and no missed steps."

"Was there money in his pocket?"

"Yes, sir, we found two pounds."

Hamish commented, "A clever man, now, he'd ha' taken the money and put it in the puir box. To confound the police."

Rutledge responded aloud without thinking. "Both of them married: Taylor and Webber. Not likely to be unfaithful, would you say?"

Weaver answered him. "They weren't likely, no, sir. Past an age for wild oats, and that. There's no jealous husband looking for revenge."

THE THIRD BODY had been found close by the crossroads where Rutledge thought he'd seen a face in his headlamps. He felt an odd frisson of cold down his spine as he got out of the motorcar, as if there were traces of something unnatural here still, a scent or lingering shadow.

Hamish, ordinarily quick to point out foolishness, was a High-lander, who understood moods.

But the corpse was a local man, not a straying doppelgänger. Harry Bartlett had gone to visit a friend who was ill—and ended by dying be-fore him.

"Bartlett wasn't what you'd call a staunch churchgoer," Weaver was saying. "He had a reputation as a hell-raiser before the war, and was the first in Marling to sign up. Told everyone he was tired of bash-ing local heads, and thought he'd try a few Germans. He was a good sol-dier, from all reports. That lot often are. But he got hung up on the wire one night that last spring of the war and when they brought him in, he was near to bleeding to death."

Hamish was asking a question. Rutledge said, "Did these three men serve in the same unit?"

Weaver blinked. "Yes, sir, I expect they did. The Kent men stayed together. Looked out for each other."

Officers had found that men who knew each other fought better side by side. They often died side by side, when a shell went up in their faces.

Rutledge walked along the road for some distance, then turned and walked back. "All right then, the war. Find out all you can about where they served, and who their friends were."

"Sir? I can't see how that might help. The war's been over for a while now."

"It hadn't ended for them, had it?"

After a last look around, Rutledge turned back to the motorcar. They drove back to Marling as dusk was falling, and the road seemed long, lonely.

Hamish commented, "A man with crutches would accept a ride."

"So he would," Rutledge silently agreed. "But why should he be saved from a painful walk—and then be killed?"

Still, it was something to consider. What had these three men had in common, besides lost limbs? According to Weaver, not much beyond their working-class backgrounds and their service in the war. Bartlett's wife, Peggy, was a girl he'd married since coming home, and there were no children.

Dowling had been right. There was hardly any evidence to build on. What had brought these men face to face with a killer? Greed? A secret that was dangerous to know? A killer wouldn't offer a man a glass of wine and then fill him with laudanum, unless he first wanted to learn something from his victim. . . . Where had they drunk together?

Rutledge, listening to Hamish in the back of his mind, wondered how many more would join this unholy clutch of dead men, before the police found any answers.

THE RAIN FELL with depressing steadiness, cold and coloring everything a bleak gray. Even the church at the top of High Street seemed dark and dreary, its ragstone facade streaked with damp, and the dead flower stalks among the churchyard stones a sign of desertion rather than loving memorials. What did you grow in the churchyard in winter besides ivy and hellebore? Rutledge wondered as he drove back to the hotel. Too late for Michaelmas daisies and too early for pansies.

He washed up and unpacked his luggage, then came down to the dining room—to find Melinda Crawford ensconced at the best table. She looked up as he came into the paneled room and smiled broadly.

"Either I'm in my dotage, or you've answered a maiden's prayers."

He laughed and came to join her. "What brings you to Marling?"

"I could ask the same of you, but I've already guessed that in your case it's murder. In mine it might well be. I've been left at the altar, in a manner of speaking."

"By whom?" he asked, surprised.

"I was invited to dine with the Masterses, but Bella says that Raleigh is in the foulest of moods and the cook is threatening to give notice, and poor Bella's at her wit's end. So I left. Fortunately I remembered that the hotel here has quite good food, and I thought I might perhaps ask Elizabeth to join me."

"And have you?" He couldn't alter the wary note in his voice.

"She wasn't at home, either." Mrs. Crawford sighed. "The one thing I hate about getting old is one's shrinking circle of friends. But here you are, quite a delightful surprise, and I'm going to enjoy my evening with a handsome young man rather than a crabby old one."

"Has Masters taken a turn for the worse?"

"I doubt his body has, but his temper most certainly did. I could hear him roaring from the front hall. If the man hadn't been such a brilliant barrister and the most charming of people, I'd say he was paying for past sins. Still, I have both my limbs, and I can't imagine what it must be like not to."

"No reason to take his temper out on his wife."

"Bella's not as cowardly as you might think. In fact, she may in the end prove to be stronger than Raleigh. If she doesn't poison him first. I think tonight I'd have had a go at it."

Rutledge felt his spirits rising. Melinda Crawford was a charming woman, possessed of wit and insight and a very clear view of human nature. At the moment, she was the perfect antidote to his depression.

The meal was excellent, and the conversation exhilarating, leaving Hamish out as if shutting the door. The Scot was still making up his mind about Mrs. Crawford.

"In another time," Rutledge heard him muttering, "she'd ha' been burned at the stake for witchcraft."

Amused, Rutledge had silently answered, "Or been the mistress of Kings."

They talked about the war, and about India, where she'd spent her childhood, and about Kent.

"Do you know what I remembered most about Kent, as a child in India?" she asked Rutledge at one point.

"That it was green?"

"No, I remembered the orchards, trees *filled* with white and pink blossoms, like butterflies, and I remembered the man on stilts with grape leaves on his head."

"Good God!"

"When they do the twiddling—that is, when they're tying the hop strings from the ground to the wires that run on the wooden framework built above the gardens—there's a man on stilts who does the high knots. It's quite a difficult task—the vines as they grow follow those strings, and mustn't be led astray. And such a man will often wear a hat to keep the sun off his head. This one had found young grape leaves—they're not unlike hop leaves, you know—and had twisted himself a Bacchus crown, to keep his head cool. We stopped at the hop farm to water the horses, and he came over to the carriage and bent down to peer in at me, making a face because I was tired and cross. I was instantly enchanted. And I wanted to see him again." She smiled. "I was quite in love. With a man on stilts."

"And what did Mr. Crawford, when he arrived on the scene, think of your infatuation?"

"He was a tall man. I've always fancied tall men. That's your claim to my affection, by the way. And he went to the bazaar in Agra one day and found someone to fashion him a pair of stilts. I was grown up by that time, and knew better than to laugh when he went headfirst into the nasturtiums."

Rutledge chuckled, and then sobered. "I think Elizabeth Mayhew has found someone to love."

"Yes," Mrs. Crawford said pensively as she poured milk into her tea. "I tried to warn you of that."

"I wasn't in danger of falling in love with her."

"No, but you'd put her on a pedestal, you know. Richard's widow. She's quite human, like the rest of us."

"Who is this man?" He heard the edge in his voice.

"I don't know. I haven't been invited to meet him. But I hear from my seamstress that he's from Northumberland, and quite handsome."

"I wasn't aware that Elizabeth or Richard had friends in Northumberland."

"My dear Ian! What does that have to say to anything?" Mrs. Crawford demanded, amused.

"I meant," he replied testily, "that it's likely to be someone she's met since the war. Since Richard's death."

"Yes, I should expect it is. He was buying a trinket for a lady. A shawl, my seamstress told me. It was described to me in great detail, because it was so lovely. And quite a harmless gift. The very next week, I happened to see Elizabeth wearing that particular shawl. I didn't ask how she came by it. Occasionally I do remember my manners." Her lips curved in amusement, but her eyes were no longer smiling. "Nor did she tell me, when I admired it."

Hamish spoke up for the first time in an hour. "She's no' happy with this match. But she willna' tell you why . . ."

They spent the remainder of the meal talking about Mrs. Crawford's years in India. In the span of her life, the subcontinent had changed enormously. The vast private holding in the hands of the East India Company had collapsed in the Great Indian Mutiny, which had seen such bloody horrors at Cawnpore. The British government had taken over the country after that, and in the course of time, Disraeli had made Queen Victoria Empress of India, equal in majesty to the German Kaiser Wilhelm. Britain had poured civilians and soldiers into the subcontinent since then, and now there were rumblings of a movement for independence.

"It will come," Mrs. Crawford said. "In time. But what will happen then is not to be thought of. I'm glad I won't be here to see it. Civil war is always the bloodiest. And this Mr. Wilson in America has pushed through the self-determination clause he was so bent on having. It will bear bitter fruit, mark me. Well-intentioned people are often blind to the results of their good deeds."

Rutledge said, "Germany is broken. And under the heel of heavy war reparations. From what I hear, people are starving in the towns, and there's no money to buy food or fuel."

"Yes. If I were a German, I would get out. Try my luck in Argentina or Chile. Sell up, beg, borrow, or steal the money for my passage, and go."

"If the best people leave, how will she rebuild? Or more to the point, how will she be *rebuilt*? In what form? I think I'd stay and fight."

"Of course you would." She nodded. "And in the end be shot for your pains. Germany isn't ready for democracy. India is better suited for change than Germany because they've learned from us how a country is run. They'd inherit our infrastructure, the railroads and the communications systems, the trained bureaucracy and so on. It's the religious issue that will tear India apart. In Germany it will be the vacuum of leadership."

Hamish said, intrigued, "My ain granny never traveled more than thirty miles in any direction. The glen was her home. She never fancied telling her menfolk how to run the world."

Rutledge answered, "Your grandmother never had the opportunities that came this woman's way."

As if she'd been a party to the exchange between Rutledge and Hamish, Mrs. Crawford smiled and added, "Politicians never heed old ladies. It's more than time we women had the vote and showed them a thing or two."

Rutledge laughed. "You'd make a superb prime minister."

"Don't be silly," she retorted. "Mr. Churchill already has his eye on filling those shoes. Gallipoli was a setback, it's true, but he won't languish forgotten for long!"

AFTER SEEING MRS. Crawford to her motorcar and placing her safely in the hands of her driver, Rutledge went back into the hotel and asked for a telephone. He knew Elizabeth Mayhew was on the exchange, but there was no answer to his call. The operator told him after ten rings, "There appears to be no one at home."

But there were servants in the house.

He found himself worrying about Elizabeth and unable to sleep. As the bells in the clock tower struck the hour of one, Hamish said, "It willna' matter what you want. It's her life, and no' your own."

THE NEXT MORNING, as Rutledge stood shaving in front of the framed mirror above his washstand, he began to feel a stirring of intuition as he reviewed what he had seen and heard about the three men who had been killed near Marling. A stirring that was just out of reach in his mind, a pattern that was on the edge of consciousness. He had felt this kind of thing before, when he was working on what seemed at first to be disconnected events and facts. For there was always a key, in murder—a logical progression of circumstance that led to the destruction of another human being.

He knew what had brought these men out into the night, to walk a lonely road home. It was the wine that was incongruous. How was it offered? And where? Under what pretense? What had happened then? Had the men been left to die on the roadside? Or had the killer watched each die, before abandoning the body? That was a macabre thought. . . .

Walking down the stairs to his breakfast, Rutledge tried to re-create the scene in his mind. Instead, he found himself intercepted by the elderly desk clerk, who had been standing behind the reception desk as if waiting for someone. For him, it appeared—

"Good morning, Inspector! There are—um—two persons who asked for you. I've put them in the small sitting room."

Two *persons*. Someone, then, not acceptable in the eyes of the hotel staff. Rutledge cast about in his memory. Elizabeth's servants, perhaps? He remembered she hadn't been at home last night when Melinda Crawford had telephoned.

"I'll see them."

He followed the man's directions to the small sitting room, usually dark and unused at this hour. But watery sunlight poured in now, and the two women sitting on the edges of the chintz-covered chairs by the hearth looked up nervously as he opened the door.

One of them rose to her feet, her red face tired and drawn. The unbecoming black hat she wore matched the threadbare black coat, giving her an air of poverty and depression. The younger woman accompanying her stood up more slowly, her eyes anxious as they scanned Rutledge's face. Her blue coat, ill-fitting in the shoulders, was a slightly different shade from the blue hat she wore with a surprising degree of grace.

The older woman was Nell Shaw. She had managed to track him down.

13

"MRS. SHAW—" RUTLEDGE BEGAN, COMPLETELY UNPREPARED to find Ben Shaw's widow here in Marling. As out of place in Kent as a blackbird would be in a gilded cage.

"I went to the Yard yesterday and asked for you. A sergeant—Gibson, his name was—told me you'd gone down to Kent to look into a murder. I thought you was looking into my Ben's murders!"

Rutledge said gently, "Mrs. Shaw, I must go where I'm sent—"

But she interrupted him again. "I've traveled all night. Well, nearly. We got a lift on a lorry from Covent Garden, and then from Maidstone came most of the way with a farmer carrying pig meat to the butcher shops hereabouts. And we walked from Helford. Why didn't you come and tell me you was not in London anymore? We've been waiting for *word*!" Her voice was accusing, on the verge of tears.

The young woman beside her blushed and looked down at her shoes. Rutledge regarded her. Taller than Mrs. Shaw, with fairer hair and a very fine complexion, she seemed out of place in the older woman's company.

Catching the shift in his attention, Mrs. Shaw added, "This is Margaret. Ben's and my daughter. She's of an age to be married, and what prospects do you think she's got, the daughter of a hanged man?

It's not fair to burden her with what they say her father done. A wrong ought to be put right!"

The flush deepened, and Margaret Shaw bit her lip, as if wishing the floor might open and swallow her.

Rutledge said, "Sit down, Mrs. Shaw. Miss Shaw. I've done my best to look into the earlier investigation, as I promised I would."

Seating themselves warily, they regarded him with doubtful eyes.

"There's nothing I can point to so far that upholds your belief that your neighbor was somehow involved. There are a number of ways that Mrs. Cutter might have come by the locket—"

"Name one!" Mrs. Shaw demanded harshly.

He hesitated. "Your husband may have given it to her."

"A *mourning* pendant? Inscribed for a man she didn't even know? And his name all over it, and no way of hiding it? You must be right barmy to believe my Ben would have done such a stupid thing!"

"Yes, I know, Mrs. Shaw. I understand—"

"You don't understand! You was like the rest of them, eager to see my Ben hang for what was done to the old ladies. *It was easier than digging out the truth!*"

He tried to keep his voice level. "As I told you earlier, there's no proof," he said, "that the locket was in your neighbor's drawer. We have only your word for that."

"Oh, yes? Because my husband was hanged, I'm a liar, am I? Well, let me tell you, if it had been in *my* house all this time, someone would have discovered it! And you searched the very rafters in the attic, didn't you? Where do you think I might have hidden it away? In the teapot? Among *my* corsets?"

The young woman winced. "Mama—"

"No, I'm being honest, that's what I'm doing! There's no one else to speak for us, love, and we can't sit back politely and hope for the *best!*"

"Mrs. Shaw," Rutledge said, "please listen to me. I must have irrefutable proof in order to ask my superiors to reopen this investigation—"

She stared at him. "Can you sleep nights, with us on your conscience?" Her voice was hard, angry. "My Ben's dead, and unjustly so.

You gave evidence against him in that courtroom, and might as well have put the noose around his neck with your own hands. I'm telling you he was not guilty, and you tell *me* that there has to be proof! When God stands in judgment of you, will you tell *Him* that there was no proof?"

Hamish stirred into vicious life. "Ye're burning in Hell already—and no' just for Ben Shaw!"

Rutledge said, "Mrs. Shaw, I'm doing what I can within the limits of my power. No, listen to me! I have no authority to open this investigation. Do you understand me? But I have asked questions—"

"You've spoken to Henry Cutter?" It was accusing.

"Not yet—"

"Let him tell you that his wife had a stroke after Ben was hanged, and never got out of her bed again! Let him tell you that her own son by her first husband was the constable on one of them streets where the victims lived! And let him tell you that George Peterson left the police force months after the trial and two years later was found drowned in the sea off Lyme Regis, where he'd gone to drink himself blind!"

There had been nothing in Philip Nettle's early reports of the Shaw investigation that had linked George Peterson with the Cutters. Nor had much official notice been taken of Peterson's subsequent death. It had been Peterson's duty to alert the Yard of any connection and he hadn't informed anyone. Why?

Rutledge said, "Are you telling me that this man Peterson could have robbed and suffocated those women, not your husband?"

He tried to bring back to mind the young constable whose patch it had been. Tall, lanky, quiet. There had been some question around the Yard about his suitability to deal with the stark reality of murder . . . but no question about his family background had arisen. And wouldn't have, if he'd used his father's name.

Hamish said, "There was a lapse—"

Yes. Philip Nettle, ill and soon to die, had been as careful a man as any on the force, covering every possible aspect of any case. But somehow the constable had never come under suspicion. Never questioned, or it would have appeared in the files. He was the Law, and not investigated, one of the hunters, not the hunted.

Dear God—how many other oversights had there been?

Mrs. Shaw was saying, "I only know the one thing, that my husband wasn't guilty, and we had no way of making anybody listen."

"You yourself believed in his guilt. I saw you turn away at the sentencing."

Mrs. Shaw sucked in a quick breath, as if the charge had been a physical blow, then said harshly. "You *made* a believer out of me. Then. I was tired and shocked and I had two children to care for all alone, and I didn't know what to make of anything Ben said or the barristers said or the judge said. That K.C. with the white hair—he stood there quoting verse and precedents and Latin, like Moses handing down the Ten Commandments. And I couldn't follow a word of it. All in a voice that would convince a saint that he was a sinner."

Matthew Sunderland . . . for whom the law was a lofty profession.

"But also a pulpit?" Hamish wondered, derisively.

She looked ill, the strain of her obsession beginning to tell, and the long, tiring journey to Kent. "Don't you think Constable Peterson would have protected his mother if *she* was the guilty party?"

"Mama?" Margaret said, leaning toward her mother almost protectively. "You're not to distress yourself like this! We'll manage, we always have."

Nell Shaw ignored her, saying instead to Rutledge, "Look at the girl. She's got her father's blood in her, the looks and the height and the graces. She deserves better than to languish in some nasty workroom where she'll be worn out at thirty and no one to care about her when I'm gone. It isn't right, and you must open your eyes and see what you're condemning her to!"

Rutledge said, "Mrs. Shaw—"

"No, I'm putting it bluntly. When you sent an innocent man to the gallows, you cursed his family, too. Where's the guilt of *that*, on your shoulders? Tell me, where's the guilt?"

She got up rather clumsily, her swollen feet heavy in her tightly laced shoes. "I'm going back to London where I belong. But if you're half the man you ought to be, you'll not sleep until you do something about my Ben. You'll find out what's behind this business, and whether there's any hope for us. But you'd better do it soon. I can't sleep nights anymore for thinking over what's right and wrong. I'd rather end up in the river, and have it all over and done with!"

She marched to the door, Margaret trailing after her, apologetic and at the same time defensive. The girl cared about her termagant mother, and she was worried.

"Please, can't you at least listen?" she seemed to say as she turned, her eyes pleading in place of her voice.

Rutledge said, "Let me make arrangements for your return—"

Mrs. Shaw wheeled to face him. "I mayn't have much else, Inspector, but I have my pride. If you won't help my Ben, I don't want your charity!"

"I will help," he heard himself saying. "But as one man, I can't promise that I'll accomplish miracles."

"We aren't looking for miracles. We're looking for fairness."

She walked away, her head high, her body chunky and compact. Her daughter followed after her, uncertain what to do, uncertain how to help. Watching her, Rutledge was reminded suddenly of her father. Ben Shaw had had that same lost-dog manner, that resigned acceptance of whatever fate had thrown at him, deserved or not. He had been afraid and wary and patient, as the law ground to its foregone conclusion of guilt, and he had not had the spirit to fight on.

Life—or years of marriage to a woman of a different class and upbringing—had defeated Shaw long before the judgment of the courts. Shaw was one of the victims, not one of the shapers of events. If he had killed those women, he had done it in desperation for the money his family needed. He had accepted the court's decision with a crushed spirit that didn't know where to turn for solace. And he had gone to his death a pale shadow of the man he could have been.

Ben Shaw had never fought. He had never tried to stem the march to the hangman in any way.

It had been seen as a sign of his guilt. His acceptance of the right of the Law to punish him for what he had done.

Hamish said, "Aye, a victim." Then, echoing Mrs. Shaw, he asked, "How will ye sleep with Ben Shaw on your conscience? I canna' follow you there—but he will."

Rutledge closed the door of the sitting room behind him and walked through the foyer of the hotel. He was no longer hungry. Standing on the street outside, he tried to decide what to do. He was in the midst of one investigation, and bedeviled by another. He should be clearheaded and have his wits about him, and instead he was having to face himself in ways that he had never thought possible.

Mrs. Shaw was a master at one thing if nothing else—she knew the demon of guilt would be his undoing.

And the tenuous connection he had been trying to build for the Marling murders had slipped, unnoticed, from his mind.

14

IN THE END, RUTLEDGE TRACKED DOWN THE SHAWS AND
drove them back to Sansom Street, himself. Mrs. Shaw had protested,
but he had swept that aside and handed her daughter into the rear of the
motorcar—to share the seat with a restless Hamish.

Mrs. Shaw was silent most of the way, her black hat and coat giving
her the air of a lump of coal capriciously shaped in human form.

"This won't change my mind," she said once. "I won't be cozened by
a kindness into forgetting what's due me and my family."

"No one is trying to cozen you," Rutledge replied. "I have business in
London."

But she made no answer to that, as if she didn't believe him.

WHEN THE SHAW women had been returned to their home, Rutledge
went in search of his sister Frances. She was dressing for a luncheon and
called to him from her bedroom, "Ian, is it urgent?"

"In a way." He went upstairs.

She came out of the dressing room wearing a very stylish suit and
carrying a matching hat in her hand. Sitting down to brush her hair, she
said, "You look tired, darling. What's wrong?"

He took the chair by the pair of windows overlooking the square and the houses that stood around it. "Elizabeth Mayhew. Has she said anything to you about a new man in her life?"

Frances's eyes met his in the dressing-table mirror. "Interesting! No, she hasn't. She's still mourning Richard, as far as I know—I've tried to talk her into coming to London for several weeks, but she doesn't want to leave Kent."

"For very different reasons, now. I think she's involved with someone who might be somehow connected to a series of murders I'm working on."

Frances put down her brush and turned to face him. "Are you sure of this, Ian? It's rather sudden, her new interest. And who is the man? Anyone we know?" The English view of acceptable social contacts: *Anyone we know?*

He shook his head. "I can't tell you his name. I do know he's from Northumberland. I have the word of Mrs. Crawford's seamstress on that." A brief smile touched his eyes and then faded. "But there's something odd here. Hackles rising on the back of the neck." He thought about that for a moment and then added, "Or jealousy, for Richard's sake."

"Your intuition is seldom wrong," she told him.

"It may be colored, all the same. It's not my place to ask questions, but if you could do it—quite casually—it might be a good thing."

Frances considered him. "There's something more here than Elizabeth Mayhew's affairs of the heart." Her eyes searching his face, she said again, "What's wrong?"

Rutledge smiled wryly. What he would have liked to say was, "I may have seen a ghost. If I have, it's no matter; I can live with ghosts," and wait for her common sense to assure him that he had done nothing of the sort. Frances had little patience with nonsense. But her intuition was often as sharp as his own. When she jumped to conclusions, they most generally were the right ones. And the war was a part of his life he wanted very much to keep shut away from her.

Instead he answered, "There's been a series of murders in the neighborhood of Marling. I've been working on the case for the Yard. No one, not even Melinda Crawford, knows who this man is that Elizabeth is attracted to. I think I've seen him once, from the back. Why is she keeping him a secret from her friends? Elizabeth could well be dragged into something unpleasant, if he's using her in some fashion or isn't quite—respectable."

"Aren't you overreacting just a little?" she asked, putting her jewelry on, her face hidden from him. "Is there any reason to think that this man could be involved in your murders? Have you good cause to believe he should be found and questioned?"

"Put like that," he answered wryly, "I suppose I'm jumping to conclusions. It's probably no more than coincidence. . . ."

Frances was settling her hat on her carefully groomed hair, adjusting it to a becoming angle that set off her face. She's an extraordinarily attractive woman, Rutledge found himself thinking, with their mother's perfect skin and cameo-cut profile, the slightly arched nose and the very intelligent eyes. Once, he'd wondered if she had been in love with Ross Trevor, his godfather David Trevor's son. Or if there was some other man who had come into her life, and taken her heart away with him. She had never spoken of it.

Just as he never spoke of Hamish, or the war, or what loneliness was.

As if reading his mind, Frances said, her eyes not meeting his in the mirror, "You know, you could do worse than Elizabeth Mayhew. You and Richard were very close. He wouldn't have minded you stepping into his shoes. Not that I'm matchmaking—"

"That's the very reason I can't," Rutledge answered after a moment. "He'd always be there. Between us."

"Like a ghost?" she asked lightly. "Well, it's time for me to leave. Would you mind giving me a lift? We can talk on the way."

But they didn't. When they reached the Mayfair restaurant, she got out, saying, "Ian. Whatever is worrying you, it isn't Elizabeth Mayhew, is it? There's more on your mind than her affairs. Or the murders. I think there's a sense of guilt somewhere. I think perhaps you feel you *ought* to step into Richard's shoes, for his sake. And because you won't, you're afraid you're letting him down by not preventing Elizabeth from getting hurt."

He considered and then rejected the possibility. "I feel some sort of responsibility, for Richard's sake. We were friends for years. But a sense of responsibility doesn't go as far as marriage."

"Then it was Armistice Day. It unsettled a good many people, you know. You aren't alone there." She was searching for clues, her father's

daughter. He had been a very fine lawyer, and he had had a strong intu-
itive streak that both his children had inherited.

Rutledge didn't answer.

"All the same . . ." She hesitated for a moment. "We all live with dev-
ils of one kind or another. I don't know how to exorcise them. Except by
surviving. Somehow, against all the odds."

It was far too close to the mark, and she must have read something
in his face, for he heard a sharp intake of breath. As if she had finally
guessed what was on his mind.

"My mistakes may go to the gallows," he told her, "the innocent
along with the guilty. And they are buried. And sometimes they are resurrected." It was said in a rueful voice, as if laughing at himself.

"The truth doesn't change," she told him. "Father always believed
that. Still, it's easy to alter the trappings of truth."

"I'll remember that."

As his sister stepped away from the side of the car, Rutledge added,
"You won't forget about Elizabeth?"

She blew him a kiss. "Darling, I won't forget."

He drove off, Hamish saying in the back of his mind, "She's no' the
common-garden variety of sisters."

"She'd have made a damned fine barrister. Better than I would
have, if I'd followed in our father's footsteps."

"Aye." There was a moment of silence as Rutledge threaded his way
through the thick of midday traffic. Then Hamish followed up on his
earlier thought. "It is no' very surprising she's no' married."

Rutledge, glancing at his watch, decided he had time for one more
call before he left London.

HENRY CUTTER WORKED at a shop where tools were designed and
fabricated. His office, high above the floor where machines made any
conversation impossible, was cluttered with invoices and paperwork,
and there were ink stains on his fingers. A thin man with a long jaw and
sunken eyes, he looked up as Rutledge entered the room, then frowned.

"I know you—" He broke off, squinting in an attempt to place the
man before him.

"Rutledge. Inspector Rutledge from Scotland Yard."

Surprise lifted his eyebrows. "That's right! You've changed—" He stopped and said, instead of completing the thought, "We all have, to be blunt about it. Is there anything wrong?"

"I've come about an old matter. Ben Shaw's conviction and hanging for murder. Mrs. Shaw worries about—er—a miscarriage of justice."

Cutter sighed. "She's got a very pretty daughter, and she's determined for the girl to marry well. She's asked me a dozen times in the last month what I remember about the police and all the questions we were asked. It's as if she worries a raw wound, unable to leave it alone. Life hasn't treated Nell kindly, you know. Still, she's a woman who draws on hidden strength and faces up to what can't be run from. I respect that."

"What *do* you remember?" Rutledge asked, interested.

"I remember how upset my wife was," Cutter answered. "She'd known the women. Well, not *known* them, if you follow me! But she'd called on them from time to time as a church visitor. Years before, when her health was better and she was more active."

"Did she believe Shaw was guilty?"

"I never asked her." Cutter looked away. "He was a very likeable man. Janet—Mrs. Cutter—was fond of him, in a manner of speaking."

Rutledge found himself thinking that Cutter was not a man of grace or charm. Plainspoken and unimaginative, a plodder. He was beginning to understand why Cutter admired Nell Shaw's strength. The question then became, was Cutter capable of murder? And why, if he had a reasonably comfortable life, should he be driven to it?

"I understand she had a son who died before she did."

"Janet was married before. Peterson fell ill of diphtheria, when the boy was almost two years old. She was expecting another child, and she miscarried. The worst part of that was, she felt she'd let her husband down by being so ill herself. And she blamed herself that the boy had been left to the kindness of neighbors while his father was dying and his mother was miscarrying. As a result she was overly protective, to the point of smothering him. But in my opinion, he was weak from the start, was George. Never could settle to anything, and in the end, killed himself." He stopped, surprised that he'd confided in this man who listened with an air of thoughtfulness that made confession easy, as if unjudged.

Mrs. Shaw had already answered his next question but Rutledge said quietly, "How did he die?"

He could feel Hamish stirring in the back of his mind.

"He drowned." After a moment, looking down at his hands, Cutter added, "Lost his footing and fell into the sea while walking by the harbor one night. That was the official finding, accidental drowning. It saved his mother from the pain of learning it was suicide. According to the police, George had been drinking heavily, and there was a suspicion that he'd been despondent. At any rate, he was fully clothed, and it was after midnight. They put as good a face on it as they could. But I always felt Janet suspected the truth. She was never the same after that."

"He was the first policeman on the scene of one of the Shaw murders."

"Yes, that's true. He came to his mother the night after Mrs. Winslow was found dead. Cried like a baby. Janet told me afterward that he had a horror of dead bodies. He didn't like touching them."

Hamish said, "It doesna' ring true. He was a constable—"

As if he'd been a party to the conversation, Cutter went on, "I could never understand that—George had elected to go into the police force, he must have known what it involved!" He shifted the papers on his desk. "I could never understand *him,* for that matter. Janet told me he took after his father. She thought that might have something to do with it. But George and I never saw eye to eye."

"Tell me about him."

Cutter said sharply, "The man's dead. You can't be worried about anything he could have done!"

"I'm interested in the man who was constable when Mrs. Winslow was killed. I've only just discovered that he was related to neighbors of the Shaws."

Taking a deep breath, Cutter replied, "Well. I don't know that it makes any difference, now. He was the kind of child who ran headlong to do something he wanted to do, and only thought better of it later. He was never in serious trouble, but he was always unsettled and unpredictable. Never really good at anything. Janet thought the sun shone out of him, and that was that. I was glad when he left home. We had a happier life then."

"Mrs. Shaw found a locket in a drawer belonging to Mrs. Cutter. Did she tell you that?"

"A locket? No, she never mentioned it. What kind of locket?" His eyes were suddenly wary. "Janet's jewelry?"

"A piece of mourning jewelry, belonging to one of the dead women. It was missing at the time Shaw was arrested." Husbands seldom rummaged in their wives' lingerie, as Hamish was pointing out.

Cutter was saying, with rising alarm, "Here, she's not trying to say my wife had anything to do with those deaths! I won't believe that! Not of Nell! You're trying to stir up trouble—"

"Nell Shaw brought the locket to me because it was missing evidence," Rutledge replied without emphasis.

"I'd like to see it!"

"I'm sorry," Rutledge answered, unwilling to tell Cutter that Mrs. Shaw had kept it. "I can't show it to you."

"Look. I can't help but feel sorry for her, she's had a rough deal. Shaw tried, but he wasn't like us—he wasn't used to hard work, his body wasn't what you'd call strong. All the same, it's far too late to save Ben or his family."

The door opened and a man stepped into the office. From the look of him, and from Cutter's sudden stiffness, Rutledge realized that he must be the owner. Holly? Was that what the Cutter maid had called him? The man stared from Rutledge to the account books Cutter had put aside, and he asked, "Something I can do for you?"

Rutledge rose. "Thank you, no. Mr. Cutter has kindly given me the directions I need." Cutter shot him a grateful glance and rose also.

Rutledge left, closing the door behind him, but he could feel the owner's eyes burrowing into his back.

Hamish grumbled, "I canna' see what's been gained."

Rutledge answered. "It's odd, that time can change the direction of an investigation so radically. *We should have known about George Peterson!*"

Hamish retorted, "It's you changed, nothing else."

There was no response to that. He made his way through the busy shop and out into the street.

IT WAS RAINING again when he reached Marling. Rutledge left the car at the hotel, realizing that he'd missed his lunch and his tea. He found a small shop down the road from the police station and went in, asking what they could provide in the way of sandwiches, late as it was. The woman behind the counter settled him at a small table for two, and bustled away to the kitchen.

Except for four women sitting at a table near his, the shop was empty, although a couple came in a few minutes afterward, laughing and shaking out the rain from their coats.

For a time the four women were silent, as if wary of the strange man almost in their midst. They couldn't know who he was, not yet. He hadn't met many of the villagers; there was nothing for the local gossips to pick up. He could almost hear the unspoken speculation about who he was and what business he might have in Marling. The natural curiosity that strangers sparked in a small town was lively. Even his voice was out of place, an educated London accent.

Rutledge's tea and sandwiches arrived. He thanked the shop owner and poured a steaming cup, watching the tea swirl up to the lip.

When they had exhausted their silent conjectures, the women quietly picked up the thread of their earlier conversation. At first Rutledge, busy with his sandwiches, ignored what they were saying, and then realized almost too late that they were in the middle of a discussion of the funeral they had just attended. Something about their cryptic references alerted him in time to hear one comment in particular.

". . . wasn't as if none of us knew the circumstances!" This from the woman who had her back to Rutledge.

"A crying shame," a woman wearing a black feathered hat replied, setting down her cup of tea and reaching for another iced cake. "I don't know what's to become of us, with the roads unsafe and murderers on the loose!"

Hamish said quietly, "They havena' said whose death it was they mourned. But I'm thinking . . ."

Rutledge cast a swift glance in their direction, noting who was speaking.

The feathered hat's neighbor on the left, smoothing her black gloves on the table beside her, nodded. "I won't let my Harold walk as far as the pub of a night. And he's fuming about it something fierce."

The fourth woman, who was wearing spectacles, agreed. "Who on

earth would want to kill a soldier back from the war? I ask you. He's suffered enough!"

"Aye," Hamish noted. "It's as I thought."

The first woman said, "It's a Bolshevik plot, that's what it is! Look
what happened to their own royal family—slaughtered along with those
pretty little girls! And the tsar a cousin of King Edward!"

"As was the Kaiser," the glove smoother snapped. "My father always
said foreigners are never to be trusted!"

Hamish agreed, "It was the same in Scotland. We looked with suspicion on the other clans, the next glen o'wer."

The woman wearing spectacles sighed. "I pity the Taylors. Alice and
her children never had two pennies to rub together, but she always put a
good face on it. What are they to do now?"

Taylor was the first man killed. . . .

The black hat nodded, setting the feathers bobbing in concert. "I've
some mending and sewing I'll ask her to do for me. She's a good needle-
woman, and taking in sewing will tide her over until the oldest boy can
work."

"It mustn't appear to be charity!" The speaker took off her spectacles, polishing them. "We must be careful about that. And we might consider ordering our Christmas goose from Susan Webber. I'm told her
poultry is very nice."

And then the glove smoother said hesitantly, "You know, young
Peter Webber might have seen who it was that did it."

Webber was the name of the second victim.

"He's only eight!" the woman in spectacles protested.

"He's got eyes, hasn't he?" was the retort. "He said something to me
at the funeral. He said there'd been a man on the road the night before
it happened, asking for his father. When Peter replied that he was working over to Seelyham, the man asked what regiment he'd been in, and
where he'd fought. Odd sort of thing to ask."

"They'd all fought together!" the first woman replied. "Everyone
knows that. They'd tried to stay together, the men from Marling and
Helford and Seelyham. Looking out for each other."

Rutledge had finished his tea and the thick wedges of egg salad
sandwiches. But he poured himself a second cup, his attention on the

table of women. Hamish, listening as well, murmured, "Ye must find the Webber boy!"

"Didn't do them much good, did it, serving together?" the woman wearing spectacles wanted to know. "My Fred says they lost more because of that."

The first speaker, the one with her back to Rutledge, said soothingly, "I wouldn't give young Peter's words any weight. Like as not he means well, but my guess is, he's hoping for a little attention. No need to upset his mother again."

There was agreement at the table, and then the feathered hat said, "We ought to do something for Mrs. Bartlett, as well. I've a bit of ham left from Sunday's dinner, and I'll take it over to her straightaway. With some of the bread and the potatoes. If you'll look in on her tomorrow, and the next day—just until she gets past the worst of it."

The woman wearing spectacles said, "I'll see what's in the gardens, that she might care for."

The mourners rose and walked across the tearoom to settle their account.

As they closed the shop door behind them, the owner spoke briefly to the new couple, and then came over to clear away the empty table.

Rutledge waited until she was nearest where he sat. "Those women," he said. "Do they live in Marling?"

The woman wiped her hands on her apron and turned. He was the stranger here, and she was debating how to respond to his curiosity.

"Inspector Rutledge. Scotland Yard," he told her. "I've a need to know."

"They're local." The owner's face remained doubtful as she studied him. "They've just been to the funeral of the man killed along the road the other night. Peggy Bartlett couldn't offer them anything afterward, though the Women's Institute had said they'd see to some refreshment. But Peggy wouldn't hear of it. I can't say that I blame her—she's beholden enough for the vicar and the coffin. I hope the police find whoever did these terrible things and send him to the gallows!"

Her kind face was suddenly grim and unforgiving.

15

WALKING TO THE POLICE STATION, RUTLEDGE DECIDED IT
would be best to speak to Sergeant Burke. The man was just settling
into his chair. He looked up at Rutledge, his eyes tired. "I expect you're
wanting Inspector Dowling, sir. He hasn't come back from the Bartlett
funeral. I was glad to escape early. It's hard to watch women cry and not
have any comfort to give!"

Rutledge answered, "Actually I've come to ask if anyone spoke to
young Peter Webber after his father's death."

Burke rubbed his forehead with a thick fist. "He was that upset, no
one had the heart to ask him anything. He's just turned eight; there
wasn't much he could tell us about his father. Webber was away most of
the lad's life. They were just getting acquainted again, you might say."

Rutledge took the chair in front of the sergeant's desk. "I understand that. But I have a feeling it might be a good idea to speak to him."

Burke said warily, "What put you onto the lad?"

"I heard four women in the tea shop discussing the funeral, and his
name came up in the conversation. Peter doesn't know me, but he'd
speak to you, I think. If you encouraged him." Rutledge repeated what
he'd overheard.

Burke heaved himself out of his chair. "Well, then, Peter'll be on his way home from school about now. We can look for him."

They found the boy trudging along the road in the rain, head down, his shabby coat dark across the shoulders. A slim child, with long hands and long feet, a promise of height to come.

Burke instructed Rutledge to stop the motorcar just ahead of the boy.

"You're wet through, lad," he called. "Mr. Rutledge here will give you a lift home," Burke said, getting out to open the rear passenger door. "Come along, then, and mind you don't set your muddy feet on the seat!"

With alacrity the boy did as he was told. It wasn't often he was offered an opportunity to ride in a motorcar. He settled quickly in the seat, but leaned forward (as Hamish seemed to do from time to time), his eyes fixed on the instrument panel.

"Could you blow the horn, then?" he asked, bubbling with excitement.

"Could you blow the horn, *please,* sir?" Burke chided him.

"Please, sir?" Peter repeated shyly, and laughed with glee as Rutledge squeezed the rubber bulb.

Rutledge thought, *Ben Shaw's son was this age when his father was hanged.* . . .

There was something about the boy, the fineness of his hands and skin, that spoke of better breeding than a laborer's child. In that lay the similarity—

Burke said, "Your mum getting on all right, is she? Enough food on the table?" He quietly gestured to Rutledge to stop the car at the next house.

Peter answered, "We're faring well enough." But he had the thinness of a growing child who was always hungry.

"Mr. Rutledge here is interested to know more about your pa, hoping to help us find the devil that did it. Did anyone come looking for him, do you think, before he died?"

The boy squirmed a little in his seat. "I don't remember!"

"Yes, you do, Peter. It won't go any further, I promise you. But it might do some good. Tell us, then."

After a short silence the boy said, "I never saw him before."

"There's a start," Burke said, encouraging. "Not from Marling, then, do you suppose?"

"No. At least, no one I'd know by sight."

"What else can you remember?"

"Not very much." As if the lengthening silence urged him to say more, Peter added, "He wasn't as heavy as you are. But tall, like the vicar." After a moment, consideringly, "He wore a greatcoat. Like a soldier. But he wasn't a soldier."

"I'd say the vicar is five foot eleven," Burke said in an aside to Rutledge. And to Peter, "What was his coloring, then?"

Peter shrugged, fingering the back of Rutledge's seat, his hands busy and his eyes on them. "He was fair. He took off his hat as he stood talking to me, smoothing back his hair. That was after I'd told him Pa wasn't at home."

"What did he want with your father? Did he say?"

"No." And then, "He just asked where he'd fought in the war, and with what regiment. As if he was looking for someone, and Pa might have known the man."

"I see. And his age, Peter, what would you say that was?"

"He was Pa's age. Thereabouts. Could you please blow the horn again, sir? My little sister's looking out the window!"

Rutledge obliged. Peter laughed again, but it wasn't as carefree as the first time. He made a movement to leave the car, but Burke sat where he was.

"Anything that set this man's face apart, that you remember? A large nose? A cleft in the chin? Eyes too close together?"

Peter shook his head and turned to see if his sister was still watching. The house was a small cottage on the edge of Marling, with a rough garden in the front and a roof that needed rethatching. Chickens and geese scratched in the muddy earth in a large pen behind the cottage. Peter began fumbling with the door, unsure how to let himself out.

Burke said, "All right, Peter, answer my question, and you can go in to your tea."

"There's nothing about his face," Peter protested. "I don't remember his face. Just his voice."

"What about his voice?"

"He sounded strange. As if he come from Liverpool, or maybe Cornwall. Different." He was fidgeting with anxiety, eager to be gone.

"Not like a Londoner, then?"

The boy shook his head. "I know what Londoners sound like! They come for the hop picking."

"So they do." Burke got out in the rain and let the boy down. "Well done, Peter. You needn't talk about it to anyone else. Best not."

Peter nodded. With a bob of his head toward Rutledge, he was gone up the walk to the door, where his little sister let him in.

As Burke got back into the motorcar, he said to Rutledge, "Not much there, I'd say. A fair man, tallish, and not from Kent. Well. I'd just as soon believe this murderer wasn't one of ours!"

It was a familiar refrain—*None of us would be guilty of such a thing. . . .*

Hamish, who had reclaimed the rear seat for his own, commented, "Yon description would fit half the men in England."

Burke was adding, "Like as not, he'd lost his way. There was a man dying that night, you know. Gassed. A good many friends came to say good-bye."

But in the middle of the week, a working man couldn't travel far. Most of the dying man's visitors would have been Kent men, their accents familiar to the boy.

Rutledge was uneasy. Fair, tallish, and not from Kent. It was a description that also fit the man he'd thought for an instant he'd glimpsed at the bonfire. And again along the road near to where the last victim, Bartlett, was found.

Hamish said with relish, "You willna' be satisfied until you find a rational answer. But there's no' likely to be one."

Burke was saying, "All the same, I'll ask for a list of the men who came to say good-bye to Bob Nester. The ex-soldier dying of his lungs. It'll do no harm."

As RUTLEDGE CLIMBED the stairs to his hotel room, Hamish said, "The Shaw woman. She's distracting you fra' your duty here."

Answering from habit, Rutledge said tiredly, "It doesn't matter. I've given her my word."

"Oh, aye? And these dead ex-soldiers. Did ye gie them your word as well?"

"What have we got so far to build with? A child's description of a stranger? The wine? The fact that all of these men had lost limbs—that they'd served together? And they died at night. It will take more than that to find a killer."

"If you were no' so distracted, you'd see another link—"

Rutledge had hung his coat across a chair, to dry. He stopped as he bent to remove his shoes, waiting for Hamish to go on.

But there was only silence.

He said, "Where they drank the wine? I've already considered that. Someone had transportation. A cart. A wagon. A lorry. A motorcar . . . In some fashion, those men were lured into traveling with someone. Or stopping somewhere with someone."

"But no' in the empty house with its stone pillars. There was no sign that the grass had been beaten down."

It was true. No vehicle had traveled up that drive since the summer. Rutledge had seen the tall grass but not registered its significance.

"If you were a weary man walking home on a cold night, and someone offered you wine for warmth and courage," Rutledge said, pacing the room, "would you take a drink?"

"If I knew him, I'd no' be suspicious. Except to wonder how he'd come by the wine, if he was poor, like me."

"Yes. I agree. But if he was a stranger—"

"Aye, it would be different."

And the difference would be the manner in which the wine was offered.

To drink enough to die from the laudanum, a man would have to be well on his way to being drunk. . . .

Apropos of nothing, Hamish quietly quoted an old toast: *"Here's tae us. Wha's like us? Gey few, and they're all deid!"*

Rutledge shuddered. *". . . all deid."*

The words triggered a memory that had no beginning and no end, that was only an unexpected glimpse through the shadows of Rutledge's mind. A resurrected image that made no sense and yet was as clear in that instant as it must have been in a very different venue.

The man by the bonfire—he ought to have been in uniform. But not an English uniform. A torn and bloody *German* uniform . . .

HIS ROOM WAS suffocating, closing in on him. Rutledge lifted his coat, still wet, from the chair and pulled it on again.

Better the out-of-doors, even the rain, than staying here and smothering.

He couldn't understand why these bits of unrelated memory seemed to jump into his mind and then lead nowhere. What was triggering them? What was bringing them to the surface when—whatever they represented—they had been buried in the depths of a past the conscious brain rejected?

Dr. Fleming, who had saved his sanity, had warned him that there would be flashbacks from time to time as the mind sorted through the dark recesses and found a way to cope with them.

"It's only natural. Nature abhors a vacuum, you know," Dr. Fleming had said, far more cheerfully than Rutledge had thought warranted. "The mind's amazing. It will bury something it can't face—and then begin to resurrect it to fill in the empty places of memory." He had studied the haunted man in front of his desk. "You don't remember the end of the war, do you? You don't recall where you went, what you did, or why. I've got some of the pieces; they came from your military file. But they don't make much sense. Only you can fill in the blanks. And eventually you will. How you will handle it will depend on how strong you are emotionally—how stable your life seems at the time. All I can offer you is this: an open door. Come and talk to me. I'll do what I can to make it more comfortable for you."

Rutledge pulled out of the hotel yard and turned north. Even if he *could* simply walk in on Fleming and sit down in his office, what would he say? That he was afraid of someone he'd seen, someone who was dead—who was German?

How many Germans had he killed? he wondered wryly. He should be haunted not by one face, but by thousands. . . .

Without consciously addressing a destination, Rutledge drove out the Marling road and soon found himself close by the place where the first ex-soldier had been killed. It was as if one part of his brain had continued the conversation with Hamish about the murders, and the other had wandered into a No Man's Land of its own.

He could see the leaning stone pillars through the rain and slowed the motorcar. It was true—the tall weeds and grass growing up the drive had that tangled, springing airiness that told him no vehicle had passed over them in some time. Weather had beaten the stalks down here and there, without breaking or crushing them.

It was nearing dusk. He drove on toward the line of trees, searching for any other means of reaching the house in the distance. But it was an unlikely possibility—Dowling and his men would already have taken note of any attempt to go through the grounds.

His head was turned, and so it was almost peripherally that he saw the woman standing at the side of the road in the rain, staring up at the gray laden clouds visible between the trees.

Rutledge's first thought was that it was Mrs. Shaw, waylaying him again, for this woman wore a dark coat that seemed to engulf rather than fit her, her silhouette shapeless and without grace. He saw as he came closer that she was wearing a man's greatcoat, and that it swallowed her slimmer figure. She clutched it close to her throat as he touched the brakes.

"Is there anything you need?" he asked, drawing even with her.

Her face was pale, the line of her brows like charcoal smudges above the dark-circled eyes.

"I'm all right," she said. And then as an afterthought, "Thank you."

He shifted into neutral, uncertain, and then switched off the engine. Opening his door, he stepped out into the road. She turned away, as if trying to ignore him. "I don't like leaving you here. It will be dark soon. My name's Rutledge, Inspector Rutledge, from London. If you will let me take you to your house—or to the police station—"

She turned at that, her eyes seeming to bore into him. "London, is it?" She took a shuddering breath. "Well. It won't bring Will back."

"Will?"

"Will Taylor. He was my husband. They found his body just here,

they said. I've come to see it for myself. I didn't want to before. But I—"
She stopped.

Rutledge said gently as he walked toward her, "Perhaps it wasn't
the best of ideas . . . to come to this place. Not in the rain, surely."

"I never really knew him, you see. We were married and then he
went off to war. He came home twice, once with the broken arm, and
then again when the Germans blew his foot off. They kept him in hospital then, and I'd go and sit by the bed, but the ward was full. There
was no privacy. You couldn't talk. Not really—*talk*."

"I understand," he said.

"No, you don't," she said bitterly. "Nobody does! He had more in
common with *them,* the other men in that ward, than he did with me,
his wife. They'd all lost a limb, too. He wasn't—different—there. Still
one of the lads."

She took a deep breath, fighting tears. "I was beginning to think
there were no whole men left in England—"

Rutledge said nothing. There was no comfort he could offer.

Mrs. Taylor looked him up and down, as if assessing his wounds.
They weren't visible, and he felt himself flushing, as if guilty of being
whole. "You were in the war, were you?" He nodded. "You came home
with nothing missing. It's all right for you, you didn't have to find a new
way of learning to live, to earn your keep. Will had to do that, and even
when he was sent home the last time, we weren't—comfortable—
together. It was like having a stranger in the house. I hardly knew what
to say to him! Nor he to me. Loving him wasn't the same. I couldn't get
used to no foot. It hadn't healed well, the stump. And we had no common ground of any kind, except the marriage and the children."

She was speaking not so much to him as she was to the place of her
husband's death. As if excusing to the shade of Will Taylor what had
gone wrong in their fragile postwar relationship.

It would bring no comfort to Mrs. Taylor to tell her that he'd seen the
other side of this coin—hasty romantic weddings, a patriotic fervor, and
in the beginning, dozens of love letters that flew back and forth like doves.

How many men standing watch in the night had cleared their
throats and gruffly admitted, "I'm worrit. There's a difference in her

letters noo. I think there's someone else . . ." Darkness shielding anxious eyes, voices low-pitched.

"She doesna' write sae often. And she says she hardly kens what I look like, anymore. But then I have only a wee photograph, mysel', and she must ha' changed in two years. I've begged her for another, but she canna' find anyone with a camera. She says . . ." A cough, as if denying the unspoken fear.

They had sometimes come to him, to beg for leave. Not just the married men, but the single ones who had left someone behind. One soldier had stood there clutching in his hand a scrap of newspaper bearing the photograph of Gladys Cooper, the actress. Pointing to it, he'd said earnestly, "She's mair real to me noo than Maggie. What am I to do?" Anguish sharpened his face and his eyes had pleaded.

Where he could, Rutledge tried through channels of his own to find out what had happened to the wives at home. But sometimes the truth was more bitter than the suspicion. And he had concealed that.

Rutledge said now, "Mrs. Taylor, I think I ought to take you home. It won't help, standing here in the rain."

"Surprisingly, it does," she told him forlornly. "I feel closer to him here than I do in the churchyard. I was afraid, when Sergeant Burke came to the door, that Will had—" She faltered.

"Surely the other deaths proved that he wasn't—didn't kill himself."

Alice Taylor shrugged. "Only Will knows that." She brushed her wet dark hair out of her face and began to walk slowly to the motorcar. Turning her head once, she looked back at the line of trees. "I wish I didn't feel guilty. As if I'd driven him to whatever it was happened to him."

Rutledge held the door for her and she climbed into the motorcar.

As he got in after cranking the motor, he said, "Did anyone come to see him before he died? A stranger? A man you didn't know."

She turned to him. "I don't know, to tell you the truth. Will took to walking out while I was doing up the washing-up after dinner. As if he didn't have anything left to say to me. Or I to him. One night he came back and asked if I remembered Jimsy Ridger. I said I did, and I was sharp about it. Jimsy was no friend of Will's. And he said someone was looking for Jimsy, but he'd given the man false directions. He didn't like his cut."

"Those were his words, 'I didn't like the cut of him'?"

She nodded, flicking wet hair out of her face again. In her own way, she was a pretty woman, with such white skin and dark coloring. Welsh, perhaps, or Cornish.

"What did he mean by that, do you think?"

"I can't say. I wasn't interested in Jimsy Ridger. He was in Will's company, and I never liked him very much."

"Why?"

"He was something of a scoundrel, Jimsy was. Light-fingered, like. He never stole anything from us, that I know of, but he wasn't someone I quite trusted. I was afraid he might be hanging about looking for money."

"Where is Jimsy Ridger now?"

She looked out across the wet fields. "In hell, for all I know. He didn't come back to Kent after the war. He'd been to Paris, and won money at cards. So it was said. Kent wasn't for the likes of him, after that. But then who knows, with someone like Jimsy?"

RUTLEDGE TOOK HER to the small cottage she pointed out as hers. It was half-timbered, of a style popular in the late Victorian era. But the plaster between the black beams needed paint and the chimney sagged. She looked up at it.

"Will was going to find someone to repair the chimney. I suppose that'll be up to me now."

He came around to open the door for her and she stepped down into the wet grass that met the rutted road in an irregular verge.

"I'll do my best to find your husband's killer," he said.

She had walked up the muddy walk before she turned. "I don't know that it matters," she answered him. "Will didn't much want to live, anyway. Maybe the murderer did him a favor."

MRS. TAYLOR'S VOICE lingered in Rutledge's mind as he drove down the roads that led out of Marling and toward the nearest villages, then back again, forming a mental map of the ground where the three murders had occurred. As darkness fell, he could see the lights springing up in the windows of farms and cottages off to either side, none of them close enough to matter.

"They would ha' been dark again, the occupants in their beds and sleeping soundly," Hamish said, "when the killing was done. Country folk aren't likely to keep late hours."

Yet someone had.

He found himself wondering if Mrs. Bartlett and Mrs. Webber had felt as estranged from their husbands as Mrs. Taylor had done. It was hard to believe that one suicide had sparked two more as desperately tired men gave up trying.

He himself knew the fierce silent urge toward death, when there was no hope left.

But Hamish, always practical, said, "Where did they buy good wine?"

That was always the sticking point. The wine.

He drove in the early dusk toward Marling, his headlamps picking out the overgrown hedgerows and the dark pockets of thick grass between trees that sometimes marched in avenues for a little distance. Vistas that in summer were glorious with a patchwork of green were now brown and dry, and the long sweep of the land had lost much of its charm.

He was not more than a hundred yards from the first cottage marking the outskirts of the town when he saw someone quickly moving into a clump of trees edging a field. Moving as if afraid to be seen.

Pulling hard on the brake, Rutledge brought the car to a halt, and got out, running toward the faintly seen outline of a human form. The trees thinned almost at once as he plunged into them, and brought him out into another field. His feet sank heavily into the wet, plowed soil, where the summer's crop had been turned under for the winter. Cursing, he tried to pick up his pace, but it was useless. Then the figure ahead of him stumbled and fell and swore harshly.

Rutledge reached him before he could flounder to his feet.

Hardly a murderer, he thought in disgust as the thick miasma of drunken breath hit him in the face before he could put out a hand to help the man to his feet.

"Leave me alone!" the man shouted, struggling to shake off his grip. "What've I done to you, to chase me off the road, then!"

He was standing now, a man with dark, sweaty hair and filthy work clothes. Rutledge realized that one shoulder was different from another, saw that the man had a useless left arm. It hung without life, clumsily and straight. Catching Rutledge's glance, the man clapped his right hand over the shoulder in a protective action that was clearly habit now.

Rutledge said, "What are you doing out here?" It was the voice of command.

"Looking for a quiet place to sleep it off. If it's any concern of yours!"

"Men 'sleeping it off' have been found dead the next morning. Or haven't you heard?"

"I'm not drunk enough to die. I'm not drunk enough to stop hurting, either. What's that to you?" The slurred voice was bellicose. The man stood his ground, with nothing more to say.

"Come on," Rutledge said, tired of argument. "I'll take you to the police station, where you can sleep until you're sober enough to go home."

"I don't have a home anymore," the man said, beginning to feel sorry for himself. "She said if I got drunk again, not to come back. But it's all there is now. Getting drunk." His hiccup turned into a sob. By the time they'd reached the edge of the first field, the man was on his knees, sick by the base of a tree.

Rutledge waited impatiently for him to finish and then got him to the motorcar and inside it.

"Where do you live?" he asked, when they were moving toward Marling. "What's your name?"

"Bert Holcomb, if its any of your business. From Seelyham. But if I drink in the pub there, the barmaid goes to my wife. I come here, and tell her I have two days' work." He groaned. "That was good beer I lost. I can't afford no more this week."

"What happened to your arm? The war?"

"Caught it on the wire. Like all the other poor bastards. The doctors saved it, but it's worthless now. I can't move it on my own." He leaned his head against the back of the seat. "God, my mouth tastes something terrible."

"Did you know the men who've been killed outside of Marling? Taylor, Webber, Bartlett?"

"We were together through most of the war. Men of Kent. We were proud of that. I'm going to be sick again—!"

Rutledge brought the motorcar to a swift halt and waited again. When the man crawled back into the vehicle, he groaned wretchedly. "I never could drink the way the others could!" A shudder ran through him.

"Do you know a man called Jimsy Ridger?"

The ravaged face turned toward Rutledge. "What do you want to find him for? Good-for-nothing bastard!"

"Where does he live?"

"Second person to ask me that today."

Rutledge said, "Who was the other person?"

"I don't know. He gave me money, and I drank it."

"Where did you meet him?"

"Walking over from Seelyham."

"Did you tell him where to find Jimsy Ridger?"

There was a gurgling laugh. "Now how could I do that? I don't know myself. But I wanted the money badly enough to make up a good story!"

16

AFTER DEPOSITING THE SODDEN HOLCOMB AT THE MARLING station, Rutledge went on to The Plough. He felt tired and restless, a man at loose ends. Afraid of his past now, and afraid for his future. He had been very certain he was right in the Shaw case. How many others had he botched, in blind belief that his experience and intuition were infallible? Would he botch this one as well? He felt like getting as drunk as the man on the road. Except that he knew it would not buy peace.

Hamish said, "Judgment is no' a safe profession."

"My father said that to me once," Rutledge remembered as he walked up the stairs toward his room. "He said the law was only as good as the men who devised it and the men who carried out the burden of it."

He turned down the passage, stopping before his door and staring at it for a moment before opening it. *What is there about the Shaw case that isn't satisfactory? Why have I been digging into the past and doubting everything that was done?* He shut the door behind him and walked to the window. It looked down the back garden, bleak in the November darkness, with the stumps of cabbages and the withered leaves of carrots and the ferny yellowed wisps of asparagus. As dead as his spirits tonight.

The answer was not hard to find. *When self-doubt awakens, it feeds on itself.* . . .

Rutledge said aloud, under his breath, "Shaw was guilty. I know that for a certainty."

Yet he'd uncovered other possible motives now. It was Pandora's box, an overturned case where everything that spilled out pointed accusing fingers at him for not seeing them before. . . .

Hamish reminded him, "Mrs. Shaw is a verra' persuasive woman."

That was true. The fact that she was unattractive in every sense, and that he had disliked her from the start, had perhaps shaped his view of her and of events. Then and now. But she had aroused such guilt in him—such a fierce doubt of his own abilities—that he was unable to see his earlier actions as clearly as he had done when Philip Nettle's death had first thrust the affair into his hands.

Rutledge turned away from the window and fumbled for the lamp on the desk, watching the flame bloom and brighten his room. The brass bed gleamed, and the white china of the washstand pitchers reflected a golden light.

With Bowles baying for results, there had been unnatural pressure on the investigating officers. Results, results, results. They had worked nearly around the clock, interviewing, cataloging statements, going back again to ask other questions, trying to sort through the simple lives and the tangled activities of everyone who had had contact with the elderly victims for the previous two years. The dustman, the man who brought the coal, the grocer's boy who delivered boxes of goods, the butcher's boy, the woman who came to clean and to cook one meal a day, the man bringing the post, the visitors from charities and churches, nurses who came to see to bedsores or bathe their patients. The chimney sweep—It had been an endless task, sorting through the sheets of closely written notes collected from all the officers assigned to the murders.

And yet Shaw had slowly emerged, slowly been identified, his life probed, his activities examined, until the timing had damned him.

He had maintained that when he left, each of the women was still alive.

But coincidence could be stretched only so far. And Shaw's way of life had been changed by the small pieces of jewelry and silver frames and bits of flatware that had been sold to men whose own livelihood lay in convenient memory loss and a rapid dispersal of questionable goods to other dealers.

Not one of them had described Ben Shaw. The man was forty. Young. Graying. Balding. A woman, they thought. Working-class. No better than she should be. Shabbily dressed and poor, but with a posh accent. Hard to trace, these remnants of a dead victim's life, without help. But one or two had come to light in the windows of small shops, noticed by eagle-eyed young constables eager to make their mark. . . .

One of those constables had been Janet Cutter's son by her first marriage. George Peterson. The suicide . . .

Rutledge paced the floor, his mind absorbed in the past.

Hamish scolded, "Ye canna' solve the problem, gnawing at it like an auld dog wi' a shinbone! There's work to be done here. You canna' ignore it!"

Rutledge recalled Mrs. Taylor's weary face, and the uncertain future of young Peter Webber.

Hamish was right. This was not the first time he'd had to juggle cases, when there was heavy pressure for answers. There had been times before the war when he hardly slept at all. And one of those times was the Shaw case.

Where had that mourning locket spent the last six years?

He looked at his watch, decided Dowling might still be at his desk. Leaving the room, he ran lightly down the staircase in the main lobby, and strode out the door, turning toward the police station. The evening was beginning to clear, a sharp wind brushing out the rain. *Brushing out the cobwebs as well?* Hamish wanted to know.

Inspector Dowling was just turning to walk home. Rutledge called his name and the man stopped, looking around.

"I'm late for my tea," he said, "and I'm tired."

"Come to the hotel and have dinner with me. I need to talk to you, and this is as good a time as any."

Torn between his obligations at home and the chance of a fair meal, Dowling stood there in the street, his face a picture of his struggle. "Yes, all right, then. I'll meet you at The Plough. I ought to tell my wife I'll be late."

He walked on, and Rutledge retraced his steps to the hotel. Halfway there, he encountered Elizabeth Mayhew on the street.

"Ian!" she said, startled. "What on earth—"

"I'm in Marling for the present. Assigned to deal with these murders."

"Oh . . ." She bit her lip, as if uncertain what to do, whether to invite him to dine with her—or perhaps to stay at her house for the duration.

Reading the dismay in her eyes, he said gently, "I've a room at the hotel. Come and dine with me one night. But not this evening, I've got a meeting with Dowling."

"He's a good man," she said distractedly. "I'd heard they had sent someone down from London. I never dreamed it might be you!"

"And the puppies. They're thriving?" It was the first thing that came into his head. Their old easy companionship had evaporated like the evening's mists, and he felt nearly as awkward as she evidently did.

"Yes—they're growing—they're quite adorable, actually, playful and sleeping less now that their eyes have opened—" She stopped, as if after such an enthusiastic report she felt she ought to invite him to come and see Henrietta's brood for himself. The silence stretched out, as she searched for something else to say.

"I mustn't miss my meeting," he said. "Will you leave a message at the hotel desk, when you'll be free for dinner?"

Relieved, she replied, "Of course. I'm—I'm glad you're here, Ian. I look forward to dinner—"

And then she was gone, a quick smile begging for understanding as she went on down the street in the direction of the church.

He turned to look after her, saddened by the change in their relationship. But if there was someone, a new man in her life, then there would be little room left for Richard's old friends. And he could appreciate that sea change. If he were courting a young woman whose late husband's friends were in the picture, their presence would cause a certain degree of unease. Particularly judging whether the widow was yet free of the past, and what his own role would become if she wasn't. . . .

But he wasn't courting Elizabeth. He was watching her fade from his life, a pleasant memory that was no longer his to enjoy.

Richard, Rutledge said to himself as he turned again and walked on to the hotel, *it's not my place to play dog in the manger. Elizabeth must make her own way.*

But the sadness lingered. And a certain unacknowledged responsibility. He remembered what his sister Frances had said: *"You're afraid you are letting Richard down . . ."*

Hamish remarked, "She's no' on her way to the altar. Only in the direction of yon kirk."

And it was true. Time enough to worry later.

DOWLING REGARDED THE Plough's menu like a starving man faced with a banquet.

Rutledge watched in amusement as the inspector chose very carefully, as if half afraid such an opportunity might not come his way again.

After they'd ordered, Dowling leaned back in his chair. "Sergeant Burke has told me about Peter Webber. How much faith do you put in what the boy had to say?"

"I don't know," Rutledge answered honestly. "But it's a place to begin. Tell me, do you know someone called Jimsy Ridger?"

"Good God, how did you come to hear of *him*?"

"Apparently someone has been asking for him."

"As in, someone who might be our murderer?"

As their soup was set before them, Rutledge replied, "It's hard to judge. But rather a coincidence, don't you think? Tell me about Ridger."

Dowling spooned up the carrot-and-onion soup with great gusto, then said, "He's not local. Never was. As a boy he came with the hop pickers out of Maidstone, a rough sort of child with a bullying nature and a particularly unclear concept of personal property. There were innumerable complaints about him. The hop pickers often camped or caravaned, you see. There were precious few things worth stealing, but it was easy enough if you saw a man's pipe you fancied, or a silver bangle forgotten on a bench, even a bit of ribbon for the hair. Most of the adults, and the children who were old enough to work, were too tired to be overly troublesome, but the younger ones, with too much energy and too little guidance, were always skirting trouble. Ridger might have become the ringleader, if he'd been clever enough to go about it in the right way. But he was always out for himself. For our sakes, I was always glad he hadn't seen his golden opportunity."

"He came in the autumn, then, for the picking?"

"And sometimes the haying before that. Depended on the weather, you see, when one finished and the other began." He finished his soup with a sigh of satisfaction.

"At any rate," Dowling went on, "Ridger was soon off to fairer fields of endeavor. He ran away to London with an older boy, and his mother didn't have the energy to care. Nothing was ever proved against Ridger. But there was a trail of near misses. Petty theft, some minor forgery, cheating old women out of their savings—the sort of trouble a boy is likely to fall into, running with the wrong crowd."

"I'm surprised you followed his career."

Dowling grinned. "Hardly that. From time to time I'd be contacted by London when they'd run out of likely places to look for him."

"He kept his ties in Kent?"

"I doubt he cared tuppence for Marling. It was more a case of going to earth when London got too warm for him. One spring he came back to work in the orchards, and after that he moved on to the hop gardens. He disappeared one day and then was back in the autumn with a swollen eye and a cut on his chin deep enough to leave a scar. I suppose he never had a home of his own in the true sense. His mother was a decent enough woman, but she produced children like rabbits and never seemed to know where half of them were. They fell into rivers and out of trees and over walls—we'd clean them up and send them back to her for a scolding."

Rutledge said, "Not a vicious man, then, Ridger."

Dowling frowned. "No, I'd not call him vicious. On the other hand, Ridger was out for himself. And that sort can sometimes turn violent."

"He was in the war?"

The woman serving tables brought them a platter of roast chicken, and Dowling's eyes gleamed with hungry relish. He fell to with an apologetic smile.

After a few mouthfuls, he answered, "He joined the army here in Kent, with the rest of the men hereabouts. He told Sergeant Burke at the time that he felt closer to them than to his friends in London. Or trusted them more, is my guess. Still, Ridger had a wonderful way with him, when it suited him. He could call the birds from the trees, as my grandmother was fond of saying. And from all reports, he was a good soldier. And the best scavenger in the regiment."

Rutledge had known more than a few of those himself. A Scot in his company, a man called Campbell, had a knack for disappearing and then coming back hours later with a full haversack. Tins, biscuits, matches, even a cold roast hen with cold potatoes, probably scooped up from some French farmer's abandoned kitchen. Campbell had found dry socks after a week of rain, and gloves in the middle of winter, and whisky for those too well to go back to aid stations and in too much pain to stand their duty. Officers tried to keep the thievery to a minimum, but what they didn't see they couldn't stop.

"What became of Ridger after the war?" Rutledge asked.

"He's back in London, I expect."

"Unless he's gone to earth again," Hamish suggested, "and someone thinks he's in Kent . . ."

The Campbells of this world, excellent scavengers though they were, occasionally forgot the rules and made enemies.

Dowling ordered a flan for his dessert, and Rutledge settled for a plate of cheese.

The inspector sighed as he put down his spoon. "I must thank you," he said with a wry smile. "I feel blissfully content."

AFTER DOWLING HAD left the hotel, Rutledge searched for the man who usually served behind the desk. Haskins was his name, and he had just finished his own meal in the kitchen, his napkin still under his chin. He pointed out the telephone, and Rutledge put in a call to London.

Sergeant Gibson's gruff voice came over the line. "Yes, sir, you wanted to speak to me?"

"I'm looking for a man named Jimsy Ridger." Rutledge gave Gibson a brief sketch of Ridger's background and history. "He's probably in

London, and he may have returned to his old ways. Or he may have acquired a new name and taken up a more respectable line of work. But someone will know how to find him, even so."

Gibson chuckled. "He wouldn't be the first to turn respectable, and find old friends on his doorstep. Anything else, sir?"

"He's a personable man, with a scapegrace way about him when he puts his mind to it." He added as an afterthought, "He could be passing himself off as an ex-officer rather than a common soldier."

Gibson noted it. "Not many of *them* in the stews of London," he retorted dryly. "I'll see what I can come up with, sir. But it will take a little time."

Rutledge gave him the number at The Plough and rang off.

As he walked up the stairs, Hamish said, "Yon Ridger is a wild-goose chase, like as not."

"True enough," Rutledge answered. "In police work, we often close more doors than we open. On the other hand, Will Taylor was killed hours after he was questioned about Ridger. And our drunken friend tonight had been asked about him. I don't want to find Ridger appearing as our cooked goose in the middle of a trial."

THE NIGHT'S DREAMS were a mixture of unsettled thoughts and emotions—the sounds of gunfire in the dark, the flashes of light, the arcing descent of flares, the first finding shots of artillery, and Rutledge was hunched behind the barrier of the trench wall, waiting for a lull to go over the top. The living Hamish was with him, and others long since dead, and he tried to keep up their courage as the minutes wore on. And then he was standing in a twilit Kent road, talking to Alice Taylor, and searching through the hop fields for the boy, Peter Webber. Mrs. Shaw was sitting in the car, a baleful presence, with her daughter weeping in the seat beside her.

Rutledge woke with a start, his body wet with sweat, his eyes searching the room for something—anything—that was familiar. He had no idea where he was.

And then the shape of the window and the pale light of a moon feeling its way through the thinning clouds brought him back to The Plough Hotel and the small village of Marling.

He got up and washed his face.

Hamish, lurking in the shadows of the room, said something, and Rutledge shook his head. Hamish repeated, "It's almost dawn."

So it was.

Rutledge said, "The summer dawns came early at the Front. You never liked them."

"There was no' much worth seeing when the light strengthened. Except for the dead, and the wire, and the men coughing with the damp."

"Or the gas rolling in."

"Aye." The Highland Scots, used to the open hills, had been good at spotting the telltale sweep of a German gas attack. All their lives they'd seen sea mists, and that particular floating gauze that was ground mist in the valleys. They knew the feel of the air before these blew in. And they knew the different feel of the air before the gas came toward them on still mornings when the wind wouldn't disperse it too quickly.

Hamish had often been the first to cry a warning. They had fumbled for their masks, shielding any bare skin, and waited for the attack to pass over them. Anyone too slow, anyone with an ill-kept mask, breathed in the fumes and felt the linings of his throat and lungs burn with a fire that was unforgiving. The damage, once done, lingered for whatever remained of a man's life.

Looking back at the past in that odd moment, there was something besides the haunting voice and the haunted man in the quiet, dark room. That bond that held together soldiers over millennia, the shared experience of the devastation of war.

17

RETURNING TO BED WAS USELESS; IT WOULDN'T BRING
sleep. Rutledge bathed and shaved and then dressed, his mind occupied with murder in this quiet part of Kent.

Sitting in a chair by the window, he waited patiently for the hotel to
rouse from the night, and then went down to breakfast at the appointed
time. The dining room was empty, and a yawning girl was just opening
the drapes that shut off the view of the street.

She looked up, smiled, and said, "I expect you'd like your tea."

"I'd be grateful," he said, returning the smile. She blushed and
looked away, hurrying to the door that led through to the kitchen.

As he turned to the window, he saw a man driving a familiar motorcar pulling up at the hotel. The man, too, was familiar.

It was Tom Brereton, whom he'd met at Lawrence Hamilton's dinner party. A guest brought by Raleigh and Bella Masters. The man
whom Melinda Crawford was thinking of including in her will.

Brereton came striding into the dining room, and didn't at first recognize Rutledge. His eyes were on the kitchen door, and when the girl
serving tables came through with Rutledge's tea, he called, "Do you
suppose you could manage toast and a pot of that for me as well?"

She led him to the table just beyond Rutledge's, and it was then that

Brereton peered at the man from London and paused, as if trying to place him.

Rutledge greeted him by name, and reminded him of the dinner party.

Brereton nodded. "Yes, that's right. The policeman from Scotland Yard. What brings you back to Kent? The murders here, I suppose. Do you mind?" He gestured to the other chair at Rutledge's table.

"No, please join me." Brereton nodded to the girl and she went off to fetch his tea.

"I'm half asleep," Brereton said, sitting down. "Bella was worried that Raleigh had finished his drops and finally sent one of the servants down to my cottage to ask if I'd mind coming in this morning to ask the doctor for a new supply."

"For his pain?"

Brereton grimaced. "It's more for his moodiness. They've given him a new foot, you know, and it hurts like the devil. Both physically and psychologically. If he could manage it, he'd have his ravaged one back."

"I expect that giving up his practice would weigh heavily on a man like Masters."

"Yes, that's probably more true than we know. He lived for the law, and he's at sixes and sevens now."

His tea and a plate of toast arrived, and Brereton added as he poured hot milk into the cup, "I don't suppose Masters has ever been easy to live with. He's a remarkably clever man. Nothing else has ever touched him the way the law did, and he's having trouble filling all those empty hours. Bella fusses, which doesn't help. But then she's worried sick about him. They end up aggravating each other to the point of scenes." He shook his head. "It's rather sad."

"He's not likely to take up growing vegetable marrows," Rutledge agreed, smiling. "I'm surprised that he hasn't thought of writing about his career. At the Hamiltons' dinner party he spoke warmly of Matthew Sunderland. He must have known or worked with a number of famous men."

"Interesting possibility! I ought to drop a hint along those lines. Sunderland was Raleigh's mentor and his standard. You'd think the man walked on water, the way Raleigh extols his virtues. I wonder if he could be objective—Sunderland made his share of mistakes, from what I've heard!"

Rutledge said, "Did he!"

"There was a famous case just at the turn of the century. Hushed up, of course, but Sunderland was reportedly too—er—fond of the wife of the man he was prosecuting. There was an odor of vengeance about the proceedings, as if he'd gladly see the man punished not for the alleged crime but for marrying the woman Sunderland had fancied for himself. Naturally I've never asked Raleigh if there was another side of the story."

"Where did you hear this?"

"It was during the war, I had taken a train back to hospital after leave, and I found myself seated with an elderly barrister. We talked about the law for most of the journey. And he made a comment about the famous Mr. Sunderland having feet of clay. Apparently there was a lampoon that showed the Q.C.—as he was then!—as David, sending Bathsheba's husband not to the forefront of battle but to prison for life. In any event the jury decided otherwise, for whatever reasons, and it was one of the few cases that Sunderland ever lost."

Hamish added dryly, "I canna' see him taking a fancy to yon harridan."

"I saw Sunderland in top form during the Shaw trial. He was impressive."

"Shaw? Oh, yes, the man hanged for murdering women in their beds. It was another trial that created a good deal of publicity. Sunderland died within the year, I think." Brereton smiled wryly. "Bella tells me Raleigh all but went into a decline."

"There was no suggestion of illness or impairment in the courtroom."

"According to Raleigh, it was a sudden death. Sunderland's heart simply stopped. He was sitting at his desk dictating letters to his clerk, and between one word and the next, he was gone." Brereton took out his watch and peered at it intently, as if having trouble reading it. "Another half hour before the doctor's likely to be up!" He put the watch away carefully. "The truth is, the man you saw at the dinner party is a far cry from what he once was. Raleigh has lost the edge that made him a superb barrister. He probably wishes he could die as swiftly as Sunderland did. In all likelihood, he won't live out the winter."

"It's sad to watch a man deteriorate," Rutledge agreed.

"It's Bella I worry about. She's going to wear herself into illness if she isn't careful. And he doesn't seem to notice. Or to care."

"There's a self-centeredness in dying," Rutledge pointed out.

Brereton looked up at him. "So there is in blindness, too. The difference is in age. And perspective. I've still much of my life ahead of me, and I don't fancy spending it tapping along the pavement with a cane!" He said restively, "I must go. Bella—Mrs. Masters—will be anxious. I may be able to persuade Dr. Pugh to let me in."

He stood and looked around for the girl who had served him, then went to the kitchen door to call to her. After settling his account, he came back to the table. "I live in the cottage just down the road from the Masterses' house. If you find yourself in the neighborhood, stop and have a drink with me."

Rutledge thanked him and, after Brereton had gone, finished his own tea. But it was still too early to call on Elizabeth Mayhew, and when the serving girl came back to clear the table, he ordered his usual breakfast.

By that time the other guests in the hotel began to arrive, and the room took on new life as voices filled the spaces. He sat by the window, watching the street come to life as well, as carts moved among the shops, bringing in chickens and cabbages and beets and loaves of bread fresh from the bakery. A small cart filled with baskets of apples rolled past, the farmer's cheeks as round and red as his wares, his bald pate gleaming in the first rays of the late-rising sun. Through the glass, Rutledge could hear the clock in the church tower strike the hour faintly. Brereton, driving out of Marling, was hunched over the wheel, intent on avoiding an accident.

How had Brereton felt about the murdered ex-soldiers? Rutledge wondered. Had he understood their suffering better than most, and felt the irony of their death in a peaceful country finished with war? Or had he secretly envied them their quiet and painless end?

Hamish said, "He isna' blind yet. Ask him in five years."

Which was more to the point.

His breakfast finished, Rutledge set out to do what had been on his mind since dawn.

Elizabeth Mayhew was surprised to see him at this hour, but he apologized with the reminder that he was in Marling on Yard business.

"You've lived here since well before the war," he said as he followed her into the small reception room off the entry hall. "Do you remember hearing of a Jimsy Ridger?"

She frowned. "The name isn't familiar at all. Richard would have known. He knew better than most what went on. He had deep roots here. People talked to him, confided in him." She looked around her at the comfortable room, her home since her marriage. "I'm considering selling up. There are no children to inherit. I might as well let the house go to someone who can keep it as Richard would have wished."

Startled, he said, "But it's been in his family for—what? Seven generations, at the least!"

"I know. There's a cousin somewhere. Out in Kenya, I think, if he's still alive. A remittance man. I'm not sure Richard would have liked the idea of his inheriting."

Black sheep in a family were sometimes paid handsomely to take themselves out of England, with a monthly stipend to smooth their road and nip in the bud any fond thoughts of returning home uninvited.

Elizabeth smiled wryly. "If you'd married Jean, you'd have been looking for a country place, wouldn't you? This house would have suited you—and that would have suited Richard. But we seldom know how our lives will turn out, do we?"

"Where would you go?" Rutledge asked, keeping to the main point. "To London?"

"I had thought about traveling—" she said vaguely.

"Europe is in a shambles. And I don't quite picture you in the wilds of America or the missions of China. Like Melinda Crawford."

One of the puppies, awakened by their voices, yipped from the other room, and Elizabeth turned the subject by saying quickly, "Oh, you must come and see how they've grown!"

Which in fact they had. But Rutledge was not to be distracted.

As she handed him one of the puppies to hold, kneeling by the box on the cold hearth, Elizabeth said, "Canada, perhaps." And then caught herself as she remembered too late that Jean, too, had gone to Canada.

Rutledge pretended he'd made no such connection and admired the puppies. Then he said, "Will you do something for me? You know the Masters family better than I do. Can you ask—skirting the reason why—what Mrs. Masters recalls of a case in London before the war?" He described the Shaw murders for Elizabeth, and the brilliant prosecution that Matthew Sunderland had mounted.

"What in particular do you want to know?" she asked, confused. "This has nothing to do with the murders here, does it?"

"It's an old case," he said lightly. "But one I was assigned to when I was young and far from wise. I'd like to know if Sunderland described it to his friends. Or if Raleigh Masters ever discussed it with his wife. At the time it attracted considerable attention—it would be natural to relive it."

Elizabeth nodded. "Oh—yes. Weren't you about to ask Raleigh when he had one of his spells? I'll try to see what I can learn." It was as if she was grateful that the request was impersonal. "But I don't know that Bella can tell me much, if it wasn't Raleigh's case—"

"I understand that. A shot in the dark, if you will."

Her eyes probed his face. Then she said, unexpectedly, "Ian, is something about this case worrying you? You haven't been quite the same since you were here the last time, you know. I shall do this, of course I shall, but if there's a reason you aren't telling me, I want you to know that you can trust me—"

He could have told her that she was the one who had changed. Not he.

Hamish said, "Aye, but who planted the seeds of doubt in your head?"

It had been Melinda Crawford . . .

"It's not the case itself," he answered Elizabeth now. "It's the people who were involved. I've been reading through their statements again."

And as he left the house, he thought they'd come to a sad pass, he and Richard's widow—lying to each other as they never had before.

DOWLING HAD LEFT a message for him at The Plough. Rutledge walked on to the police station and learned from Sergeant Burke that the Marling inspector was already on his way to Seelyham.

Rutledge asked, "Has anything happened? Am I to follow him?"

Burke shook his head. "I doubt there's any new development, sir, or I'd have heard it as soon as I came on duty. Constable Smith informed me that Inspector Grimes over in Seelyham had sent a man along to fetch Inspector Dowling, but there mustn't been any urgency, sir. The inspector waited half an hour at the hotel for you before setting out. I expect it's no more than a meeting to consider next steps, and Inspector Dowling included you as a courtesy."

"You shouldna' have lingered on your ain business," Hamish scolded. "It's no' right to muddle the past wi' the present."

When in Rome—Rutledge thought, but this was Marling . . .

And it was an opportunity to meet Grimes, in Seelyham.

He thanked Burke and was gone.

But he'd no more than turned the crank and started the engine when a young woman stepped out of the hotel's side door and paused, as if waiting for him to drive on. It wasn't until he'd climbed behind the wheel that Rutledge, his thoughts far from London, realized he knew her.

It was Nell Shaw's daughter.

She simply stood there, prepared for rejection.

"Miss Shaw?" he said tentatively. He dredged his memory for a name, and somewhere in the mists of the past, he remembered that she was called Margaret.

Her face, clouded with uncertainty, cleared as he recognized her. "It's my mother," she said hurriedly. "I'm so terribly worried about her."

With a repressed sigh, he asked, "Is she ill? Shall I ask the doctor to come to the hotel?" Nell Shaw was, he thought, a better tactician than half the generals at the Front—But then, as Hamish was pointing out, perhaps she had a better cause. After all, Rutledge was the man who had brought her husband to judgment—and thus to his death. Shifting the burden of his self-doubt to her shoulders, blaming her for demanding what she perceived as justice, was shirking his duty to himself and to the Law.

"I'm sorry—No, she's in London. I came down alone."

Thanking God for small mercies, he said more sharply than he'd intended, "I must drive to Seelyham. My business there can't wait. I'll have to take you with me. We can talk on the way."

She hesitated, as if half afraid of him, gnawing her lip like a child.

"Margaret," he said more gently. "Would you prefer to wait here until I come back? I can't promise how long it will be. On the other hand, if you drive with me, there won't be any distractions or interruptions. We can discuss what's wrong with your mother along the way, and I'll see you safely home from Seelyham."

Flushing with embarrassment and gratitude, she nodded, and Rutledge handed her into the passenger's seat before turning toward the main road out of the village.

As they passed the ironmonger's, a man leaning wearily against the wall stared blearily at them. Rutledge recognized the drunk, Holcomb, from the night before. Belching heavily, the man turned on his heel and shambled on.

Rutledge wondered if the man was sober enough to make any better sense now. But he couldn't stop.

Picking up the thread of Margaret Shaw's earlier remark, he asked, "Why are you worried about your mother?"

"It's like an obsession," Miss Shaw told him earnestly, as if relieved to find someone who would listen. She was not as hard as her mother, nor as intelligent, he thought. Sheltered—by choice or by circumstances—she was not worldly, in the true sense. And he wondered if she really understood why her mother was so adamant that the past be expunged.

"Clearing your father's name?" He glanced toward her.

Her face reddened again. She had that kind of fair complexion that registered shifts in emotion easily. "She's convinced Papa didn't kill anyone . . . she can't sleep, she can't eat—it's all she thinks about!"

"How long has this been going on? All these years? Or since she found the locket?"

"She's always railed against the jury. But since the locket she's been like a madwoman."

"Tell me about finding the locket."

"There's nothing to tell. She went next door to help Mr. Cutter as he'd asked, and when she came home she looked sick, as if she was about to lose her dinner. She was that upset, she locked herself in her room. I've only known her to do that twice before. The day Papa was taken away, and the day the letter came."

"What letter?"

"I never saw it. But after she read it, she cried for hours. Then she came out of her room and was herself again."

"A letter your father had written?"

She frowned. "I don't see how it could be. It only came this autumn. But I overheard her tell Mr. Cutter that a cousin was dying. She said, 'Everyone is gone. There's no one left.' "

"And what has been your feeling all these years? About your father's guilt?" he asked quietly, without judgment.

She shook her head. "I never cared whether Papa was guilty or not. It didn't matter. When they took him away, I wept all night. I hated the police, I hated you. He was my *father*—I didn't know how we were to get along without him! And indeed, it's been the hardest thing we've ever had to face. Nobody *understands!*"

Hamish said, "She would ha' been at an age where she doted on him."

It was true. Rutledge recalled the stricken, white-faced child standing in the doorway, staring up at her father, waiting for him to tell her it was all a mistake, that he'd be home by the morning. And Shaw had looked at her, pain in his eyes, and said nothing.

The boy, her brother Ben, had been belligerent, beating his fists against the young constable escorting his father, crying out to let him go, he'd done nothing. But the girl had been unable to speak, crushed by events, not even coming forward to kiss her father as he turned a last time on the road and looked back at her.

"It's important to realize that your mother may be wrong. That she's going to be disappointed," Rutledge began, slowing in the wake of a lorry. "I know she's desperate and afraid and clinging to hope. But what if there is none? So far I've found nothing, no real proof to support her belief that this new evidence—"

"That's no' true!" Hamish thundered. "It's no' the truth!"

Rutledge silently defended himself. "I will not give her false hope! It won't help her mother, and it won't serve her!" he said adamantly. "Nothing is black and white—it's more often shades of gray!"

Hamish replied defiantly, "Aye, so you say!" His upbringing in a barren, harsh land, compounded by his rigid faith, had always set out the lines of battle cleanly. One faced and dealt with life, and if necessary, with death. It was what had led him to refuse a direct order in the field, this stubborn, suicidal belief that compromise was unacceptable. Hedged in by exhaustion and disgust and grief, he had had nowhere to go. And so had chosen execution rather than lead even one more man to his death in the teeth of the German guns. . . .

"—evidence," Rutledge went on, overriding the protest, "is sufficient to satisfy either the police or the Home Office that this file should be reopened."

"But there's the locket! Mama says you haven't spoken to anyone— that you've come here about other murders, and forgotten us." The girl bit her lip again, and turned to look out at the fields. "Mama says—" She broke off as her voice quivered. Pride forbade her to cry in his presence.

"I know what your mother says," he told her, more gently. "And I *have* spoken to people who remember your father and his trial."

"And nobody wished to help," she said forlornly. "I'm not surprised."

"Who else could have killed those women?"

There was a long silence.

He hadn't expected an answer. He said, finally, "I can understand why your mother took the locket from that drawer—it was human nature, it was vindication, and she didn't think beyond that possibility. Still, Mrs. Cutter is dead. We can't question her about how it came into *her* possession."

"But I don't think Mrs. Cutter intended to harm Papa, when she told the police about the change in our circumstances. I think when George—that was Mrs. Cutter's son from her first marriage—told her about the murders, she saw a way to make trouble for Mama. Because she wanted Papa to come to her for help."

"Your father worked in the victims' houses, not your mother."

"But Mama was always after Papa to ask pay for what he did. And he wouldn't hear of it. Mrs. Cutter told me one afternoon that Mama would go round to the houses herself and say that we were desperate for whatever they could spare. Mrs. Cutter told me that Mama would ask to be remembered in their wills, if the old ladies couldn't pay much."

Nothing in the original testimony suggested that Mrs. Shaw had had any contact with the victims. Was this the truth? Or a fabrication?

"How did Mrs. Cutter know these things?"

"I don't know. I was afraid to ask her!"

Her son George?

"Did you ever speak to your parents about her accusations?"

Margaret shook her head vigorously. "Oh, no. It was shameful to think of Mama begging."

Which might have scuttled Janet Cutter's intentions.

He drove with only half his mind on the road. It would be easy to believe that Mrs. Cutter had simply used the killings to her own advantage—except for that locket. The locket put an entirely different complexion on the interactions between the Shaws and the Cutters. Would Janet Cutter have asked her son George to bring her a small token, some property of the dead that she could use in her persecution of Nell Shaw? And instead the police had taken her literally and investigated the husband, not the wife! She'd have buried the locket away, then, for fear it would condemn the wrong Shaw—

Mistaking his silence, Margaret Shaw turned to face Rutledge. "It will break Mama's heart if you fail her. I don't know what I'm to do then! Mama has always been that strong! How will my brother and I survive without *her*?" Her voice ended in a wail that made him flinch.

Rutledge swore to himself. He mustn't—he couldn't—afford to find himself entangled in the emotional turmoil of the Shaw family. His objectivity slipped with every encounter. The locket was damning—but where had it come from? That was the crux of his dilemma.

Where had the locket spent the last six years?

It couldn't have been in the possession of Janet Cutter's dead son. Unless he'd sent it to her in a final and desperate need to justify his suicide—

"It would be a tidy answer," Hamish interjected sourly.

The whole case was revolving around Janet Cutter. And she was dead. . . .

Rutledge said, "Your mother means well, Margaret, but she's living under the delusion that the police and a jury and a judge were wrong in their findings. And that doesn't happen very often—"

"That's what Mama said to us—'It doesn't happen very often—but they wronged your father, and they wronged me, and they wronged you—' Mama was there in the courtroom. She could see that a jury believes what the lawyers tell them. What the police tell them. But Papa never said a word in his own defense. Who gave his side?"

The defense had put up the best arguments it could. But the most damning evidence had been Shaw's refusal to deny his guilt when the police had questioned him.

Hamish said, "If Mrs. Cutter had told him what she told the lass, and he believed her lies—"

"—he would have taken his wife's place in the dock, for the sake of the children. . . ." Rutledge completed the thought.

Miss Shaw was silent for a long breath. Then she said stoutly, "I never liked Mrs. Cutter. There was a slyness about her. She'd be very kind, offering tea cakes or hair ribbons. And then once I was lulled into accepting, she'd begin to pick and pry. She'd ask about my parents, about my father. I didn't know how to stop her, or turn the questions. It was like being pinned, the way insects were in a museum display I saw once—"

"What sort of questions?"

"What Papa and Mama talked about together. If they had arguments. What my father had given my mother on her birthday. It was as if she couldn't bear for them to be happy together."

ON THE OUTSKIRTS of Seelyham oast houses lined the fields, like misshapen windmills lacking their sails. Miss Shaw asked about them, staring over her shoulder. "I was never much in the countryside," she said artlessly. "I don't know anything about flowers or trees. But I like them."

Rutledge, thinking of the shabby, cheek-by-jowl houses of Sansom Street, replied, "I expect you do. You should consider going into service in the country." If he'd been on better terms with Elizabeth Mayhew, he could have recommended this girl to her. But she was considering selling up, and there would be no place for Margaret Shaw, when new owners took over.

The pretty face turned to him, brightening. "I could, couldn't I? If Mama doesn't find a way to help us. I learn quickly, if I'm taught."

Hamish said, Covenanter to the bone, "It's no' a very fine future, service."

"For many girls with no other place to go, it provides a home," Rutledge pointed out.

At that Hamish snapped, "And salves your conscience, aye."

ON THE OUTSKIRTS of Seelyham was a huddle of half-timbered cottages with thatched roofs that led into a broadening of the road, a few side streets, and a small green with two- and three-story brick buildings on either side, one of them half covered with ivy and sporting a sign identifying it as the Seelyham Arms. Around the corner stood a small public house with a pair of benches on either side of the door. The church was set on higher ground where a lane branched to the right, and the churchyard wall ran along the lane for some distance beyond, sharing it on the other side with a rather shabby house that rambled into three wings, its plaster faded to a soft cream and the pointed windows reflecting the church tower. The police station, a farmer walking his dog informed Rutledge, was just beyond the pub.

Rutledge left Miss Shaw in the parlor of the Seelyham Arms, ordering tea and sandwiches for her, before walking along to the station. It was crammed between a pair of shops, one with meats hanging in the window and the other a bakery displaying an array of cakes and bread.

He found Dowling talking with a heavyset, red-faced man who was introduced as Grimes, the local man on the scene. The small office, stuffy with the heat of bodies and the smell of stale food, was almost claustrophobic in atmosphere. Rutledge quickly found himself wanting to leave the outer door standing wide.

Gruff and to the point, Grimes declared, "I've just been acquainting Mr. Dowling here with the names of men who'd be included on any list of possible victims if our murderer widens his range. Seemed to be a good idea to say something to each man, and we've just done that."

Rutledge wondered how many able-bodied men had gone marching off to war out of the village's tiny population. He sat down in the chair offered him and replied, "I take it that they served with the Marling men?"

Grimes looked him over, the height, the thinness of the face, the haunted eyes. But something in Rutledge's appearance made up his mind for him. "That's right. Except for two that went to sea." He sighed. "The farmers got used to their being away, managing somehow. But it's not the same—never will be. And no money to mechanize."

"What did these men have to say?" Rutledge asked.

"Not what you'd call helpful information. Dowling sat there and watched them, and he's of the same mind: Nobody seems to know anything we don't." Grimes passed a list to Rutledge, who scanned it quickly. None of the names were familiar. "What's more, I'd already spoken with the rector. Comparing impressions, you might say. He knows Seelyham as well as or better than I do. And there's been no indication of secrets or trouble that he's aware of." He stirred in his chair, glancing briefly at Dowling. "All the same, the men and their families are worried. You could see it in their faces."

Hamish said, "If there's trouble, they're no' likely to confide in either priest or police."

And Hamish was right. Men who had stood shoulder to shoulder in the terrifying bombardments, leaning against the slick mud of the trench walls as they waited for the signal to go over the top, were as close as brothers. What passed between them was kept to themselves, and they looked out for each other. The Scots under Rutledge were as feuding a lot as he'd ever come across in civilian life, but they'd close ranks before an officer, turning bland faces his way and swearing that all was well.

Admirable in some ways, this silence, and infuriating in others.

It could well turn out to be deadly now.

Grimes was saying, "I've asked about strangers as well. Not one of these men has seen someone hanging about."

"There was a boy who came down with the hop pickers. A Jimsy Ridger. Has someone from their ranks been searching for him?" Rutledge asked. "Ridger might not be viewed as a stranger if they'd served with him."

"If there was, no one spoke up. I recall Ridger, as a matter of fact. An unlikely lad to settle down to a decent living. To my knowledge, he hasn't been around since the war ended a year ago." Grimes picked up the thread of his discussion. "But the women, now, they're a different story. And that's where we were heading when you walked through the door. If you want to come along, I'd ask only that you let me do the talking."

Taking acceptance of the invitation for granted, Grimes got heavily to his feet, and Dowling said diffidently, "Ought I to wait here? Too much officialdom—"

"No, you might as well hear what's said."

The three men walked briskly in the direction of the brick cottages that stood in a cluster where the High Street ran into the Marling Road. For the most part the homes were well kept, sedate with white curtains at the windows and pots of flowers set in the sunny doorways.

"Mrs. Parker lives here," Grimes was saying, indicating one of them. "You can see how that pair of windows in the front room overlooks the street." He tapped lightly on the door, and stood back.

An elderly woman opened it a crack and peered out at them. "Now, then, Mrs. Parker," Grimes said with gruff affability, "I've brought Mr. Dowling and Mr. Rutledge here to listen to what you told me you saw the other night. If you'd not mind repeating it for us."

She was swathed in shawls, stooped and breathing with noticeable difficulty. She didn't offer to invite her visitors in; she stood her ground in the doorway, clutching the frame and the edge of the door as if to support herself. A brief gust of wind stirred her thin gray hair and she stepped back into the shelter of the entry. She spoke to them from there, like a frail ghost of the woman she must once have been, her large frame shrunken with illness and age.

"I don't rest of a night, as you know very well, Bill Grimes! I sit by my windows"—a gnarled finger pointed out the one he'd indicated earlier—"and sleep in my chair when I sleep at all. It was last Tuesday night, I think it was. There was someone walking by, and I leaned forward to tap on the glass."

"Did you know who it was?"

"Well, I thought I did. I thought it was Tommy Jacobs, and one of the twins had taken ill."

"And was it?"

She glared at him. "You know very well it wasn't. You went straight to his door after you left here, and asked him yourself!"

"I know, Mrs. Parker," Grimes answered patiently. "But these gentlemen don't."

"If it'ud been Tommy, he'd have stopped and told me what he was doing out at that hour. Instead he crossed the road there, head down, and hurried off, as if he hadn't heard me."

"And how would you describe him?"

She pressed her lips together, trying for breath. "He looked like Tommy Jacobs," she said after a moment. "Tall. Good shoulders. He had on a heavy coat and his hat. It was cold that night. That's all I saw."

"I'll let you step in out of the wind, then, Mrs. Parker. Kind of you to talk to us, I appreciate it." Grimes tipped his hat again.

She looked from him to Dowling, then to Rutledge. "I've seen him before," she said, indicating the inspector from Marling. "But not *him*."

"Mr. Rutledge has come down from London," Grimes informed her.

She gave Rutledge a toothless grin, her bright blue eyes suddenly dancing. "From London, is it? Mr. Parker was from London. I always fancied London men!"

With that she shut her door firmly, and left them standing on the street.

"Do you believe her?" Rutledge asked Grimes.

"I think I do. She's not well, but her eyesight is keen enough, and so is her mind."

Dowling said, "Her windows are near enough to the street for a clear look at the man."

They considered the story for a moment longer before walking on.

"If her testimony was the only one we had, I'd be more chary of taking it seriously," Grimes said. "The next woman in a way corroborates what Mrs. Parker saw. But before we walk on, notice the direction of the church from here."

Rutledge and Dowling turned to observe that the church was closer into town.

"Now, look down there, the house set back from the road in the trees."

It was on the outskirts of Seelyham, a good fifty yards away, and rather finer than the cottages. Rutledge thought it might have been at one time a Dower House, judging by the low brick wall in front and a handsome portico.

Grimes set off with determination, explaining as he went.

"Miss Judson and her father live in that house. It's called The Swallows, and it's too far off the road to see who's coming and going. But that same Tuesday night, Miss Judson went out to fetch the rector to her father. He isn't well, and sometimes he takes a bad turn and wants to make his peace with God. She does what she can to keep his spirits up."

Rutledge said, "They live together, then."

"Oh, yes. Miss Judson is what you might describe as a mature lady. I'd guess Mr. Judson is well past his three score years and ten."

They had reached the property and were walking up the drive when a woman with a dog came out of the house, went down the stone steps, and stopped to stare at them with interest before moving in their direction.

"Inspector Grimes," she said, nodding to Dowling and Rutledge. A tall, angular woman in her forties, with clear gray eyes and a no-nonsense manner, she waited with composure for Grimes to explain himself.

"I've brought Inspector Dowling from Marling to speak with you, and Inspector Rutledge, from London. I'd like them to hear what you told me."

Frowning, Miss Judson said, "You attach more importance to it than I do."

"I daresay we do," Grimes agreed affably. "But in police work, it's the small things that sometimes loom large in the end."

She faced the other two men and explained in her abrupt fashion, "I had gone to fetch the rector to my father. As I walked down the drive and turned toward the rectory, I passed a man coming out of Seelyham. It was late, and I didn't expect to find anyone else on the road. I nodded as I passed him, and went on to knock on Mr. Sawyers's door. When the two of us walked back, the man was nowhere to be seen."

"Did you recognize him?" Rutledge asked.

"Indeed not."

"How was he dressed?"

"Well enough to be a gentleman. Certainly not shabby enough to be a beggar, even though he was on foot. We're the last house, you see, and I thought perhaps he might have been staying at The Arms and couldn't sleep. I suggested as much to Inspector Grimes, here."

"Could you see his face or judge his coloring?"

She smiled. "There was no moon, Inspector—Rutledge, is it? I wouldn't know him again if he came to tea. Except that he had a good bearing. I thought perhaps he'd been in the war."

They thanked her and took their leave. As Grimes walked back to the main road he told them, "I asked at The Arms. There was no one who might have taken it in his head to try the air well after midnight. Two ladies visiting a cousin, and a pair of travelers too drunk after their dinner to have made it down the stairs again without breaking their necks."

"Then we have a man walking out of Seelyham on a Tuesday night. No one was murdered on a Tuesday," Rutledge pointed out.

"But there was on a Saturday," Grimes reminded him. "And here's the other bit of the puzzle. Another woman was walking through the churchyard around nine o'clock Saturday evening. She was coming home from sitting up with a child with croup. Rounding the corner by the church she walked straight into a man coming out of the bushes. He was living rough, she thought, and she didn't care for that. She walked on, and came to find me. But by the time I reached the churchyard, he'd taken the hint and moved on."

"She spoke to him?"

Grimes laughed. "Miss Whelkin would ask the devil who he was roasting over the fires of hell. If we'd sent her to fight the Kaiser, the war would have been over in two years."

Rutledge smiled. Such women were the bane of ordinary villagers, and the delight of policemen.

"She stopped stock-still and wanted to know if he was waiting for someone. There's a young girl here in Seelyham who is no better than she ought to be, and Miss Whelkin was of the opinion the man was loitering for a chance to meet her. She asked him outright, and he answered that he'd come a long way and was tired. He'd fallen asleep when he went into the church to pray. She was fairly certain he was from Cornwall."

"Has she visited Cornwall?"

"My guess is that she hasn't," Grimes replied sourly. "But she swore he could pass for Tristan. Whoever *he* might be when he's at home."

Rutledge, who had been studying the churchyard, turned to look sharply at Grimes.

Tristan . . .

His first thought was the opera. But he doubted Miss Whelkin had ever set foot in a London theater. She was not likely, from Grimes's description, to be a lover of foreign works.

"How old is she, this Miss Whelkin?"

"Fifty-five if she's a day," Grimes declared. "Her father was schoolmaster here for most of her life."

"Then she'd have known the *Idylls of the King*—" Tennyson's romantic series of poems about Arthur and his Court. They had brought the Round Table knights back into fashion, and all things Gothic. *Tristan* . . .

Grimes's face cleared. "Tennyson," he nodded, recalling his school days. "I had to learn a good bit of his poems by heart."

Dowling was talking to Grimes, and Rutledge shut out their voices as he dredged his memory. There had been a painting just before the war, very popular with Londoners. C. Tarrant's portrait of a young, fair man on a narrow, grubby back street of a Midlands town, staring up at an aeroplane overhead. Ignoring the signs of poverty all around him, the young man's eyes were fixed in wonder on the miracle of flying. Earthbound, he longed for the skies. Like a Grail Knight blind to the misery of the world in his vainglorious search for the miraculous Cup. And the artist had called it *Tristan*.

There had been two schools of thought on the intent of the portrait, and much had been written about it. The show had been a triumph. Much later, Rutledge had met the man who might have posed for that knightly figure. . . .

Miss Whelkin would probably have agreed with the artist about the depiction of Tristan. There had been reproductions of the painting in bookshops, and she might even have seen one of them. But why had she connected that Tristan with a stranger from Cornwall?

Hamish said, "You canna' be sure she did!"

Rutledge said aloud, "I think we ought to speak to Miss Whelkin."

"You'll have to come back, then. She's off to her sister's in Canterbury for the week. Miss Whelkin visits her every November, like clockwork. They don't get on together. It's a trial for both of them. But she's bent and determined to do her duty by her kin."

DOWLING WISTFULLY SUGGESTED luncheon at the hotel before returning to Marling, but Rutledge still had to address the problem of Nell Shaw's daughter. Grimes and Dowling set off toward the police station, where Dowling had left his bicycle, and Rutledge walked on to the Seelyham Arms.

Margaret Shaw had managed to reach Marling on her own, but it was necessary to find her safe transportation back to London. With promises that he would not forget her mother and would visit her as soon as possible, Rutledge handed her into the carriage of an elderly and respectable greengrocer driving to London to see his dentist. He also gave her fare for a cab to take her across the river from Charing Cross.

There was trepidation in her face as she asked, "But what must I do about Mama? I can't go home and tell her there's nothing new, and watch her worry herself into one of her blinding headaches! She'll be fit to be tied, if I come back empty-handed!"

Rutledge said, "Did she send you to me?"

The girl shook her head. "No, but she'd want to know where I've been and who I saw. She's that strict! I'll have to tell her—if I lie, she catches me out, and it's all the worse. Last night she sat on the side of my bed and told me she was at her wit's end. She had that pinched look about her eyes, as if the lamp was too bright." She stared around her at the village of Seelyham, her gaze wandering to the stone church tower, green with moss, and the hummocky ground of the ancient churchyard. "Do you believe Papa killed those women? *Truly* believe it?"

As her eyes swung back to his face, she read the uncertainty there before he could control the doubt that had plagued him since the day her mother had walked back into his life.

"It doesn't matter what I believe," he said wearily.

The key to this muddle was very likely the stroke Janet Cutter had had shortly after Shaw's sentencing—and shortly after her son's suicide, come to that. But which piece of news had destroyed her? If the truth were known . . .

"Did you know George Peterson?" he asked then.

Margaret was surprised. "Hardly at all. He was grown up when I was a child, and I was rather afraid of him."

"Because he was older?"

As if digging into her memory, she answered slowly, "He was a policeman, and Mama would threaten to call him to come and take us away if we were naughty."

It was a common enough threat—in many households, the police had replaced the devil as a deterrent to bad behavior. Rutledge smiled.

Following her own train of thought, Margaret Shaw said, "I don't know why Mrs. Cutter cared for Papa. He was whimsical. And I think she must have liked that."

"How did Henry Cutter behave toward your mother?"

"Oh, he was always asking her advice. I think he admired Mama's strength, and Papa liked Mrs. Cutter's softness. She reminded him of growing up somewhere else, not Sansom Street. It was almost as if they'd all married the wrong people. I don't expect to wed," she added with a candidness that was a measure of her own lost childhood. "There's too much heartache. It seldom comes out right!"

RUTLEDGE DROVE INSPECTOR Dowling back to Marling. Halfway there the inspector began, "We don't see many murders in this part of the country. Not like some of the towns, where there's an uncertain element. Maidstone, for instance. Or Rochester. Dover sees more trouble, being a port where all kinds mix. The last murder in Marling was just before the war, a son who killed his father before the old fool could marry again and change his will. I understand that kind of violence. The son felt he was being cheated out of his inheritance, and the father was bent on having a pretty young wife. *She* knew a good thing when she saw it, and if there was blame anywhere, it lay at her door. She was greedy, not to put too fine a point on it. She saw the father could give her more than the son. Without her stirring up the pair of them, that farmer would be alive today. But the courts can't take such behavior into account. If they could, a jury would have hanged her along with the dead man's son."

It was, in some ways, the story of the Shaws. A wife wanting what she couldn't have . . .

Rutledge said, "It's straightforward, at least. I once had an investigation that hinged on a lamp. Where it had actually been placed before the crime. Through a window the murderer had seen something in the room that triggered an explosive anger, jealous anger. But only because the lamp's light illuminated it in that position. Once the lamp was moved, we saw nothing out of the ordinary. There was nothing to give her away."

Dowling glanced at Rutledge. "Where's *our* lamp, then?" he asked. "I understand what you're saying, but I can't apply it to our situation."

"The roads," Rutledge answered. "Each of the dead men had a family at home. Other eyes to see whatever transpired. It put the men out of reach, in a sense. But they were always accessible along the road. The question is, what drew each of these victims into the killer's net? Circumstance? Opportunity? Or trickery?"

Dowling turned his head to consider the road behind them. They had nearly reached the trees where one of the victims had been discovered. Taylor. The first . . .

"It can't be theft," the inspector said, ticking off the possibilities on his fingers. "These three had little worth stealing. No one stole what they did have. And no one stands to gain from their deaths, as far as I can tell. The murders took place on different roads, different nights.

That's a vote for opportunity, not circumstance. They had the war in common, of course."

"And there's Jimsy Ridger," Rutledge said.

"If someone was looking for Jimsy, he wouldn't have to kill a man to ask where to find him."

"He might kill a man he thought would warn Ridger."

"Then I think it's time we found out where Ridger is, and what he knows about this business."

18

IN THE EVENT, NEITHER DOWLING NOR RUTLEDGE HAD TO search far for the missing Jimsy Ridger.

Sergeant Gibson had left a message at The Plough. It read, *"In regard to the man you want: he's not in London. Rumor has it he's dead. My guess is that he's in hiding. No one is prepared to say where."*

Rutledge's reaction was, *I'm not surprised. . . .*

Hamish said, "Aye. It stands to reason he'd go to ground, if there's someone looking for him. And the man searching for Ridger may be a step ahead of you. He may ken that Ridger is in Kent . . ."

"Yes, it makes sense." Rutledge took the stairs two at a time and spent the next half an hour finishing his notes about the conversation with Grimes in Seelyham. He debated driving to Canterbury to look up Miss Whelkin, and then decided against it. She would be home again in a few days.

Closing the notebook, he sought out Sergeant Burke and asked the man to draw a rough map of Marling.

IT WAS NEARLY TEATIME when Rutledge pulled into the drive at the home of Lawrence Hamilton and his wife, Lydia. They had been his hosts when he met Raleigh Masters, and Rutledge was certain they would know as much about this part of Kent as Richard Mayhew had done.

He was surprised to find that Bella Masters was already there. She looked tired, unhappy, but her face brightened as Lydia Hamilton welcomed the newcomer and offered him a cup of tea.

Mrs. Masters said, after the courtesies had been observed, "I've come to invite Lydia and her husband to dine with us tonight. But they have another engagement. Could I persuade you to join us, Mr. Rutledge? There will be only six, I'm afraid. Tom Brereton, Mrs. Crawford, Elizabeth Mayhew, and you, but I can promise you a fine dinner and lively conversation."

Lydia's face, turned away from Mrs. Masters, pleaded with Rutledge to accept.

It was not common for a policeman to be invited to dine. It was, indeed, a measure of Mrs. Masters's desperation that a stranger and a lowly inspector would be acceptable at her table.

For his own reasons, Rutledge agreed. "I'll call for Elizabeth, if you like," he said.

"That would be lovely!"

Lydia put in, "I think I hear Lawrence—"

Rutledge said, "If you don't mind, I'll meet him in the hall. There are a few questions I'd like to put to him."

She nodded, and then a look of alarm spread over her face. As if his words had touched a wellspring of concern that was swiftly hidden.

He thought ironically that it was the policeman she dreaded. . . .

Lawrence was coming down the stairs when Rutledge stepped into the hall and shut the sitting room door behind him.

Hamilton held out his hand and greeted him with a smile. "I hear we have another guest."

"Mrs. Masters. I've accepted a dinner invitation in your stead," Rutledge answered lightly. "In return, I need a favor."

"I hope to heaven Bella's made peace with her cook! Or you'll be back demanding my firstborn," Hamilton retorted humorously, leading Rutledge into a small study. Closing the door, he said in a more serious tone, "What's this about? The murders? I'd heard you'd come down to help the local people. Any progress?"

"None." He took the chair that Hamilton indicated and looked around the room. It was a study-cum-office, where open law books and stacks of paper indicated an ongoing brief.

Hamilton gestured wryly and said, "I can't find a reference. It's there somewhere, but I can't put my finger on it. I asked Raleigh if he recalled it, but he said I'd earn my keep if I find it on my own."

Rutledge said, "He may have forgotten it himself."

Hamilton laughed. "The man's memory is famous. Matthew Sunderland taught him that, early on. To cultivate a good memory. I sometimes think that Raleigh would be pleased to discover that Sunderland was his father. It would be the crowning moment of his life."

"Tell me about Sunderland."

"He was one of the best men of his day. Toward the end there was something that wasn't noticeable early on. An arrogance. A certainty that he was never wrong. It persuaded judges, sometimes. I never discovered whether this was a pretense or if Sunderland actually believed strongly in his own judgment. Needless to say, he was convincing as hell! Did you ever work with him?"

"The Shaw case. And one other before that. Most of my cases were not of a caliber to rate Matthew Sunderland, K.C."

"Yes, well, he was a watchword for years. Almost an assurance of conviction, when he was prosecuting. Now, tell me, what is it you need from me? Certainly not the past history of a dead man."

But it had been what Rutledge needed. Still, he said, "I wonder if you recall someone named Jimsy Ridger."

"Good God, Jimsy was an eel. Convicting him of anything was impossible. He never came my way, of course, but I've heard enough tales about him. Most particularly since he'd spent a goodly part of his life where I lived, and no one in London let me forget it. He wasn't actually from our part of Kent, but he had a habit of popping up here at the least likely moments."

"Tell me about him. Not his criminal history, but what you know of him."

Hamilton got up to offer Rutledge a glass of whisky and then, sipping his own, said ruminatively, "He came with the hop pickers. A wild lad, with no sense of fear. And no one, really, to look out for him. Consequently he fell in with the wrong people. Or they fell in with him."

It was almost word for word the description that Sergeant Burke had given Rutledge. "I need a picture of him as a man," he said, studying the amber liquid in his glass but not drinking.

"I doubt that anyone can give you that. Jimsy was as charming as a snake, and as quick. But no one got through the charm into the person behind it. He had more energy than most, and had learned to skirt the law with impunity. Underneath the surface, I always thought he was lonely. No, lonely isn't the word. I think—" He paused, trying to find the right explanation. "Jimsy was one of those people who never successfully formed friendships. He was too devious and too questionable in his character for most people to like him. He never got close to anyone that I know of. And as a result, he was dangerous. There were no ties, you see, to hold him. In a way, he was like Matthew Sunderland—odd though it might sound. He walked in his own shadow, and showed the world only what he thought it fit for the world to see."

RUTLEDGE STOPPED BY Elizabeth Mayhew's house to leave a message that he'd be collecting her in time to drive to the Masterses' house for dinner.

She was waiting for him in the hall, when he came to lift the knocker on her door later in the evening. She opened it herself, and said, "Ian, I could have had myself driven over, you needn't have come!"

"I came because I'll enjoy your company more than my own thoughts, tonight."

She looked up at him as he closed the door behind her and ushered her down the walk to his car. A fitful moon slipped in and out of the trees and a bank of thinning clouds, its thin crescent cold in the November air.

"You're tired, aren't you, Ian? I wish you hadn't let Bella persuade you to dine with them. Come to that, I shouldn't have, either. But Melinda Crawford will be there, and I couldn't let her down."

"Nor I." He settled her into the motorcar with a rug for her knees as before, and then went to crank the engine. As he climbed in beside her, she sighed. It was as if she had had other plans that she'd changed, and regretted having to do so.

Rutledge said as they went down the drive, "Did you ever see the Tarrant exhibition in London before the war? There was a painting there that caused a great deal of comment. The name of it was *Tristan*."

"Richard liked it. I wasn't fond of it," she replied. "He was drawn to flying, you know. I thought the painting made it seem far too glamorous. Or to put it another way, I wasn't eager to praise anything that would encourage his attraction." She laughed bitterly. "I was afraid that flying machines would take him from me. I couldn't even imagine then that war would do that, and I'd be helpless to prevent it. It's not wise to love too well."

Hamish said, "She didna' ken what you were asking about yon portrait."

It was true—Elizabeth had taken Rutledge's question at face value, remembering her husband, not reminded of anyone else.

He said, as if moving on, "No, not wise at all. But Richard was intrigued by the concept of flight. He'd told me once that he would like to see the Downs as a bird could. And how the Weald stretched beyond the horizon we were limited to. He was intrigued with maps, and this was the ultimate opportunity to draw the face of the earth."

"He once talked for hours with Melinda about the project to map India. I think, under different circumstances, he'd have been among the first to volunteer. He was drawn to adventure. Perhaps I never really had him in my heart the way I thought I did."

"He loved you very deeply. It made dreaming very safe, because you were there to come home to."

She moved restlessly. "I'd rather not talk about Richard just now."

He changed the subject, and as they drove through the night reached a truce in whatever silent war lay between them.

RALEIGH MASTERS GREETED his guests with a chilly courtesy.

Rutledge saw his wife glance at him several times, an uneasiness in her eyes. But their host was pleasant and made an effort to draw out his guests. They were seated in a drawing room where the elegance was growing shabby around the edges, as if there was no money to renew the drapes or the gilding in the plastered ceiling. The house, Georgian and foursquare, possessed a beautiful staircase in the entrance hall and a collection of exquisite Venetian glass displayed in cabinets between the doors. The light from the lamps caught the colors and gave them a depth that was jewel-like. Whether the collection was valuable or not, Rutledge couldn't judge, but the quality was there, in shape and design.

Bella had gestured toward the cabinets as she ushered him into the drawing room and said diffidently, "My father's hobby. Glass. My mother traveled to Italy every winter for her health, and in his free time, my father roamed the old markets in Venice, searching for unexpected treasures. Raleigh doesn't care for Italy."

Nor for the glass, Rutledge thought.

Melinda Crawford, looking rather tired, greeted him with warmth and kissed Elizabeth's cheek as if delighted to see her. Brereton, standing by the hearth, shook hands with Rutledge and asked quietly, "Any progress?"

"Early days yet," Rutledge told him. It was the standard formula. But even as he spoke the words, Hamish was reminding him how empty they were.

Brereton said, "Kent has always had an independent spirit. My guess is that whatever people may suspect, they won't point fingers."

Rutledge was saved from answering by a query from Elizabeth regarding a mutual friend in London. Twenty minutes later, as they were finishing their sherry, dinner was announced, and Rutledge found himself escorting Mrs. Crawford. She pinched his arm, as if in warning, as they followed their host and hostess through to the dining room.

"Even if this meal is inedible, you must swallow every mouthful for Bella's sake!" she hissed under her breath.

He smiled and said, "I'll try."

But it appeared the cook was intent on making amends. The roast of pork, seasoned with rosemary, was as delicious as any Rutledge had ever eaten. As the conversation flowed around him, he listened to two threads that seemed to intertwine and then separate.

Local gossip of the ordinary variety, to be heard at any country dinner table in England—and an undercurrent of speculation about the newcomer from Leeds who was buying one of the larger houses in Marling. Whether he intended to live there or if it was purchased for a son or daughter, whether he was the sort one would wish to meet or the sort one ignored.

"There's money," Bella was saying. "And I hear from John Sable that he's renovating the house and gardens."

John Sable owned a small construction firm in Helford, Brereton explained to Rutledge across the table.

"He won't come cheaply," Elizabeth responded. "I'd asked John about working on the drains, and he sent a note quoting an exorbitant sum."

Brereton said, "Too bad our Leeds friend's not interested in the old property out on the road to Seelyham. The one with the stone gates. Shame to see it go to rack and ruin. But I suppose we must wait on the lawyers to sort out who inherits."

Bella nodded. "I remember going to a party there, oh, well before the war. It was Mrs. Morton's seventieth birthday, and her husband wanted to cheer her up a bit. There were lovely old pieces in that house. I remember she was mourning the fact that there was no one to pass them on to. Only a distant relative out in New Zealand, I think it was. Influenza took both of them last year. And the house has stood empty ever since. There'll be damp and dry rot, and heaven only knows what else, before it's finished. And who'll pay for that, I ask you?"

Rutledge found himself thinking that people like the Mayhews and the Hamiltons, and indeed the Masterses, with their declining income and rising prices, would be hard-pressed to keep their homes as once their ancestors had. But the new money, the war money, would manage quite well. The man from Leeds, for one.

"Has anyone actually met this man?" Brereton asked, looking around the table.

After a moment of silence, Elizabeth said tentatively, "I think I may've."

Everyone turned to stare at her, and she went pink. "It was quite by accident and very brief," she said, stumbling over her words. "I'd gone to Helford at the end of last month to meet someone taking the train down from London. And a man was asking the stationmaster about transportation to Marling. He had a rather loud voice, although he was dressed well enough—" She broke off, shrugging. "I didn't see his face."

Rutledge, his attention caught, listened to Elizabeth Mayhew but said nothing.

Hamish murmured, "Ye ken, no one would think to ask the likes of Mrs. Mayhew about strangers . . ."

Raleigh Masters, ignoring the small glass containing his medicine that stood beside his plate, was finishing his fourth glass of wine instead.

The glitter in his eyes was the only thing that betrayed him. He sat like a toad, waiting. Hamish, alert to Rutledge's own watchfulness, growled, " 'Ware!"

As Elizabeth paused, glancing around the table uncertainly as if she'd gone too far, Bella opened her mouth to speak and then closed it sharply.

Raleigh said, "We are an odd lot, we English. We judge a man by his voice. And the price of his clothes. God help us, if we are born brilliant but poor, and have nothing to indicate the quality of our minds."

Elizabeth said, haltingly, "I didn't mean—"

"No, of course you didn't," Melinda Crawford interposed bracingly. "Raleigh is simply reflecting on our propensity to judge from outward appearances. A barrister would certainly not fall into *that* pit."

She was, Rutledge realized, drawing fire on herself.

Masters said, rather nastily, "He won't last long if he does. All the same, there is something to be said for a man's upbringing. It generally tells in the end. As the old saw would have it, you cannot make a silk purse out of a sow's ear."

"I shouldn't care to try," Mrs. Crawford retorted.

"You would tell me, then, that your friendships are all of a sort that reflects well on your judgment of people?"

"I never choose my friends because they reflect well on me. I choose them because they're interesting. I consider boredom far more soul-crushing than the Seven Deadly Sins. And so I have made a point throughout my life never to be bored. It has, I think, kept me young."

But Masters apparently wasn't to be deflected from whatever was on his mind. Rutledge, watching him, was reminded of a prosecutor waiting to pounce. It was, he thought, a natural mannerism in a man who had spent his life judging others.

Masters's eyes swept down the table to his wife's face. "And I, I think, shall never grow old. We learn to put up with distasteful things, at the end."

"Raleigh, it's hardly the *end*—" Bella protested, her voice anguished.

As if he didn't believe her, Masters swept on. "I know whereof I speak, my dear. Otherwise, I shouldn't be reduced to entertaining a *policeman* at my table. People are not overly fond of watching death creep up on themselves or others. But perhaps Mr. Rutledge is accustomed to it."

There was a moment of stunned silence, broken only by the sharp intake of breath from Bella Masters. Her face was pale with embarrassment. Rutledge could feel himself reddening at the insult.

Hamish said starkly, "You canna' quarrel with him."

But before Rutledge could speak, Melinda Crawford was there ahead of him.

"Raleigh," she said in a voice that brooked no argument, "illness is not an excuse for bad manners. You will apologize to all of us for your rudeness!"

He glared at her. She returned the stare with the authority of a woman who has spent a lifetime learning her own worth.

Rutledge thought, *She faced down the Mutineers in India. Masters has forgotten that.*

After a moment Raleigh said, "Why should I apologize, I ask you? He comes to dine in the guise of a guest, but who knows what actually brings him here? Policemen don't have social lives. Or if they do, I've never heard of it. And behind my back he asks questions of a derogatory nature about a man whose boots he is not fit to lick! Matthew Sunderland was my friend and my mentor—"

Rutledge turned to look at Bella Masters. Guilt was written clearly in her appalled expression.

He knew instantly that Elizabeth had spoken to her at his request—and she had passed the query on to her husband.

He replied, "I'm afraid you've misunderstood. I've never spoken derogatorily about Matthew Sunderland. I have expressed an interest in one of his cases. One in which I myself was involved."

"Odd, don't you think?" Masters inquired of the table at large. "Generally when a policeman has a question concerning a trial, he goes to his superiors. This means, I fear, that Mr. Rutledge is afraid he had not prepared his case well enough and wants the reassurance that he is right in his assumption of guilt!"

It was too damned close to the truth, and for an instant Rutledge found himself thinking that Chief Superintendent Bowles had been in touch with Raleigh Masters. But that was not very likely.

Hamish was roaring in his ears, telling him that Masters had seen through him and he had nowhere to turn.

But Rutledge responded with courtesy, "As you were not a party to the trial, sir, I'm afraid I must rely on the opinion of others."

Before his host could frame a retort, Mrs. Crawford was on her feet. "*Raleigh!* You are not only rude, you are very drunk." She turned to the maid standing stricken behind Mrs. Masters's chair. "Will you summon my driver, please? I am leaving. Bella, I must tell you that I will not dine with you again until your husband has apologized to me and everyone present."

Bella, her voice trembling, said, "Mrs. Crawford—Melinda—"

But her husband's voice cut across hers. He was standing now also. Something in Mrs. Crawford's face had finally penetrated the alcoholic haze and touched him.

Or else he had fired all the salvos he'd intended.

"Ladies and gentlemen, I beg forgiveness for my behavior. If you will excuse me, I shall retire. Mr. Rutledge, you have been a gracious and pleasant guest in my home. I don't know what possessed me to attack you, but you must put it down to my intemperance."

Raleigh bowed, retrieved his cane, and walked steadily from the room, closing the door softly behind him. Rutledge had the feeling that he was very nearly sober. . . .

Bella was almost in tears. "I don't know what to say—" she began.

Melinda Crawford replied briskly, "It's better if you say nothing. There is never any defense for rudeness." She signaled to the maid. "I think we're ready for our tea, if you please. And I believe the gentlemen will join us in the sitting room tonight."

She nodded to Elizabeth and Brereton, then said to Rutledge, "You behaved with generosity. My father would have commended you for keeping your temper. But I will tell you that the man who insulted you is not the man I have known for some years. Now, we shall put this behind us and have our tea!"

With a sweep of her skirts, she ushered the still-trembling Bella toward her own sitting room, with Elizabeth at her heels. Brereton said, following them with Rutledge, "It's true. He *isn't* the same man. But that hardly changes anything—"

Rutledge, still seething with anger, smiled and said, "I *am* a policeman, you know. It must be the first opportunity he has had to break bread with one. And it marks a dramatic change in his circumstances."

"All the same—" Brereton began, and then went on, "I would have believed Raleigh Masters was guilty of murder before I would have believed what has become of him."

He stumbled, catching his foot on the edge of the carpet in the hall, and swore. The loss of his eyesight, Rutledge realized, must be worse than Brereton admitted, even to himself.

They drank their tea dutifully, and kept the conversation bright and reasonably unforced. When a proper length of time had passed to do so gracefully, the guests took their leave and left.

Rutledge's last glimpse of Bella Masters's face as she closed the door herself on her departing guests caught the mask of civility slipping and a black despair behind it.

ELIZABETH SAID, AS they reached the road to Marling, "I was never so appalled in my life! Raleigh has been unbearable—but never insulting."

"Don't think about it," Rutledge told her. "He will have to make amends to his wife, now. She'll be hard pressed to find any dinner guest willing to put up with his temper."

"I don't think it's temper," Elizabeth responded, considering it. "It's something else. I don't know . . . death creeping up."

"Enough to make any man despair," Rutledge agreed.

But Hamish was saying from the rear seat, *"I willna' believe it. It's no' death. Nor the wasting. Something else."*

Rutledge tended to agree with him, and returned to the possibility that Chief Superintendent Bowles knew Masters—it wasn't unlikely—and had dropped a hint of some sort. But that didn't make sense, either.

Elizabeth was finishing a remark that he'd missed, ending with "—I shall have to invite Bella to tea. Without Raleigh. To let her know I'm not blaming her for her husband's behavior. She's never quite known how to cope with his moods, you know, but she adores him. There isn't anything she wouldn't do for him."

He was reminded of what Margaret Shaw had said about marriage—that it seldom works out the way it ought to. "What is the medicine he takes in that glass? Laudanum?"

"I suspect it is. For pain initially, of course, but it helps with his—moods."

Or created them?

Elizabeth sighed. "Why do so many people hurt each other?"

He had no answer to that question. And in the silence that followed he remembered the conversation about the house in Marling that had been sold to a wealthy merchant. "Tell me about the man you saw. At the train station in Helford."

"There's really nothing more to tell. He was exceedingly well dressed; you could almost smell expensive tailors. But his voice was overloud, and it grated. New money. That was my first thought."

"Describe him physically."

"I'm not sure I can. It was a nasty evening, and he was wearing a heavy coat and a hat. My guess is that he was fair." She looked across at him. "Tallish, I'd say, but not as tall as you. A bit on the heavy side, perhaps, but with the coat it was difficult to tell. He came rushing into the waiting room, spoke to the stationmaster, and then went out again. I'd been standing inside, out of the weather, but Richard's motorcar was waiting by the gate. He must have seen it! And so I turned away, for fear he might ask if I was driving in the direction of Marling." She smiled ruefully. "He seemed to be the sort who might be—*encroaching.*"

It was inbred in an Englishman's nature, this dread that someone casually met might brashly overstep the unwritten rules of acceptable behavior. It was, perhaps, at the root of Raleigh Masters's abhorrence of a policeman in his house. . . .

A visit to the stationmaster then, tomorrow morning, to follow up on this man Elizabeth Mayhew had seen.

They had reached Elizabeth's house and she was thanking him for driving her. He saw her to her door, and then turned to go.

She called, "Ian."

He turned again. "Yes?"

But whatever it was she was planning to say, she changed her mind. It was visible in her face, however much she tried to hide it. "Perhaps we can have lunch one day. While you're here." Brightly spoken.

"I'd like that," he said. And watched the door close quietly before walking back to his motorcar.

THE LOBBY OF The Plough was empty when he came through, a night lamp burning by the desk and another by the stairs. But when he opened the door to his room, he found a sheet of paper slipped under it. One of the staff had taken a telephone message for him.

It was from Sergeant Gibson. *In regard to the person you'd inquired about. He made it home from France and then ended up in the river. There's a grave to prove it in Maidstone.*

So much for tracking down Jimsy Ridger, Rutledge thought, as he shut his door and began to take off his coat. Yet someone was combing the countryside trying to run the man to earth. Someone without Sergeant Gibson's resources—someone who hadn't discovered the Maidstone grave.

But why was this same person killing men?

"You canna' know it's the same man doing the killing," Hamish reminded him.

"That's true," Rutledge said, answering aloud from old habit when he was alone. The voice seemed so real then that he could almost hear it echoing around the walls.

————

HELFORD WAS A small village, with a tall spired church and a churchyard set behind a low stone wall that boasted the remains of wildflowers in the crevices, a pretty sight in the spring. The main street wound
down a hill, houses and shops spread on either side of it, before curving
away in the direction of Marling. The railway station sat on the northern outskirts, as if added as an afterthought. Which it had been, Helford
itself predating the train by some four hundred or more years. Hop gardens and farms encircled the town, picturesque in the brightening
morning light. Several very nice old houses faced the main street, one of
them pedimented and the other boasting an elegant bay window. There
had been money here, and an air of gentility lingered. The Tudor gate-
house of a sizeable manor house lay at the bottom of the hill, tall and
graceful, with a battlemented facade and an assortment of shields an-
nouncing the proud heritage of the family within. Its aged stone church
lay just up the hill, green lawns and half-buried tombstones visible beyond its wall.

After a courtesy call on Inspector Cawly, Rutledge went in search of
the stationmaster.

The man was still at his breakfast.

"The next train isn't due for another hour," he told Rutledge when
he'd been tracked down to a cottage not far away. "You can wait at the
station, if you like. It's open!"

Rutledge explained his interest in a traveler who had arrived from
the coast one evening at the end of October, during a rainstorm. "He's not
a local man. He was looking for transportation to Marling," he added.

The stationmaster, idly stroking his graying Edwardian beard,
stared at the floor. "Heavy rain, was it? We had only one passenger on
the nine-forty from the south, and the ten-ten was late by two minutes
coming in from London. You're asking about the nine-forty, then, because there was a lady here to meet the passenger on the ten-ten. I've
seen her before, traveling to London on occasion."

A lady. Elizabeth Mayhew . . .

"That would be right."

"He was what you might call a turnip in velvet. And he made a right
nuisance of himself!"

"Indeed."

"After the train pulled out, he came into the station and told me he needed to reach Marling that night. I said I doubted he'd find anyone who would drive him at that hour, in that weather. 'I'm willing to pay whatever is asked. All you have to do is send for someone.' 'Send who?' I wanted to know. I wasn't about to get wet through, running errands for the likes of him. He wasn't best pleased, I can tell you. 'I have to reach Marling,' he said again, as if I was deaf, and finally I told him he'd have to put up at the hotel for the night, and in the morning have Freddy Butler send for one of the lads who regularly take the goods wagon over to Marling. Well, *he* wasn't about to arrive in Marling with the chickens and cabbages, he said. He wanted a proper carriage." The stationmaster chuckled. "If he'd been the gentleman he thought he was, I'd have told him the smith kept a carriage he could have in the morning. He left, cursing under his breath."

Rutledge smiled. "Did he indeed go to the hotel?"

"He didn't. My guess is he was smarter than he looked and knocked on the first door he came to. They'd have sent him to the smith."

"Was there anything more that you noticed about him?"

"He had blue eyes. I'd not have remembered that, but Freddy Butler's son John had eyes the same color, like the summer sky. John didn't come back from Arras."

"How would you describe him? Educated? A Londoner? From the Midlands?"

"And how am I to guess that? He's not a Kent man, I can tell you. I know what a Kent man sounds like!"

"Had you seen him before that night? Or after?"

"He came back this way a day or two later, didn't he, to take the train again. And he looked like the cat that supped on cream. Whatever his business in Marling, he was that pleased about how it went. Cheeky bastard!"

19

AFTER SOME DISCUSSION WITH SERGEANT BURKE AND A HALF
hour of searching, Rutledge ran to earth the agent who was handling the
sale of the house in Marling that the Leeds merchant allegedly had his
eye on.

Mr. Meade was alarmed to be faced with a policeman across his
desk. And a policeman from Scotland Yard at that.

"For if there's anything untoward about this man, the sale will not
go through—" He fiddled with the papers on his desk, fastidiously edging them with one side of the blotter, before moving several envelopes
in the other direction and adjusting the position of the inkwell.

Rutledge said blandly, "I've no reason to believe that he's involved
in any crime. On the contrary, I'm after information that will close
doors, not open them."

Meade was not reassured. "He doesn't live in Kent. At least—he
will, when the sale is completed. I can't see how he could help you. And
I hope it won't be necessary to contact him. It could put him off living
here, to find Scotland Yard on his doorstep about murderers loose in
Marling!"

"All the same," Rutledge persisted, "I need to know whatever you
can tell me about him."

With a sigh, Meade said, "Wealthy. He's prepared to sign for the house, and on his behalf I've already spoken with a man in Helford who can begin renovations immediately, as soon as the paperwork is completed. And that's not all—he wants to restore the gardens. The house was once noted for its gardens. But that's in the spring, of course, when the weather—"

Rutledge said, interrupting, "Describe him, if you will."

"Younger than I'd expected, considering the fact that he's done as well as he has. Fair. Putting on the weight of prosperity, I'd say. I'm told he made his money up north, in Leeds or thereabouts." Meade was clearly more impressed with the man's money than anything else about him.

"Name?"

"Aldrich. Franklin J. Aldrich," the agent responded reluctantly. "The firm originally belonged to his father-in-law, I believe. Mr. Aldrich lost his father-in-law and his wife to the Influenza, and has decided to sell up and move away."

"Why did he choose Kent?"

"The better climate. That's what he told me. I daresay now he's made his money, he'd like to enjoy spending it. And no doubt there's a desire to put some little distance between himself and his roots, if he's looking to set up as a gentleman." Meade seemed to run out of virtues to extol and looked out the window at the busy street.

"How often has Aldrich traveled to Kent?"

"Most of our negotiations have been by letter, through his bankers. He came one weekend at the end of October, to view the property I had described. I'd actually offered him two or three possible choices, but he seemed to be in no doubt about the kind of house he wanted. It explains his success, I should think. Knowing what he wants."

"How did he make his fortune?"

"I haven't—er—felt free to ask him. He's a very private person, actually. He did tell me once that the war had treated him well, and from that I assumed he'd been in manufacturing of one sort or another. That's where most of the money was made."

Aldrich wasn't the first to make a fortune from the war. But even Meade seemed to feel uncomfortable with that. He added, almost as an afterthought, "It's no bad thing for Marling, to have fresh blood coming in." As if in apology for his own eagerness to conclude this sale. "A widower, of course—"

Hamish observed, as Rutledge finished his questions and rose to go, "Yon Aldrich will be good company for Raleigh Masters, when there's no one left to dine wi' him."

Rutledge smothered a smile.

THERE HAD BEEN no time to consider lunch, and Rutledge had bought a pork pie and apples at a small shop on the High Street before calling on Mr. Meade. He finished the apples as he made his way back to the scenes of the killings, drawn by reasons he couldn't explain.

The roads were quiet at this hour of the day, and clouds were building to the east, over the Downs, threatening yet more rain. A cold wind had blown up as he came to the line of trees where Will Taylor had died, and he reached for his coat as he left his car.

What was there about these stretches of country roads, out of sight of witnesses, that had invited murder?

Rutledge had always depended on intuition, on a sense of what was there beneath the surface, unplumbable unless the mind was open to receive whatever swam up from the depths and into the light. He had no way to describe his intuition; he had never really questioned it. But something was there. Not on command—intuition was never amenable to conscious will. It simply responded in its own fashion, with an unexpected knowledge.

He walked the length of the line of trees, and tried to feel some response that would help him understand the terrible thing that had happened here. But nothing came, no small whisper of knowledge or breath of emotion. It was as if these trees, older than he was, open to the wind and elements, to time and space and seasons, had nothing to offer him except mute witness.

Here a man died. We don't know why—

Smiling wryly at his morbid imagination, he went back to the motorcar and turned toward the other two scenes.

Hamish, always at his shoulder, unseen but never mute, had nothing to say, his mood dark.

Rutledge stood at the place where Kenny Webber had died, and listened to the soft soughing of the wind in the bare trees. He was standing so still that a small meadow mouse crept out of the high grass to stare at him before scurrying off to safer ground.

There was nothing, Rutledge told himself, that fitted any particular theory well enough to support it.

But the Shaw case had been much the same. . . .

No clues to the killer of women who had little to steal but whose pitiful treasures had offered a poorer man hope. It had been sheer accident that the police had stumbled on the name of a man-of-all-work who had come to help and ended up killing.

Would it be the same thing here? Would these two cases, seemingly so similar to a man tormented by the past, end up with the wrong suspect hanged?

He shivered at the thought, and turned back to the motorcar.

And Hamish, the practical Scot, whose family tree boasted feuding clansmen through centuries of bloody warfare, insisted, "It isna' the same in the light. It isna' the same . . . The murders happened at night."

Rutledge stopped in his tracks.

And he was walking here in the light, where everything was different.

Even on the battlefield, the night had been different from the day. You could see what was coming in the daylight. You could prepare yourself for defense or attack. At night, sounds seemed to roll in from nowhere; movement was hidden and stealthy. A wind jangling the wire, a man coughing, the unexpected stirring of the rats—nerves, raw and alert, jumped like live things, and eyes watered with trying to pierce the darkness for the first sign of anything that could kill.

Rutledge said, "It's true," and bent to crank the motorcar, his mind already busy.

In the country it was not uncommon for people to walk long distances. There were few means of transportation as available as shank's mare. And a good many of the horses kept for carriages or riding had been swallowed up by the war, to die dragging heavy artillery or wagons in the mud of France, work many of them were not accustomed to.

Bicycles were a common means of getting about in the country—clerics used them, police constables, boys delivering groceries and housewives pedaling into the villages to market.

A bicycle, then, for a man unaccustomed to country distances . . .

And he thought he knew where to find one.

RUTLEDGE WALKED THROUGH the hotel doors and turned toward the dining room, in search of a cup of tea.

The man behind the desk said, "Inspector? There's a letter for you. It came in the morning post."

He turned back, and the man limped around the desk to meet him halfway.

Glancing at it, he couldn't place the writing. It was rounded, curlicued, as if the owner had been at great effort to conceal his or her normal hand.

Going through the dining room door, he tore open the envelope and unfolded the letter.

It had come from Mrs. Shaw.

This woman, he thought tiredly, would haunt him like the husband he'd sent to a doubtful death.

Dear Mr. Rutledge,

I am hoping you are making some progress in the matter of my husband's innocence. I cannot think why you have not come to see Henry Cutter and look for the chain to the locket that is still lying in Mrs. Cutter's chest, where I left it. The locket is proof that someone besides my Ben killed those women, and I don't know why it is taking so long to bring the truth to light! My heart is breaking with the weight of my worry, and yet nothing is happening to help my family recover from this terrible burden. You mustn't let us down! We are counting on you to save us. It is poor recompense for not being able to bring my Ben back to life, but it will give my children a chance to live properly when the stigma is removed from our name. I do not want to die of hard work and hopelessness. It must be God who rectifies the wrong done to my poor husband, but you have it in your power to give something back to me and mine.

    Your trusting servant,
    Nell Shaw.

Rutledge swore under his breath.

She was a master at touching him on the raw. She seemed to see into his soul and find the most certain way of stirring up guilt and mistrust of his own judgment. She had brought her daughter with her, she had come on swollen feet to hunt him down, and she held over his head like the sword of Damocles the knowledge that he may well have failed her and her children.

And yet he was beginning to see, too, the will that must have driven Ben Shaw to murder, to satisfy the needs that this woman had felt were rightfully hers. Middle-aged and far from attractive, Nell Shaw still had a power that was intransigent and unyielding.

And yet Henry Cutter had admired her strength. . . .

He read the letter again. She pleaded as well as any K.C., he thought bitterly, her abilities wasted by her station in life and her limited opportunities.

But was she telling the truth?

He didn't know. Nell Shaw believed it. And that was all that mattered to her.

RUTLEDGE SLEPT FOR four hours. Rousing himself at the end of that allotted time with the internal clock that more than one soldier had taught himself to use—when a lighted match to see the face of a watch spelled death from a waiting sniper or machine-gunner—he dressed in dark clothes and pulled a heavy black sweater over his head. Lacing his boots, he went through a mental checklist. Satisfied that he was ready, he descended the back stairs and slipped out to the hotel yard.

The night porter kept his bicycle there, and from casual observation Rutledge had noted that it arrived at the same time every evening, departing at the same time every morning. In between it was never moved.

Availing himself of it, Rutledge tested the tires and the brakes, and then, reassured that it would serve him well enough, mounted it and rode out into the quiet High Street.

It was a little after ten-thirty by the clock in the church tower as Rutledge looked up at the Cavalier on his plinth, pleased to see that the face was shadowed by the broad-brimmed hat, and the bronze was lackluster in the pale light of the stars. The heavier clouds had blown through as he slept, leaving behind wet roads, a colder wind, and clearing skies.

He pedaled steadily, without haste, a nondescript man on a nondescript bicycle, head down as if tired and looking forward to home and his bed. On the outskirts of Marling he turned toward Seelyham, his eyes already accustomed to the dim light and his ears picking up the night noises: the bark of a fox, off in the fields, an owl calling his mate from the deep shadows close to the trunk of a spreading oak, the whisper of wind through the autumn grasses and the dead stalks of summer. His tires made a rhythm of their own, soft and sibilant, never intrusive.

When he had reached Seelyham, he turned at the crossroads for Helford, a lone traveler with no company except his own. From time to time he whistled, not for his own sake, but to throw off any suspicion that he was himself the elusive murderer. The last thing he wanted, as Hamish had warned, was someone mistaking him for a killer and trying to get in the first blow.

Hamish, unhappy over the heavy shadows and fading moonlight, was wary, as watchful as he had been leaning against the trench walls in France. He'd had a keen eye for movement, while their best shot had stood at his side, with his rifle ready to fire where his corporal pointed. But there was no one here with a rifle, no one to stand guard.

Rutledge had once loved the night. He had been at home in the open spaces of the Downs or the dales of Yorkshire or the valleys of Wales. Like many Englishmen of his time, he had found walking a means of reaching out-of-the-way places where he was completely alone, open to the sounds and smells and mysterious moods of a land inhabited over centuries stretching back in time. Self-sufficient and capable of protecting himself if need be, he had never thought twice about the dangers or the loneliness. Neither superstitious nor overly fanciful, he had felt safe in the dark, however strange the place, however far from civilized society it might lie.

This, after all, was England. . . .

France had taught him a different kind of night. With star shells and artillery fire and snipers and dread of the first faint glow of morning when the gas came over. Night didn't cloak; it concealed, and death lay in the blackness of a shell hole or behind the blasted trunk of a tree. Death came out of the night as often as it came out of the day, but in the night it could break a man's nerve.

Such memories were only just beginning to fade a little. The space of a year had taken the edge off the tension and the watchfulness but had failed to put them behind him. The year had given Rutledge back the ability to sleep through a night, and to look people in the eye without wondering what they could read in his face. But Hamish was still there. His uncertainties were still there. And unexpected shocks still threw him into the chaos of self-doubt, an awareness of the changes that had not yet come. Might never come.

Hamish reminded him of the Roman candles at the Guy Fawkes bonfire, and Rutledge winced at the memory. It was stupid to react irrationally to fireworks. And yet fear and its blood-brother, self-preservation, were so deeply buried in the very marrow of a soldier's bones for so long that they were hard to root out. To start at sounds and sudden movement, to act primitively and quickly, was the difference between living and dying. Even when he had wanted so badly to die, the body—and bloody luck—had taken the choice out of his hands.

Fear and courage—and boredom. The three faces of battle.

Rutledge threw off the past and concentrated on the night. But there was no one abroad, not on the roads he had chosen to take.

He paused from time to time, standing astride his bicycle and listening. Feeling the darkness, feeling the loneliness. The three men killed here were at home on these roads; they knew them intimately. And this familiarity was their shield—as well as their gravest peril. They considered themselves to be safe—and so they would be vulnerable, unsuspecting.

A farmer passed with a sick calf in the back of his cart, calling to Rutledge with the cautious voice of a man who was worried about strangers on the road, after three murders. Rutledge answered him, say-ing, "Far to go?"

"My son's a better cowman than I am. He's willing to try his hand at saving her."

"Good luck, then."

"Thank'ee. I may have need of luck before the night's done." The farmer spoke to his horse and, before he was out of sight, turned down a narrow lane toward the distant shapes of a barn and a house.

Rutledge rode on, already beginning to think he was on a wild-goose chase and needed good fortune himself. But now he knew that whoever stopped these men had been considered by each victim to be "safe. . . ."

With Hamish carrying on a conversation in the back of his mind, Rutledge reached Helford and then turned back toward Marling. The muscles in his legs were beginning to complain about the unaccustomed exercise, and he ignored them.

This part of Kent was vast enough that three roads hardly touched the sum of choices that he could have made. Still, Rutledge had passed all three murder scenes, waiting for his senses to be tweaked, for some-thing in the quiet night to speak to him, but there were only the foxes and owls and once a hunting cat, frozen in a tense crouch as he came upon her. With a twitch of her tail, she had jumped into the tall grass and vanished. Dogs barked at his passage, desultory and without feroc-ity, as if merely doing their duty.

The wind had picked up, cold knives cutting through his sweater.

A motorcar was ahead of him for a short distance, turning off into a side lane that Rutledge hadn't noticed before. On the map it had ap-peared to go nowhere, down to a wooded stream and up the hill beyond to a field. He pedaled on, staying with the main roads rather than break off from his triangular sweep.

In the end he came back to Marling empty-handed. Tonight there was nothing in the darkness that wanted to be found. . . .

He would have to try again.

20

RUTLEDGE SECURED THE NIGHT PORTER'S BICYCLE WHERE he had found it, and wearily made his way to the back door of the hotel. It was still unlocked, just as he had left it hours earlier. So much for the night porter's rounds. The man would most likely be asleep somewhere warm and quiet.

Rutledge was thinking too that somewhere warm and quiet would be inviting, as he moved through the empty kitchens and service quarters to the door that led into the lobby. Letting it shut silently behind him, he strode swiftly down the passage and rounded the stairs with one hand on the newel post.

"*'Ware!*" Hamish spoke sharply in his mind.

A woman coming down the steps toward Rutledge, her coat open in the warmth of the hotel, gasped in startled disbelief at what seemed to be a dark and sinister figure hurrying toward her.

In the same instant Rutledge recognized Elizabeth Mayhew and stopped stock-still in surprise at finding her here of all places, and at this hour.

"Ian?" she said uncertainly. "Is that you?"

"Elizabeth?"

"Ian, you must come—for the love of God, you must come! I don't know what else to do—!" she said with breathless intensity. "Oh, please—!"

She reached him where he stood at the bottom of the stairs, her fingers clutching the thick, dew-wet knit of his sweater, pleading with him. Her face was streaked with tears and tight with fear.

"I didn't know what to do—I knocked and knocked—you weren't there—*I didn't know where to turn!*"

He took her hands in his, holding them firmly. His were cold from the night air, but she didn't seem to notice. "Elizabeth. Take a deep breath and tell me what's wrong."

"There isn't time—could we go in your motorcar? I ran all the way from the house. I don't think I have the strength to *walk* back!"

Indeed, she looked to be at the end of her tether. Rutledge led her to one of the lobby chairs but she refused to sit. "No, we must go! *He's bleeding!*" The last words came out with a sob.

Rutledge said, "The motorcar is in the hotel yard. This way." He took her through the kitchen passages, where he himself had just walked moments before, and out through the small flagstoned entry that led to the back gardens and sheds.

She sat huddled in the car as he drove fast down the High Street, and he glanced at her once or twice to see if she was all right. As they pulled up in the drive beside her house, she was out and running before he could stop the engine. Swearing under his breath, he followed her.

She came to a halt at the main door, bending over something on the front steps. Rutledge was beside her in time to see a man's face lift up from the cradle of his arms, the features twisted with pain. Even in the faint light of the stars, the face seemed unnaturally pale. The man's hair was dark with sweat, and it was hard to judge its normal color.

"Who is he?" Rutledge asked Elizabeth. "How did he get here?"

"I had gone to Lydia Hamilton's for a women's committee meeting, and when Lawrence brought me home—he was *here*! Oh, please, do something!"

"Did Lawrence see him?"

"No! No, I told him I could find my own way—"

Rutledge knelt down beside the figure. "Are you hurt? Tell me where."

Elizabeth said, "His shoulder. His chest. I don't know. When I tried to help him to his feet, there was blood everywhere. It was *horrible!*"

"Knife," the man managed to say. One hand groped toward his left side.

Rutledge pulled away the heavy cloth of the man's coat and felt the hot warmth on the sweater under it. His hand came away black with blood.

"We've got to get him inside, and send for a doctor," he said.

"No—" The injured man's voice was firm as he spoke the single word, echoed almost immediately by Elizabeth's breathless "No!"

"Nonsense," Rutledge responded briskly, and held out his hand. "Your key, Elizabeth."

She hesitated. Then she gave it to him, torn between worry and what seemed to be a fear of bringing the stranger inside.

Rutledge was already heaving the man to his feet, noting with relief that he seemed to have both arms and both legs. And there was no wine on his breath—

There was a small lamp burning in the entrance hall, left for Elizabeth's return. Beyond that table was an ornate Jacobean chair, and Rutledge got his burden lowered into it just as Henrietta, the spaniel, began to bark ferociously from behind the closed door of the sitting room. Distractedly Elizabeth called to the dog to hush.

"Go to her, or you'll have every servant in the house down here to see what's happening," Rutledge commanded. And Elizabeth hurried off, calling the dog's name and shushing her.

The man slumped in the chair seemed to be slipping in and out of consciousness, his head rolling on his shoulders. Rutledge, working swiftly, managed to get the coat off and was just lifting the sweater to rip it and clear the wound when his eyes met those of his patient. He froze, staring.

Gentle God! It was the face from the bonfire—it was the German!

In the poor light of the stars, with the grimace of pain distorting the man's features, Rutledge had failed to notice any resemblance.

And even as he stepped back in alarm, the pain-filled blue eyes stared back at him, recognition—and resignation—in them.

———

THE MAN STARTED to say something, shook his head, and then found the words in English.

"A long way from France." His voice was quiet, pitched so that Elizabeth couldn't hear him. Her soothing words to the spaniel had roused the puppies, and they were whimpering.

Rutledge, with Hamish hammering at the back of his mind, asked harshly, *"Who the hell are you?"* A dozen images pressed and overlapped and faded with such speed that he was unable to sort through them or comprehend their significance. He was on a road—a road filled with figures, men he didn't know—there were caissons and lorries, abandoned where they stood—voices he couldn't understand—confusion, and a blank, impenetrable haze. . . .

"Don't you know? I've come—" The man winced, caught his breath, and went on, "—I've come back from the dead."

"You don't belong here—"

"True. Yes. I know that."

Rutledge's mind was reeling, fighting shock and disbelief.

And then relief surfaced, the realization that what he'd seen on Guy Fawkes Day two weeks before had been no hallucination, no slippage of the mind into madness. The man was real. *He was real.*

Rutledge had no idea who he was—or where he had come from—except out of the darkness of war.

And Hamish was saying, *"But he's deid. You said yoursel' he's deid."*

"I thought you were dead," Rutledge found himself repeating aloud. "I watched you die!"

"Yes. Well. I am hard to kill." The man shivered, and Rutledge came back to the present, staring at the warm blood on his fingers, at the sweater thick with it. He reached out and fumbled for an instant, lifting the heavy wet wool, then found his pocket knife and began to cut it away. With his hands busy, his mind seemed to anchor itself, as if rejecting anything but the work that needed to be done.

He could hear Elizabeth walking back down the passage, her feet hurrying.

The man cautioned hastily, "We will talk about the war another time. Not now."

She came into the hall, moving quickly to help Rutledge pull away the last of the ripped yarn, gasping at the dark wet blood all over the man's shirt.

Rutledge cut the shirt in its turn, saying to Elizabeth, "Water. Hot if you can manage it, and cloths. Bandages. Then send someone for the doctor." His voice sounded different in his ears, strained and brutal.

She went away quickly to do his bidding, but not before he'd seen the glance exchanged between the German and Elizabeth.

"Leave her out of this," the German was saying. "She has nothing to do with this. I will go with you to the doctor. You must not bring him to this house. It would cause—" He stopped and caught his breath again. "—It will cause comment. Talk. What do you call it?"

"Gossip. You should have thought of that before passing out on her doorstep."

"I had very little choice. I was nearer this house than where—where I am living now."

"You're a German national." Rutledge was still trying to sort through it.

The man managed a smile. "Even German nationals need a—need a roof when they travel. This hurts like the very devil!"

The knife blade had slashed down from the shoulder across another, older wound that had scarred over on the man's chest. Deep, but not dangerously so. Rutledge, working carefully, explored the wound.

"Someone didn't very much care whether they killed you or not," he told the German. "What had you done to him, to deserve this?"

"I had done nothing. I was walking along the road, my coat over my—over my arm. There was a man at the side of the road. As I came closer, he hobbled out and struck. Then he was—he was gone."

Sweat was running down the man's face. His jaw, set now against another wave of pain, quivered with the effort to keep himself alert.

Elizabeth came back with the water in a kettle, and cloths with which to bathe the wound lying across a basin. She handed them to Rutledge and stood back, looking close to fainting herself.

"Go find the doctor," Rutledge told her, pouring the water into the basin and dipping a cloth into it. Almost too warm, he thought; the stove must have just been banked for the night.

But she stood there, mesmerized, unable to move.

Rutledge cleaned up the wound as best he could, unable to staunch the bleeding even with the water and pads of cloths. In the end, he simply packed it and wound strips of linen around it. It reminded him, more than he cared to admit, of his own wound, hardly a month healed.

"The cook," Hamish was saying, "willna' know where her tea towels have got to."

And Rutledge saw the embroidered initials on one of the strips. An absurdity in the nightmare. Like all nightmares, he thought to himself. . . .

"Give him something to drink. Whisky, with a little of the hot water to dilute it," he said to Elizabeth, and like a sleepwalker, she turned away to do as he asked.

The German drank it down gratefully, when she handed him the crystal glass, and he gave it back to her with a wry smile. "However will you explain this to the servants tomorrow?" he asked, glancing at the bloodied cloths and the basin full of dark red water.

It was as if he were trying to tell her to get rid of the evidence of his presence. Elizabeth, starting awake from her shock, said, "I'll—I'll deal with it." She bent down to lift the basin of water at Rutledge's feet and nearly dropped it as she looked into the bloody depths.

As she walked away to pour it out, forgetting the kettle sitting on the floor by the chair, the German said, "You have a motorcar? I thought I heard one before you came."

"Yes. It's in the drive."

"Then if you will get me out of here, I will tell you whatever you want to know."

"I'm taking you to the local doctor, and then to the police station."

"No, I think you will not do eith—either of these things once you—once you have heard what I have to tell you." He tried to stand, to pull his coat over his bare shoulders. But the effort was too much. He sank back in the chair, saying ruefully, "I think you must help me again. I don't quite seem to know—to know where my feet are!"

Elizabeth came back, picked up the bloody towels and strips of clothing with distaste, and carried them away with the kettle.

She said, returning, "I put the cloths in the stove. It's an awful smell!

But they'll burn." She looked up at Rutledge expectantly, as if waiting for him to solve all their problems.

Hamish said, "She wants him to go. But she isna' happy with his going."

Indeed, she seemed to be torn, her hands gripping each other tightly, the knuckles white as the silence in the hall lengthened.

Rutledge said peremptorily, "Elizabeth, go to bed. I'll see to him. You look as if you'll fall down any minute. He's not dying. There's nothing more you can do. He needs better medical care than this—" He gestured to the rough bandaging.

Rousing herself with an effort, she said angrily, "Just because you're a policeman—" And then she stopped, thoroughly ashamed.

"It's because I'm a policeman that I'm telling you to go to bed," he answered without heat. "Leave this to me. He will live, and I'll see to him."

She stared at him for an instant longer and then, without looking at the German, walked to the staircase.

21

It was with some difficulty that Rutledge got the wounded man out of the Mayhew house and into the motorcar. Afterward he walked back through the open door and looked around the room. There was no sign that they had been there, neither blood nor bits of cloth nor shifted furniture. He went out again, shutting the door firmly behind him.

The man in the passenger seat was slumped to one side, as if trying to cushion the torn muscles of his shoulder.

Hamish was asking, "Where does your duty lie, then? Ye canna' protect the lass from this folly."

It was true. Throw the German into a police cell, and by morning Elizabeth would be pounding on the door demanding to see him. Folly indeed—

"She's no' the only person who has seen him," Hamish reminded him. "He canna' go free!"

There was the Webber child, for one. And certainly Miss Whelkin, in Seelyham, who had described Tristan. And the drunk on the road? Holcomb. Would he be able to identify this man? Witnesses indeed. And even though they had failed to place the accent the German strove to conceal, they were all certain that he was not a Kent man.

"They wouldna' know him for a German. He speaks verra' well!"

Rutledge cranked the motor and got in, thinking rapidly.

The wound was clean enough, and bandaged well enough despite the simple field dressing he'd applied to stop the worst of the bleeding. There was time—time to decide whether he carried this man to the doctor, or directly to the police station, leaving it to Dowling to summon the doctor.

Hamish was muttering behind him—loudly enough, or so it seemed, to be heard by all but the very deaf.

"I can't deal with it now," he silently responded. "Leave it!" He pulled out of the driveway and drove back into the center of Marling, stopping his vehicle under the gaze of the Cavalier.

Beneath the broad brim the eyes seemed to bore into Rutledge's, as if judging him.

Rutledge looked away and took the car out of gear, setting the brake. He turned to consider his companion.

As if sensing his attention, the other man struggled back to alertness.

"I know who you are." Rutledge spoke with more confidence than he felt. "You're a German officer. That much has come back to me. I don't know why you should be in Britain, much less here in Kent. I don't know why a man should stab you without provocation. If I'm to decide what to do with you, I need the truth."

The man said nothing. And in the lengthening silence, under the barrage of Hamish's complaint, Rutledge was thrown back to another time—another place . . .

THERE HAD BEEN speculation since the beginning of the month, the first of November, a year ago now. The Allies had made great strides—the Germans were in disarray—Berlin had been taken over by a Revolutionary council—the Kaiser was to lead his troops out of France to restore order at home—there was widespread famine in Germany—negotiations for a truce had begun—broken down—It was impossible to separate truth from rumor.

The only certainty was that the fighting and dying hadn't stopped.

And then, on 11 November, word came down just after nine in the morning that a document had finally been signed and an Armistice would go into effect at the eleventh hour of that day. Not a victory. A truce to end the stalemate.

The news had left Rutledge in emotional turmoil. Torn between an unspeakable relief for his men and an overwhelming weight of guilt for failing so many of them—the thousands who hadn't lived to see this day—he moved in a fog of mental exhaustion. Faces, living and dead, seemed to crowd his mind, and the wording of the kind letters he'd written to parents of men he hardly knew, killed before they had had a chance to serve as more than cannon fodder, seemed to float in his brain. For more than two years, he'd seen himself as a dead man, like them; it was only a matter of time before he joined them. And now the war was ending. While he was still alive—

As watches moved slowly toward the appointed hour, the fighting never faltered. And then—without fanfare or flourish—it ended. Men were standing in the trenches, half dazed by the silence, uncertain at first, some openly weeping. Exhausted, weary beyond the ability of sleep to renew their spirit, they were wary of celebration, lest it lead to another disappointment, another grief. Numbed and unprepared, they had nothing to say.

Then one or two men climbed warily over the top for the last time, moving to stand by the first rolls of wire, staring across the devastated landscape that was once the rolling green farmland of northern France, before tons of shells and thousands upon thousands of bodies had been ground into the earth by the madness of war.

Men began to touch each other, began to laugh with nervous humor, began to acknowledge that they were alive, that they had survived— and then looked around as if half expecting to find the shades of the dead staring sadly back at them. Soldiers came to wring Rutledge's hand and thank him for bringing them through. Others were hugging each other in a rising euphoria, and then stopping, as if not knowing what they should rightfully be doing. Ashamed of feeling at all.

A few Germans had come out of their trenches, staring at the English lines, their faces grim, their shoulders slumped with despair and relief.

Someone called across No Man's Land; someone responded in the other lines. And then it was quiet for a time, as if men who had fought so long and so hard had nothing else to do with their lives, and felt the emptiness of nothing behind them, nothing ahead of them.

Rutledge began to issue orders, parroting the instructions he'd been given. A single voice pitched to normal levels sounded strange without the backdrop of battle or the silence of anxious waiting. One by one his men turned to listen to him. These soldiers who would, if the war had gone on for another week, another month, have died soon, and by his hand—led out to fight and suffer while he himself survived—were finally going home.

War *was* suffering. For the wounded, for the survivors, for their families at home, for the bled-out land around them and the dead horses and stark blasted trees that bore no resemblance to anything living.

As he spoke, it began slowly to dawn on him that he, too, was going to survive. After all, he would not die. It was such a horrific realization that he couldn't cope with it. His mind went blank, and even the voice of Hamish MacLeod, his constant and unrelenting companion since the summer of 1916, was stilled.

He had no memory of what happened after that. Where he had gone, what he had done, how he had managed to simply walk away. This man, bleeding in his motorcar long after the war had finished, knew more than he did. Dr. Fleming at the clinic must have known a little about the blank days from official reports. There had been compassion in the doctor's eyes, and it had hurt Rutledge more than the truth might have done. But Fleming had refused to tell him. It was, the doctor felt, far safer for his patient to come to it naturally. . . .

THE GERMAN WAS watching him. "I saw you at that ridiculous bonfire. And again on the road, when you tried to run me down. As a matter of interest, why did you leave me, back there in France? I was still alive!"

Rutledge said, holding on to reality with a grip that was iron, "I don't remember the end of the war. I don't remember you—or, yes, I do, a little, but only since the bonfire."

"You don't remember anything about ending up deep behind our lines? What the devil were you doing there? We looked up and there you were, standing within feet of us. Terrified us; we thought at first you were a dead man—some apparition out of hell! Someone spoke to you—"

Rutledge closed his eyes, and in the blackness there, like a flickering scrap of film, he found images. He had been walking—he had no idea where he was going, or why. And eventually he'd come to a road, for there were men all around him and voices buffeting him, making no sense—

He had stood there, waiting to be shot . . . waiting for oblivion.

The German beside him was saying something, but Rutledge couldn't shut out the images now.

All he had wanted was for the pain to end. For the blessed release of a single shot. Instead, some half a dozen soldiers had turned toward him, a montage of faces with moving lips, defeated, tired eyes, and the filth of the trenches filling the cold November air.

One of the Germans had stepped forward, staring hard at Rutledge, then mimicking reaching for a cigarette to offer him. And then he took his hand back again with a shrug, when Rutledge made no move to accept it.

He didn't want a cigarette—he wanted to be shot.

An officer came then, looking closely at his irregular visitor. And then he was saying something to his men.

The two of them were walking side by side, away from the rest. Rutledge thought, *He doesn't want to shoot me in front of them* . . . and was content.

There were so many soldiers at first. And then the road seemed empty, and darkness was coming down. Not the darkness in his mind, but the early dusk of November. He found himself wondering if this was still the eleventh, and where the officer was taking him. One body lying along the road here would be anonymous, forgotten.

His sister would probably never know what had become of him. Just as well—it would spare her the shame—

He lost track of time. He couldn't be sure whether he'd been following the German for a few minutes or for far longer. The only anxiety he felt was whether the man would lose his nerve and not shoot.

There was some sort of exchange—furious and loud-voiced. Unexpected, jarring. And as Rutledge struggled to make sense of it, there was a shot at close range.

In the split second after the report, as the echo faded, Rutledge gratefully waited for the pain, for the spreading agony and for the death that would end it.

But it didn't come. There was nothing—

He turned toward the German officer, confused, unable to understand how the man had missed—and watched the German fall in slow motion to the ground, a dark red bloom opening on his tunic.

"No!" He had shouted the single word in disbelief. Somehow they had shot the wrong man—

And then with the swiftness of habit, he was on his knees, ripping open the buttons, fumbling in his pocket for a dressing, stuffing it into the bubbling wound. But before he could staunch the bleeding, the German officer sighed and went limp.

Rutledge became aware that there was someone standing over them. Rutledge looked up, seeing him clearly for the first time. A refugee—an old man—

"I need dressings—a doctor—*un médicin—vite!*"

"Il est mort," the Frenchman said contemptuously. *"Bien sûr."* And then in rough English, "One less Boche."

Rutledge looked down and saw that there was a pistol in the old man's hand, still pointed at the German's throat.

"You should be glad, Englishman. They killed enough of you. They killed my wife and my child in the bombardment, these bastards."

Rutledge staggered to his feet, his mind suddenly clear and fury wracking him.

The Frenchman shrugged. "They nearly took Paris that time. I said I'd get even. God has been good. He has offered me many chances." The venom in his voice was as shocking as what he'd just done. The German hadn't even had time to draw his Luger in self-defense.

He spat on the still body. Stooped, his hair a straggling gray under an old beret, a twisted foot, with hatred burning in his eyes and the madness of revenge burning in his soul, he looked a last time at his victim. Then he walked on, as gnarled fingers began to reload the pistol, stroking it like a mother fussing over her child.

Rutledge found his own pistol and raised it to bring the man down—and then held his fire.

There had been enough killing. *Enough. Enough—*

He tried to revive the German, and when that failed, he walked on.

"I THOUGHT YOU were dead," Rutledge told the wounded man. "I watched you die." He had said the words before—this time he understood them.

"I lost consciousness. From the collapsed lung. Thank God someone else came that way, and got me to hospital. Did you kill that old fool? He was insane!"

"He'd lost his family," Rutledge said tiredly. "You were there, and he shot you. Because you were wearing a German uniform." He didn't add the final irony, that the old man's family had died forty years before, in another war. It didn't signify anyway.

The German sighed. "And what the hell were *you* doing, coming through the German lines like a sleepwalker! Scared the hell out of us! Was it a head wound? I've never seen such agony in one man's face. You just stood there, as if you wanted to be shot and put out of your misery."

"I did," Rutledge said.

After that shooting, he must have walked until he was too exhausted to carry on. He never knew for certain where or when he'd been stopped. Someone had given him strong coffee, and let him sleep, and soon after he must have been turned over to a doctor and a pair of nursing sisters. He remembered the bitter odor of disinfectant on their clothes as they took him in charge: a silent, gray-faced officer with no visible wounds and no way of communicating.

He was shipped to England finally, a tag pinned to his coat giving rank and name and destination. Like so much baggage. He knew he'd crossed the channel—the smell of the vomit of seasick men filled the compartment.

After that, nothing. A man with no memory save for a voice in his head that no one else could hear, and nowhere to go that wasn't another living hell. A man who was already dead and had not found a way to die. Until one doctor, found by his distraught sister, had unlocked the silence and made him feel again.

It was the one thing he had prayed would never happen. *He had not wanted to go home. . . .*

22

TRYING TO CLEAR HIS HEAD, TO CONCENTRATE ON THE PRES-
ent and leave the past, Rutledge reached across the motorcar and examined the bandaging on the German's chest. "You're bleeding again.
Which is it to be, the doctor or the police? I'm too tired to care."

"I don't want either. I want to get out of Marling and back where I
belong—"

He stopped, as if he'd said too much.

"Where *do* you belong?" Rutledge asked. The cold night air was beginning to smell of dawn. He wondered how many people, looking out
their windows, had seen the odd sight of a London policeman and a
wounded German ex-soldier sitting together in a motorcar in the middle of the square, for all the world like old friends.

"I belong in Germany, damn it. But there's nothing there. No food,
no work, no hope. I came here using a cousin's papers—Gunter Manthy
is Dutch, but through our mothers, a Friesian, like me—because I was
looking for something stolen from me during the war. It happened—"
He stopped, swallowing the pain. "It happened when I was briefly
taken prisoner by a unit from Kent. The thing's valuable. At least to my
family it is. I shouldn't have carried it with me when I went to fight, but
it had belonged to every soldier in my family since the time of Frederick

the Great. It was a talisman, to bring me home safely. If I can find it I shall have to sell it. I have nothing else of value—except a farm which no one can afford to buy and that no one will work with me unless I can pay them. The money will take me—me and my children—to Chile or Argentina, away from Germany. I must find it. I can't go home empty-handed. You don't know what it is like there now."

"And that's why you've been killing these ex-soldiers, because they didn't have it? Or won't tell you who does? How many more have died, that we know nothing about?" He thought, *How shall I tell Elizabeth—*

"I haven't killed anybody, damn it!" the German retorted wearily. "But who—whoever it was nearly got *me* killed tonight! I tell you, he was stabbing me before I could even throw up an arm to stop him! It was worse than the war—in the war, you *knew* to be on your guard!"

Rutledge rubbed his eyes. They felt as if sand had scoured them. "Don't lie to me. I've proof that you've been searching for Jimsy Ridger!"

The German stared at him. "Who told you that?"

Rutledge waited.

After a moment, the German said, "Yes, all right. His name was given me when I protested to an officer as we arrived behind your lines. 'Ask for Jimsy Ridger. Tell him it's an order. He's to give it back.' But Ridger had returned to the trenches. And no one could tell me how to find him there."

"What did he take from you?"

"A small silver traveling cup. Very beautifully chased. And the—the story told in my family is this: Since the Friedrichtasse came into our possession, we've survived every war we've fought in. I wanted very much to come home again. And I foolishly carried it with me."

"How valuable is it?"

"In pounds? I can't tell you. I was hoping I might sell it to a museum, or to the Treasury in the church at Oldenburg, I don't know. But to the highest bidder, certainly." He let his head fall back on the seat. "I'm hurting like hell. What are you going to do with me? I can't sit here any longer."

Rutledge took a deep breath. "There are witnesses. A woman in Seelyham . . ."

"Yes, in the churchyard. A busybody. I left there as soon as she was out of sight."

"A child . . ."

"Yes, yes, he was very nice. I did him no harm."

"But he believes he saw his father's killer."

"His father was dead before I could find and speak with him."

"And a drunken ex-soldier you stopped on the road."

"He told me a lie. But I suppose I'd have done the same in his shoes."

"It's evidence enough, given a good prosecution, to see you hanged." But there was another agenda besides hanging. And Rutledge had come face to face with it. "Where are you living?"

"If I tell you," was the wry retort, "you'll have grounds to take me in charge anyway."

"I haven't rejected the idea. With Mrs. Mayhew?"

"God, no. In an empty house. Out on the Marling road. Close by where the first soldier was killed. I told you, it was grounds—"

Rutledge put the engine in gear. "I want to see for myself."

"There's not much to see. Except in the kitchen, where I have made a bed for myself. I'm not a vandal. I needed a safe haven, and I can't afford to pay for it."

"Is that why you're courting Elizabeth Mayhew?"

The German moved too quickly and swore furiously. "I am not going to hurt her! But she has been kind, and I didn't know where else to turn tonight."

I'm not going to hurt her—

How many men had said that—and then had done it anyway?

Hamish insisted, "I canna' believe a word he's told you!"

"You've already hurt her," Rutledge replied as he turned the motorcar. "She's vulnerable, and she thinks she's in love. Is there a wife back in Germany?"

"She died when my son was born. I have not made love to Mrs. Mayhew!"

"No. But you didn't need to. She's already compromising herself for your sake. If you don't find this cup of yours, will you convince her to marry you, and use her money instead?"

"I tell you, I have not hurt her! I can't—I won't. I've come— believe me or not as you choose. But I swear she will come to no harm through me!"

The damage, Rutledge thought, had been done. Small wonder that Elizabeth Mayhew had never had the courage to tell him where her heart lay.

IT WAS ALONG the Marling road near a burned-out oast house that the German roused himself, and said, "Just there. I was stabbed there." He pointed clumsily with his good arm. "See for yourself, there is no body lying about—not even mine!"

Rutledge stopped the motorcar and got out to examine the road in the light of his headlamps. But there was not much to see. Several scuff marks, but no blood.

Hamish commented, "The sweater would have soaked first."

Which was true enough.

Rutledge walked along the verge on either side of the road, finding himself a sturdy stick with which he could probe the tall grasses and bushes, laying them aside to look beyond them. If a body had been left here, it was gone now. Or had crept away—

He got back into the motorcar, and the German demanded, "Did you see?"

"I'll come back at first light. There's nothing now. Neither your blood nor anyone else's."

The German grunted. "Then you must be blind," he accused. "Or else determined not to see."

Rutledge made no comment, driving on into the night.

"I DON'T KNOW your name," Rutledge told the man beside him as the motorcar turned down the dark and rutted drive that led between the stone posts and up to the empty house, the dry grass thrashing against the coachwork.

"Hauser. Gunter Hauser," the German said, rousing himself again. "If there is whisky in that house, I shall drain the bottle!"

He directed Rutledge around to the rear of the house, where a yard door had been pried open, then held closed again with a bit of wire.

For a manor house, this one was small—a country squire's home rather than a grand estate—with gardens along the south front and out-buildings in a courtyard formed by the stables on the west. There was an air of solidity about the house, and at the same time a forlornness, as if the last owners had not foreseen the straits to which it had come: wait-ing for the lawyers to settle the family's affairs and find a relative who had probably never seen nor ever wanted the responsibility for the fam-ily dwelling. The gardens, standing out in the headlamps as Rutledge turned the car, were overgrown with a summer's weeds, their outline no longer sharp and clear. Nature had already begun her efforts to reshape the manicured paths between the beds, and grass lifted seed heads like small rockets in the darkness. The paint on the outbuildings had begun to flake and peel, giving a scabrous look to the walls where the head-lamps spread them with light. A window high in the stable had blown in from a windstorm, and the air of decay all around the yard seemed to promise a dreary interior.

With some difficulty, Rutledge managed to get the German into the stone-flagged kitchen and, after the man had lit a lamp on the table, de-posited him in the nearest chair. Hauser's face was gray with pain and ex-haustion. Rutledge himself felt like falling asleep where he stood. Instead, he walked along the passage toward the formal rooms of the house.

The stairs ran up into blackness beside him as he reached the main hall; paintings or mirrors, carefully shrouded and secretive, climbed the wall beside the steps.

Dust sheets covered the furniture like shadowy ghosts, looming out of the darkness without sufficient definition to betray what was beneath them. Here, he thought, in the drawing room, must be a piano, and over there, a square table. And a cabinet or a chair here . . .

He lifted that sheet to look under it, and found a drinks cabinet with cut-glass decanters still half full. Taking up a pair of them, he walked back to the kitchen.

He found Hauser leaning on his good arm, lips tight against the pain.

"Here." Rutledge set the decanters on the table beside him and crossed to the cabinets to find something to put the whisky in. "In for a penny, in for a pound. I don't suppose anyone will care, anyway, if we drink all of it."

The dishes had been packed away. Settling for two clean jam jars, he came back and poured a stiff drink in one of them, a smaller amount in the other. Adding water from a metal pitcher, he pushed the full glass toward the German.

The man drank, shuddering. "Thank you. I should have seen that doctor, after all. But there would have been too many questions."

Rutledge was silent.

"So." After a moment, the man said, "What is it you want with me? There's something. Or you would have handed me over to the local police." The blue eyes, narrowed with effort, studied Rutledge intently.

Unwilling to be led too far too soon, Rutledge said thoughtfully, "There's enough evidence to hang you. You know that. We haven't found any other explanation for these murders. Witnesses. Motive. Opportunity. Only what points to you."

"I haven't come here to kill Englishmen. I was sick of that long before the war ended."

"There may be good wine left in the cellars of this house. Did you use it to trick your victims? There's your weapon." He watched the face before him with interest. "A good K.C. could bring a conviction." Suddenly he could see an image of Raleigh Masters in a courtroom, using his voice and his dry wit to shape the thinking of a jury. . . .

"You can't kill men with wine." The German's voice was bitter.

"No. But you can with laudanum."

"I have no laudanum."

"You're resourceful. You'd find it if you wanted it. A few drops in the glass, to start with, and then more in the second glass. The victim would be drowsy by then, and not realize how dangerously close to disaster he was. Especially if he's already taking the medication for pain. Did you bring them here, and kill them?" Rutledge looked around the kitchen, with the bedclothes heaped in one corner, nearest the stove. "You could drag them out and find some means of carrying them off. A bicycle. A horse borrowed in the night. A handcart. Leaving them beside the road, where someone would discover them sooner or later . . ."

The German said appreciatively, "It's a clever picture you've drawn. A jury would no doubt believe it. As a matter of interest—having left me for dead once—would it sit well with your conscience if I was hanged?"

Rutledge flinched. "No." And then as if the words were drawn out of him against his will, he said, "Where did you find me? When the war had ended?"

He tried to keep his voice steady. He failed.

Hauser looked at him. "You really don't know? No. If I had a map, I could probably show you. One of my men asked you if you had any English cigarettes. We had none, and no beer either. But you merely stood there. Damnedest thing I'd ever seen! And you don't remember?"

"Very little."

"What was it? A head injury? We couldn't see a wound. And nobody wanted to touch you, to try to take your cap off."

"Something like that," Rutledge agreed. The tension in his body almost choked off his breath.

Hauser nodded. "That's the conclusion we came to. Someone said, 'You'd better get him back to his own lines,' but no one volunteered. We didn't care, in a way. The war was over for us, and we didn't care about much, to be honest."

"And yet you took me back?"

"I took you as far as I could. Too far, as it happened. I stopped a Frenchman, an old man, to ask if he'd guide you back to the English lines. He gaped at me as if he didn't understand me. My French is fairly good—accented, but good. Instead, he pulled an ancient pistol from his pocket, and shot me!"

The astonishment of it was still in his voice. "I saw you kneel and start to do something with a dressing. And then everything went black. I thought he'd probably kill you as well, but when I asked the men who'd found me, they said there wasn't another body. Just mine. I decided you'd simply walked away, and never looked back."

Rutledge drew a harsh breath. "I don't know what happened after that. I suppose someone thought at first I was a released prisoner. Later—back in England—someone came to visit me in hospital. Out of curiosity, I expect. Or the doctors may have sent for him. But I couldn't make sense of what he was saying. And the nursing sister came and took him away." He cleared his throat.

He couldn't tell this man, dressed in ordinary civilian clothes and a long way from the Front, how badly shell-shocked he'd been. How confused those months in hospital had been.

"Head wounds," Hauser was saying. "They do strange things." He made as if to shrug it off, as if it were too far in the past to matter anyway. "The question now is, what are you to do with me?" He swallowed the rest of his whisky at a gulp, set down the jam jar, and waited, his eyes fixed on Rutledge's face.

23

RUTLEDGE GOT TO HIS FEET, ONE OF HIS LEG MUSCLES CRAMP-
ing, and lifted the dressing on Hauser's chest. The blood had stopped
running and was beginning to make dark clots along the edge of the
wound. He thought, *It must be painful for the man to breathe.* . . .

Hamish said, reversing fields, "If ye take him to the police, they'll
clap him in irons and close the case."

Silently arguing, Rutledge said, "He's probably guilty."

"Aye. But first ye find the one that did the wounding . . . and why."

Aloud Rutledge answered the question Hauser had asked. "I could
take you in, let them charge you, and come to the hanging. Or I could
leave you here until I've looked into your story. I don't think you're up
to walking far."

Hauser gave a grunting laugh. "Not tonight. I won't promise tomorrow."

Rutledge turned and examined the cupboards. The German had
brought in tins, bread, a sausage, and a bowl of apples. There was
cheese wrapped in a cloth, and the pitcher for water.

Watching him, Hauser said, "I couldn't risk a fire. Smoke rising
from the chimney would have attracted attention. I've bathed and

shaved in cold water. No different from life in the trenches, when you think about it. Although we were a damned sight more comfortable in ours than you were in yours."

Which was true.

"I'll leave the decanters here. For the pain, not to give you Dutch courage for an escape. Does Mrs. Mayhew know where you are living? Is she likely to come here searching for you?"

Outraged, Hauser swore. "*Mein Gott, nein!* No!" He struggled to get to his feet and failed. "She and I have met, yes, but she knows nothing about me. I have Dutch papers. She came into the church in Marling, where I was trying to stay warm, out of the wind. She thought I was praying. We talked about the greenery she was bringing for the service that Wednesday evening. I'd seen something much like it in the gardens around this house, so I thought she might have come here. I was worried. But she had found them on her own property. Then we talked about the flatness of Holland, and the tulips. I met her again on the train to London, quite by accident. We talked about the war, and books, whatever we could think of. We have only talked."

But for a lonely woman, Rutledge thought, companionship was precious, and a meeting of minds was but a stepping-stone to wishful thinking. . . .

He left then, still unsure how far he could trust the German, and drove back through the gates, toward Marling. Tired to the bone, he ignored Hamish and concentrated on the road. Dairy cows were making their way to pasture, streaming across just ahead of him, forcing him to stop and wait. There was no one with them, but the cow at their head knew her way as well as any farmer. Plodding with empty udders, they ignored him, except for one young heifer who stared with dark and friendly eyes, as if the motorcar was a curiosity.

Had he made the right decision about Hauser?

Dawn had broken as Rutledge drove into Marling. He felt grubby, his beard rasping against the sweater under his chin. Leaving the motorcar in its accustomed place behind the hotel, he went in through the yard door and up to his room.

The bed was inviting, the room cool enough for sleep. But he shaved and bathed, then dressed for the day, noting that there was blood on the cuffs of the shirt he'd taken off. He washed it out himself, and left it to dry by the window.

Breakfast was a hurried affair, a mere restoking of the fires of energy, and a second cup of tea gave him a second wind.

When Rutledge walked into the police station afterward, Sergeant Burke said affably, "Mrs. Mayhew was here, asking for you."

Alert, Rutledge said, "And what did she want with me?"

"Something about urgently needing to find you. She looked as if she hadn't slept. Anything wrong?"

Burke was too sharp to be put off with excuses. Rutledge said, "She had an alarm in the night. Tell me, who might be walking down the Marling road late? Besides a killer?"

Scratching his jaw thoughtfully, Burke answered, "Well, now, there's not so much traffic as once there was. People being wary, eager to be home as fast as they can. The gentry in motorcars and carriages don't mind as much." When Rutledge didn't respond, he added, "It's hard to say, sir, without an hour to judge by."

"After midnight."

"Lord love you, sir, there's not much likelihood of anybody being on the road then. Not with three dead already!"

Hamish said, *"Aye, it may be the killing has stopped for that reason."*

Rutledge responded silently, "Or someone has discovered that Jimsy Ridger is dead."

To Burke he said, "If you hear any news of trouble, get in touch with me as soon as you can."

"That I will, sir, but there's no report so far," Burke answered doubtfully.

Hamish agreed. *"Aye, who'll tell the police he stabbed a man, even out of fear for his own life?"*

ELIZABETH MAYHEW WAS in her sitting room, her eyes red with lack of sleep and tears.

"Where is he?" She got up from the comfortable chair by the fire, looking forlorn and far younger than her years.

"Safe for the moment." Rutledge had sat in this room with Richard and Elizabeth many times. The bookshelves, the hearth, the table where they'd taken their tea when there were no guests—it was all sadly familiar. The carpet was worn in one corner where, long before the war, one of the young dogs had chewed at it. There was a photograph on the east wall that he himself had taken of the house, and Elizabeth had framed. Familiar . . .

"I thought you might have turned—" She stopped. "Is he at Dr. Pugh's surgery? I couldn't think of an excuse to call there."

"He's not at the surgery, nor is he in a cell at the police station. You shouldn't concern yourself with this man—"

She flushed with anger. "I haven't *concerned* myself with this man—"

But before she could rashly commit herself to something she would regret, Rutledge interrupted brusquely. "He's safe, Elizabeth. For the time being. I haven't decided what to do about him. But you should understand that he's a suspect—"

"Nonsense! He's staying in a hotel in Rochester. They'll vouch for him there, and tell you he's a respected Dutch citizen here on personal business."

"Is that what he's told you?"

She began to pace the floor. Rutledge silently remained on his feet as well. Elizabeth turned on him. "You're trying to make me believe that such a man could be guilty of murder! I won't listen. If you turn him in to Inspector Dowling, I shall swear that he was with me when the murders occurred—"

It was like an obsession, her blindness. She believed in this man she thought was Dutch, and she would place her own reputation in jeopardy to protect him.

"You can't. I was here the night the last man was killed." Rutledge stood there, watching her, thinking that he didn't have the kind of experience to cope with this. He considered Lydia Hamilton, and rejected that idea. Lydia was a friend of the Mayhews, yes, but she would come to see Elizabeth in a vastly different light if she knew what was happening—and it would stand as a barrier between the two women after Elizabeth had come to her senses.

His sister Frances, then?

But she, too, was a friend. And Elizabeth would find it even harder to face her, because Frances had been very fond of Richard. . . .

Melinda Crawford? He couldn't bring himself to worry her.

Hamish warned, "It isna' wise to interfere—"

"I'd like to see him," Elizabeth said, flushed. "And this safe place you've found for him. I'd like to go there. Now."

Putting his own friendship with Richard's wife on the line—and realizing with a bitter sense of loss what he risked in doing this—Rutledge said firmly, "No. Not now. Not later. I've told you, he's a suspect in these local murders, and until he's cleared—until I can clear him of suspicion, you cannot openly befriend him. It would ruin you—"

"I don't care about ruin. I do care about this man—"

It had been put into words. Her infatuation.

They stared at each other, and fear crept unbidden into her eyes. "Ian—"

He shook his head. "I've had no sleep," he said, more curtly than he intended. "And you've had very little yourself. I'm leaving before one of us says something we can't take back."

Walking out the sitting-room door without waiting for an answer, he saw her face before he could take his eyes away from hers. And read in them her determination to search on her own for Gunter Hauser.

RUTLEDGE WENT BACK to the vicinity of the burned-out oast house to look for signs, but even in the pale sunlight he could see nothing that either supported or refuted the German's story. Looking around, he saw that it was an ideal spot for an ambush. Another of those empty stretches of open land. He himself had passed here on the night porter's bicycle a good hour before the attack.

Hamish said, "He could be lying."

But if there wasn't an attack here—who had slashed the German's chest with a knife? And where?

Fatigue was catching up with him as he drove back into Marling. The road seemed to dance in the watery sunlight, and the trees flickered like a fan. As he swerved to miss what he thought was someone in the high grass along the verge, only to realize it was the shadow of his own motorcar passing with him, he knew rest was essential.

He stopped for petrol, then carried on to the hotel and allowed himself two hours of restless sleep. And he was on the road again, turning between the stone pillars and down the overgrown drive to pull up outside the kitchen door.

The house in the midday light was a richly shaded brick, with stone forming the portico and steps and facing the front windows. A family home, made for light and laughter and children, not for pretensions and grand aspirations. A quiet residence set in the countryside and surrounded by its fields and pastures and woodland, shielded from the road by old trees and great banks of rhododendron that were now sadly in need of trimming.

Crows flew up from the chimney as Rutledge got out of the motorcar and stood looking around him. This was the England he had fought for. And it was already dying. The crows might as well be vultures.

Shaking off his somber mood, he walked briskly toward the kitchen door, knocking once before opening it.

Hamish called, "'Ware!"

But there was nothing to be wary of. Gunter Hauser, far from a threat, was lying on the makeshift bed, deeply asleep and snoring like a drunk.

Before Rutledge could step forward and shake him awake, the man came out of his sleep with the abruptness of a soldier, instantly cognizant of where he was and that danger was approaching. And definitely not drunk.

Opening those blue eyes, he fixed Rutledge with a feverish stare and said, "You, is it?"

Rutledge came in and took off his outer coat. "You look like the very devil."

"Yes, well, I feel like it. I couldn't sleep for hours. When I finally did, it was like the sleep of the dead." Forcing himself to sit up, he regarded Rutledge quizzically. "Am I to be taken into custody?"

"Not yet. I'm taking you to the doctor in Marling first."

"Over my dead body. Sit down, it hurts my shoulder to look up at you."

Rutledge pulled out a chair from the table and sat. After a moment he chose his opening gambit. "You're the best suspect I have. I'd earn a commendation for solving these murders so quickly, you must see that. You're here in England under false pretenses, and that's only the first strike against you. What's more, there's business in London that needs my attention." He kept his voice level and his eyes hard.

"It would not be to your glory to find out in a courtroom that you were very wrong. As a matter of interest, have you ever hanged an innocent man?"

It was too close to the mark. Rutledge looked away before he could stop himself.

"So." There was a pause, and then Gunter Hauser asked, "It was a shocking experience for Mrs. Mayhew, finding me bleeding all over her steps. Has she recovered?"

"I expect she's out searching for you. With a first stop at the hotel in Rochester, where she's certain you are staying."

It was Hauser's turn to look away. "So. She will quickly be disillusioned."

"Lies have a way of coming home to roost."

"Like the crows on the roof, which should have awakened me, and didn't. Is there any more of that whisky? I'd prefer schnapps, but beggars aren't choosers."

"It won't settle well on an empty stomach." Rutledge got up, taking out the bread and the sausage, cutting off a chunk, adding a slice of cheese to make a sandwich for Hauser. Then he went out to the motorcar and brought in the Thermos of hot tea he'd asked the hotel to put up for him.

Hauser eyed it with interest, but laughed when Rutledge poured it and he saw it was tea. "How the English can drink tea is beyond a European's imagination. But it is hot, and just now, I am grateful."

Rutledge laced the tea with a little whisky and passed it to Hauser. "Tea-drinking Englishmen defeated your armies, if you remember."

"No, it was the Americans did that. We couldn't fight all of you. What do they drink, the Yanks?"

"Bourbon, I expect," Rutledge answered, and was silent while Hauser got down the food and most of the tea.

Seeming to be a little stronger after that, the German said, "You don't know what to do with me. I'm a problem, like a dead horse."

"The truth is," Rutledge told him, "I have you just where I want you. For the moment. We can't seem to lay hands on the man who stabbed you. Is he up the stairs under one of the sheet-shrouded beds?"

Hauser laughed. "See for yourself. No one will stop you."

"The outbuildings, then?"

The laughter faded. "I have killed no one. I was the one who was assaulted, if you remember."

"Describe him, then. This man."

Hauser frowned. "He was perhaps my height. And there was something wrong with the way he walked—I overtook him easily. Or perhaps he was intoxicated."

Rutledge considered the drunk he himself had brought in. Had Holcomb armed himself with a knife, since then?

Hauser was saying, "At any rate, I was soon catching him up. He crossed the road then, and I expected to pass by on my side with no more than a nod."

"Did he speak to you?"

"No. When I was even with him, he came at me with the knife. I didn't see it in his hand at first. He was on me and the knife was already cutting my chest. I've told you this already—" The frown deepened.

"What is it?"

"I don't know. I would have said he was not a common laborer on his way home. He—There was something in the way he moved. I don't know—"

"Where did he go after he stabbed you?"

"I have no idea. He was there—and he was gone."

"On foot?"

"I was too busy just then to care." Hauser finished the tea and then, setting the cup aside, he said, "I've been wounded before. I know the drill."

"Yes."

Hamish was stirring in the back of Rutledge's mind.

Hauser said, "What is it that haunts you? I ask, because whatever it was, it nearly got me killed in France. And it could very well get me killed here."

Rutledge stood up, searching in the cupboards for a pitcher. "Will you be able to manage for a few more hours? I'll draw some water for you, and set the tins of food on the table with the bread and what's left of the sausage, where you can reach them."

"That's very kind of you." Still watching Rutledge, Hauser said, "Is it because I know about France that you're afraid to take me to the local police? I've had some time to think about this matter, you see. It's either that, or you're worried about Mrs. Mayhew's reputation."

"Or perhaps," Rutledge said, walking toward the door, "having killed one innocent man, I've found it the easiest way to do my business. Like a tiger that's tasted the meat of a human being, I've learned to like it."

Hauser waited until Rutledge was about to close the door, then said, "I had nightmares long before the war was finished. I saw the dead come back for me. And my weapon jammed, and I realized that I couldn't stop them anyway, they were already dead. I woke up screaming. I lied and said that I hated rats running across my legs. I don't know whether my men believed me or not. I suppose the blood of heroes had run thin by my generation. I was not the stuff of soldiers. I was a farmer, like the man who must have built this house. I understand him far better than I understand generals."

It was in a way a confession, but Rutledge couldn't in turn bring out the shadows that tormented him. He couldn't speak of Hamish and the Somme. Or that blind and terrible walk through the German lines.

Shutting the door behind him, he could still hear the voice of the man in the kitchen. "You will not heal until you face your nightmares. A priest told me that, and he was right."

Rutledge found the pump and brought the filled pitcher back to the kitchen, setting it on the table.

"Not all demons can be exorcised," he told Hauser.

"No. I do not envy you, my friend!"

Rutledge ignored the German's parting shot.

RUTLEDGE SPENT HALF an hour making a concentrated search of the outbuildings. Blotting out his fatigue and the emotional upheaval that was the aftermath of reliving his own disgrace, he felt clearly the numbness of a year ago, as if in bringing it into the open, he had released the pent-up mass of it into the present.

What did it matter? he thought wearily. *I've failed so often, what does it matter?*

There was work to be done, and he could do that. Try to do that. Until someone found out how hollow he was, and replaced him . . .

"And Ben Shaw?" Hamish asked quietly.

"I don't know. God, I wish I did!"

There was nothing unexpected hidden in the sheds and stables. For that matter Rutledge would have been surprised to stumble over a body— Hauser was cleverer than that—but thoroughness was never wasted.

"And yon German knows verra' well what ye're doing out here."

It was part of the game. . . .

But there was one interesting find after all. In the carriage house Rutledge came across a motorcar, with worn tires—and a small amount of petrol in the tank. There was no way to tell how recently it had been run. A brief examination told him that it could still run. . . .

Hamish reminded him, "The grass wasna' beaten down on the drive until you came here. He was on foot when witnesses saw him."

"And the townspeople in Marling would recognize the Mortons' motorcar, if Hauser drove it there. I'll ask Meade if there's another way in here. Still, it's interesting, isn't it?"

"You could move a body verra' well, in a motorcar at night."

"Or offer a tired man a lift."

DRIVING BACK TO Marling, Rutledge gave some thought to what to do about the German. He couldn't ignore the fact that he was aiding and abetting a fugitive, whatever reasons he might summon to explain it away. Hauser was an educated, clever man. He had been a German offi- cer. And Rutledge was well aware that he himself was vulnerable to the man's manipulation of whatever had happened in France. He still wasn't sure he had the whole truth of it—or whether Hauser had simply used the bits of memory Rutledge did possess to cast himself in a hero's role.

Hamish had his own view. *"It's the deid on your conscience that torment you. No' the German. You havena' made peace wi' the ghosts."*

"I killed them. I counted the dead that unspeakably long night be- fore you were shot. Someone ought to have put *me* up before a firing squad—for murder! They were hardly more than boys—when they lay wounded or dying, they called for their *mothers*! It was slaughter, and I couldn't tell them."

"No," Hamish answered tiredly. "It was better to die believing they were no' wasting their lives. It was better for their families to feel it wasna' in vain. The cruelty was knowing, as you and I did. It's the reason you willna' face the Shaw case—he was defeated, and died a broken man. And you see yourself in him!"

Rutledge said, "You weren't there. You don't know."

"I wasna' there," Hamish agreed. "But Jimsy Ridger is deid, and if yon German didna' kill *him*, he still could ha' killed the ithers."

In the end Rutledge went to the police station and sought out Inspector Dowling.

Without preamble, he said, "I'd like to pose a theoretical question."

"Theoretical, is it?" Dowling asked, regarding his counterpart from London with curiosity.

Rutledge took the chair across from Dowling's desk. "If you were on the roads outside Marling last night, and someone attacked you, would you report it?"

Dowling frowned. "Most people would, I think. Were there theoretical wounds?"

"Let's assume there were."

"Well, then, the doctor would be your first thought. After that, it's out of your hands, isn't it? The doctor will be reporting to the police, anyway."

"And what about the attacker? What would he do?"

"Go home and pretend nothing has happened. As he may have done three times before."

"What if he isn't the killer we're after? What if he attacked out of what he saw as self-defense—a terrified man striking first, for fear of becoming victim number four? In the dark, our theoretical man might have seemed threatening, or appeared to be deliberately following him. An honest mistake, as it were."

"He'd still go to ground." Dowling rubbed his chin. "To tell you the truth, I've been afraid something like this might happen. But *strike*, you say. As with a cane? A knife? A pitchfork?"

Rutledge smiled. "Strike as in assault. Theory doesn't disclose further details. We'll have to find this man and ask him."

"Why not find the victim first? If he's still alive, he's a witness."

"The victim has his own secrets. He won't come forward of his own accord."

Dowling said, "I should think, considering this theory of yours, that the hands of the police are tied. I don't care for that. There are men dead, after all."

"If," Rutledge said, "the victim here is a red herring—and there may be reasons to think so—to bring him forward would overshadow the search for the real murderer. People would be eager to believe it's over, and let down their guard."

Dowling leaned forward in his chair, staring at the Londoner. "If you've made up your mind, why tell me this cock-and-bull story?"

"Because," Rutledge answered, unsmiling, "I don't want to be seen as going behind your back. But for various reasons, it's best for the theoretical attack to be kept quiet. At the same time, I need to hear any rumors or gossip that might begin to float about. And you need to know how to listen for them."

"I don't like working in the dark!"

"You aren't." Rutledge got to his feet. "Find out, if you can, who was on the Marling road last night near a burned-out oast house, and why he was armed, and what made him strike first. The theoretical loose ends." He waited, wondering if he'd misjudged his man. Wondering, in truth, where Dowling would stand—with him or against him.

Hamish predicted grimly, "He will stand wi' ye—for now. And then turn on you."

There was a strong possibility of that.

Dowling studied Rutledge for several seconds. "All right," he said finally. "I've not been able to solve these murders on my own. That's why the Chief Constable sent for you. I'll find the answers to your questions. But by God, when I do, I'll expect the answers to mine!"

"Fair enough," Rutledge replied. "You might begin with our drunk from Seelyham." And then, earnestly, he added, "If I tell you the whole story, people are going to jump to conclusions that will only muddle the facts. I need your help, but I don't want it prejudiced by my suspicions.

There's probably enough circumstantial evidence to charge my theoretical victim, but when we do, the real killer will be the one who goes to ground. And the chances are, we won't winkle him out again."

"You've an odd way of putting it, but I see your point," Dowling answered reluctantly. "On the other hand, I heard from London that you were a secretive bastard who played his own game. Perhaps there's more to that than I was ready to believe."

Rutledge smiled. "Not secretive. Merely careful. You'll still be in charge here long after I'm gone. If I'm wrong, you won't be brought down with me."

HE WENT BACK to the hotel and made an effort to sleep for a few hours. But his usual ability to close his eyes and ignore the world around him eluded him, and for a time Rutledge lay there on the bed, rigid, one arm flung over his closed eyes, and his mind wrestling with one image after another. He could feel the tension in his bones, and for a while he thought he would never sleep again.

It began to occur to him that there was one grain of good in the disaster of his war. A single saving grace. He knew now he'd never abandoned his men before the fighting ended. He hadn't walked away from the line while they were dying. Whatever else he had been and done, he had not forsaken them.

And with that, he drifted into a restless sleep.

It was sometime later that he was summoned to the lounge. Elizabeth Mayhew was waiting there. She was beyond anguish now, her eyes burning in a pale face, her hands tightly gripped together as if to keep them from shaking.

"I've looked everywhere. I telephoned the hotel in Rochester. There's no one registered under that name . . ."

He sat down on the small footstool beside her chair. "What name do you know him by?"

"Gunter Hauser, of course!"

"Has he ever shown you his papers?"

"No, why should he? Do you go about showing people yours?" She remembered that he was a policeman. "I mean, at dinner parties or a cricket match?"

"Of course not." Looking at her dark blue coat and the patterned silk of her collar, he was reminded of the Shaws and their faded, ill-fitting clothes. And that reminded him in turn of something that Melinda Crawford had told him. "Did Hauser give you the gift of a silk shawl?"

Elizabeth turned her head. "It's none of your business."

Which answered his question. "You know he was married? And that he has children?"

Her eyes came back to his. "It doesn't make any difference. What kind of life will I have as Richard's widow? Shall I travel, as Melinda Crawford did after her husband was killed? Or take up charity work? Set my cap for someone like you, who was Richard's friend long before he was mine, because I'd rather have a safe marriage and children than none at all? You don't know what it's like, Ian, you aren't a woman! It's so easy for you to find love!"

Was it? He said only, "I'm not criticizing you, Elizabeth. I *am* trying to protect you. What if this man is a murderer? I've got witnesses who could identify him, people who will swear that he's been stopping ex-soldiers and asking them for information about Jimsy Ridger. It casts a very bad light on his activities, when there've been murders among this same group of men. If you love him, of course I'll do what I can for him. But if he's guilty of murder, I can't let him walk free! Nor should you expect me to."

She seemed to shrink into herself, suddenly small and defenseless and very afraid in the overlarge chair. "Oh, Ian, how did we ever come to this?"

He could see the tears in her eyes. And the sorrow. He didn't have an answer to give her.

"If Richard had only come home, none of this would have mattered, would it?" she asked. "But he didn't, and I have to accept it and try to forget and look out for my own future. Gunter is a man very like Richard, you know. In many ways. He likes music and books and poetry, and he loved his farm. He's described it to me—how the brick house and barn form one great building, how smoky the chimneys are when it rains for days, how the windmills keep the land drained, so that crops can grow, how he hunted ducks along the canals when he was young."

"He's not Dutch, Elizabeth. He's German. He must have been describing his cousin's way of life, not his own. The papers he carries belong to his cousin. They aren't his, either."

Elizabeth stared at him, appalled. "No! It isn't true—"

"I—saw him during the war, my dear. He was a German officer. There's absolutely no doubt about that fact."

She began to cry, the tears spilling through her lashes, her eyes awash. "If you're lying to me, I'll never forgive you," she whispered. "Never!"

He reached out to take her hands in his, but she pulled them away, tucking them around her out of sight.

Rutledge offered her his handkerchief and after a moment added, "I think you should go to stay with Mrs. Crawford for a few days. It would be best. She'll be happy for the company."

She fumbled with the handkerchief then, and wiped her eyes. "I've got to go *somewhere*. I can't bear to walk into that house now, where his blood was all over the floor, and Richard's memory is everywhere I look."

"I'll drive you, if you like."

"I've made a terrible fool of myself, haven't I?" Her eyes begged for a denial.

"No. I think you were ready for comfort and love and warmth again. I'm sorry it isn't possible." He stood up, looking down at her. "I'll take you home, and then come back in an hour—two—and drive you to Mrs. Crawford's."

"What will you tell her?"

"I won't tell her anything. She won't ask why you're there. She never does. The rest is your decision."

"Do you think she loved anyone else after Major Crawford died?"

"You'll have to ask her that," he said gently. "I never have."

24

RUTLEDGE WENT BACK TO THE HOUSE WITH THE STONE gateposts while he was waiting for Elizabeth to pack her cases.

The German was sitting up, his face washed out by pain but his eyes alert. The fever seemed to have abated.

"How is she?" The question seemed drawn out of him by something in Rutledge's face.

"Upset. I'm taking her to a friend's house for a few days."

Hauser nodded. "That's best. So. It's safe now to bring me to the police."

"Have you driven the motorcar in the carriage house?"

"I've been afraid to. Someone might recognize it. I walk wherever I need to go. Or hire a carriage. I'm considered quite respectable in Marling, you know. I've told them that my ancestors came over with William of Orange—your king William the Third. London was overrun with Dutchmen then. They owned land here, some of it very valuable." He smiled wryly. "I wish it were true, but my ancestors lived in Friesia, with its heath and sand and the North Sea wind. We didn't meddle in politics. Except for the Friedrichtasse, we've never consorted with kings."

Rutledge looked at the bread and sausage on the table. "You'll need more to eat. I'll see to it. Meanwhile, what about the doctor? I warn you, it's the first step toward a prison cell. I can't prevent that. But God forgive me if I let you die. Elizabeth Mayhew won't."

A flash of sadness swept over the handsome face. "She isn't in love with me. Not yet. But she could have been. In a very different world from this. No, I'm going to be all right, if the fever doesn't come back again. I'd like more water, if you don't mind. I can't work the pump yet."

Rutledge brought him a pitcher of water. "More whisky?"

"No, it's making my head thunder." Hauser paused. "Look. Why should I have killed those men? It's Ridger I'm searching for. Do I give the impression I'm someone who would be overcome by a murderous fit of temper? Laudanum isn't hot-blooded enough for that!"

"Ridger is dead," Rutledge told him. "Buried in Maidstone, where he was born. I doubt you'll find your cup. His sort would have sold it long ago."

Hauser sighed. "I'd thought about that." His face wreathed in a self-deprecating smile, he added, "On the other hand, I might have got those men drunk in the hope they'd tell me what they knew about Ridger—and then misjudged how much would kill them."

"I don't know why you killed them," Rutledge replied. "Yet. Revenge, perhaps? All three served with Ridger. That cup is a very good story—but I have only your word that it exists. And so far, your lies have been plentiful and extremely persuasive. But they're beginning to catch up with you."

And with that, he was gone.

MELINDA CRAWFORD WAS delighted to see them.

And there was another guest at the tea table—Bella Masters—who was decidedly not.

She greeted Rutledge with a flush that rushed up under her fair skin like a burn and said with embarrassment, "I was just leaving. But this offers me another opportunity to say—"

"Mrs. Masters." He interrupted her with a smile. "I hope you'll stay and enjoy Elizabeth's company. There's work waiting for me in Marling, I'm afraid, and I've only driven her over as promised."

He turned to Elizabeth, standing beside him with a worried expression on her face, as if wishing Bella Masters at the devil. "I'll come for you, whenever you say the word."

"You'll—you'll keep me informed?" she begged.

"I will."

Melinda Crawford, no fool, had caught Elizabeth's expression, and looked at Rutledge quizzically. "Now tell me you won't have a cup of tea, Ian! One cup! And then I'll walk you to the door myself. Elizabeth, dear, do sit down. You look as if you're feeling a little sick from the motorcar."

Elizabeth crossed to the hearth and held out unsteady hands to the blaze. "I'm cold, that's all. Bella, it's wonderful to see you." Gathering her wits and her social graces about her like a cloak, she smiled. "Raleigh's better, I hope. He was abominable the other night. I've only just decided to forgive him!"

Bella seemed to relax a little, her eyes still on Rutledge. "He has his good days," she agreed. "The truth is, he's not content with an invalid's role, and it grates more than we probably know. I ache, sometimes, watching him try to manage. A far cry from the world of the courts—" Trying to hold back tears, she picked up her spoon and vigorously stirred her tea.

Mrs. Crawford had poured tea for Elizabeth, and now handed Rutledge his cup. It was hot and strong and sweet, without milk.

"She'd have added a discreet drop of something stronger, if she could," Hamish said, beginning to get Mrs. Crawford's measure. "My granny would ha' done that."

Elizabeth was saying something about time lying heavy on her hands as well, and turned to Mrs. Crawford. "I've come to stay a few days, if you'll have me—"

"My dear, I'd like nothing more! Ian must have told you how much I've complained lately about no one to talk to. I'd go up to London, if the weather weren't so cold. I feel it now, more than I did. Used as I was to a hot climate."

Rutledge drank his tea, standing by the small inlaid Chinese desk that sat out of reach of the sunlight pouring through the window.

Bella, regaining her composure, said, "Raleigh prefers a good fire these days. I can remember when he insisted that the windows be opened wide each morning. It was outrageous, but he couldn't bear to be too warm. I'd slip around behind him, closing them as soon as he left a room."

They laughed. Melinda Crawford's eyes met his, and he dutifully commented, "I've never quite understood how men fought in wool in India."

"They dropped dead of heatstroke," she said. "Silly fools."

He drank his tea and set down the cup. "I really must go. Elizabeth's cases are in the boot—"

"Then I'll come and see that they're carried up to her room," Mrs. Crawford replied.

Rutledge took his leave of Mrs. Masters and kissed the cheek that Elizabeth tentatively offered him. Then he followed his hostess into the echoing hall. She caught his arm and pulled him into the music room.

"Now tell me what this is about," she hissed. "Elizabeth looks as if she's been crying—"

"Let her explain in her own fashion. She will, after Mrs. Masters has gone. But I found out about the silk shawl. And I'm not sure I can keep Elizabeth's name out of what's about to happen. I brought her here, and you must find a way to hold her."

"I'll do what I can. Even if I must take to my bed for a day or two. You look as if you haven't slept at all. Nobody's dead, I hope."

"No." He thought, watching her expressive face, that he would like nothing more than to stay here himself, and put everything else out of his mind.

Her hand reached up to touch his cheek. It was cool and smooth, like silk. "Ian. Strength is a wonderful thing, you know. But sometimes a man can have too much of it. You can't save the world from itself. If people are intent on destroying themselves, they will. And sometimes they don't care if they bring others down with them. That's selfish but it's human nature."

"I'll remember." He turned toward the door, and then stopped. "I need cloths, clean but old and lint-free. And some laudanum, if you have it. And whisky. And your promise to say nothing about any of this."

She asked no questions. "Go see to Elizabeth's luggage. Take your time over it. I'll have everything ready."

He made a great fuss over bringing in the cases, carrying them up the broad stairs himself as Shanta came running, protesting vigorously that he must do no such thing.

By that time, Mrs. Crawford had returned with a small, oddly bulging sack. "I've added some soup," she said breathlessly. "It will do no harm."

He kissed her hands, and was out the door. But before he had shut it behind him she was already opening the door to the sitting room, saying briskly, "The most stubborn man! He insisted on taking up the luggage himself . . ."

HAMISH GRUMBLED, "YE'RE digging your ain grave deeper. It's no' verra' clever—"

Rutledge had debated his best course of action, driving with a silent Elizabeth huddled in her seat staring out at nothing.

But once he committed Gunter Hauser to the police, saw him taken into custody and charged, it was out of his hands. This whole affair. And right or wrong, solid evidence or not, it was all too likely that the German would go to trial, and the case against him as an imposter in the country on false pretenses would make the murder charges far more believable. It was one thing to bring in the guilty. It was another to doom the innocent.

Like Ben Shaw, for one.

He swore.

Hamish said, "I canna' find a reason for his killing those men."

"Nor can I. Yet. If it wasn't the Friedrichtasse, what was his business with Jimsy Ridger?"

"Something else stolen, that he canna' name."

Rutledge turned at the crossroads for Marling, passing a dogcart that held a pretty girl and two younger sisters. Her fair hair was almost hidden by a tam, the long blond tendrils blowing in the wind, her cheeks pink with cold. It could have been 1914, before the annihilation of a generation.

It was dusk when he turned into the drive of the manor house. Hamish complained, "Ye canna' keep coming here—someone will ken a motorcar's driven through the gates now."

Rutledge said, "I'll deal with that later, when I have the time."

Hauser had lit the candle on the table, and as Rutledge walked up to the door, he heard the scrape of a chair's feet on the stone paving of the kitchen floor.

"It's Rutledge," he said as he came through to the kitchen.

Hauser, haggard and unshaven, snapped, "You scared the hell out of me. I'd fallen asleep in the chair!"

"I've brought soup—a beef broth, I think—in this Thermos. And new dressings, and more whisky. In the boot are bread and pork pies and apples, along with more cheese."

Hauser sniffed hungrily at the Thermos and exclaimed, "My God, it's like the broth my grandmother used to make! Where did you find it?"

"Sit down and let me look at the wound."

Hauser did as he was told, and grimaced as Rutledge peeled the blood-caked dressing away from the skin. Looking down, he said, "It's not infected, thank God."

"Not yet. It's clean enough. There's a good chance you'll live." Rutledge used one of the precious cloths to bathe the wound, and then re-bound it, this time with more finesse than he'd used in Elizabeth Mayhew's house. "That should do. I've brought something besides the whisky, if the pain keeps you from sleeping."

"Or to keep me from wandering? I could drive away in that motor-car. I wasn't able to do it today, but by tomorrow—"

"Yes, you could do that," Rutledge agreed impassively. He found a kitchen bowl that would hold the broth, and a spoon. Handing both to Hauser, he said conversationally, "All things considered, what will you do now that Ridger is dead?"

"There's no choice but to go home. I haven't the money to waste on wishful thinking."

The crows flew up in noisy protest, and Rutledge stepped to the door to look out. But there was no one there, only a prowling cat.

He came back to the kitchen, satisfied. "Tell me, why do you think these ex-soldiers were killed?" Seating himself on the edge of the heavy wooden table, he said, "You must have known about them. Did you think that because you were whole, no one would touch you?"

"I didn't have the luxury of waiting the killer out. I told you. Money is short. When it's gone, I have nothing, and nowhere to turn." He ate the soup with relish. "Men kill for passion, and they kill for money. And they kill to keep a secret. Take your pick."

"They kill for revenge."

Hauser regarded him for a moment, spoon in midair. "So. You have been asking questions about me!"

Concealing his surprise, Rutledge said, "The old Frenchman shot you for revenge. It's common enough in wartime."

"Still. You must know about my brother." A pause. "Did you bring the laudanum so that when the police come, they will find it in my possession? Oh, yes, I looked in the sack while you were seeing to the crows. I'm a suspicious man."

"I told you. It was brought to help you sleep. I want the hangman to find you healthy enough to break your neck as you fall through the trapdoor."

Hauser put the cap on the Thermos of broth, leaving half of it for later. As if he'd lost his appetite.

Rutledge said, "Tell me about your brother."

"There's nothing to tell. Except that after the cup was stolen, my brother Erich was killed." He looked away. The wound was still rawer than the slash on his chest. "Perhaps if we had had the cup, he would still be alive. Call it superstition, if you will. So. I had every reason to kill Jimsy Ridger. But no one else."

"And yet you claim you'll sell the cup, if you find it."

"If we stay in Germany, my son will be old enough to fight in the next war. There's always a next war. If I take him away from Europe, he won't need the protection of the cup. He'll be safe."

Hamish cautioned, "He would make a verra' fine chess player. But I wouldna' turn my back on him!"

Rutledge, rising from the table's edge, conceded the point.

―――――

RUTLEDGE WAS WALKING down the passage to his room when the maid, her arms full of brooms and mops, a bucket clutched in one hand, smiled at him. "Mr. Rutledge? Mr. Haskins at the desk asked me earlier if I'd seen you. There's a telephone message for you!"

It was from Chief Superintendent Bowles. When he had been located, his voice came down the line affably. "I've had no word on the situation in Marling. No progress to report, eh?"

"So far, there's nothing new. But the killing has stopped. For the present."

"The Chief Constable will be grateful for that blessing. But it's not good enough. There's bound to be something to point in the murderer's direction! What does the local man have to say? Dowling."

"Murder at night on a deserted road leaves very little to be going on with. By the time police reached the scene, morning traffic had already obliterated any tracks or other evidence."

"Not good enough," Bowles repeated. There was a pause. "The Chief Constable informs me you've dined with the great Raleigh Masters. Rumor says the man's dying."

Rumor, Hamish was pointing out, had clearly said a great deal more.

"He seemed lively enough," Rutledge replied, trodding carefully. "He was reminiscing about Matthew Sunderland. I remember him from the Shaw case."

"Ah! So that's why you were looking at the files! Indeed."

"It was a matter of luck," Rutledge agreed, "to hear someone of Masters's caliber discuss the legal implications of a crime. Particularly one I'd worked on."

Wary, Bowles's voice changed. "And what did he have to say?"

"He's of the opinion that Sunderland was one of the most brilliant legal minds of our age."

"I would have to agree with him. Dining out is all well and good, you know, but you're there to find a cold-blooded murderer. I'd prefer to see more progress made on that front!"

"Indeed, sir!"

Bowles rang off, and Rutledge hung up the telephone with unusual care.

Hamish said, "He went through your desk. Or someone reported to him."

"But he isn't quite sure what brought Mrs. Shaw to the Yard . . ."

"Else, he's waiting for your heid to be well into the noose—"

RUTLEDGE WENT TO call on Mrs. Bartlett and Mrs. Webber. Alone and overworked, the widows looked older than their years.

Hamish said distastefully, "I'd no' want to be a policeman. I'd no' want to question the grieving."

"It's the only way to find a killer. Sometimes."

"Oh, aye? And ye'd be happy telling your ain secrets?"

Susan Webber, brushing her auburn hair back from her forehead with one hand, was holding on to the shy little girl burrowing into her mother's skirts with the other. Peter's sister . . .

"It was kind of you to let Peter ride in your motorcar," she said as she led Rutledge into the parlor and turned up the lamp. It smoked, as if it needed trimming. A basket of folded laundry sat on a table in the passage, and there was evidence that cabbage was part of their dinner menu. He could smell it boiling.

"I'm sorry to trouble you," he said, "but I'm sure you are as eager to have an answer to your husband's death as we are."

She said, "What good will it do, then? It won't bring Peter's father back, and it won't make my life any easier. Kenny might as well have died in the war. I'd got used to him being away, after the first year. Then he was back, and he needed more care than these two."

He looked up to see Peter standing quietly in the doorway.

"Is there anything you can tell me, Mrs. Webber, that might be useful? Did your husband have any enemies—or any friends he didn't trust?"

"Kenny wasn't back home long enough to make enemies! And his friends were in the war with him. Or dead. I don't know why anyone would want to hurt him. Or us. And why would he stop along the road somewhere and drink wine? He never liked wine, it made his stomach raw."

"He may have learned to like it in France."

She shrugged. "Kenny learned to like a lot of things in France, didn't he, that I didn't know about. The French pox, for one. He was cured. He said. It was Jimsy's doing, that's what I was told. Jimsy got him a surprise for his birthday. It was a surprise, right enough."

"Did you know Ridger well?"

"Him?" Her voice was contemptuous. "He was one of the hop pickers. My mother would have locked me in my room if I'd shown any interest in that direction! One summer when Jimsy was twelve, he helped Kenny's pa to build a fence, and Kenny's ma was kindhearted and let him stay to supper many a night. I don't think Jimsy ever forgot that, and he was always respectful of Kenny. That's what Kenny said when I railed at him about the whore. That Jimsy knew he was homesick and down, because they was going into the line again the next morning and Kenny had a premonition he'd be killed. But he wasn't, was he?"

As Rutledge left, Peter followed him out into the front garden, staring longingly at the motorcar at the gate.

Rutledge showed him how the crank was turned, and let him peer into the driver's seat at the gauges on the panel. When Peter hopped down to the road again, Rutledge got behind the wheel.

Peter said, "One night I saw my pa come home in a motorcar. He'd been working out on one of the farms. I was at the window watching for him. He said he liked riding in it and would do it again, if he got the chance."

"When did you see this motorcar? Do you remember?"

The child smiled shyly up at him. "One night. I don't know when."

"Can you tell me about the driver?"

Peter shook his head. He wasn't interested in anything but the vehicle.

"Did you see your father in this motorcar again?"

The fair head shook again. "It was the only time he came home early."

"Did your mother see the motorcar?"

"No. She'd gone to sit with Mrs. Goode, who has a baby."

As Rutledge pulled away, Peter said, running along beside the motorcar, "I think it was a woman. Older than my mother. Old . . ."

———

MRS. BARTLETT, SITTING by her kitchen fire, looked up at Rutledge with swollen eyes. The handkerchief in her hand was crumpled, sodden. "I miss him most at night, you know. Because he'd come home, then, and I'd not be alone anymore." The tiny kitchen, scrubbed clean, had an emptiness about it, as if Mrs. Bartlett had given up on cooking. "When Harry worked somewhere and stayed the night, I never could sleep the way I should."

"When you heard he was dead, did you suspect anyone? Did you think of anyone who might want to harm him?"

She looked up at Rutledge with complete bewilderment. "No. It was a murderer. It wasn't someone we knew."

Rutledge changed his tactics. "Mrs. Bartlett. I'm trying to find something that connects the three victims. Their service in the war, for one. And the fact that they lived here in Marling. Can you think of anything else?"

She considered the question. "It doesn't make sense that anyone would want to hurt Harry. He was a good man. They were *all* good men, and it was cruel when they'd already suffered so much!" And then, unwittingly, she quoted Nell Shaw. "I don't know what I'm to do without him. I don't know how I'm to get on!"

"Did your husband know someone called Jimsy Ridger?"

"How should I know?"

As she broke down completely, Rutledge asked if there was someone he could bring to her. She shook her head.

And so he made her a cup of fresh tea, and she drank it gratefully. He wondered if she had eaten all day. As she settled into a calmer state, he took his leave.

Where were the women of the church tonight, when she needed their comfort? At home with their own families, and unaware . . .

THE NEXT MORNING HE FOUND HAUSER SHAVED, DRESSED, and waiting for him. The wound looked dry and as if it had begun to heal. Changing the dressing, Rutledge said, "It's nearly time to make a decision about you."

"Mrs. Mayhew. Is she all right?"

"She's in good hands."

Hauser nodded. "I'm happy to hear it." But he didn't sound happy.

He ate a good part of the food Rutledge had brought with an appetite. "A farmer's breakfast," he commented, finishing the last of the bread and bacon. "Very good. So. Have you found the man who knifed me? It won't have proved an easy thing to do! He was a coward; he'll hide himself well."

"Not yet." Rutledge toyed with a bit of eggshell, drawing imaginary lines on the table.

Hauser said, "Come now! You are a good policeman, are you not?" There was humor in the man's face. But not in his cold eyes.

"I don't know," Rutledge said, getting up from his chair to rinse out the Thermos and set it on the drainboard by the sink. "I've learned that when a man wants something very badly—as you say you want this cup—he will measure the cost carefully. And if it comes down to it, he'll willingly pay whatever price is demanded. The important thing is to understand the consequences. You were in the war. You know better than most what it's like to face death. I think you'd go to the hangman with few regrets—except perhaps for your children."

Startled, Hauser had the grace to flush. "It would be very easy to hate you," he said after a moment.

"No. We were out there. In the trenches." Rutledge heard a rough edge to his voice. "On different sides, but we were out there. That's a soldier's bond."

Hauser got up and walked to the window. "I'll have to move on, you know. People will see where your car has been. They'll be suspicious." He sighed. "It's going to be damned inconvenient."

"His Majesty's Government won't house you as well," Rutledge agreed.

Hauser said in a different voice. "You know I never killed them. You won't hang me for the sake of your career."

Rutledge collected the Thermos and walked to the door. "Tomorrow. After that, it won't be in my hands, anyway."

He left, wondering if he were making a mistake. Hauser could walk away now. Is that what he wanted, deep in his own soul?

In Marling, he found a note waiting from Melinda Crawford. It read simply, *I think you'd better come.*

Reluctantly he drove to her house on the Sussex border. He wasn't in the mood to be questioned about Hauser. Shanta opened the door to him, saying quietly, "You are to go upstairs."

He followed the direction of her eyes, walking up the stairs and turning to the left. In the back of the house, Melinda Crawford had made for herself a comfortable sitting room that overlooked the gardens. She was waiting for him there, standing by the window.

As he opened the door, she turned.

"Ian."

"What has happened?" he asked, relieved to see that she herself looked well enough except for the deep concern on her face.

"Elizabeth. She left this morning, without telling me. When Shanta went in to bring her her morning tea, the bed was empty. We waited for a time, thinking she might have gone for a walk. But there's a horse gone from my stables as well, and my groom tells me that it must have been taken sometime close to dawn."

Rutledge swore under his breath. "Did she tell you? About the German?"

"Yes. I think she's afraid you're going to hang him. Foolish girl! But there you are." Mrs. Crawford examined him critically. "You look terrible. You did yesterday, but I put it down to this business with Elizabeth. It isn't, is it?"

"I'm tired, that's all. I've been bicycling over the countryside and then dealing with her German."

She rang the small bell at her side, and Shanta came in almost at once with a tray, glasses, and decanters. Mrs. Crawford poured a whisky for him and passed it to him. "Drink that, my dear. Tea built an empire—we need something stiffer to see us through Elizabeth's histrionics. She had the feeling you knew this man. Is it true?"

"Yes."

"From the war."

He nodded.

"She thought there might have been some ill feeling between you."

"Not . . . ill feeling." Rutledge fell back on the old cliché. "He was the enemy."

Melinda Crawford considered him for a moment, and he felt like a schoolboy squirming under the gaze of a stern schoolmaster. "What happened to you in France, Ian? You were on the Somme, were you not?"

Rutledge could see his hand trembling as he lifted the glass. He set it down again and said, "Trench warfare."

She smoothed the fabric of her skirt, as if she knew he didn't want to meet her eyes. "When I was in India, I watched people die. Sometimes peacefully—sometimes quite horribly. Not just in the Mutiny, you know. It was a poor country, and people simply died. Along the road, in the courtyard of a mosque, in the shelter of a banyan tree. I have seen the Taj Mahal, one of the most elegantly beautiful shrines in the world. I've lain in a blind in the middle of a night to watch a tiger walk softly down to the river and drink. But I had nightmares for years about the butchery at Cawnpore, where the women and children were massacred in the Bibighar. I heard my elders describe how some of the murderers were blown from cannon rather than hanged. Do you think you can shock me?"

He said, boxed into a corner and trying to shift the conversation, "Did you offer to drive one of the Marling victims home one night? Did you take him up in your motorcar?"

"Yes. I saw him limping down the road and instructed my driver to stop. Hadley was horrified, but I didn't care. Compassion takes many forms."

"You should have told me!"

"Why? I didn't murder him. I only saved him from a long walk home."

Rutledge said, "All the same—" And then, he answered her question in the only way he knew how. "I can't tell you about the war. Please don't ask me to tell you about it."

"Does this German know what you won't tell me?"

"Only a very small part of it—" He reached again for the whisky, and nearly spilled it. *"For God's sake, don't ask me!"*

"Then there is nothing that this man can tell Elizabeth that would harm you? Or that she could use against you?"

"No—nothing." It wasn't completely true, but he could think of no one who could profit from the knowledge that Gunter Hauser possessed.

"Then you are free to do whatever is required, to take him into custody if that becomes necessary, and there will be no repercussions?"

He could feel himself beginning to breathe again, the tightness in his chest no longer bands biting into the flesh. "I can't believe—" he began, and then realized that he didn't know Elizabeth any longer.

"I think she must have gone to find him—and Elizabeth isn't stupid, she can put facts together exceedingly well. She must have some idea where to look."

He hadn't considered that. "She thought he was living in a hotel in Rochester. It was a lie; he'd been living in the kitchen of an empty manor house on the Marling road. The Morton house—"

"And you took him back there. I find myself wondering why."

"I took him back there because I needed information. I don't know if that was right or wrong. Still, it was a personal decision, not a professional one."

"Yes. I see that. Did you owe him your life, Ian?"

"Not precisely. But I nearly got him killed after the war had ended."

"My dear, I can't imagine that you would have taken the man anywhere but gaol if you truly believed he was a murderer."

"I don't know," he said with honesty. "I can't be sure."

"As far as I can see—and I have known you much of your life—your judgment is no more impaired than mine. Whatever transpired in France, you must never let it conquer you. Do you understand me?"

"Understanding is one thing—living up to that standard is another," he said wryly.

Melinda Crawford said, "I recognize courage when I see it, Ian. Now, what are we to do about Elizabeth, before she makes an utter fool of herself?" She took his glass and added to it.

He was able to lift the whisky to his lips this time. And the warmth seemed to spread through the icy grip of tension.

"I'll have to go back to Marling—"

"And I shall go with you. If I'm there, we can probably salvage her reputation."

They left ten minutes later.

WHEN RUTLEDGE REACHED the Mortons' drive, he already knew what he would find in the manor house kitchen.

In the event, he was wrong.

Elizabeth Mayhew sat at the table where Rutledge had left Hauser only a matter of hours ago. She faced him with a shaky calmness.

"He's not here," she said. "I told him to go back to Germany, while he could. I told him that for Richard's sake, I couldn't marry a German. But I promised I'd find that cup for him. Somehow. My penance, if you like."

"You shouldn't have interfered!"

"Because you believe he's a murderer? I don't know the answer to that question. I don't care. I want him out of England. Out of my life. Out of my mind."

"For God's sake, there are three men *dead*—" Rutledge began, the stress of the morning leaving him short-tempered.

"Then find out who killed them." She got to her feet. "I told him to take the horse as far as the Helford railway station. I'd send someone later to fetch it."

The outer door had opened and Mrs. Crawford stepped in, distastefully regarding the signs of occupation in the kitchen—the tins of food, the bedding on the floor, the water pitcher next to jam jars, and a whisky decanter on the table.

"You should have told him to come to me, Elizabeth. I'd have taken him in and kept him until this business has been sorted out," she said. "You've put Ian—and yourself—into an extremely difficult position! You aren't in love with this man, you know. You've fallen into an infatuation. You haven't known him long enough to destroy other people's lives on his account. Now I suggest we all leave this place as quickly as possible. I'll understand, Elizabeth, if you would rather not return to my house."

She lifted her skirts to walk gracefully out of the kitchen, leaving the two of them standing face to face.

Hamish was saying, "I'd search the house, if I were you."

But Rutledge was aware of the emptiness around him, of the sense of someone having walked out of a room just before one walks into it. Hauser was no longer here. . . .

RUTLEDGE DROVE ELIZABETH Mayhew in to Marling, and left her at the door to her house. It was clear that she didn't want his company or anyone else's at the moment. When he walked out to the motorcar again, Melinda Crawford told him, "We've missed our lunch. If you ask me to dine at the hotel with you, I won't say no. I shouldn't worry about Elizabeth if I were you. She's feeling quite self-righteous at the moment, but it won't last."

As they drove past the Cavalier on his plinth, Mrs. Crawford gestured in the statue's direction. "My husband's family," she said. "He was quite a hero, defending Charles the First to the death. It was seen as a brave thing, at the time. But the family lost its title and its lands under Cromwell, and never recovered."

When they arrived at the hotel, Rutledge offered to order a room for her, to rest.

"Nonsense. I'm not as fragile as I look, my dear."

"I'd like to speak to Inspector Dowling before we go to the dining room. Do you mind waiting? It's a matter of unfinished business."

"I understand. I'll sit comfortably in the lounge and beg a glass of sherry from the clerk."

Feeling as if he'd been ground in the mill of the gods, Rutledge walked on to the police station, to find a grinning Inspector Dowling sitting behind his desk like the Cheshire cat.

"Your theoretical victim walked in half an hour ago and gave himself up."

Stunned, Rutledge said, "Why on earth—" and stopped himself short.

"He said he was innocent of murder, and wanted his name cleared. He said he was attacked on the road north of Marling by someone who mistook him for the killer. From the look of the knife wound in his chest, someone was very nervous indeed!"

"I'd like to see him."

"He's in Dr. Pugh's surgery at the moment, with Sergeant Burke in attendance." The grin disappeared. "What do you know about this business?"

Hamish hissed, "Walk softly!"

"Hardly more than I've told you. As for why I didn't bring him in, the first reaction of everyone in the county would have been, We have our murderer. He's a very fair candidate. The newspapers will be full of righteous condemnation."

Dowling sighed. "Yes. And you were right, reputations will fall over this. But now he's given himself up, and what am I to do with the fool?"

"God knows. Keep him here for a few days, let him help you with your inquiries."

"Is it true that Jimsy Ridger is dead?"

"So I'm told."

"Then," said Dowling, "if I can't charge this German, and Ridger is dead, we've got no case at all. We're back where we started from when the Yard sent you to Marling."

AT THE PLOUGH, the lobby was full of luggage. A steamer trunk with labels from expensive European hotels and ocean liners was surrounded by matching cases in calfskin, some six or eight of them. A uniformed driver was crisply instructing the housekeeping staff on what went where.

As Rutledge walked toward the sitting room, he found Mrs. Crawford watching from her chair by the door.

She said, "You'd require seven camels for that."

Rutledge laughed. "Camels are thin on the ground in Kent. Who is the new arrival?"

"So far there's only the driver on view. Judging from his demeanor, we're being honored by no less than a duke."

"The man from Leeds?"

"Very likely."

They went into the dining room together, and after Rutledge had ordered for them, he said, "Hauser has turned himself in to the local police. But not under his own name. He's using that of his Dutch cousin. He's presently at the doctor's surgery."

"Pugh? He's a good man." She sat back in her chair and sighed. "Hauser is just the man for Elizabeth after all," she declared. "Quixotic. They'll be quite happy together."

"I thought you would be opposed."

"For Richard's sake, yes. But that's water over the dam now. We must learn to let go as well. I shall miss her. I can only hope that she'll be happy. An English stepmother might not sit well with little German children. What will the police do with this man?"

"I don't know," Rutledge answered as their first course was set before them. The dining room was filling up, with market-goers coming in for their meal.

"I can't see what reason he might have had for murder. The monetary value of that cup is all well and good—"

"After the cup was stolen, his brother was killed in action."

"Revenge." She considered the possibility. "But a cold revenge, don't you think? Without passion or satisfaction."

"Hauser said much the same thing."

"I lived in the East for a very long time, Ian. I suppose I've absorbed a little of their way of thinking. To kill in this fashion—with wine and then laudanum—you must apply yourself to the task. You must watch and weigh. Enough? Too little, and the victim will live to describe how he came so close to death's door. Too much, and the victim empties the contents of his stomach before the drug has been effective. I think the question you need to ask yourself is why anyone would do such a thing. It's far more grim, in my view, than using a weapon."

It was an interesting point. But where did it lead?

As if she'd read his mind, Melinda Crawford said meditatively, "It would suggest that your killer is mad. Or that he derives some satisfaction from watching the process of death. As if to acquaint himself with it . . ."

Hamish said, "She's no' so verra' far from death herself. She spoke no' so verra' long ago of her will—"

Rutledge heard him.

He couldn't remember the rest of his meal. The conversation had taken another turn, this time to less dramatic topics, but in the back of his mind, he couldn't shut out the words tumbling over and over, like stones.

"As if to acquaint himself with it . . ."

26

RUTLEDGE WENT TO THE POLICE STATION AFTER DRIVING
Melinda Crawford back to her house.

Gunter Hauser was sleeping, but he heard the door to his cell open.
Without opening his eyes, he said, "The doctor praised your handiwork.
And asked me repeatedly who had seen to the wound. Should I tell
him?"

"Elizabeth expected you to take the train to London."

"Yes, well, she'll be very disappointed." He opened his eyes and sat
up stiffly. "A bargain, Mr. Rutledge. We both have secrets, you and I. I
would be very happy to keep yours, if you keep mine."

"Early days to decide that." There was a single chair in the room,
and Rutledge hooked it with his foot, then sat down.

"I asked Dowling. He says there's been no progress on finding your
attacker."

"You can hardly think I wounded myself!"

"Hardly. No, I'm of the opinion he's not going to surface. He's no
fool; he can't be sure who he slashed."

"Yon drunk you questioned," Hamish pointed out, "is a verra'
strong possibility. In the dark, he may have mistaken Hauser for you."

"He doesn't fit Hauser's description—"

"Aye, well, you canna' be sure o' that!"

Rutledge concentrated his attention on Hauser. "At a guess, you didn't tell Dowling how long you'd lived rough at the manor house."

"It is one thing to confess. Another to confess everything. I learned that in the war, you know. There's no certainty that others will see a situation quite as you do."

Rutledge got up to leave.

"Elizabeth will blame you," the German said. "But there's not much either of us can do about it."

"I'm not in love with her, if that's what you're asking." It was true.

"No, but you feel a Cavalier's responsibility. Elizabeth is stronger than you think."

Rutledge went out the door without responding.

TIRED AND IN no mood to talk to Dowling or anyone else in Marling, Rutledge found himself driving toward the small cottage where Tom Brereton lived.

It was old, a half-timbered yeoman's house with a crooked roof beam and a massive wisteria twining up the porch and into the thatch. Boasting only a few rooms upstairs and down, land enough around it for a pretty cottage garden, and an atmosphere of sturdiness that belied its age, it was ideal for a man living alone. At the gate a small sign next to a bicycle identified it as Rover's End.

He left the motorcar on the grassy verge and went up the short walk to the door.

Brereton opened it, surprise in his face when he saw who had come to call.

"I'd offer you a warm welcome, but from the look of you, whisky would be more acceptable."

"I expect it would."

Rutledge had to bend his head to step through the door, and inside, the beams were hardly more than an inch or two above him. The room was small, but there were windows at either end, and a fire on the hearth. Bookshelves, chairs, tables, and chests were crowded in upon each other, as if Brereton had crammed the contents of two houses into this tiny space.

"For a man going blind, it isna' a verra' safe place to walk."

Rutledge found a chair by the hearth and watched a gray cat rise up from it, yawning with arched back. It blinked at him and then leapt to the floor, tail high, as if reminding him that his use of the chair was at most temporary.

"That's Lucinda. She came with the furniture. Both inherited. But I don't mind, she's company of a sort. Sit down."

Brereton poured two small whiskies and handed one to Rutledge. "It's prewar. I inherited that, too. An aunt raised me, and she detested sherry. Like the late Queen Victoria, she preferred the smoky flavor. What brings you here?"

Rutledge sat and stretched his legs out to the fire. "What do you know about these murders?"

"What do I know?" Brereton sounded surprised. "Only what I hear. And that's generally what gossip considers worthwhile passing on. Are you looking for information?"

"No. Peace."

Brereton chuckled. "You'll find that in plenty out here. The only house near Rover's End belongs to Raleigh Masters. And as neighbors go, he's invisible. I can step out into my garden of an evening and hear nothing but birdsong or the cry of an owl. I like it. Most people would find it daunting."

Most people, Rutledge thought, would find approaching blindness daunting. But as Hamish was pointing out, what was the alternative?

"How is your neighbor, by the way?"

"He just went up to London, to visit his doctor. I drove him. Bella—Mrs. Masters—didn't accompany him. There's no change in his condition. But colder weather won't help his circulation. Six years ago he might have considered the south of France during the winter. Not now, not so soon after the war." Changing the subject, Brereton added, "How are Elizabeth's puppies faring? I ought to go see for my- self, I suppose."

Something in his voice, the way he looked away, caught Rutledge's attention. A yearning. Was there an attraction there, carefully concealed?

"Thriving," Rutledge replied. "What will Lucinda make of a dog joining the household?"

"She'll whip him into shape, just as she did me."

A comfortable silence lengthened.

Rutledge toyed with his whisky, watching the firelight in the swirls of amber liquid. He thought, *If I gave up the Yard, I could live like this—but for how long? How long would I be content?*

"Of an evening lately, I've been thinking about your murders," Brereton said after a time. "And I've come to a possible answer."

Rutledge set his glass down on the table at his elbow, and said with interest, "I'd like to hear it."

"Yes, well, I'm no policeman. But it was a gentle death, was it not? As murders go, I mean."

"Suicide? Is that what you're thinking?"

Brereton frowned. "Not exactly. But an—easing—into what the murderer might see as a better world."

Unbidden, the image of Melinda Crawford's face rose in Rutledge's mind. "How does he choose his victims?"

"I don't know. So far his compassion extends only to ex-soldiers. It may be that he was one himself."

Hamish was pointing out that Melinda Crawford had nursed wounded men during the Mutiny. Rutledge shut the voice away.

Remembering Mrs. Parker struggling for breath and sleeping upright in her chair by her window, he said, "Then you're suggesting that he doesn't have a wide circle to choose from. Or that he's wary of approaching people in their houses. For example, Bob Nester, who died of burned-out lungs."

The logs shifted on the hearth, throwing Brereton's face into the shadows. "Or your presence in Marling has deterred him before he could widen his net."

"All right. We'll accept that. Why does he use wine, do you think?"

"The wine doesn't worry me. For all we know, it's what our man prefers anyway. If you'd found an empty bottle, now, that might help narrow the field. You could ask wine merchants in the larger towns who purchased it. No, what intrigues me is the merciful death."

"It's a chilling idea," Rutledge agreed. He wondered where

Brereton was taking his discussion. At first it had seemed no more than an intellectual exercise. Now . . .

"Is it? Chilling, I mean. We're looking at it from our own viewpoint, aren't we? The murderer may see it entirely differently."

"Raleigh Masters has lost part of a limb. He's very likely to lose the rest of his leg. He'd have a better understanding than most of what Taylor, Webber, and Bartlett were suffering."

Brereton laughed. "Raleigh doesn't have compassion to spare for his own wife. I doubt he'd give much thought to ex-soldiers struggling to scratch a living."

"There's your blindness . . ."

"Yes, well, it won't ease my suffering to kill blind men. However much I may sympathize. I'll tell you what started me down this road, though. Mrs. Crawford once remarked that as a child during the Lucknow siege, she learned what deprivation was. For a very long time afterward she felt terribly guilty about wasting even a scrap of food or a drop of water. If she couldn't eat a crust of bread, she'd feed it to the birds—the ants—even the monkeys that sometimes came into her mother's garden. Later, she was sure this obsession must have driven her mother to distraction, but the point is, she had to deal with this guilt in her own fashion. What other kinds of guilt are there, and what other ways have people found to work through them?"

"Mrs. Crawford is not a likely suspect," Rutledge answered.

"No, of course not. But she proves a point, in a way. What if someone can't bear to watch these men hobbling down a road, and finally decides to put an end to it?"

She had given Peter Webber's father a lift home, in her motorcar. . . .

Brereton said, "For the sake of argument, how do you feel as you stand over a murder victim? You can't be objective; you have to feel something. Passion, possibly. Anger? Disgust? Vengefulness?"

"A policeman can't afford to feel," Rutledge answered slowly. "He mustn't let emotion cloud his observations. First impressions are important."

"All right, bad example. Let's take interviewing suspects, then. You pry into the deepest, darkest corners of their lives. And what you learn is disturbing. But it turns out neither they nor their secrets have any bearing on the case you're working on. How do you walk away from that?"

"It isn't always possible," Rutledge conceded, picking up his glass and drinking from it.

"And if you've learned something that *could* be set right, even though you betrayed a secret, would you do it?"

"No. I'm not God. I can bring the guilty to justice, or try to. I can't go around righting wrongs."

Brereton smiled. "But there must be a great many people who don't have that discipline. It must be tempting after a while, to play God."

"And you think someone is doing that, in Marling?"

"I don't know," Brereton answered. "But it's an interesting thought. Isn't it?"

AFTER THE CLAUSTROPHOBIC atmosphere of the cottage, Rutledge was glad to drive away. The cold air swept past his face and he felt he could breathe more easily.

It had been an odd conversation.

Hamish said, "Ye noted the bicycle leaning against yon garden wall."

He had. It provided all the transportation that Brereton needed to go where and when he pleased.

It was possible that Brereton was confessing, after a fashion. . . .

Was it likely?

Rutledge couldn't find in the man's background anything that would translate to murder. But London could tell him more about that.

Tired, he turned at the crossroads for Marling.

HALFWAY THERE, HE stopped by the trees where Will Taylor had been found and got out again to stand and look at them.

He had been here in the dark. He'd been here during the day. And there was nothing he could learn from this place. Where had these men died? Where they'd been found—or somewhere else?

Even if Brereton was right, and these were merciful deaths, there was no dignity in lying in a ditch to be found by some passerby. . . . Why had the murderer cared about the man—but had no qualms about abandoning the corpse?

This, Rutledge thought, was the major problem with Brereton's theory.

A motorcar approached from Marling, a last errant ray of sun catching the windscreen and flashing across the trees in a bright glare. Uncertain whether the driver had seen him, Rutledge stepped nearer the verge of the road, waiting for him to pass. Instead, the vehicle slowed, and stopped; after a moment, a man got out, retrieved his crutches, and with difficulty walked toward the Londoner.

Rutledge could see that Bella Masters was in the rear seat, a dark shape whose hat was all that betrayed her gender. She stayed where she was, behind the chauffeur.

As Raleigh approached him, Rutledge waited to see how the man would open the conversation.

Instead, Masters paused to look at the stone columns and the flattened grass of the drive.

"Someone's been here," he said. "The New Zealander, I expect. Someone's taken over a whole floor at The Plough. With that kind of money he won't think much of the Mortons' estate."

"You've met him?" Rutledge asked, curious. "I thought he was from Leeds."

"Leeds? That could be. The staff was atwitter when we stopped at the hotel for tea. You'd have thought God Himself had arrived. Service was terrible."

"I saw the luggage," Rutledge said. "He's here to stay, at a guess."

"Yes, well, it's a wonderful facade, all this fuss, isn't it? Even if he's poor as a church mouse. An entrance, an actor once told me, is half the play."

There was a silence. Masters moved nearer Rutledge and regarded him thoughtfully.

"Why are you so fascinated by Matthew Sunderland?"

"I've told you. I was one of the men assigned to the Shaw case."

"And that was disposed of. Six years ago."

"So it was," Rutledge answered neutrally. "It was an interesting trial. I should think it would be one that Sunderland himself would have talked about from time to time."

Raleigh stared at him, the flush of anger mottling his face like a change of skin.

"Damn you! You know as well as I do that he barely finished the trial before he was taken ill! That was the *last* case he'd have enjoyed discussing with anyone!"

Stunned, Rutledge said, "I didn't—he showed no sign of ill health. It was a classic performance!"

"You didn't know him! You didn't have any concept of what he was capable of. How could you judge a man like that? You weren't fit to wipe his boots—"

"Perhaps you're more sensitive to his problems because you did know him well. And therefore saw lapses the rest of us—"

Masters cut him short. "Are you trying to overturn the Shaw decision? It won't do you much good. The villain's dead. Leave him to rot!"

"I'm trying to get at the truth," Rutledge told him bluntly. "I'd like to know whether the evidence is as strong in hindsight as it was at the time."

He thought Masters was going to have an apoplexy. "He was my mentor, the man I admired more than any other. I won't stand by and watch you destroy his reputation for the sake of some"—he fumbled for a word— "some modern desire to cleanse the conscience—"

"Hardly that—" Or was it? "What if there is new evidence?"

"*New* evidence? Are you mad? How could there be any new evidence!"

"A locket has turned up. One that was included in the list of Mrs. Satterthwaite's possessions but was never found."

Masters was silenced. The color began to drain from his face, leaving him white and shaken.

"I won't let you do this, do you understand? You're easily broken, and I shall take pleasure in arranging it."

"Break me if you like," Rutledge answered. "Will that change the truth?"

Raleigh walked several steps away, his crutches stabbing the earth, then turned back. "It was a fair and just verdict."

"I'm sure it was. With the information available. What if that's changed? Would you rather Sunderland's reputation stand undeservedly?"

"You don't know what he went through, you don't know anything about the pain and the courage and the sheer will that carried him through the last year of his life!"

Hamish said, "It's no use. His mind's made up."

"I don't want to destroy Sunderland. I want to find out if we misjudged Ben Shaw."

"How very considerate of you. How very enlightened." The words were chill and offensive.

"We aren't going to solve this," Rutledge replied. "If you like, I'll sit down with you and present my findings. And you can be the judge."

"No."

"If you tell me that I'm wrong—"

"No."

"Then I'm afraid there's nothing more to discuss."

Rutledge turned to walk back to his own motorcar.

Masters said, "Don't walk away from me, Inspector." It was a warning.

Rutledge half turned. "We have no common ground. It will do no good to savage each other."

He walked on.

Masters said, "I know about your sister." His voice was low, pitched not to carry beyond Rutledge's ears.

Rutledge stopped, not sure he'd heard correctly.

He faced Raleigh Masters again. "You don't even know my sister."

"That's true. I don't *know* her. But she and your dear friend Richard Mayhew had an affair just before the war. They were very much in love. Mayhew betrayed his wife for her. And would have gone on betraying her, if the war hadn't sent him to France."

Rutledge, cold with anger, said, "You're lying."

"Am I? Richard Mayhew, alas, is dead. You must ask your sister, if you want the truth. If you dare. Or—perhaps you'd rather spend the rest of your life wondering . . ." Masters smiled. "Now you know how it feels to see your idol stripped of his honor."

27

RUTLEDGE HAD NO REAL MEMORY OF THE REST OF THE DRIVE to Marling. He had stood there watching Raleigh Masters return to his motorcar and climb painfully into the rear seat. It moved off, as if Rutledge no longer existed, as if he were no more than another tree standing rooted at the side of the road.

It isn't true.

That was his first thought.

And then came niggling doubt. How fond Frances had been of Richard Mayhew, how well she'd known him, long before Elizabeth had stolen his heart. How close they had been over the years. How devastated Frances had been when the news came that Richard had been killed in action, her letters to her brother at the Front full of grief. How willingly she had faced loneliness . . .

It wasn't true.

The man was a master manipulator. It had been the signature of Raleigh's success in the courtroom.

Hamish said, "It doesna' signify. It had naught to do with you. What they did. Ye're no' their keeper."

And that *was* true. . . .

It was something that lay between his sister and his best friend. It was not his business. Opening it up would only hurt Elizabeth Mayhew.

But the painful doubt had taken root, all the same. And he tried to find a way to accommodate it, and still love two people who were an infinite part of his life. . . .

He could see why Raleigh Masters had used this final weapon.

To explore it would hurt the wrong people.

"A lesson in the cost of opening up the past?" Hamish asked.

AT THE HOTEL, there was a quiet madness.

The dinner hour attracted a large group of diners, eager to glimpse the man who had arrived with such fanfare. The room was crowded.

The woman seating guests said affably, "I'm afraid it will be an hour at best. We're quite busy tonight. Marling hasn't seen this much excitement since the war ended."

"I hear you have a guest from New Zealand."

She frowned. "New Zealand? I hadn't heard that he'd gone there."

"The man with all the luggage—"

"Oh, no, he's from *Leeds*! He's just bought the Hendricks house near the church."

Rutledge dredged in his memory for the name. "Mr. Aldrich?"

"Yes, that's right."

"I was misinformed, then. Where is he?"

"In his room, I expect. Cook says he's ordered a tray sent up." She smiled conspiratorially. "Everyone will have a good dinner and no satisfaction."

"Shy, is he?"

"I wouldn't know. I haven't seen him myself! But I'm told he's just sent for Mr. Meade."

Amused, Rutledge said, "He can't stay in his room forever."

"True. If you'll have a seat in the lounge—"

As Rutledge took her advice, Hamish said, "You willna' have to travel to Leeds to speak to him."

"That's a small consolation."

Most of the dinner guests had come in pairs or in groups. He felt a wave of loneliness. He was shut off from Elizabeth. Melinda Crawford was at her house. . . .

It was odd to find himself questioning her role in a murder investigation. It made him uncomfortable and uneasy.

Someone spoke behind him. "Good evening."

He turned to find Inspector Dowling.

"My wife's gone to stay with her sister for a few days, to look after her. Gallstones."

"Painful," Rutledge agreed. Beware what you wish for, he chided himself.

Dowling sat down in the next chair. "I oughtn't be here. She left a meat pie in the oven. But I fed it to the dog."

Rutledge laughed. "And how is the dog?"

"The last I saw, he was groaning in the back garden." Dowling sobered. "I shouldn't disparage her cooking. A man has to accept what he can't change. The dining room is full. What's on the menu tonight?"

"Gossip for the first course. Have you met Marling's newest resident?"

"As a matter of fact, I haven't. Sergeant Burke has. In his opinion, this man Aldrich will do. A rough diamond, but he'll settle in. The gentry won't care much for him, but the merchants will profit." Dowling paused. "My prisoner swears he's not involved in murder. I brought young Webber in this afternoon to have a look at him. The boy recognized him. And I've sent word to Inspector Grimes to have Miss Whelkin brought down when she returns to Seelyham. I daresay she'll have no difficulty identifying him."

"I won't argue with that."

"Is he a murderer? Or simply clouding the water?"

"God knows." Rutledge turned to look out the window at the dark street.

"My men have been asking questions. It appears this man had lunch one day with Mrs. Mayhew. And that he's met other important people in and around Marling, on apparently legitimate business—an exploration of his family's activities after coming to England with William the Third. There will be repercussions if he's innocent. There's the Dutch government to consider as well."

Rutledge said, "I warned you he would complicate the investigation."

Dowling took a deep breath. "And we're no closer to finding a killer."

"I met Raleigh Masters today, on the road. He seemed to think the man who is heir to the Morton estate is here in Marling as well."

"I expect he misheard. But I'm told John Boyd, the Morton solicitor—and Mr. Masters's as well, I daresay—has had a letter from the heir. He's made a fortune in New Zealand and has no interest in the bequest. The house and land are to be sold."

"A pity—" And it was, Rutledge thought. The house deserved better.

The clerk from the desk came into the lounge, looked around, and then walked quickly toward Rutledge.

"Inspector Rutledge? There's a telephone message for you." He held out a folded sheet of paper.

Rutledge opened the sheet and read the brief message.

You must come at once. It's urgent. And it was signed *Margaret Shaw.*

"Was there anything else?" Rutledge asked the clerk.

"No, sir. But the young woman was in tears, very upset indeed."

Dowling said, "Is this another case?"

"In a way." Rutledge stood up. "I'll have to see to it—"

Fifteen minutes later, he was on the road to London.

THE SHAWS WERE not on the telephone. Short of contacting the Yard and asking that men be sent to the house to find out what the emergency was, Rutledge had no choice but to go himself.

It was a long dark drive, and weather was moving in from the east, a damp wind laden with the promise of heavy rain before dawn. Staying awake was a problem. And he was nearly certain that this was a wild-goose chase, another dramatic reminder from Nell Shaw that her husband's fate ought be his foremost priority. On the other hand, he couldn't risk ignoring Margaret's cry for help.

To fill the time he turned to the past.

What had really passed between Shaw and the women he had been accused of smothering? Why had he been tempted to kill each of them? Need? His wife's ruthless prodding to provide more and more opportunities for their children?

Hamish said, "You canna' know the answer to that. But at a guess, he comforted himself with their condition."

"Yes, I can understand that. Those women weren't going to recover, and they were probably afraid of dying alone and neglected, of lying there until someone came in and found them. They must have looked forward to his visits." He'd learned early on that murderers often could convince themselves of the rightness of what they had done.

"Still, there's the connection with Mrs. Cutter. Was her son involved? Was she trying to protect him? Or did she use him to try to put the blame on Mrs. Shaw?"

"Aye, the locket. George Peterson could have pocketed that. To gie to his mother."

"Yet she never used it against the Shaws. Why did Peterson kill himself? Because he didn't like police work, as we've been told? Or was there more to the story?"

"He wouldna' be the first policeman to die by his own hand."

It was true. After the first long months of working with the worst of human nature, of seeing violent death and recognizing evil for what it was, a callous disregard for the lives and property of others, either a policeman developed a hard shell against the nightmare of his job or he began to drink. Sometimes when the shell cracked or the drinking failed to dull the mind, a man withdrew into himself, and built not a shell but a wall against any emotion at all. Or he put an end to all of it.

Rutledge himself, drawn to law enforcement because of a firm belief that the police had the power to give the dead a voice, to offer in a courtroom the evidence of the scene and the body, had discovered soon enough that he was losing his objectivity. And it had been a long, difficult climb to a level of professionalism that had allowed him to function without losing his humanity.

Young George Peterson might never have succeeded in reaching that level. . . .

As the lights of London came closer and he could see the city shining in the misting rain, the smell of the river borne on the wind and the heavy odor of coal fires hanging between the clouds and the rooftops, he turned toward Sansom Street and finally pulled up in front of the Shaw house.

Every light seemed to be burning, the house startlingly lit like a beacon. In the West End, it would signify a party. In Number 14, Sansom Street, it was an omen.

Rutledge got out of the motorcar and stretched his shoulders, postponing the moment of walking up to the door and lifting the knocker.

Margaret Shaw was there as if she had been waiting just on the other side, and he walked into the narrow hall.

A passage led to the back of the house, with narrow stairs climbing to his right and doors into rooms standing open on his left.

Margaret was in tears, her face red and streaked, as if she'd been crying for hours.

"Mama is upstairs," she said. "I've been that frantic. I think it's her *heart!*"

"You should have called a doctor, not me," he said, and then regretted it.

"The doctor came," Margaret told him. "And left. He said it was something she's eaten. He gave her a digestive powder—she won't touch it, she says it's poison, and she just lies there clutching her chest and asking God why he deserted her."

"Where's your brother?"

"Mama sent him to stay with a friend. I don't know what excuse she made, but they agreed to keep him for a day or two."

Rutledge followed Margaret up the stairs and into a bedroom that faced the street.

The bedclothes were rumpled and tossed, half on the floor, half covering the fully clothed woman lying in their midst. Her hair was a bird's nest, tangled and spiked with sweat, her shirtwaist and her skirt wrinkled and twisted.

As he walked toward the bed, she turned her head to see who was there, and froze.

"Dear my God!" she cried, staring at him, and sat up with such hope blazing in her eyes that Rutledge turned away.

He said to Margaret, "Bring your mother water and towels. A brush for her hair. Then put her in that chair—" He gestured to the single chair by the door. "I'll wait downstairs."

"No—!"

"Mrs. Shaw, for your own sake and your daughter's—you're in no state—"

Nell Shaw stretched out her hand. "No, don't leave me! You've got to help me. I can't do it all myself. I can't anymore!"

"Mrs. Shaw—"

"What does it matter to them? Janet Cutter is dead. Her son George is dead—It won't matter to them if the slate is wiped clean for my Ben, and their names are substituted for his!"

"I can't perjure myself—"

"Is it perjury? Look at my girl! Am I to put a dead woman ahead of my living flesh? It *could* have been that bitch next door! It could have been her as easy as it could have been my Ben! And they can't hang *her,* can they? They won't dig up her corpse and hang her in the prison yard! All you have to do is tell the police that you was wrong, that there's proof now that she did the murders—"

"They'll want to know how she did it—what opportunity she had. *Why* she should have killed the women—there had to be a *reason*—"

"Her son, then! Good God, he's a suicide, he must have had it on his conscience, and after my Ben was hanged, he couldn't bear it any longer—he took his own life." She was on her knees on the mattress, begging. "There's the locket, you saw it! Love—in the tall chest there, the top drawer! Give it to him and let him take it to the Yard. He can tell them what the truth is, and get the verdict reversed, and clear your father's name. *Give it to him!*"

Margaret went to the drawer and opened it, her hands trembling as she searched among the handkerchiefs and gloves. Finding what she sought, she brought it to Rutledge, her face strained and on the verge of tears again.

Rutledge opened the handkerchief to look at the contents. The locket fell through his fingers and onto the floor. As he bent to retrieve it, cold metal and stone in his hand, he thought, *God forgive me. I don't know what to do!*

And yet he did. Out of the shadows had come an answer. The only answer he had failed to explore. He had examined the possibility of the Cutters—of Janet Cutter's dead son—even of Mrs. Shaw herself being the true killer. He had never looked at Ben Shaw, except as a victim. . . .

As he straightened up, he said, "Mrs. Shaw. Where had your husband hidden this locket?" There was a different note in his voice.

Hamish said, " 'Ware!"

Rutledge thought she was going to die then.

"We searched the house," he said implacably. "We never found it. Where was it?"

Nell Shaw crumpled before his eyes.

Covering her face with her hands, she lay back in the bed and thrashed, moaning, from side to side. From an angry demanding harridan, she had become diminished, a woman without spirit and without hope. Margaret ran to her, throwing an accusing glance at him.

Hamish said, "It canna' be true—!"

Rutledge answered grimly, *"You weren't there!"*

He left the room, and went down the stairs. In the kitchen, the remainders of a meal lay on the table, greasy plates, scraps of sausage and bread. He took the kettle, filled it with fresh water, and set it on the stove, then opened cupboards until he found cups and saucers.

As he took them down, he could see that his hands were shaking.

Guilt—

He thought then about what Tom Brereton had said about guilt—about the need to work it out.

But why had Mrs. Shaw suddenly taken it into her head to remove the locket from its hiding place and put it in among Mrs. Cutter's clothing?

Why?

To what end?

Yes, it would make a difference in her children's lives as well as her own to clear her husband's name, but the passion driving her had been ferocious—

He reviewed everything he knew or had learned about the Shaws. And Margaret's words came back to him . . .

"She went next door to help Mr. Cutter as he'd asked, and when she came home she looked sick, as if she was about to lose her dinner. She was that upset, she locked herself in her room. I've only known her to do that twice before. The day Papa was taken away, and the day the letter came."

"What letter?"

"I never saw it. But after she read it, she cried for hours. Then she came out of her room and was herself again."

The teakettle sang a cheerful note, startling Rutledge back into the present.

Mrs. Shaw had judged him well, he thought. And with a cleverness born of desperation, she had found the one chink in his armor: his understanding of Ben Shaw's broken spirit, his fatal willingness to doubt his own judgment.

Like a tightrope walker fighting for his balance, he had been swayed by the wind of her vehemence, uncertain, unable to ask for help or support from his superiors, a man caught in a dilemma that cast doubt on the one part of his life he needed most to believe in—his career. The perfect foil to Nell Shaw's intentions.

But *why*?

Hamish said, "She learned that you had survived the war—"

Rutledge shook his head. It went beyond that.

He poured three cups of tea when the pot had brewed, and set them on a tray with sugar and milk, then took it upstairs.

NELL SHAW WAS sitting slumped in the chair by the door as Margaret struggled to make up the bed alone. Rutledge set the tray on top of the tall chest, carrying a cup to her.

It was hot and sweet, and she drank it thirstily.

Margaret, with the bed straightened up, sat forlornly on one end of it and sipped at her tea as if afraid it might be poisoned. She looked old, worn, an image of herself far into the future. Rutledge felt sorry for her.

He said, taking his own cup and going to stand by the window, "I think we need to get to the bottom of this matter."

Nell Shaw, drained of emotion, said, "You've destroyed us. You know that."

"No. That began when your husband murdered three helpless women."

"He done them a favor. You don't know the truth. You don't know how they lay there day after day, with nobody to talk to, nobody to see to them except my Ben and the old charwoman who cleaned a little and cooked a bit. He'd come home of a night and shake his head with the pity of it. He said, once, 'It would be a mercy if they was released from this life. I've prayed that it would come.' But it never did."

"Where was the locket hidden?"

"It was pinned to my corset, under my petticoat. In a little sack along with some other money he'd picked up as well."

"Why in God's name did you try to shift the blame to Mrs. Cutter?"

"I never liked her! And that son of hers, the policeman, he stole more from those houses than my Ben *ever* did. Some of the possessions listed as missing we never had. But there was no way to prove what we suspected. That bitch betrayed me, to save her precious George, and he went and killed himself from shame. It got her back, a little, for him to die almost the same week as my Ben. I didn't see any reason why, with both of them dead, I couldn't use them the way they'd used us!"

Hamish broke in. "You canna' be sure that's the truth, either!"

Rutledge said, "You could have told one of us—one of the officers here to find evidence—what you suspected."

"Not without letting on that we knew which he'd stolen, and which he hadn't. We was afraid to. George was a policeman—who would have listened to the likes of us?" She raised her head and stared at him. "You can still set this to rights. With a little help, we could still clear my Ben."

"Why is it so important to you?"

"I told you—my children! Look at that girl of mine, and tell me I was wrong!"

"And what about the letter?"

For the second time that evening, her face turned gray with shock. Her lips tightened; she said nothing.

Hamish, already ahead of Rutledge, said, "That letter wasna' to *her*—it was to her deid husband!"

"You might as well tell me," Rutledge said. "I've guessed most of it. Ben's cousin who went to Australia is coming home, and you thought he might be willing to help you, if you could prove you'd been wronged. . . ."

She glared angrily at him. "That's charity!"

"Then what did this man want?"

"He didn't want anything. Neville was dying, and he wrote to Ben to tell him that he'd always admired him for staying home and making a good life for himself here, carrying on the family name with pride. He was ashamed of the way he'd spent his own youth, and he said God had punished him for that, taking his son at Gallipoli. We never even knew he'd married! But he must have, and he took the loss of his son hard. And he wanted to leave his money, all of it, a whole bloody *fortune,* to Ben—for old times' sake!"

28

HER BLEAK, RED-RIMMED EYES STARED AT RUTLEDGE, DAR-
ing him to pity her.

"Ben predeceased him—" he began.

"That's right. You can't leave money to a dead man. But if I could
prove that he'd been wrongfully hanged, if I could show he'd have been
alive still if he hadn't been taken from us, I thought I might stand a
chance at the inheritance. Neville didn't know, you see—he hadn't kept
up with Ben or us, he hadn't ever heard of Margaret and young Ben. He
was leaving it all to Ben, *and Ben was dead!*"

"And that's when you decided to risk claiming you'd found the
locket next door, in Mrs. Cutter's possession."

"I was afraid if it all went wrong, the police might think I'd taken
it, and I'd be clapped in jail. But then I heard you was back at the Yard,
and I thought, if I got to Mr. Rutledge, he might listen to me. With
George's suicide, it was easy to believe Janet Cutter's son was guilty of
something. And with her stroke coming when it did, it would be easy to
think she knew more than she should and was guilty of letting Ben die
in her son's place."

Hamish said, "Mrs. Shaw nearly succeeded."

"It was wrong of you—" Rutledge began.

"Wrong be damned!" she cried, with a little of her old blazing spirit. "It was my family I cared about. Wouldn't you fight for yours, if you had to?"

Hamish reminded him, "You fought for your men—but you didna' fight for me!"

Rutledge retorted, "You refused to listen—you preferred to die!"

Struggling to collect his thoughts, he said aloud, "If you spoke to a lawyer—"

"And where's the money for that to come from, I ask you! I could scarcely pay for my way to Marling, much less hire a solicitor who knows his arse from his elbow. I was desperate, and something in your face when I came into your room at the Yard made me think you'd listen. That I could make you believe in Ben."

She had nearly done it. She had shaken him to the core, and driven him to listen to her demands, to ask questions, to revive, at least in his own mind, the trial that had left its mark on so many people.

"It was a near run thing," Hamish was saying. "With yon Matthew Sunderland ill, and the constable guilty of theft, and Mrs. Cutter knowing what he'd done, it might ha' turned out differently."

"Differently, yes." Rutledge answered silently. "But it was still Ben Shaw who put the pillows over the faces of defenseless women and smothered them!"

"Then why did ye no' uncover the rest of the story at the time?"

"Because when George Peterson was taken on, he hadn't told the Yard that his mother remarried. Nobody knew of his relationship to Mrs. Cutter."

"Because he and his stepfather didna' see eye to eye?"

It was one explanation. There might have been other reasons . . . Who could say what had tormented George Peterson?

As if she'd heard Rutledge's thoughts, Nell Shaw said, "I never knew what possessed George, but something did. He was always looking for something—somewhere to belong. He was like one of them icebergs. You never saw what was below the surface, only the little bit at the top."

She looked across at her daughter, forgotten in the anguish of the last hour. Margaret was quietly crying, lost in misery.

"You shouldn't have heard any of this, poppet. I'm that sorry."

29

Rutledge left half an hour later. As he came out into the street, he found Henry Cutter standing by the motorcar, staring up at the Shaw house.

"What's happened?" he asked, his face pale and shaken. "I heard such terrible screams. What's happened?"

"Mrs. Shaw wasn't well. Her daughter sent for me."

"For the *police*?" Cutter asked, frowning. "Not the doctor?"

"He came and went," Rutledge said. "But this wasn't within his province."

"I don't think she's ever got over what happened to Ben."

"No." He was on the point of telling Cutter about the locket. Instead he asked, as if merely curious, "She told me that your stepson also was troubled beyond the ordinary."

"I never understood him. Janet claimed I never tried, but he made it too difficult, and I gave up. I thought everything would be better after he'd killed himself. But it wasn't. It killed my wife, too. That and Shaw's hanging. She took that hard. She had airs and graces, my wife did. In some ways she should have married Shaw, not me. I've always been a plain man." He looked up at the brightly lit windows again. "Are you sure they're all right?"

Rutledge would have liked to tell him the truth, but again he stopped himself. "You might call in the morning, and ask if there's anything they need."

Cutter said doubtfully, "I don't know . . ."

Rutledge moved around him to crank the motorcar and then climbed behind the wheel. "No. I don't expect you do," he said in resignation and, after a moment, drove away.

HE STOPPED AT the end of the quiet street, and rubbed his face with his hands. His eyes burned, his very soul felt dry and warped.

Remembering the question that Brereton asked him—about the secrets he uncovered in people's lives, and how he dealt with them—he thought, *I can't pass judgment on what Nell Shaw wanted to do.*

Hamish replied, "Her husband sowed the wind, and she reaped the whirlwind." It was a very black-and-white interpretation of tragedy. And, in its way, true.

Rutledge dropped his hands to the wheel again. "I'll speak to Lawrence Hamilton. He might be able to help her."

"It's no' your business. The murders in Kent are."

The murders in Kent—

He ought to be pleased that he hadn't been wrong in his judgment of Ben Shaw. But that was no consolation. Nor did it offer insight into these other deaths, or a sense of purpose and renewed dedication. There was only emptiness.

Judgment had its well of sorrow.

And compassion had its pitfalls.

All the same, he was glad he hadn't walked away from Nell Shaw, as he might have done. It would have been the coward's way.

For a moment he considered going to his sister's house in the city, and staying the night there. It would offer him peace and a little comfort.

But before the evening was over, he was afraid he'd blurt out Raleigh Masters's accusation about Frances and Richard Mayhew. And that was not to be borne tonight.

Instead he turned toward Kent and his empty hotel room, where only Hamish shared his mind. That was where he ought to be.

IN THE EVENT, there was no sleep to be had.

Dowling had left a message under his door.

The Chief Constable called tonight after you left, wanting to speak with you. He believes there's sufficient evidence against this Dutchman to charge him with the murders. It's out of our hands—

Rutledge read the words again and then crumpled the sheet of paper into a ball.

Damn them all! he thought.

Five minutes later, instead of trying to sleep in his bed, he was walking to the police station and asking the constable on duty for the key to the prisoner's cell.

If Hauser had been asleep, he showed no signs of it as Rutledge unlocked the door.

"Wait, I'll find the lamp," the German said, and after a moment light bloomed in the dark room, shadows falling across Rutledge's face.

"Good God, man, you look worse than I do!" Hauser exclaimed.

"I live an exciting life. As you will, shortly. The Chief Constable is preparing to charge you with the murders of three men."

"On your evidence?"

"There's damned little of that. No, on circumstantial evidence."

"There's wine in the cellars. But there's no laudanum. I poured that out, before I left the house yesterday morning, and threw the bottle into a field on my way into Marling."

Rutledge laughed bitterly. "I never meant for it to convict you."

"No. I know you didn't. I'm beginning to get the measure of you."

"I wish I could say the same for you," Rutledge answered.

"The problem is, you're an honest man. And you know that I am not. I am safe in believing you. But you may find yourself in trouble if you believe me."

"Exactly. Did you kill those men? There are no witnesses here. Not even outside the door. And any confession is your word against mine. A good barrister could claim that I had very good reasons to want to see you convicted."

"Elizabeth? God, I hope she won't come into this!"

"She has already. Dowling has found out that she lunched with you at the hotel one day and has been seen several times speaking to you."

"They will say I used her, to buy respectability. Yes. All right, if you want me to swear I'm innocent, I shall. On my brother's soul."

His face was sober, the blue eyes intense in the lamplight.

Hamish pressed, "Do you believe him?"

Rutledge answered, "Does it matter?" Aloud, he added, "Tell me, does this cup of yours exist?"

"There are records in my family. Letters. I can probably prove it was with me during the first years of the war, if someone can track down the men serving under me. But that would lead to the truth that my brother died after the cup was taken from me. It gives me a reason for murdering ex-soldiers from Kent who were in the unit that captured me. Better to believe I was here searching my family connection with England."

"You've made a tangle of your life."

"So I have," Hauser answered regretfully. "But then I expected to be gone in a few days. Find Ridger, demand the cup be returned, and home again. It seemed quite simple, when I borrowed my cousin's papers."

Rutledge turned back to the door. "Is there anything—anything at all you can tell me about these dead men?"

Hauser rubbed his jaw with the tips of his fingers, feeling the beard there. "I've thought of little else shut away in here. Elizabeth was right, you know. I should have taken the train to London and the next boat to Holland."

"It would help if you'd seen something suspicious out there wandering around in the dark."

"I couldn't even identify the man who stabbed me! But think about this. If you offer a man a drink that is drugged, a drink he's not accustomed to—this wine of yours—how would you go about it?"

"I'd have a drink first myself. To show the bottle was safe."

"That's because you're aware that it's drugged. No. You would offer him the wine to keep out the cold. You may have driven these roads, but you haven't walked them long after dark, as I did. At first the exercise warms you, and then you begin to feel tired. Your shoulders ache, and then your face grows cold, and your hands. The feet last. You'd be glad of a drink by and by. I cursed myself for not bringing a flask with me."

It was an interesting approach.

"All right. Anything else?"

Hauser yawned. "You're the policeman. You'll think of something."

RUTLEDGE SLEPT HARD. When he awoke to a cold and raw Thursday morning, he lay in his bed, trying to bring his mind to bear on the day's work ahead.

As he shaved he sorted through all the possible motives that he had uncovered—Hauser's revenge for Ridger's actions; guilt; compassion; and a pure and callous evil. Not the work of a madman, nor of a passionate man, but of a wary one.

What drove ordinary people to the point of murder?

He considered the three women who had been married to the victims.

Had there been some collusion among them? To rid themselves of a husband who had become a stranger and a burden they hadn't bargained for in the glamorous, exciting days of sending a soldier off to fight the Hun?

If so, they had concealed it very well.

And yet Mrs. Taylor had called her husband a stranger. Mrs. Webber had confessed to Rutledge that her husband had been unfaithful in France. Mrs. Bartlett spoke of being afraid to be alone, but perhaps she preferred it in some objective and well-disguised corner of her mind.

How easy would it be to kill your own husband? Or had they drawn lots, each taking on the responsibility for a man not their own?

Was that why the deaths had occurred on a dark road at night? Was the wine a gamble that had sucked the victim into conspiring at his own death?

"Ye're avoiding yon Crawford woman—"

"I'm doing what I have been sent here to do—"

"Oh, aye—"

"Then I'll talk to Mrs. Crawford. I won't destroy a friendship on a whim."

AS IT HAPPENED, Rutledge's first item of business was a brief encounter with Lawrence Hamilton.

They had met in the triangular square within touching distance of the Cavalier's broad back.

"What brings you to Marling at this hour?" Rutledge asked after greeting him.

Hamilton shrugged. "An errand of mercy, I expect. Elizabeth has asked me to act for this man Dowling is holding for the murders."

"Indeed!"

"I'm not happy about it. But Elizabeth was adamant. And distraught. Do you know what this is all about? Lydia is very worried, I can tell you!"

"It's Elizabeth's place to answer that, not mine. The man Dowling is holding is trying to keep her out of it." He carefully avoided giving Hauser a name.

"What's between them? How serious is it?" Hamilton prodded.

"There's nothing between them as far as I know. I think Elizabeth is—infatuated."

"Yes, I gathered that. And the man?"

"He's not what you expect. In other circumstances—who knows?"

"Well. Damn the war, anyway! If Richard had come home, this wouldn't have happened."

As he started to drive on toward the station, Rutledge laid a hand on the car. "I've a favor of my own to ask."

"What's that?"

"A Mrs. Shaw. London, Sansom Street. She's got no money, and probably no hope of any. It's about a will. She needs someone to act on her behalf, to protect her children's interests."

Hamilton chuckled. "You're a dangerous man, Rutledge, do you realize that? I haven't known you a month, and now I'm dragged into a murder case and asked to take on a questionable will."

Rutledge smiled, and it touched his eyes, lighting them from within. "Yes, well, we're neither of us in the law for peace of mind."

"Richard always said you were a philosopher." With that he drove on, leaving his motorcar in the hotel yard.

AS HE WALKED through the gate up to the Webbers' door, Rutledge found himself thinking of Peter and his younger sister. What would become of them if their mother was a murderess?

Would they suffer as the Shaw children had done? Or were there relatives to take them in and give them comfort?

This was the distasteful part of his work. On the other hand, who had spoken up for the dead men? Who had heard their voices? Dowling was more concerned with a killer on his patch than he was with men who had slipped into oblivion. They were a blot on his record, and one to be removed. . . .

Rutledge knocked lightly on the door.

It was Monday morning, and Susan Webber, sleeves rolled up, was elbow deep in her tubs. She greeted him with surprise, and said, drying her arms on her apron, "I'm just finishing the wash."

"I'm sorry to interrupt. I must ask a few more questions."

She led him into the room where they had talked before, sitting stiffly in a chair facing him.

Hamish said, "You'd think she had a guilty conscience. . . ."

But Rutledge put her nervousness down to talking to the police at all.

"You told me you couldn't think of anyone who might harm them, your husband or the other men. And you were not prepared to believe your husband had killed himself."

"Yes, that's right. What for? Kenny knew we had little enough, with him alive!"

"You'd managed throughout the war without him. Perhaps it would be easier to go on that way."

She stared at him. "Bringing up two children, without a man? Go and speak with Bobby Nester's wife! He died of the gas, and she's making do as best she can. She'd dreaded the day when he was gone, and she'd got nothing. And nobody! Or try talking with my Peter, when he wants to leave school and help me. And I'm telling *him* that schooling is his only way out of this life. People have been good to us, and I'm not denying it. Kenny would have been proud of that. But it's not the same. It'll never be the same again. Who'll marry a woman with two growing children, and take on that burden?"

There was a sincerity in her voice that made him ashamed of how little a grateful country—a war-bankrupted country—could do for its soldiers and their families. But with hundreds of thousands dead, and so many wounded to care for, proper compensation was out of the question. Even a pittance was better than nothing. . . .

"It's part of my duty to ask unpleasant questions," he told Mrs. Webber. "Inspector Dowling would have done it better—"

"No," she said tiredly, "he wouldn't have asked at all. But then he knows me and Peggy Bartlett and Alice Taylor."

"Or thinks he does?"

She smiled faintly. "Yes, there's that, too. I understand, Inspector. But I didn't kill my husband. What's between us is between us. Or was. Better or worse, the vows read. And I didn't make it easy for Kenny to kill himself, either. Whoever did that never thought about those Kenny was leaving behind, did he? I expect the one you want doesn't have children to bring up. Or he'd have thought of *us* before handing the wine to our men."

"At one time, I was fairly certain that Jimsy Ridger had a hand in it."

"That one? Jimsy always lands on his feet. His kind generally does. I can't see him coming back to Marling. We're none of us good enough for him now. Jimsy did well in the war, I expect. Kenny told me once that Jimsy found a teakettle full of gold buried in among the onions in some Frenchie's garden. I expect it's true, though Kenny swore he never saw it. Luck follows the Jimsy Ridgers of this world."

"Not always," Rutledge told her. "I've learned that he drowned in the Thames and is buried in Maidstone."

"Did he now!" she said, with some surprise. Something in her face changed. "What I wouldn't have given to be there, at his funeral!"

RUTLEDGE HAD NO better luck with Peggy Bartlett or Alice Taylor. Though Mrs. Taylor was more unsettled by his questions.

"I don't understand why you'd want to believe any such thing!"

"It isn't what I believe," he answered. "It's what I must do, ask unpleasant questions and suggest unpleasant possibilities."

"Yes, well, you must be desperate to think one of *us* turned murderer."

"I *am* desperate," he admitted. "I need to find the truth before there's another death."

"I heard there's someone taken in charge. If that's true, why are you wasting time over the likes of me?"

"Because the evidence against him is not satisfactory."

"Whose fault is that?" she demanded. "Not mine!"

RUTLEDGE DROVE FROM his last call, the Bartlett house, toward Melinda Crawford's home on the Sussex border.

She was in a chair by the windows watching the play of light across the lawns and the distant Downs.

"It's very beautiful," she said, turning as Shanta ushered him into the sitting room. "I don't know why. I've seen far more exotic landscapes in my time. How is Elizabeth?"

"I don't know." He sat down in the chair she indicated and closed his eyes. "Will you answer a question honestly?"

"Of course. You know that."

He opened his eyes. She saw the wretchedness in them, and caught her breath for an instant.

"Was there ever anything—anything between Richard Mayhew and my sister?"

She regarded him for a moment. "Who told you there was? Elizabeth?"

"I'd—rather not answer that. Not yet."

Melinda Crawford said, "I can tell you truthfully that I never saw any relationship between them that exceeded the bounds of friendship. I think they cared greatly for each other. But that was all."

He couldn't be sure whether it was a denial—or an affirmation that she herself had not witnessed any untoward relationship in spite of her own doubts.

It troubled him.

"It's not precisely the answer I wanted to hear," he said after a moment.

"Are you asking me if they were lovers?"

"Yes," he replied baldly.

"I don't know, Ian. But I can tell you that they never gave *me* any cause to suspect them of misbehavior." She smiled. "My dear, do you think either Frances or Richard would be so stupid as to arouse suspicion, if they were intent on adultery?"

"I'd always wondered why Frances hadn't married. It never occurred to me that she couldn't marry the man she loved."

"Ian, who told you this? You must always consider the source when there's malicious gossip."

"That's just it. I have. And I don't believe it, I don't want to believe it. But it's there, a worm niggling in the back of my head, and I can't walk away from it."

"Someone has set out to hurt you. I ask you again, was it Elizabeth?"

"No. If she'd even suspected, I think I'd have guessed. She's not a very good liar."

"Well, that makes me feel a great deal more cheerful!" She glanced out the window again and then said, "And the murderer. Have you found him yet?"

"Not yet." There was a wariness in his voice. He couldn't prevent it.

"And our German friend?"

"I haven't got any name to put forward in place of his. The Chief Constable is eager to close the investigation, and he will. After that, it's all in the hands of the courts."

"Who is taking the brief?"

"Elizabeth has asked Hamilton."

Mrs. Crawford nodded. "Yes, a good choice. I do rather wish she'd asked Raleigh Masters."

Surprised, Rutledge said, "I thought his health had forced him to give up his practice."

"So it did. But he needs such a challenge right now. It might be the salvation of him."

"At the German's expense," Rutledge answered ruefully.

"Why are you so ambivalent about this man?"

"Am I?" he asked, startled.

"I think you are. I've never known you to be indecisive. What did you do to Hauser in the war?"

"I nearly got him killed," he answered, getting up to pace the room.

"But he didn't die, did he?"

"No."

"Then you don't owe him a life, do you?"

"I expect I don't." *Except perhaps my own, for what that's worth* . . .

"Have you a stronger suspect than Hauser?"

"No. Yes."

She smiled. "You'll do the right thing, Ian. You always do."

But how could he, he thought, when the choice could very well lie between this woman he cared so much for and a man he didn't want to see hanged?

30

IT WAS LATE AFTERNOON WHEN RUTLEDGE REACHED MAR-
ling, and he found three messages waiting for him at the hotel—frantic
requests from Inspector Dowling for his immediate presence.

Without preamble Dowling said as Rutledge walked into his office,
"Thank God you're here! There's been another murder. We'll take your
motorcar, if you don't mind."

"Where? Who is the victim?" He was already following Dowling
through the office door, down the passage to the street.

"Mr. Brereton, I'm afraid. Out the Marling road. The house where
he lives has been turned upside down, and there's blood everywhere.
Where have you been!"

"When did you learn about this?"

"Not a quarter of an hour ago. A man called Adams, delivering firewood for the winter, reported it. I've been trying to reach Inspector
Grimes in Seelyham, to ask him to block the road north. Sergeant Burke
has already put men at the crossroads, and I'm damned shorthanded!
And this morning we had to let that Dutchman go—Mr. Hamilton is
that clever, he even spoke to the Chief Constable, and in the end, we had
no choice but to agree to release him."

"Where is the man now?" They had reached the hotel and were walking swiftly around to the yard.

"God knows. Sergeant Burke saw Mr. Hamilton at The Plough, but he was alone. That was at noon."

"Did this man Adams see the body? So far all the murders have been at night, on the road. It's a different pattern."

"It's different, yes. But I'd lay odds it's the same killer. Who else could it be? Marling is not so cosmopolitan that we can boast of two murderers running amok in the same month!" He cranked the motorcar for Rutledge and climbed in. "Adams didn't search the house, and rightly so. He came straight here, crying murder. Sergeant Burke is at the crossroads, and I've sent Weaver to fetch Dr. Pugh. It will be crowded in the back, but we can take them up with us."

Rutledge, driving out into the square, said, *"No—!"*

Dowling said, "Be sensible, man, we need them. Adams carried Burke to the crossroads, and he'll be staying there, with another man."

But where would Hamish sit—!

Rutledge fought down sheer panic, reminding himself that it was an illogical reaction. Hamish lived in his head, however often the voice seemed to come from just behind his shoulder. And yet he was so accustomed to the reality of Hamish in the seat behind him that he couldn't breathe at the thought of men crowding him out, sending the dead Scot to jostle with Dowling for space in front. Rutledge had lived in dread for three years that he would turn one day and come face to face with the voice whose owner he never saw, that no one heard, that was the Nemesis in his mind—

It took a formidable act of will to accept Dowling's proposition.

They found the young constable, Weaver, his face shiny with nervous sweat, standing at the gate to the doctor's surgery, and even as they drew up and the constable stepped into the motorcar, Pugh came running out his door, bag in hand, to join him in the rear seat.

Dr. Pugh was a slim man in his fifties, with a high forehead and an air of competence. "I've had to put off the rest of my patients," he said. "I hope this isn't a mad scramble for nothing. Weaver says Adams didn't see the body."

They drove quickly out of Marling, and at the crossroads—where Harry Bartlett had been killed the night Rutledge was driving Elizabeth Mayhew home from the Hamiltons' party—he could recall clearly the German's face in his headlamps, eyes wide and alarmed. *Where was Hauser now?*

Burke nodded to the two men manning the block across the road, and climbed into the motorcar beside the doctor. Rutledge could feel the springs dip under Burke's weight, and he felt, too, the claustrophobic sense of humanity crowding in around him, cutting off escape and air, thrusting Hamish into the forefront of his brain.

Burke was saying, "—It's not likely we'll find our man at the cottage, sir; by now he's more than likely well on his way to wherever it is he goes to earth."

"That's as may be," Dowling answered sharply. "But this is the closest we've been to him. We'll make the best of it."

Silence fell, and the sound of the motor was clear in the fading light, a reminder of speed. But not fast enough to satisfy Rutledge, as Hamish grumbled incessantly from the direction of Sergeant Burke's lap. Rutledge drove grimly, increasing his speed in spite of the wet and rutted road.

He had passed fields, several farms, and was coming up on the small stand of trees that led to Brereton's cottage when Dowling said, "We ought to pull up here. No need to spoil whatever prints may be there."

Rutledge stopped the car, and waited as they all alighted. As the cool air blew through the open vehicle, he could feel relief sweeping over him as if a veil were being lifted. The chiding voice in his head subsided, and he shook himself like a dog, half a shiver, half a shudder.

Getting out to follow the others, he kept his eyes on the road. Among the wagon tracks, droppings, imprints of tires, and the footprints of a man in heavy boots, there was nothing of interest. Their killer would have been too clever to leave his mark in the mud when he could walk on the grassy verge—he'd already shown himself to be careful and elusive . . . adept at escaping detection.

Rutledge caught the other men up as they turned in the gate. The bicycle was gone, and he pointed this out to Inspector Dowling.

"Then he's well ahead of us, I'm afraid," Dowling answered with a sigh.

The door was ajar, apparently the way Adams had left it in his haste to report to the police. A neat stack of firewood covered with a tarpaulin stood to the east of the house, and Adams must have looked in to ask for his money after delivering it.

As they began to push the door wider, Lucinda came to greet them, her tail high as she made a sound of welcome. Sergeant Burke scooped her up and held her against his chest as he stepped into the cottage.

The room was not wrecked, as Rutledge had expected, but there were unarguable signs of a struggle—books scattered, a lamp and chairs overturned, a table on end, and what appeared to be blood drying in front of the hearth; Lucinda had stepped in it at some point: her prints led across the patch and back onto the bare floorboards.

There was also a smear of blood on one wall and streaks on an overturned chair, drops scattered here and there as dark spots on polished surfaces and the floor.

Of Brereton, alive or dead, there was no sign.

But most telling was a bottle of wine spilled on the table and running down to puddle on the edge of a bit of carpeting. Two glasses sat next to the bottle, one of them still a quarter full.

As Sergeant Burke, putting down the cat, moved heavily toward the other rooms calling Brereton's name, Dr. Pugh saw the wine and went over to lift it, sniffing the contents.

"Laudanum?" Rutledge asked.

"I shouldn't be surprised, but I'll have to test it to be sure." The doctor put out a finger as if considering tasting the wine in the glass, then prudently changed his mind.

Dowling was squatting by the pool of blood on the hearth. Weaver, following Burke, looked rather green.

Rutledge said, "Judging by the blood we've seen so far, how seriously wounded was Brereton?"

"It would depend on where the wound was located. Not an artery, of course, there's no pattern to show that. Still—" Pugh turned to walk on into the kitchen and stopped short. "Look. It would appear someone dragged himself across the floor here!"

Burke was already examining the drying streaks. "But they stop just outside the kitchen door there," he pointed out. "And Mr. Brereton's body isn't in the house."

Rutledge stepped around the doctor and looked at the smears. Were they drag marks, where something heavy had been pulled toward the door? Or had someone crawled, half dragging himself, toward the only means of escape?

"The question is," he said, "where's Brereton? Trying to hide in the woods—or already half buried in the leaves somewhere out there? Would the killer have taken the time to hide a corpse? Or was he interrupted by Adams arriving on the scene, and Brereton got away?"

Inspector Dowling, scanning the trees beyond the garden, said, "We'll need a score of men to search out there."

Sergeant Burke reminded his inspector, "We can't wait for a search party. He might be bleeding to death right now."

Dr. Pugh said, "I'll make a cursory search." With the constable at his heels, he stepped beyond the smears and out the door, moving along the grassy path that bordered the small kitchen garden and the herb bed. Stopping at a garden shed, Pugh peered inside, pulling the door open only as far as needed. He looked up again at the men in the kitchen, shaking his head. Taking care to observe where he put his feet, he moved rapidly toward the boundary of the cottage and the beginning of the wood. "Nothing so far," he called to the watching men. "I can't see anything to indicate there's been a body dragged along here. Still—even if Brereton had passed out, he might have come to his senses and managed to walk away under his own power."

Burke stepped back into the house. "The odd thing is," he said, "that *this* attack happened well before dark today. Not like the others. Sir, should someone be sent along to Mr. Masters's house, to be sure there's been no trouble there? It's little more than a mile by the road."

"With servants in the house, Sergeant, they shouldn't be in immediate danger. Our priority right now is Brereton. Unless there's a path that Brereton might have taken through the woods, trying to reach help?"

Burke shouted the question to Weaver, still searching, and got the reply "No, sir, no path that I can see." Unsatisfied, Burke said, "I'll just have a look on my own, sir, as it's getting on toward dark."

Rutledge crossed to the sink in the kitchen and saw that there were no dishes waiting to be washed up, possibly indicating that Brereton cleared away after his luncheon. And the stove was banked. But then Brereton often dined with the Masterses rather than make his own evening meal. The buffer between Raleigh's temper and his wife's anxiety . . . A high price for a good dinner.

He tried to picture the scene as it might have occurred. Had Brereton answered the door, expecting to find Adams arriving with the wood? And instead was greeted by someone else standing there, smiling and expecting to be invited in?

Hamish said, "You canna' tell. The fire's no' lit, he may have been in the garden, clearing out a place for the wood."

Rutledge called to Dowling, who was inspecting the rest of the house. "How trustworthy is this man Adams?"

"Completely, I'd say. Church sexton, thirty years a farmer. His sister is the housekeeper to the rector. I'd as soon believe Sergeant Burke was a murderer."

Lucinda came to rub against Rutledge's legs, recognizing a familiar scent.

"She's verra' calm," Hamish said.

"Yes, I'd observed that as well," Rutledge answered him thoughtfully. "But then whatever happened here is over. There's nothing to frighten her now—no loud noises, no angry, raised voices."

Burke, coming back through the kitchen door, reported, "If there's a path, I can't find it."

Dr. Pugh, following him, added, "There's no sign of Brereton—and I called out, identifying myself. Weaver is still searching, but the light has gone, and it's dark under the trees."

Cleaning his feet on the scraper by the kitchen door, he walked back into the sitting room and shook his head as he studied the signs of struggle. "I've met Tom Brereton. He's come to me on Mrs. Masters's behalf a number of times, and I know of course about losing his eyesight. All the same, he was a soldier, and I'd say he was well able to defend himself.

Unlike the other victims, who had to deal with crutches. Hurt, of course—there's the blood in the sitting room. Still, even assuming he drank any of that drugged wine, he must have inflicted some damage of his own. But where is he now?"

Rutledge said, thinking aloud, "We don't know how badly his attacker was hurt, do we? Brereton might well have turned the tables and gone after *him*."

Sergeant Burke was making notes, a rough diagram of the house, then the sitting room sketched in and an X marking the location of each visible bloodstain. He said, "Mr. Brereton's a clever man. He would have come directly to Inspector Dowling and reported the identity of his assailant. My guess is, he was dragged into the kitchen while Adams was stacking the wood, and then was carried off to hide the body." As Weaver walked back into the house, Burke added, "We'll have to have that stack of wood taken down. Weaver? Get on it, man!"

Dowling, coming back into the sitting room, nodded. "I agree."

But Hamish, who had spent the last ten minutes arguing in Rutledge's head, did not. "He talked to you about the wine," he reminded Rutledge. "He would ha' been suspicious as soon as he saw it."

Rutledge, standing to one side, was reviewing his last conversation with Brereton in light of Hamish's adamant stand.

He had wondered then if Brereton in his roundabout fashion was making a confession. If the man was already contemplating disappearing, would he have staged his own death?

It would have had the opposite effect. Another murder would have galvanized the police into furious action. It would be far simpler to say that he needed more specialized eye care and to make arrangements with Raleigh and Bella Masters for the care of the cottage and of the cat.

No, very likely Brereton was what he seemed. A victim. But why in the daylight? Rutledge came again to that question, and Hamish answered it.

"Here it's as isolated as anywhere on the road. And I canna' believe he'd open his door after dark, but in the daylight he would—he did when you called. He had all his limbs, aye, but he was going blind. Nearly as bad as losing a leg—if the murderer canna' abide the sairly wounded . . ."

But why would Hauser come here and slaughter Brereton? Was he truly searching for Jimsy Ridger, or had that been a ruse from the start?

Rutledge walked through the house again, looking with care at the scene in the sitting room.

Dowling was searching now for the weapon, poking about behind the furniture, looking in the hearth.

Brereton would have let the German into the house, if Hauser had used Elizabeth's name. Yet the bottle of wine would have put him instantly on his guard. He himself had told Rutledge that wine was key to the investigation.

Unless Elizabeth had sent Hauser to Brereton, surely against Hamilton's orders to stay out of it, and Brereton, jealous, himself had brought out the wine.

"He fetched Raleigh Masters's medicines for Mrs. Masters. Laudanum for pain and the moodiness . . ." Hamish suggested.

Rutledge turned to Dr. Pugh. "Did you prescribe laudanum for Mr. Masters?"

Pugh, watching the drawing Burke was completing, said, with some surprise, "Dr. Talbot in London prescribed it, among other drugs. It was agreed I'd see that the supply was replenished as needed. Going back to Harley Street so frequently was difficult for Mrs. Masters—sadly, her husband sometimes refused to allow it."

Brereton—victim—or murderer? Either way, Melinda Crawford would be distressed. She had intended to remember Brereton in her will, because of his approaching blindness. Pitying him, as she had once pitied Peter Webber's father and taken the tired ex-soldier to his house in her carriage.

Hamish said, "Aye. One soldier will trust another. Brereton would find it easier than most to walk a distance with a man on crutches, and then offer him a drink to pass the time."

It was falling into place.

Rutledge felt an urgent need to find Elizabeth Mayhew and make certain she was safe.

Dowling had finished his search. Rutledge said to him, "I'm going back to Marling. Is there anything or anyone you need to be brought back here?"

Dowling turned to Pugh. "Doctor, are you ready to go back?"

"I've already missed my afternoon hours. I'll stay until we are sure Brereton doesn't need me."

"Weaver's just finishing up. I'll send him with you, Rutledge. He can find us some six or a dozen men to walk through the wood back there. They'll need to bring lanterns, oil, all the torches they can lay hand to. If Mr. Brereton's out there somewhere, the sooner we find him the better. Alive or dead."

THE YOUNG CONSTABLE was silent most of the way back to Marling. Tired and grubby from unstacking the wood, he picked at a splinter in the palm of his hand, looking up once to say to Rutledge in disbelief, "We've not been away more than an hour!" After a bit he added, "I was glad not to uncover him amongst the wood. The others were asleep, like. Not bloody. Do you think he's dead, then?"

Rutledge, busy with his own thoughts, had no wish for conversation. But he said, remembering Janet Cutter's son George, who had not liked touching dead bodies, "I wish I knew."

He dropped Constable Weaver at the police station and then drove on to Elizabeth Mayhew's house.

She greeted him with open hostility.

"He's not here. I don't know where he is. Lawrence made me promise I'd not try to contact him. I ought to hate you."

"No," he said, with more gentleness than he felt. At least she was safe—"You know I haven't had much choice in any of this."

"You can't blame *duty* for callousness."

He let it go. "Elizabeth. Tom Brereton's missing—"

Her face tightened with shock. "What do you mean—*missing*?"

"Just that. The cottage is empty, there's furniture overturned, blood everywhere, and no sign of him. Or of whoever came to call on him. And there's a bottle of wine on the table. Most of it spilled out onto the floor, but there's probably enough left to tell us if anything has been added to it."

"Because of his *blindness*? But I thought only amputees were being killed!" Her hands covered her mouth. "I don't understand—have you come for Gunter again—because of Tom?"

"I've come on my own. Inspector Dowling is still at the cottage, and they're searching the wood that lies behind it. The problem is, we don't know anything at this stage, but people will start pointing fingers soon. And it would be much better if I found Hauser myself, rather than wait for Dowling to do it. Time's short, you see, and the longer it takes to catch up to him, the more suspicious it will look."

"I tell you, Lawrence forbade me to speak to him—"

"Then I'll go find Hamilton."

"Take me with you!" Before he could argue, she ran for her coat and came back again, pulling it on with urgency.

Hamish reminded him, "Better under your eye!" It was true.

As they got into the motorcar, Elizabeth said, "Ian, I'm sorry. Lately we've been at each other's throats, and I think it's worry, and the strangeness of all of this business."

And the fear, he thought but didn't say aloud. She wouldn't hear a word against Hauser, in her foolish certainty that he was all she believed him to be. But beneath that determined defense was, Rutledge knew, the niggling fear that she could be wrong.

When he didn't at first respond, she went on. "I love you dearly, I always have. I always will. But I'm not Richard's *wife* any longer. We can't go back to that old comfortable life again—and you can't protect me from the consequences of his death. I have to make my own way." Then she added forlornly, "It's just that nothing seems to be working out the way it should—nothing seems to be *right*—"

LYDIA ADMITTED THEM to the Hamilton house, startled by Rutledge's grimness and the pallor of Elizabeth's face. She led them to the room that Hamilton used for his study and, after a nod from her husband, went out again, shutting the door behind her.

Without preamble, Rutledge said, "Do you know where I can find your client?"

"He said he was going to Maidstone. Something about searching there for a relative's grave."

Jimsy Ridger's, more than likely. Or looking for any of Ridger's surviving family, who might have that damned cup?

"Is he coming back here?"

"He's promised to return in the morning." Lawrence Hamilton pulled out his watch and looked at the face. "It's a long journey. He was hoping to find a lorry or a carter going that direction. Why? What's happened?"

"It's Brereton. He's missing. And there're indications of a violent struggle in his cottage. The police are there now, mounting a search. I want to find Hauser before Inspector Dowling thinks about looking for him."

"Good God!" Hamilton was on his feet, staring at Rutledge. "You're not telling me that this man could have anything to do with Brereton going missing? Elizabeth—you assured me he was perfectly respectable!"

Elizabeth said, "I've already been through this with Ian. No, he just thinks it's best to find him—"

Over her head, Rutledge's eyes met Hamilton's. "Keep her here," he ordered. "I'll know where to reach you both—"

"Yes. Yes, I understand. You'll send word as soon as you can?"

"As soon as there's anything to tell you."

He turned and was gone, leaving behind him a flurry of questions, Elizabeth's voice higher with worry, Lydia coming in, begging someone to explain what had happened.

Hamish said, as Rutledge put on his headlamps, "Ye're no' going to Maidstone! You'll never find him!"

"No. I've a feeling he may be closer than that. Where he was before. The Morton house."

RUTLEDGE WENT BACK to the crossroads, and turned for the Morton estate on the Seelyham road. In the distance behind him he could see the lights of another vehicle—Weaver, very likely, ferrying men back and forth to Brereton's cottage in commandeered motorcars.

Rutledge turned through the stone gates, driving to the stableyard and leaving his motorcar in the shadow of one of the sheds. The grass was still thick and high around it in the beams of his headlamps—the Morton motorcar was still inside. As he switched the lamps off, it seemed that absolute darkness fell, blacker than before.

There was no moon and the night was quiet. The crows, long since gone to roost in trees beyond the house, were silent. And the house loomed black, bulky, and uninviting.

Walking briskly, he went to the kitchen door.

Inspector Dowling—or someone—had latched it more securely now.

Working by feel, he spent several minutes on the length of wire, until he had it open. If Hauser was indeed here, he'd already heard the motorcar coming up the drive. He'd be waiting, but not in the kitchen. Otherwise he'd never have rewired the door so firmly. Rutledge's efforts had given him time to prepare, to select his own arena for confrontation.

If he was here. And not in Maidstone, minding his own business. . . .

The kitchen was in darkness.

"Hauser? It's Rutledge."

He stood there, listening to his words trapped against the walls and ceiling. There was no response. After a time, he began to move around the room. His probing hands, outstretched, found the lamp. It was cold when he touched the chimney. The matches were just beside it. Nearly tripping over a chair as he stepped closer to work with the shade and the wick, Rutledge swore silently.

Light bloomed, a bright and golden glow that sent the shadows in the kitchen fleeing into corners.

There was no sign of occupation in this room. No food on the table, the pitcher back on the sideboard where it belonged, the bedding returned to whatever room it had come from. But then a man like Hauser wouldn't be caught twice like a rat in a hole.

Rutledge waited until the wick had caught well, and then he took up the lamp and moved out into the passage. He could hear his own breathing in the confined space.

Swinging open the door, he said again, "Hauser? It's Rutledge."

The light preceded him out into the hall, picking out the sheets and the shrouded furnishings, giving an odd life to the long flight of stairs, and to the rooms he walked into one after another. He was clearly visible in the aura of the lamp, and took care to give no appearance of hostility.

It was an eerie experience, the silence fraught with nothing, the urgent whisper of Hamish's voice in his head, his quiet footfalls as he moved slowly, carefully, examining any place large enough to hide someone. The lamp was growing heavier in his hand, the heat warming his face.

Anyone in the kitchen could have heard him fumbling with the latch—anyone in the house would have heard him stumbling against the chair. And there were many ways to disappear here. If Hauser was innocent, why should he hide? But then he'd learned to his cost that the police were not as sympathetic as Elizabeth Mayhew had been. . . .

Rutledge stood in the hall and called Hauser's name again, then listened to the stillness around him. After a moment he walked on, methodically investigating, making certain that each room was empty before moving on to the next.

He was beginning to think he'd been wrong. That Hauser wasn't here.

Rutledge climbed the stairs, no longer on guard, yet unwilling to stop until he was certain. He went into the first of the bedrooms, found nothing, and moved on. In the third, deep inside a man's wardrobe, was a small valise. He set down the lamp and opened the bag. Inside were personal items, clean clothing, a pipe and some tobacco, and a worn photograph of a smiling woman standing by the gate of a barnlike house, her fair hair shining in the sun. And documents in the name of one Gunter Manthy, of the town of Gronigen, in Holland. On a square of paper someone had sketched a likeness of a chased silver cup, with details laboriously added. It was very convincing.

A prop—or an heirloom?

Hauser had never really left this house. He had given himself up— but he had concealed his belongings, including the photograph, where they wouldn't readily be found. The safest place he could think of. Someone had cleared away the bedding and food in the kitchen, to give the impression the house was no longer occupied. Allaying any suspicion that he might return.

Which meant he expected to come back and retrieve his possessions.

Had Hauser gone to Maidstone, just as Elizabeth believed he would? In the slim hope that Jimsy Ridger had passed that silver cup on to someone in his family?

"Then what's become of Brereton?" Hamish asked. "If yon German is still alive and out of harm's way?"

"A very pressing question now!"

He was at the end of the passage on the second floor when he heard something. The sound traveled far in the empty, silent house.

Hamish said softly, " 'Ware!"

Brereton? Or Hauser? Who had followed him here?

31

RUTLEDGE STAYED WHERE HE WAS, LISTENING. HIS HEARING had of necessity been acute on the battlefield, where sound was a betrayer. And Hamish had always heard what he could not.

He asked, into the silence of his head, *"Where?"*

"On the ground floor . . ." came the reply after a moment.

And as Rutledge held his breath for an instant, to listen more intently, he heard it again.

—thump—

AT FIRST IT sounded as if someone had bumped into a chair in the dark—as he himself had done in the kitchen. And then as his brain processed the nature of the noise, identified it, documented and explained it, he was not prepared to believe it.

His first reaction was *"No—!"*

And yet—it made a dreadful sense. Here was the hidden killer, the murderer seemingly with no motive. One not driven by familiar emotions—not guilt nor compassion nor greed nor vengeance. A hidden face, turned inward toward a grief that had no means of expression. And how in the scheme of things, had that grief turned to murder?

Hamish pressed, "Are ye verra' sure?"

"It has to be. There's no other answer," Rutledge responded grimly. "We looked at the wine, and not the laudanum. We looked for any connection with victims, and there was none. We looked for opportunity, and didn't see how it could be accomplished. We told ourselves it was the darkness that mattered—we told ourselves it was the road—we believed it had to do with men who'd fought together. And in the end it was none of these things. It all came back to *dying . . .*"

The sound came again. A footfall, too heavy to be concealed, echoing through the silent house and rising up the open stairwell.

"In the hall, then,"

"Yes."

"Aye."

Rutledge stayed where he was, furiously thinking through his experiences in Marling.

Chief Superintendent Bowles had been aware of his revived interest in the Shaw case—and had laid his plans accordingly. He'd used the Chief Constable and Raleigh Masters to keep his eye on Rutledge, and he'd isolated his troublesome inspector in Kent, where he could do no harm. But it had backfired, this stirring up of passions and fears . . .

Raleigh Masters, whose own obsession was Matthew Sunderland, had been primed to dislike and distrust the man sent down from London. And he'd had no qualms about showing it publicly.

But the fear that drove Raleigh Masters had nothing to do with Matthew Sunderland.

Raleigh Masters had already suspected who the killer was, and had done his best to throw Rutledge off the scent. A subtle legal mind's misdirection . . .

It had succeeded admirably, because Rutledge had been thoroughly blinded by Nell Shaw's vehement determination, driven and cornered and harangued into half believing her web of lies. He'd been distracted by Gunter Hauser and Elizabeth Mayhew. By that sudden return of a missing part of his memory and the truth about the end of his own war. He had been vulnerable, and Masters, the wily barrister, had recognized that.

But what had Raleigh Masters seen that he hadn't?

A multitude of small signs, the first withering of the spirit, eyes that looked away, a silence where there had been conversation, an empty bed, the sound of a motorcar in the night . . . Little wonder that Rutledge had missed them: He hadn't been privy to them. And whenever there was a chance that he might see too much, he'd been passionately attacked by Masters, driving him out.

He set the lamp down in the room nearest him, where the door was still ajar, and with great care he closed it behind him, shutting off the light.

Walking with the quiet tread of a soldier accustomed to the stealth of night attacks, Rutledge went down the passage and then descended the flight of stairs to the first floor.

The darkness seemed absolute after the brightness of the lamp.

And he could feel, like pressing ghosts, the presence of someone else, standing below him, looking up toward him from the hall.

"Rutledge?"

The voice was pitched to carry.

"I'm here."

"So you are." There was an inflection of satisfaction. "Odd place to find you, I couldn't think why you'd come here. But it suited me well enough, too."

"Did you follow me?"

"With great difficulty, I'm afraid. Yes. And I'd seen you outside the gates before this, if you remember. The grass was beaten down."

Rutledge began to descend the stairs. "Do you know where Brereton is?"

"It's my blood, not his, flung around the sitting room. If that's what you're asking. I believe he went up to London on a private matter. Last week he'd mentioned something to that effect. It had slipped my mind."

"Where is she?"

"I'd like you to see for yourself. What did you do with the lamp? I could follow it through the windows."

"It's in a room upstairs. A delaying tactic, if you will."

"Leave it then. You must drive. I've done all that I can this day."

Rutledge came down the last half dozen steps. In the darkness, the face of Raleigh Masters was shadowed with grief and pain, a caricature of the man who had ruled courtrooms like his predecessor, Sunderland.

They walked together through the hall, into the kitchen passage, and out into the night. Masters was limping heavily, leaning on his cane, as if in great pain.

The night air smelled of damp, as if rain was on the way. Underfoot the scurrying of mice rustled the leaves. There was no wind; the trees were stark against the black sky.

Rutledge cranked the motorcar, while Masters heaved himself with difficulty into the passenger's seat, drawing his bad leg in after him.

The other vehicle stood halfway down the drive, where Masters had left it, and Rutledge was forced onto the lawns to drive around it.

"Did she use the motorcar, offering them a lift? And a little wine to keep out the cold? I didn't know she could drive. You always had someone do that."

"She learned, when my leg first began to trouble me. Porter, the chauffeur, is half senile. We use him only when there's no one else."

They had turned out of the stone gates, passing the tree where Will Taylor had been found.

Neither man spoke of it.

After a time Raleigh Masters said, "I would like very much to kill you, you know. It's strange to admit, after years of serving the law, that I could so easily break the most weighty of them."

"It's all too easy to kill," Rutledge answered, remembering Hamish.

"That was the war. It's not the same."

Rutledge didn't argue.

Silence followed them the rest of the way. At the Brereton cottage, a lonely constable stood guard, touching his hat as he recognized Rutledge's car. Somewhere among the trees the search for Brereton must be continuing, but there was no sign of lights or men. A mile or so farther on, as he turned into the drive that led up to Raleigh Masters's house, Rutledge said, "Tell me about Brereton."

"She went to kill him, you know, but he wasn't at home. She believed, after you'd called on him, that he must surely have witnessed her coming and going. The wine was there on the table, the first glass poured, when I walked in. She'd just sat there, waiting. She looked so tired. We argued, and when I reached for the wine, to pour it out, her face seemed to fall apart, like shattered porcelain. It was rather horrible. I tried to calm her down, and instead she fought me, like a tigress. As if taking her fear and her grief and her anger out on me. I was hardly her match. And I really thought she intended to kill me there and then. I fell twice, and the last time I lay on the floor as still as I could, until she'd gone."

The scene, violent and shocking, was vivid in Rutledge's mind.

Masters took a deep, shuddering breath. "I suspected. I didn't know. But I suspected—"

"It was a practice for death."

"Yes. She thought—God forgive her—she thought that it would be easier, when they removed the rest of my leg, just to end it. But she wasn't sure how to go about that. It took her two attempts before she got the mixture right. The first man, Taylor, was hours dying—she told me this afternoon. It must have been dreadful to watch. And I had a nurse— she dared not risk arousing the woman's suspicions by making me unexpectedly ill. Webber was easier, but to make absolutely certain, she tried again. Bartlett, that was. She chose men who were suffering. As I was. Not someone who was healthy—until Brereton. But there was his blindness, you see. It would have masked the real reason for killing him."

He stopped.

Hamish demanded, "Do you believe him then?"

Rutledge silently answered him. "I'll see what his wife has to say first. If she's coherent. Please God, Dr. Pugh is still at Brereton's cottage!"

"Aye."

As the motorcar drew up in front of the house, Rutledge asked Masters, "Where are the servants? Is someone with her?"

"They were given the day off, early on. She didn't want them to see her walking down the drive to Brereton's cottage. Since Porter—our chauffeur—was gone as well, I had to drive myself there. Which meant I had to put on this damned false foot! And even so it was unbelievably difficult."

Raleigh refused help getting out of the car. His heel rang heavily against the metal frame as he tried to manage the long step to the ground. Swearing, he stood there grimacing against the pain, and then walked steadily up to the door of the house.

In the light from the hall, shining through the narrow lancet windows by the door, Rutledge could see Masters's hands clearly for the first time. They were cut and bruised, where he had tried to stave off blows. His face was bloody from a head wound that was still oozing from under his hat and dripping down his temple to soak into his torn collar. A slit cheek had swollen grotesquely.

Acknowledging his stare, Masters said impassively, "She used my cane. She took it from me and broke my grip with it, when I tried to hold her."

Rutledge said again, "Where is she?"

"Go on," he replied wearily. "Go in and see your handiwork. *I wish to God you'd never set foot in Kent!*"

He slumped against the doorframe, his back to the house, looking ready to drop. There was no color in his skin, except for the ugly streaks of blood. But he watched with venomously cold eyes as Rutledge opened and stepped through the door.

" 'Ware!" Hamish warned.

The staircase ran up the center of the hall as it always had. The glass cases of Venetian splendor stood where they had always stood. A beautiful room, lighted with candles and lamps.

But as he looked up, Rutledge could see, swinging slowly from a carefully fashioned noose, the dead body of Bella Masters. She had used the upper balustrade as her gallows, and was hanging free in the stairwell. Her face, shielded by her disheveled hair, was turned away from him, but her neck was broken. The angle of her head seemed obscenely coquettish.

"*Murderers hang . . .*" The words ran through his mind like an epitaph.

It shook him as few things ever had.

For several minutes he stood there, Hamish silent at his shoulder, simply looking up, watching the pendulumlike motion of Raleigh Masters's wife.

Aloud, he asked, "Did you do this?" It was hard to keep the anger out of his voice.

"No. While I was at Brereton's, trying to collect my wits, she came back here. She did what she had to do." Then he said with difficulty, "My enemies would have enjoyed prosecuting her."

"Did she want you dead so very much?"

"I don't think it was that. It was just that she knew me so very well, and she was terrified, at the end, that it would be up to her—deciding when it would happen. And so she tried to accustom herself to death, and perfect the means of death. She didn't want me to suffer. Instead, she suffered for me . . ."

His voice broke. Masters added after a moment, "It wasn't pity. I don't think it was pity. In her own way, she saw it as love." But there was doubt behind the tentative words.

He pushed himself away from the wall and started to walk awkwardly toward the motorcar. "For God's sake, shut this door and leave her. For tonight. Take me somewhere where no one knows me."

"I can't. I must report this."

"Take me to Melinda Crawford, then. While they do what must be done here."

Rutledge forced himself to look away from Bella Masters. The sight was already seared in his mind.

This was how Ben Shaw had looked. And so many others . . . But without the terrible indignity of the hangman and the warden and the witnesses.

"I'm sorry." It was all he could find to say. He wasn't certain whether the apology was to Bella Masters, or her husband. He walked out of the hall, and closed the door behind him.

Masters said, "It doesn't matter, you know. The doctor told me the last time I was in London that the infection is moving quite rapidly. I won't live to see Christmas, even if they cut off my leg. It's taken hold, the gangrene."

"Brereton told me you were improved—"

"He wasn't in the room during the consultation. And I lied to him afterward. I didn't want Bella to travel to London with me, you see. I didn't want Bella to know the truth. Not yet. Not until I'd made peace with it myself. I was afraid."

Rutledge, grateful for the blessed darkness of the drive, asked, "Why didn't you stop her? If you knew what was happening, in God's name, *why did you let it continue!*"

Raleigh Masters turned to face him across the bonnet of the motorcar. "I didn't know in the beginning, not until Webber was already dead. The second victim. She came up late to bed that night, smelling of wine—depressed, on the verge of tears. And then—suddenly I didn't want to know. I didn't have the courage. I told myself the time might come when I would be glad to drink wine by the fire and go to sleep forever. But the time *has* come, you see. And it's too late. She was right. I could never kill myself."

He opened the passenger door. "If there's any mercy left in you, get me out of here!"

But the lights from the hall seemed to pursue them down the drive until the trees finally blotted them out. And still they blazed brightly behind each man's eyes.